MW00479419

MISTY MASSEY	JONATHAN MABERRY
EMILY LAVIN LEVERETT	ROBERT E. WATERS
MARGARET S. MCGRAW	TONIA BROWN
FRANCES ROWAT	JAMES R. TUCK
WENDY N. WAGNER	LIZ COLTER
GAIL Z. MARTIN	SCOTT HUNGERFORD
LARRY N. MARTIN	JOHN G. HARTNESS
BRYAN C.P. STEELE	DIANA PHARAOH FRANCIS
R.S. BELCHER	KEN SCHRADER
DAVID SHERMAN	FAITH HUNTER

THE WEIRD WILD WEST

EDITED BY
MISTY MASSEY, EMILY LAVIN LEVERETT
AND MARGARET S. McGRAW

eBooks
Stratford, New Jersey

PUBLISHED BY
eSpec Books LLC
Danielle McPhail, Publisher
PO Box 493,
Stratford, New Jersey 08084
www.especbooks.com

Copyright ©2015 eSpec Books LLC
Interior Art Copyright ©2015 Jason Whitley

ISBN (eBook): 978-1-942990-05-5
ISBN (trade paper):978-1-942990-01-7

"Abishag Mary" by Frances Rowat. © 2015 Frances Rowat.
"Blood Tellings" by Wendy N. Wagner. © 2015 Wendy N. Wagner.
"Ruin Creek" by Gail Z. Martin and Larry N. Martin. © 2015 Gail Z. Martin
    and Larry N. Martin.
"Via Con Diablo" by Bryan C. P. Steele. © 2015 Bryan C. P. Steele.
"Rattler" by R. S. (Rod) Belcher. © 2015 R. S. (Rod) Belcher.
"Rocky Rolls Gold" by David Sherman. © 2015 David Sherman.
"Son of the Devil" by Jonathan Maberry. © 2015 Jonathan Maberry.
"Mungo Snead's Last Stand" by Robert E. Waters. © 2015 Robert E. Waters.
"Frank and Earnest" by Tonia Brown. © 2015 Tonia Brown.
"From Parts Unknown" by James R. Tuck. © 2015 James R. Tuck.
"Sundown" by Liz Colter. © 2015 Liz Colter.
"Fifteen Seconds" by Scott C. Hungerford. © 2015 Scott C. Hungerford.
"Redemption Song" by John Hartness. © 2015 John Hartness.
"Grasping Rainbows" by Diana Pharaoh Francis. © 2015 Diana Pharaoh Francis.
"The Faery Wrangler" by Misty Massey. © 2015 Misty Massey.
"Haven" by Ken Schrader. © 2015 Ken Schrader.
"Eighteen Sixty" by Faith Hunter. © 2015 Faith Hunter.

All rights reserved. No part of the contents of this book may be reproduced or trans-
mitted in any form or by any means without the written permission of the publisher.

All persons, places, and events in this book are fictitious and any resemblance to actual
persons, places, or events is purely coincidental.

COVER CREDITS
Steampunk Skull on Parchment
© AlienCat - Fotolia.com
Brown leather textured background with side light.
© Costin79 - Fotolia.com
Silhouette of a horse from a tree © nutriaaa - shutterstock.com
Graphic elements © mhatzapa - shutterstock.com

Copy Editor: Greg Schauer
Interior Design: Sidhe na Daire Multimedia
            www.sidhenadaire.com

ACKNOWLEDGEMENTS

There are so many people to thank for making this book happen — Danielle Ackley-McPhail of eSpec Books, our great Kickstarter backers, and all the incredible authors and artists who agreed to be a part of the show. And a nod of thanks to each other — we three couldn't have asked for better partners!

Misty: Most of all, thank you to Todd and Bleys, my wonderful guys, who always believe in me even when I think I should give up and go live in a cave. I couldn't do it without you.

Emily: I would also like to thank Oliver for being my support, my sounding board, and my friend. Without you, I wouldn't be able to do the things I love to do!

Margaret: Be careful what you wish for, like an anthology of weird wild west stories. I can never say thank you enough for the support and encouragement of family and friends. And for my daughter Emily, who inspires me to be better. Namaste, y'all.

photo credit: Frank Bennett Fiske, October 23, 1950

DEDICATION

This book is dedicated to the memory of Dr Luther R. Zehner and Frances T. Zehner, who lived on and served the Standing Rock Reservation in North Dakota for three years and were adopted into the Lakota Tribe in 1950.

Their legacy lives on through their daughter, Gail Z. Martin.

TABLE OF CONTENTS

ABISHAG MARY

FRANCES ROWAT

THE PIRATE MADE LANDFALL AT MIDNIGHT IN THE DRY STRETCH OF THE midwest, and staggered forward until dawn. The sun rose behind her to gild the land, and she followed her shadow forward, more or less, until it puddled at her feet. The air was crisp with heat, and the uneasy weight of the treasure she had stolen dragged at her heart.

Each step she took left a wet bootprint on the ground. When she stopped to gather her bearings, judging the sun or the wind or the lay of the land, a puddle would begin creeping sulkily out from under each sole.

Her name was Abishag Mary, and she walked into an idea of the West.

When her shadow was starting to bleed out behind her again, she crested yet another hill and stumbled down toward a cabin, although not the kind she was used to. Despite the distance she'd walked, she hadn't found her land legs, but that was part of the curse; the sea was always and ever two steps behind her, waiting to fill the air with roaring wet breath. So Abishag Mary was a stranger to land, and when she saw a small square block with no deck or hull below, it took her a minute to find the word 'cabin'.

She'd had a better cabin, once. The windows had been larger.

A woman came out, cast-iron pan in hand, frown on her sun-weathered face. She stopped when she saw the pirate, and the two women stood that way a long moment; Abishag Mary with her feet planted wide and her hands a little akimbo for balance, and the woman with the frying pan half-raised as if a shield, staring frankly over the round black circle of it.

"Where did you come from?" the woman said after a moment.

"The sea out east."

The woman's eyes were storm-brewing grey. They measured out Abishag Mary, weighing her white-as-salt hair against her walnut-shell skin, all rumpled and weathered by years at sea and now dried into something that'd never be smooth again. They took in the salt-stained boots and the travel-grimy clothes and the wide hat. And the saber on one hip, balancing out the pistol on the other. It was a very odd pistol to see in the West, a great thing of black iron and redwood chased with bright brass inlays.

They weren't sharp enough to see the treasure Mary carried, and that suited Mary fine.

"You mean me harm?"

"No ma'am." Abishag Mary was no saint of any kind, but she was footsore and hungry and not minded to start a fight. And the woman's eyes were less like clouds brewing a storm and more like the sea under those clouds, and it touched something in Mary's heart to see them.

"Well," the woman said, "suppose you can visit, then. I'm Grace O'Regan, and this is my home."

The inside of the cabin was neat and dim, floored with split planks. Mary's boots left footprints, but not wet ones. Only setting foot on land proper could bleed away the sea creeping up toward her heart.

"You often get people stopping by?"

"Not like you," Grace O'Regan said. "But I prayed for help, and I guess you'll do."

Mary looked out one of the windows. The gold and brown land was as wide as any sea she'd seen, and on the horizon were low rising foothills, blue with distance.

"Well," she said, "I could stand to do a little good, measure of my deeds. Afore we turn to what help is it you're needing, where the hell *am* I?"

"New Mexico."

Mary blinked and stared out of the window again. She'd been many things, but landlocked hadn't ever been one of them.

Still and all, perhaps it wasn't the worst place to be, given how she'd left things with the sea. They were on bad terms.

"Jack came out here," Grace said over a thin meal. None of it tasted of fish or coconuts, and Mary was tearing through it. "He had a land grant, for settling; he worked it pretty well, the first two years. He's a family friend, and things were hard, back in Boston. So I came out here and we were married."

Grace hadn't prepared a third plate or left anything in the pot.

"What happened?"

"It was a bad year," Grace said. "Not enough rain. And a long winter. He went to town, in spring, but he never came back." She scraped the spoon around the edge of her plate. "I walked out there, a week later. They said he'd been heading back, but..." She shrugged. "Where'd you come from?"

"I was shipwrecked," Mary said. It was true, if not all the truth. "We'd been searching for a—jewel. And we found it, but a storm came up and battered my ship to pieces in the cove, and all hands on it as well. I went inland. I was there... Not sure how long. It wasn't a very big island."

"Does that matter?"

"There wasn't much to eat."

"Oh," Grace said. She hesitated, then pushed the meal's bread toward Mary, who set aside her cleaned plate and set to.

"It was peculiar," Mary said. "I had to eat my bird. I was fevered. I thought I saw the sea, waves and woman all together. And my ship's figurehead drowning in it, dragged down by my crew. Last there was a man with a sextant, with the Polestar in his left eye, who told me that if I kept walking I could get off the island. So I did, and came to be here, in the morning sun. And then I found my way to your front door."

Grace nodded placidly.

"Grace," Mary said after a moment, "when you prayed for help, who were you praying *to*?"

Grace only shrugged, but Mary kept staring at her, jaw set. After a long moment Grace rose, and went to poking at the fire. "Whoever it was," she said, "he sent you."

"What help are you needing?" Mary asked. "You can walk to town; you've got family, back in Boston. Wouldn't they take you in?"

"If I could make it back to Boston," Grace said, "then yes, out of pity." Her mouth grew ugly at the thought. "But pity or not, they can't pay my passage home. Nor can I. If I can settle my claim to this land, I'll at least have *something*."

"Who questions your claim?"

"There's a man called Hutchins," Grace said. "The land's worth something, even if the field's gone fallow. If I've got a homestead here when the surveyor comes, Jack's deed will be mine."

"A deed's enough to keep Hutchins off?"

Grace smiled a little; Mary could see the corner of it. "I think so."

"Well," Mary said, "hoping you're right. So Hutchins would see you off your land?"

Grace nodded. "Offered to buy me out, and then made it clear I should move along. I promised I'd sell, to put them off, and I've spent the last three days out in the land, praying and hoping they'd think I was gone. But the surveyor will be here tomorrow, and I need to be here then; I can't let Hutchins argue my homestead's been abandoned."

"So it's only one night you need help?"

"I'm thinking so."

"Well," Mary said after a moment, looking away from the hope in Grace's grey eyes. "I'll take dog's watch — I'll keep watch till dark. Don't suppose you've got a drink?"

"There's the pump outside."

Mary sighed.

"Tobacco?"

Mary went out, leaving Grace within to load the long gun her husband had used for game. As soon as her feet crossed from floor to land, a puddle fell out of each boot, spreading and sinking into the dry earth. Mary imagined a cheated hiss, like the tide pulling back over rocks, as the sea that had been creeping up to her heart bled away.

She paced once around the cabin, making sure her footprints weren't growing wetter, then leaned back against the door to light a cigarette and take off her hat. It had a weather-bleached handful of tail-feathers in the band, bloody in the setting sun. She picked the Polestar out of the darkening sky, and it told her where she was, relative to the seas — farther west than she'd ever been before.

She smoked her cigarette, and then another.

The men came as dusk had near given way to dark.

They were not carrying a lantern among them, but Mary could see them against the low stars. It was a clear night, and they made her out as they drew near enough to greet.

She stepped forward, putting on her hat.

"The hell're you supposed to be?" said one of them.

"Move on," Mary said, reaching cross-body to rest her right hand on her saber's hilt. There were three of them, each taller than her though one wasn't quite as wide. They heard her voice and glanced between themselves; she guessed they hadn't been expecting a second woman.

The one who'd asked what she was supposed to be shrugged and came forward, putting a hand on her shoulder to push her aside. Mary whipped her saber out and he howled and scrambled back from its bite. There was heart enough to his bellowing that she guessed he'd live.

The other men were cursing in shock. Mary was drawing a line in the dirt with the tip of her saber when they shot her.

The guns roared as if there were a full dozen men firing on her, and Mary lit up with pain, holes boiling at face and shoulder and chest and gut. She fell back, head bouncing off the cabin's doorsill. Her mouth was full of foulness, and when she blinked only one of her eyes was working. The other was a red roaring pit of agony.

She saw one of them come toward her, pulled her pistol clumsily from her right hip, and shot him.

Her gun's roar was briefer than theirs, but louder and closer. The man went down like an anchor, and the one she'd cut took to his heels.

The third man only stared.

Mary wasn't sure if anyone was screaming or not; her ears were ringing madly, and the pain was gonging in her skull. She sat up, stiffly, and a flood of foul water spilled out of all the holes they'd shot in her. She wiped some of it off her face with her free hand and found that the sight in her left eye was coming blearily back.

She spat out a mouthful of something like thick bilgewater and tried to brandish her pistol at the remaining man, although it came out as more of an ominous waggle. He was staring at the gun as if he thought the devil had reloaded it with powder and shot while neither of them was looking.

"Move along," she said again.

He fled.

Grace came out a moment later, and Mary went sprawling as the cabin door slammed into her back. The younger woman had the long gun set against her shoulder, and she didn't drop it when she saw the bleeding body in the starlight.

Grace helped Mary inside, bolted the door, and lit an oil lamp. Mary still couldn't close her left eye, but her vision was clearing. She looked down at herself, and the wracked tatters of her shirt and vest.

"Still no drink?" she said, trying to smile at the younger woman.

"Are you going to die?" Grace was staring at her. "You have holes *everywhere*. And your blood stinks. And..."

"I don't think that's blood," Mary said. The leaking liquid smelt foul as if she'd been gutshot, but was watery and salty and didn't have much red to it. Bilgewater came to mind again, and she managed to blink.

She mopped some of the ooze away with the remains of her shirt. Her skin was scarring white over her wounds. "Get me something to clean with."

Grace backed away, still staring, and found a clean rag. Mary wiped the blood and bilge off herself, and by then Grace had found her a shirt. Mary guessed it had been Jack's.

"How are you still alive?"

"I took something from the sea," Mary said. "It was a fountain, like, and a star, and a jewel. But it was her heart, as well. I went looking for the heart of the sea because I loved her, and I took her heart for my own."

"You stole the heart of the sea?"

"Aye." Mary thought of saying more, and worked the buttons on Jack's shirt, instead. The collar was too high and tight, so she left the top ones undone.

"How do you know... I mean, did you see her?"

"I've seen her all my life," Mary said, "and sailed her, and loved her in all her moods. It wasn't enough. So I found my way to the island where she'd walk when she chose to, and I found her heart at the bottom of a sun-struck lagoon, and... Well. I'm not a good woman, I guess."

But she couldn't have passed it up, and that was the truth of it. The sea's heart had been blue and green as the Caribbean, and grey as the light striking across the water and under the clouds when a storm breaks mid-morning, and hot as a red sky at night, and immortal as the waves.

"I knew that if I took it..."

"She'd love you?" Grace interrupted.

Mary tried to keep the exasperation from her voice. "No-one who's had their heart stolen can love. I knew that if I took it I could be always close by her, and live near as long as her, and it seemed worth it." She sighed. "It was a fool's choice, I guess. Didn't work out so well."

"I suppose," Grace said awkwardly. "But... Will you still help me? Until tomorrow's all I need."

Abishag Mary looked up into the younger woman's eyes, the steady sea-grey of them, and nodded.

The night had gone full dark and the moon had risen by the time Mary saw the men coming. Grace identified Hutchins by the tails of his coat. There were four others with him, and two were carrying small packs. That worried Mary more than guns.

Grace was inside with her rifle, watching through the small holes they'd gouged between the chinked logs. The windows gave a better view, but anyone could aim for shutters. Mary slipped out, got up on the far side of the roof, and fired.

Then there were three other men with Hutchins.

Tomorrow, Mary thought, meant half a dozen hours until dawn at least, and then however long until the man Grace was pinning her hopes on arrived. She'd have sworn they had no chance, except Hutchins was here and that seemed desperate. She'd have thought he could have buttonholed the surveyor back in town.

The men were shooting, and she ducked behind the roof, reloading and wishing for better light. She could hear them coming around to either side; the six-shot pistol of the man she'd shot at dusk would have been of some use now, but Grace had nothing to load it with.

Mary picked the best-lit of the men she could see and fired. She couldn't tell if she'd hit him or if he'd merely dived for cover. She slid down from the roof, sea-water splashing out from her boots as she landed, and ran staggering toward a man rounding the end of the cabin. He fired as Mary barrelled into him, knocking him over more with her speed than with the saber. She stabbed downward and kept running. Grace was firing, and someone was screaming commands. Mary rounded the corner of the cabin to see one of the men had dropped a pack by the door, saw a coiling fuse, smelled gunpowder—

She snatched it up, throwing it away from the cabin as the fuse burnt down, and felt herself lifted in a roar.

Everything was a mist of wet fragments and dirt and splinters. The ground was soaking into mud underneath her, and Mary smelled rot and salt and all manner of putrid things, but she saw smouldering light and dragged herself toward the cabin. Its wall was embers and splinters, crawling with smoke. She couldn't see putting it out near quick enough, but—

She felt a clock, chiming.

The creeping embers froze on the cabin wall, and the moonlight grew brighter. Grace came to the cabin's tattered doorway, and a silhouette waited at the doorsill. It was darkness neatly cut into the shape of a man, and the eye that she could see glinted with a lodestone light.

Abishag Mary knew it for the one who'd shown her the way west.

She'd thought of tomorrow as the next day's dawn, but for a thing that held to measurements and lines, that could map the quadrants of the sea and cut a path from the heart of the sea to the brown and gold plains of New Mexico, *tomorrow* came at midnight.

She understood why Hutchins hadn't waited in town.

The thing—the surveyor—didn't have the sextant any longer; he held a brass circle and bar in his hand, with little stiff arms pointing up from each end of the bar. But his left eye still gleamed with the Polestar, and when Abishag Mary looked to the sky, she saw only darkness at the lynchpin of the night, and felt the world tilt around her until she looked back to him instead.

"I am arrived," he said calmly, and looked at the doorway where Grace O'Regan stood.

She curtseyed.

He smiled, and the embers crawling on her cabin winked out.

Hutchins showed more mettle than Mary would have guessed and came forward with a nervous smile. "Sir," he began, bowing slightly. "I hope that you will settle the matter of the claim on this land. As a representative of the railroad, set out and driven along your measured lines..."

"I see a homestead." The surveyor's voice was sharper than Mary's saber. "Belonging to the woman who petitioned for my attention."

"*You* petitioned—" Hutchins looked at Grace O'Regan, and stepped back.

The surveyor set the brass thing in his hand aside to rest on the air. He pulled a sheet of white vellum from his jacket, and shook it out with a sound like a dead bird landing in the grass. Mary pulled herself to her knees as he ran a long narrow fingertip across it, and she saw letters blossom under his touch.

"Grace O'Regan, nee Bailey, born in Boston and landed in New Mexico, by writ of my hand, the homestead land grant provisionally extended to Jack O'Regan is yours. Jeremiah Isaac Hutchins, bear witness."

"Sir, I—" The surveyor turned to look at Hutchins, who went white as a drowned man. Mary imagined she might've looked the same, once, if she'd ever though to argue with the sea. "Yes, sir, I bear witness."

"The hell is going on?" one of the men standing by Mary said quietly. He was holding his arm; she thought he might be the man she'd run into, coming off the roof. She staggered up to her feet.

The surveyor was explaining to Hutchins that, having come there in person, it would be considered a personal slight if the land deed granted to Grace O'Regan was not respected.

"Your captain lost," Mary said.

"Your boss won?"

"She's not my boss." Mary watched as Grace took the vellum, the deed sending back its own white light under the moon.

"It's mine?" Grace said, gazing up at the surveyor's, and Mary's stomach pitched to see Grace's young face so close to the Polestar, her eyes still alight as a grim sea.

"It's yours," the surveyor confirmed, and smiled, and then he touched his brass land-sextant, folded himself up like one of his own deeds, and vanished into the night air.

"I'm drunk," the man standing next to Mary decided. "I'm drunk and I'm going home. Hutchins, sir, we leaving?"

"Just a minute," Grace said, her mouth hard. "Hutchins, I want to sell."

Mary's stomach went from a sharp yaw to an utter drop.

"*Now* you want to sell?" Hutchins looked like he'd eaten bad cheese. "I offered you a fair price in spring, and you said—"

"You offered me nothing. *Now* you'll offer me a fair price, or you'll try to run me off my land and answer to him."

"You sniveling whey-faced little—"

"You're standing on my land," Grace said sharply, and Hutchins shut up.

"Grace," Mary said. It came out thin as her bird's voice when they'd starved, before she'd wrung his neck and plucked him. "Grace, you wanted this land. You said that if you had claim to it—"

"Then at least I'd have something," Grace said. "And I do. The railroad lives by maps and grades, by all the lines drawn over the land and the surveyor's sufferance. Hutchins won't shortchange me, and they'd have a fair ways to go to find someone who'd dare. The land they want is worth enough to pay passage home, and have my own house in

Boston besides. Nothing grand, but I won't be beholden to the pity of my sisters." She looked at Mary, and surprise crossed her face. "You thought I meant to stay? No, to hell with that. But I won't leave you stranded here. I can book you passage east, or south if you want to go down to the coast. I don't know what ships cost. I don't think I can buy you one."

"I wasn't thinking to go back."

Grace looked puzzled, then shrugged and turned back to Hutchins. "I'll see you in town tomorrow," she said. "We'll meet at the land office, and then send a wire. You speak for the railroad; you can arrange to have me paid some now, and have the rest waiting. I want a stagecoach ticket to Santa Fe..."

Mary closed her eyes as Hutchins and Grace walked off, discussing details.

The man next to Mary coughed, and then offered her a cigarette.

"Are you sure you wouldn't like a ticket east?" Grace said. She was looking at Mary with a sort of interested courtesy. That was all it had ever been, Mary guessed, with maybe a little fear thrown in. People looked like they cared about you if they thought they needed you. Couldn't help it.

Grace's eyes were still dark and grey as a sea getting ready to storm. It was only that Mary had forgotten for a while, in the gold and brown land, how cold that sea could be. Cold enough to crush the air from your lungs if you fell into it, and stop your heart besides.

"I'll settle for a mule," Mary said. Grace O'Regan had bought her new clothes, and heeled boots, with a jingling spray of spurs. She'd kept her hat, and her pistol and saber. An odd mix, although she was deep enough in the landlocked southwest that people only thought *odd* and had no nevermind of what it meant to be a pirate.

"Well, as it suits you," O'Regan said. She offered her hand, and Mary took it after a moment's hesitation.

Nothing had been promised, after all. She'd only hoped.

And then O'Regan boarded the stagecoach, and Mary set on her way. She had no particular place to go, and so she headed out of the town and down the trail, and deeper into the golden idea of the West.

Blood Tellings

Wendy N. Wagner

"Boy, I need your help." Sheriff Toomey took a seat on the boulder beside me and wrapped his arms around his knees. The wind stirred the winter-dried bunchgrass stems so they hissed and rattled all around us, the voice of Granddaddy Rattlesnake looking for all his kin what got killed during the harvest. Out by the lake, Deer Maiden looked up from her browse and nodded at me. I knew the sheriff didn't see the half-deer, half-woman spirit. He just sat staring out at the lake, his face gone gray, and unhappiness seeping out his pores like some strange sweat.

I bent a grass stem between my fingers, wondering why it had to be now. My fourteenth birthday weren't for yet another four months, and I was a long way from being man enough for what was coming. I caught Deer Maiden's eye, and she smiled, the light that surrounded her flaring up reassuring-like, and then pushed back the brown old cattails with her slim hands. The spirit waded out into the water until her horns disappeared beneath its green surface. Spirits always leave when I most want their help. Ma says that's just their way.

I tightened the grass stem around my pointer finger until the fingertip went purple with pent-up blood. Weren't no way to take the blood out of my mind or my eyes, though. My blood had set my seeing and feeling apart. My ma's blood, her granny's blood, a long line of folk what talk with spirits. I sighed.

"This about Paul Tucker, sir?"

The sheriff looked surprised and more than a little awed. I didn't want to give him the wrong idea. My kin talk to spirits. We ain't fortune-tellers.

"I heard my folks talking about it when they thought I was in the outhouse," I said. "Reckon that's why my pa's gone off to Davenport. Maybe getting some men together."

Sheriff Toomey swallowed, hard, like he had a crab apple stuck in his throat. "They want to hang him, Will. And I can't blame them. What happened in that house..." he shook his head. "Dear God, what a nightmare."

I nodded, not wanting to ask for details, but knowing with sick certainty that I'd see it for myself soon enough. This morning I'd stood on the porch listening to my parents, not moving even after the ugly story came to an end. I'd heard them like the rattle of the bunchgrass in the wind: spirits telling me my boyhood was done.

Going inside, I passed Pa putting on his good coat, wearing his Stetson instead of his usual knit cap. He patted me on the shoulder, his face tired and the lines set deep. Inside, Ma was kneading bread dough on the counter, her eyes red.

"You hear all that?" she asked.

I nodded. Neither of us spoke, and I could hear the hiss and rattle of the grasses and sagebrush, like the wind was pacing, anxious. Louder than that, we heard the creak of our front gate as Pa rode out.

Ma looked up from her dough. "The blood will tell, William Fergal. And yours is saying you're ready for this work. I've been waiting for this day with a heavy heart."

"I know, Ma." I'd been waiting for this moment, too, ever since the day I realized nobody else talked to glowing horned women with deer legs or kept playing with their puppy after its body had been buried.

"You'd best wait outside for it. Whatever's coming to you, it'll find you faster in the open air."

"Yes, Mama." I hadn't called her "mama" in years, but she didn't seem to mind it none, especially when I put my arms around her and buried my face in her warm, bread-smelling neck.

And so I walked out of my boyhood and came to sit on the lake shore with only the company of Deer Maiden and a few shy pygmy rabbits. I was looking at a new life I knew I didn't want—but the powers in me were stronger than my will.

The sheriff tossed a pebble, pulling me out of my own thoughts. "I've known Paul Tucker ten years, Will. He's a good man. Loves his family. Not a mean bone in him."

I worried the grass between my teeth.

"I know what you're thinking. What everyone's thinking—that this is about my Lura. Sure it is. When two horrible things happen in the same house, you've got to think there's a connection."

He sighed. "You don't know what I'm talking about. Keep forgetting you were only a kid back then." He looked sideways at me, rubbed the gray shadow of his day-old beard. "Shit. You're still just a kid."

"Ain't nothing for it, is there?" I sounded tougher than I felt. My ma and pa's conversation roiled at the back of my brain like a stockpot left on too hot a stove. I could already almost picture what it would be like at the Tuckers' house. It made my stomach twist round itself.

I got to my feet. There weren't no point sitting here thinking on it any longer. Sheriff Toomey looked up at me, surprise written all over his face.

"You sure, boy? You really sure?"

I felt tears prickle up against my bottom eyelids. It was one thing to help Pa with the cows and the hay harvest, or even castrate the steers. That kind of growing up wasn't so bad. But looking at evil with only the spirits to help me—well, I wouldn't wish that on anyone, man or boy.

We followed the little trail along the creek's edge. In spring, it'd gurgle and chortle with water spirits, full from snow pack and a few good rains. Now it was only a little greener than the gray land surrounding it. Gray land, gray brush, gray grass. Some people thought it gloomy, but I knew the different colors of gray. These were peaceful grays, warm, happy. Not like the gray under Sheriff Toomey's eyes or in the lines I'd seen around Pa's mouth.

Ma stood beside the side gate and opened it for us. Not even a chicken tried to step out. There was something in the air that warned creatures to stay home and huddle with their loved ones. But Sheriff Toomey and I couldn't stay here inside that fence. We kept walking.

Ma already had my horse saddled, and when I pulled myself up onto Fionn's back, she patted my knee. "I packed you a lunch." She took a napkin-wrapped packet out of her apron pocket. "With a few necessities."

I could smell the rosemary and sage tucked into the bundle. Necessities, all right. Powerful protection in those herbs.

She stroked Fionn's white neck. "Keep my boy safe, Fionn MacCumhal." The gelding tossed his head, his word of honor. He knew what she said. Animals always understood my mother.

She turned on Sheriff Toomey. "And you." She narrowed her eyes. With her black hair glinting in the sun, she looked hard and more than a little scary. "You listen to my boy. And keep your gun handy. Whatever spirit's causing this trouble might not like the taste of hot lead." She quirked a half-smile. "Though that's a long shot."

I smiled at her. I wished she could come with me, and knew she could not. Ma's gift was with critters and plants, the magic of life. The creatures of death and the greater spirits were beyond her control. I was alone.

I twisted my fingers in Fionn's silver mane and hoped I wouldn't throw up.

The old Bluwalter house lay on the far side of town, a good six-mile ride. The sun stared straight down at us, but there weren't no heat in its touch. Our shadows shrank under that glare, creeping under the horses' hooves like they wanted to hide. To the east, the mountains pulled down clouds to warm their snowy tops.

"I reckon you ought to tell me what you know about the house."

Sheriff Toomey startled in his saddle. "Oh." He seemed to deflate on the sound, like my words confirmed a hunch he hadn't really wanted to be true.

"Well," he started, scratching under the brim of his hat. "That house was mine for all of two years before I sold it to Paul Tucker. I bought it from Lura's pappy, Dan Bluwalter, when he decided he wanted to go live with his son over in Walla Walla. But it had another owner before him. That house is one of the oldest in this area, built by a man of the name of Kurt Schwartzkopf." He gave me a nod. "A kraut," he added, unnecessarily.

"He had all kinds of money when he came here, a widower from Germany, and he wanted to build a good house. But something happened—I heard his daughter got drug off by a bear, but that might just be talk—and he bought a house in Odessa."

"Plenty of Germans over there in Odessa," I agreed. My folks liked to ride into Odessa at Christmastime. There were always dances, and the German women made special cookies with names like the crunching sounds snow makes underfoot.

"Well, he never made it. He died trying to get his piano out the door by himself. Poor lonely old man." He shrugged. "That's all I know, I guess. It ain't much."

"All but the first owner moving out, most far away. The old man up and dying like that. And then three mighty bad things happening in that house: The daughter taken by the bear. Lura's dying. And now the Tucker family."

"I never thought about it like that. Three horrible things in a house less than fifty years old. You think that's important?"

A few days ago, I would have rolled my eyes at him, but today I was no longer a boy. Sass was a thing I would have to put behind me.

I scanned the sky and noticed the mountains had drawn up more clouds. They'd begun to fill in the far edge of the sky, crowding the weak blue. The air didn't smell like snow yet, but I wondered if it was coming.

We passed by the edge of town, where everything sat silent. Normally I'd hear the blacksmith's anvil singing to itself and the rattle of wagons coming and going from the general store. But it could well be Sunday out here, it was so quiet. Even the spirits stayed low. I felt a few eyes following me, and from their coolness, knew the spirits were measuring me up. I missed their usual chatter.

Neither of us spoke the rest of the ride. Sheriff Toomey's eyes had turned inward, their crisp blue lost in his own depths. I studied him side-wise. He wore ordinary denim workpants and the same indestructible, flannel-lined brown coat my pa wore when he worked in the cold. Sheriff Toomey was younger than my father, but the tired gray settling over his face, a deeper and unhappier gray than the bloom of beard along his jaw, was just the same as the gray in the lines of my father's face. I wondered if anyone else could see that color, or if it was a spirit shade, a color a man's own inner fire broadcast in its discomfort.

Then we came up over the ridge of Bluwalter Bluff, and down by a narrow stream a house hunched, its walls whitewashed and freshly mended, surrounded by haze of searing black no ordinary eyes could see. I had to blink away rainbows from the fierce light of it, and a greenish-white nimbus floated over my vision, shaped like a steep-roofed farmhouse. Even up here, the ugliness was so strong it stole my breath.

I stopped Fionn and took my ma's bundle from my coat pocket. The rosemary sat on top of the sandwich, green and fresh and clean-smelling. I squeezed it between my fingers and breathed in that good smell a few seconds, till my stomach stopped churning and aching. Then I tucked the rosemary sprig into my shirt pocket, as close to my skin as I could get it.

Sheriff Toomey sniffed as I caught up with him. "You know, that smell reminds me of old Mrs. Bluwalter—a mighty nice lady. She was from one of those old countries, Poland or Romania or something. While she was alive she washed the floor every day with her special herb soap. Said it kept peace in the house. Maybe she was right. Nothing bad ever happened there while she was alive."

His words made me break out in gooseflesh, and my hand went to my shirt pocket, pressing the herb until it scratched through the flannel. Three bad things had happened in that house, but none under the protective touch of rosemary. I was glad for Ma's provision.

Fionn whickered at me, almost too soft to hear. He could feel the house's ugliness as strong as I could, but he kept his walk even, just as calm as the great hero he was named for. Sheriff Toomey's horse tossed its head and shifted its weight around.

"Come on, girl, it'll be okay." He patted the horse's neck. "The animals smell the blood. They took the bodies back to town, but nobody's cleaned the place up yet."

I cleared my throat. The question I needed to ask felt too large for my mouth. "Sheriff. I got to know, before we get down there. What happened to Lura?"

He pulled short his mare and didn't look at me. "You sure you want to know?"

"I wouldn't ask it of you if it weren't important. Please, sir."

The hint of boyishness in the word "sir" seemed to strike him. From my place behind him, I saw his shoulders twitch. A boy like me should be at home finishing school work or starting some ordinary chore, like mending fence. He was the one who wanted to understand the house. He was the one who'd asked me to help.

"She was working on a baby blanket," he said, real lightly, like the words weren't so bad to say. He made a noise then, something what could have been a cough or sigh or a choked off sob. "She'd picked out some real nice wool for it. Soft, white and yellow. I can't tell you how many times she made me rub against my cheek to see if I thought it was soft enough."

I wanted to reach out to him, but I sat still.

"I keep thinking that maybe if I'd been home, I could have stopped her. That she would have asked me to stop her. I keep wondering if I did something that made her do it."

His voice dropped to a whisper, but I heard every word.

"I came home and I couldn't understand it. I thought maybe she'd fallen on the damn thing, but there's no way to fall on a crochet hook once and gouge out both eyes. Sometimes at night, I still see that damn crochet hook, sticking up out of her head, her beautiful face all covered in blood. Just like the moment I opened the front door and saw her."

The wind stirred the sagebrush, and for a second, I smelled snow. The clouds had thickened around the borders of the sky. I buttoned the top button of my coat.

"Strangest thing of all, Will, is that I never found that yarn. I can't think of what she did with it. It was so soft."

A strand of Fionn's mane fluttered up on the wind, a long string of white like an unspoiled skein of yarn. I thought of the terrible darkness of the house, that burning bright blackness.

Sheriff Toomey patted his horse's neck, then rubbed his fingers into the winter's thickness of her coat. "Come on, girl. It'll be okay," he repeated. He urged the mare forward.

We left the horses at the bottom of the bluff, tied to the Tuckers' windmill. The stillness of town had nothing on the dead silence of this place. Even the creak and squeal of the windmill seemed to come from someplace a thousand miles away, muffled by the distance. Sheriff Toomey's breaths sounded quick and shallow in my ear.

I'd never felt so alone. All my life the quiet presence of stone spirits and dust devils had kept me good company, the whispers of sagebrush and clover my constant companions. But whatever hid inside that house had somehow terrified the surrounding spirits into hiding. There was a deadness to the very earth under my boots. My heart gripped itself in my chest, stung with fear, and, yes, anger.

"I guess we'll start inside the house," the sheriff said, his voice tight. He led me up the porch steps.

"Wait," I said. I stepped forward and set my hand on the doorknob. I wanted to be first inside, wanted to see what scurried into place or out of sight before the other man disturbed it.

The knob wriggled beneath my palm like the back of a snake, cool and dry and slick. I jerked back, and the whole door rippled, laughing at me. I gritted my teeth and took hold of the knob again.

It turned easily, and the door swung open without even a creak. A smell escaped the house, a waft of a dozen ordinary smells, beeswax and cedar chips and bacon and firewood, but beneath them the stench of outhouses, spoilt meat, bull piss. The house breathed it out like a sick man breathed out bad humors. I'd never met a house with its own spirit, but this one hummed with the energy of a spirit bent on trouble.

For now, it just watched.

I took a step forward, and the sheriff fell in beside me. Mrs. Tucker had made her front room fine. White lace curtains framed the windows. A many-colored rag rug filled nearly the whole floor, and a bookshelf stood beside the wood stove. There were real books on the shelves as well as an entire zoo of whittled wooden animals. They called me to come touch them, but as I crossed the beautiful rug, something squished under my boot.

I didn't want to lift my foot.

Sheriff Toomey went pale when I did, and we saw the white shell of Mrs. Tucker's ear laying there, the soft shade of her skin a perfect match for her curtains. My gut heaved, but I didn't throw up. Barely.

The house chuckled, a low, dry sound.

Sheriff Toomey balled his hands into fists and stood there with his eyes closed a minute. "Shit," he whispered. I knew he was fighting the desire to turn around and run the hell out of this house — I had the same feeling. I wanted to set the damn place on fire and burn the darkness clean.

That would be my last option. I knew from Ma's stories, stories she'd heard from her granny: Sometimes things survived burning, and those things had a way of roaming. Whatever lived in this house, I wouldn't want to face it again.

We turned the corner into the kitchen, which was clean save for a long stripe of red-brown that Sheriff Toomey followed out into a little hall and then up a flight of stairs. The dark weight of the house pressed down upon me so that it was hard to breathe. The blood looked thicker on the steps, rich and chunky in some places.

The staircase bucked beneath my feet and I had to grab the railing as it nearly shook me loose.

The sheriff looked over his shoulder with a strange expression on his face. "You feel something?"

I nodded. I couldn't have answered if I had the breath to. I'd known that Sheriff Toomey was no unbeliever like my father. He must have felt something for the spirit world, or he would have never listened to the stories about Ma and come to us for help. But the strength of this thing was powerful enough to turn a believer into a senser. I felt a sudden liking for the man that went deeper than my respect for his badge and quiet manner.

At the top of the stairs, a black cloud rose up, leaping over Toomey to claw at my face. Cold fingers seared my skin. Iron fists pummeled my nose, my gut. I dropped to my knees, but didn't loosen my grip on the stair rail. I would not fall. I would not let this thing dominate me.

My mind hardened and pushed back with a force I didn't know I had. The black cloud snarled. There was a cold blast of rotting flesh and swamp water, and then I was alone at the top of the stairs, Sheriff Toomey staring down at me with wide eyes.

"Are you all right?" He tugged me to my feet. "I shouldn't have brought you here, damn it. Ain't no place for a boy. You shouldn't have to see this."

I realized he meant the great black puddle of blood that had dried on the landing. He hadn't seen the cloud, whatever it was. He could feel, but not see. And the thing hadn't touched him.

"I'm all right."

He shook his head.

I raised my hand. "I got to see this. All of it." I had to see what had happened to understand it, and I had to understand it to fight this spirit. It was like no spirit I had ever encountered. I had only known ordinary spirits, the animate forces of the natural world and a few dead men passing through this plane on their way to someplace else. Whatever this spirit was, it had been taken from the ordinary course of things and forced into monstrosity.

"We found little Michael Tucker up here. The blood keeps going—I reckon he was cut pretty bad in his room and then dragged out here. We had to gather up all his insides," Sheriff Toomey's voice broke, but he kept on, "because they were all spread out on the floor."

I followed the blood with my eyes, through an open door, where I could just make out a small bedstead with a blue quilt, a stuffed rabbit laying at the foot. The rabbit's ear was bloody.

"Mrs. Tucker was downstairs," Sheriff Toomey whispered.

The window of the little boy's room exploded.

We both dropped to our knees on the top of stairs as a window in the other bedroom burst. The doors to the rooms slammed shut.

Black liquid dripped from the top of the doorframes and oozed down the doors, molasses slow. Pounding sounded all around, the whole house resounding like a drum.

"Get downstairs!" Toomey shouted over the pounding, and he dragged me by the arm down the steps. We skidded into the kitchen, and the sound stopped.

I paused. The kitchen was clean, like when we first came in, everything in its proper place as my ma commended. But there was something wrong there, something what weren't there a minute ago: A black fur rug, draped over a chair back. The hairs rose on my neck. The rosemary sprig seemed to prickle and wriggle against my chest.

I didn't want to touch it, but I spread the thing out over the kitchen table anyway. The fur shone thick and lustrous in the light from the kitchen window. The pelt was heavy, and when I felt the leather of its hide, I felt a cold smoothness that rolled beneath my fingertips. I flipped it over.

"Oh," I breathed. A beaded border, all shimmering colors of mother-of-pearl and blue glass, followed the edge of the rug, and a neatly worked image of two horses and a little colt stood in the middle. It was beautiful. A treasure.

I couldn't help frowning at the ugly hole along one side, suspiciously round, like a bullet hole. A set of brown fingerprints marred one edge.

"I'd forgotten this." Sheriff Toomey put out his hand, but didn't touch the beaded surface. "Mr. Bluwalter once showed it to me. He'd found it in a closet or something. Figured it was an Indian thing, some kind of memento Schwartzkopf had left behind. It's the sort of thing you'd buy if you were getting older, I suppose. Something thick and warm for winters."

I touched it again, studying the beads. "Looks Nez Perce, maybe. And the fur ..." I broke off, remember what Toomey'd said: *his daughter got drug off by a bear.*

By a bear.

Sure felt like bear fur. The wheels of my mind spun, but something else exploded upstairs, and I smelled that smell again, thick swamp and dead things.

My eyes went back to the bullet hole and fingerprints. The fur rippled and twisted, the fingerprints going black, bright black, stinging my eyes.

"Let's get out of here," I said, and hurried out into the blessed chill air outside.

I stood on the gravel footpath leading up to the front door and stared out over the land, seeing again its dead grayness. Out here, all was quiet and clean-smelling, but the color of the earth warned me that the house's evil was spreading. The house had first forced one woman to kill herself, then a man to butcher his wife and son. Yes, it was getting stronger.

And me? What did I have? That new strength what had come out of my mind might have been strong enough to push away one of the house's manifestations, but I didn't doubt that its power was greater than any power I yet held. I was new at this. Untested. Untaught.

"What do we do?" Sheriff Toomey asked. "What's in there, Will?"

I shook my head. The only word I had for the spirit living in that house was *evil*, pure and simple.

Something nudged my ankle.

I looked down, surprised by the gentle touch. A pygmy rabbit stood on my boot, its tiny body a gray-brown that would have just matched the stem of a healthy sage bush. A faint line of light traced the outline of the rabbit's fur, the only hint that it was not what it appeared to be.

"Hello," I whispered. The rabbit nodded, just once, and sprang off my boot, bouncing off in the direction of an outbuilding I'd somehow overlooked.

"What's that?" I pointed. "Root cellar?"

Sheriff Toomey stared a moment, his blue eyes confused. "Well, shit. I plumb forgot about that. I always meant to tear it down since it wasn't doing anything." His eyes traveled from the building to my face, his usual focus coming back to them. "It's an old cistern."

I eyed the windmill and its pump. "Don't they have a well?"

"Mr. Schwartzkopf put the well in when he was preparing to sell the place. Told folks there was never enough rain to make the cistern worthwhile and that it had a leak. Pa Bluwalter said he never used it."

I saw a flicker of light by the old structure, and knew the spirits — the kinds of spirits that live in the good things of the world, my friends — had not left me. I pushed through the dead sagebrush and dried weeds to reach the abandoned cistern.

"What are you doing? There's nothing out here," Sheriff Toomey reminded me.

"There's something," I said. I pulled at on the door knob, but it wouldn't turn.

"It's locked, boy. Not safe to have these things open."

I kicked the door. I felt my stomach twisting, my skin crawling. There was something in there, something that needed out. I had to get in there.

"It's not going to come open, boy."

"Shoot it, Sheriff. Shoot the knob off!"

He blinked at me a second, then pushed me backward. "Cover your ears." He took his revolver from his holster and pressed the muzzle to the base of the door knob. He pulled back the hammer.

Even with my ears plugged, I heard the roar. The last bit of boy in me had to grin at the tremendous sound of it. He put his fingers into the hole he'd made, and then he yanked open the door.

The hinges ripped free of the wood and the door fell to the ground, hitting me in the arm on its way. I stood rubbing my shoulder, staring inside. A god-awful stink came up out of the cistern, a smell like dirt and skunk and some deeper, muskier smell I couldn't quite place. But it wasn't the smell of dead things or swamp. Whatever was in here, it was not a part of the house's spirit.

A narrow lip ran around the edge of the cistern, and a ladder disappeared going down into it. Afternoon sunshine lit the building as bright as the inside of the house. I took a step inside, leaning over the pit. Everything was black down there.

"There's a lantern on the front porch," Sheriff Toomey murmured. "I'll go get it."

I stood waiting for him, listening. Silence still lay heavy out here, but I could have sworn I heard a sound like skin moving against fabric. I rubbed my stomach. It hurt worse than ever.

"I got it." Sheriff Toomey struck a match, lit the lantern, and held it out over the yawning cistern.

The darkness below was not impenetrable. The light glimmered across glossy black curves and winked against flat black ovals. A ribbon of yellow appeared, then twisted away in a dry rustling. I knew the sound now. Snakes. Dozens and dozens of garter snakes.

"I have to go down there."

"No." Toomey grabbed my arm "No, boy, you've done enough. There ain't nothing to see down there. There wasn't anything here for you see anyway. Let's get you home."

I shook him off. "I know that whatever is in that house, it's getting stronger. It's stretching out across the land. You want that thing to come into town? You want to see what it does to other families?"

He studied my face. "Do you think that could really happen?"

I didn't laugh. I wasn't a boy anymore, to laugh at a man who doesn't want to see what's right in front of him. "I am sure of it. Sure enough to go into a snake den just to make sure there's nothing important at the bottom."

He held the lantern for me as I climbed down the ladder. Rung by rung, I felt more certain of what I was doing. I felt the strong hand of my mind reaching out to the creatures at the bottom of the cistern. Ma could have charmed these snakes into doing anything she wanted, but me, I had to work at it. I had to push and nudge and urge those cold and sleepy reptiles.

I stood in the clear space I'd made at the bottom of the ladder and looked around myself. The snakes had mounded up around the edges of the cistern, trembling with unhappiness and the need to sleep. They watched me with little fierce eyes. I could smell them clearly now, their rank and musty hibernating scent. Beneath it was the scent of water gone thick with algae, too spoilt to drink.

But the plaster-lined cistern looked dry all over, the precious water sucked up by the hungry desert air. Whatever catchment system Kurt Schwartkopf had installed, he'd taken it down when he put in the well. I knelt on the smooth tank bottom and studied the space by the faint orange glow of the sheriff's lantern.

It weren't all smooth. A little heap lay to one side, only half-uncovered by the snakes, but that half was enough for me. It was easy to make out the shapes of two skulls, one big, one tiny, a set of long arm bones curled around the little skeleton. The lantern light flickered and danced across the yellowed bone, showing the cracks and the ugly hole drilled into the biggest skull. Beside the bones, a string of beads, blue glass and mother-of-pearl, winked in the light.

I stood up, my head spinning in the stink of the snakes, the understanding settling in my mind. Wind roared around me. I felt the power of the spirits swelling my chest. Everything went dark.

"Will!" Toomey screamed.

The walls above me pounded and throbbed. Something shrieked. The clean white lines of the tiny baby skeleton glowed bright as pure sunshine.

I saw the picture on the bear fur blanket: two horses and a colt.

Something began to wrap itself around my ankle. All around me, the air trembled with the sound of hissing. I fell to my knees, too dizzy to stand. My hand landed on something soft, too soft to be a snake.

Sheriff Toomey screamed again, a horrible, pained sound.

In my mind the words kept repeating themselves: *blood will tell, blood will tell, blood will tell...*

A snake buried its fangs into the flesh of my leg. I slapped it away, felt the hot blood dripping down my ankle. I put the soft thing in my pocket and clawed for the ladder.

"Sheriff Toomey!"

The ladder bucked and wriggled in my hands. The air beat against me, pounding and clawing at my skin. The blackness burned as it spun around me. For a moment, I couldn't tell up from down.

"Will!"

Sheriff Toomey's voice. I reached up for it. Something bit into my calf, hot burning fangs. And a sudden brightness flared up beneath my feet. I had to look down.

Something shimmered like the pale light of a candle flame in a window. It stretched and bloomed, took shape, the outline of a woman. The snakes pulled back around her. The baby wriggled in her arms, all crying mouth and dark eyes and hair as thick and black as an Indian baby.

Blood will tell.

Unwilling, I reached out to them with the strong hand of my mind. *It's all right*, I said, firmly enough that it echoed in my head. *It's safe for you to come out now.*

The spirit woman shook her head.

"Will!"

Blackness whooshed down the ladder and caught me in a blast of cold air. I slid for a second, caught myself, climbed faster.

I fell onto Sheriff Toomey as I scrabbled out of the hole. The wind pummeled me and pounded the walls. The air trembled with the groan of timbers pushed too far. Half of the roof lifted free, sending shingles tumbling down onto us. I grabbed Sheriff Toomey's sleeve and staggered out of the remains of the shed.

The far wall of the shed shrieked as the wind ripped it off its foundation.

I could feel tears freezing on my face as I stumbled onto the gravel footpath and found I could not get up. Sheriff Toomey threw himself down beside me, and the wind, black and sooty, swept away the last boards of the old cistern building.

"I know you killed your daughter and her baby, Mr. Schwartzkopf!" I screamed it and I put will behind it. I couldn't see the old man's spirit in the black wind, but I knew it was there. "But now they're free! Both of them! They're free!"

The wind twisted upon itself, turning into a solid black cylinder whirling with broken boards and grit. It began to spin toward me.

I tried to reach out to it with my power. I tried to control it, tried to speak to it like I'd speak to any other spirit. But it bore down on me, thick and black and evil.

Then, deep inside the cyclone, lightning flashed. A bright white burning streak of it, the same shape as a deer's antler. And something inside the whirlwind screamed in unspeakable agony.

Then there was silence.

The cyclone went still, the boards falling to the ground in a clamor. The sheriff and I sat there, our voices gone. It was a long time before we heard another sound. It was just the territory song of a sparrow, but it cleared the strangeness from the air.

I got to my feet, as stiff as an old man. Sheriff Toomey looked worse than I did. When we reached the windmill, we had to lean against the horses' ordinary warmth and rest a moment before we could mount up. We didn't talk as we rode.

A man met us before we reached town. I knew him a little as the father of a schoolmate and one of Sheriff Toomey's deputies. He touched his hat when he saw the sheriff.

"Jake, I got some bad news. Paul Tucker's dead."

Sheriff Toomey's lips thinned. "How the hell did that happen?"

"He unraveled the blanket in his cell. Used the yarn to strangle himself. Poor bastard."

The sheriff passed his hand over his eyes. "I guess that's that."

"Yep."

"I got to see this boy home, but I'll be back at the office in about an hour. We'll talk then, all right? Meantime, I imagine it wouldn't hurt anything to let a few folks know."

We rode all the way home in silence, the sheriff looking sick to his stomach. He stopped at our gate. We sat there, neither one ready to leave the other, neither one sure what to say.

Finally, he spat off to the side of the road. "All of that for nothing."

"Not nothing, Sheriff. We fixed a place that was broken beyond the bounds of even the spirit world."

He laughed, a short sharp sad bark. "What does that do for Paul Tucker?"

I thought of the bear fur, the beautiful bracelet, the tiny baby. The picture of the three horses sewn in those Nez Perce beads. I knew in my gut what Mr. Schwartzkopf had done to his daughter and grandbaby and the Indian man who had brought them that fur blanket, but just at moment, I was too tired to explain it all.

"I don't know exactly, Mr. Toomey. But I think Lura would have." I took the soft bundle out of my coat pocket, and passed it to him.

He stared a long time at the skein of wool in his hand. It wasn't pale yellow any more, more of a grubby gray than anything else, but he still rubbed it to his cheek, his eyes suddenly bright.

"You can call me Jake," he said. "You're man enough."

I nodded, and leaned down to open the gate. I didn't look back at him as I urged Fionn homeward. I could feel the welcoming presence of my friendly spirits.

Good job, a voice whispered, and though I couldn't see her, I knew it was Deer Maiden.

The first snowflake fell as I rode toward the barn. It fluttered past me on a rustle of wind, the sagebrush rustling with the passage of Granddaddy Rattlesnake, seeking his kin.

RUIN CREEK

GAIL Z. MARTIN AND LARRY N. MARTIN

"ARE YOU SURE ABOUT THE TELEGRAM?" AGENT JACOB DRANGOSAVICH set his carpetbag down on the platform of the empty train station. "You're certain you read the time right?"

His partner, Mitch Storm, leveled a glare. "Yes, about the telegram. And yes, I can tell time."

"Then there aren't many other people taking the train to Ruin Creek, are there?" Jacob asked drolly. Their horses were stabled near the station, awaiting their return. A single gaslight burned at one end of the wooden platform. Even the ticket agents were gone by this late hour, and no other passengers were in sight.

"Not leaving from here, anyhow." Mitch began to pace. With dark hair, a trim, muscular build and a five o'clock shadow that darkened at three, Mitch looked like every penny-dreadful writer's epitome of an Army sharpshooter and secret government agent. Jacob was tall and raw-boned, with a long face and blue eyes that spoke to his Eastern European background. All things considered, a darkened train station in the middle of Arizona wasn't the strangest place they'd been sent by the Department of Supernatural Investigations.

In the distance, a coyote howled. Moonlight cast the saguaro cactus in strange shadows. Overhead, the stars seemed bright as a lawman's badge, and the darkened ridge of the Superstition Mountains loomed on the horizon.

"It's just strange, having Headquarters send us out without notice," Jacob remarked.

Mitch shrugged. "Not the first time; probably won't be the last. Things come up, especially in our business. A fellow agent calls for assistance, we go."

"If the telegram hadn't had all the right codes, I'd worry we were being set up," Jacob replied.

"You're worrying about that anyhow." Mitch knew his partner. "I triple-checked the codes."

"I don't like getting sent out at the last minute without more information," Jacob groused.

Mitch rolled his eyes. "When has the Department ever worried about telling us everything we needed to know?"

Jacob grunted in grudging assent.

The mournful whistle of an oncoming train echoed across the empty desert landscape. A silver and black train ghosted to a stop at the platform and sent a puff of coal smoke into the air. It was a small train, just two passenger cars and two boxcars behind the engine and coal car. The passenger cars were brightly lit, but as far as Jacob could tell, they were empty.

"All aboard!" A man with a conductor's uniform leaned out of the doorway to the first passenger car. Mitch grabbed his carpetbag and the long duffel that carried their weapons and hopped on before Jacob could utter a word, forcing him to catch up.

"Classy," Mitch said as they entered the Pullman car. The seats were flocked green velvet and the cars were paneled with mahogany. Brass-shaded lanterns hung from the ceiling.

"Empty," Jacob said, walking to the back of the car to check that no one was hiding on the floor between any of the empty seats. He peered through the glass in the door to the vestibule, looking into the second, equally deserted car. "I don't like this."

Mitch had already selected a seat with his back to the wall where he could watch the entire length of the car. Jacob reluctantly took a seat opposite him where he could see the other door. Mitch had a newspaper on his lap and beneath it, his Colt Peacemaker. He removed a silver flask from his pocket, took a swig, and offered it to Jacob, who shook his head. "Maybe when we get where we're going in one piece," Jacob replied.

The conductor entered from between the two passenger cars and walked toward them as if an empty train in the wee hours of the morning was the most natural thing in the world. "Tickets, please."

Mitch held out the two tickets that had been delivered to their hotel within an hour of the unexpected telegram. The conductor barely glanced at the tickets, then nodded curtly.

"Do you make this run nightly?" Jacob asked.

"Make it when we need to make it," the conductor replied as the engine started with a slight lurch. "Folks need to get to Ruin Creek, we stop here."

"I know it's late," Jacob said in his friendliest tone, "but it's pretty quiet. Where'd you come from?"

The conductor looked at Jacob as if the question didn't register at first. "Down the line a ways," he answered. "Far away. Long haul."

"I'm just surprised that the cars are empty," Jacob continued. "Seems like a lot of effort to run us out to Ruin Creek by ourselves. Isn't there another train going that way in the morning?"

"Don't know about that," the conductor said, turning away. "I just do this route. Make yourselves comfortable. Won't be long. No stops between here and there." With that, he turned away and ambled down the empty car.

"Talkative fellow," Mitch said.

"Have I mentioned that I don't like this?" Jacob said. "There's something fishy going on." In response, Mitch closed his eyes and leaned back against the tufted seat cushions. "I'll wake you up in two hours," Jacob growled, settling in with his gun handy. "Then it's my turn to sleep."

Phoenix, Arizona, where they got on the train, was a wide-open outpost, not yet twenty years old. Anywhere they were headed was likely to be even rougher. Jacob had never heard of a town called Ruin Creek before the telegram, but the West was full of tiny railroad towns that sprang up and died within a year or two as the railroad workers and their camp followers moved on.

"You don't think Ruin Creek is anywhere near Canyon Diablo, do you?" Jacob asked, ignoring the fact that Mitch was dozing off.

"Canyon Diablo is twelve miles northwest," Mitch grunted, slouching further in his seat.

"I'm just saying, two government agents riding into a town like Canyon Diablo aren't going to ride back out," Jacob warned. "I heard that town went through eight lawmen in six months. Nothing but saloons and houses of ill repute."

"Sounds like my kind of town," Mitch said, turning away from Jacob.

"We didn't bring enough ammunition to go into a town like that," Jacob continued.

"Speak for yourself."

With a sigh, Jacob settled in for his time on watch. The train was moving fast, streaking through the night as the wheels made a *click-clack* rhythm. Jacob's Remington revolver was where he could draw it quickly and so was a Bowie knife. A shotgun, Mitch's rifle, and an assortment of other weapons were in the duffel bag overhead.

The train pulled into Ruin Creek at nine. "Last stop," the conductor said, reappearing just before the train slowed. Jacob peered out of the window. What he could see was unimpressive. The station was just a small shed and an awning over a wooden platform.

"Funny. There's no one here to meet us," Mitch muttered as they walked across the platform. Behind them, the train whistle sounded and then the locomotive pulled away from the station.

"There's a note," Jacob said, pointing to an envelope pinned up on the board where schedule updates usually were posted. 'Department of Supernatural Investigation', the envelope read. Jacob took it down and unfolded a single sheet of paper.

"Sorry I couldn't be here for your arrival," he read aloud. "Cline's Rooming House is expecting you. Leave your bags in the parlor. I'll meet you there and will explain more then. Many thanks. The letter's signed, 'Ahiga Sani'."

"That's a Navajo name," Mitch observed.

Jacob nodded. "The town is technically on Navajo land. The brass had to clear it through a couple of other offices to keep from getting sideways with the tribe before they sent us."

"That, and the fact that the last agent they sent out here disappeared." Eli Bly, the agent who had sent a telegram asking for back up at Ruin Creek, had not been heard from since that brief, urgent message.

"If it were easy, they wouldn't pay us big salaries to figure out what's going on," Jacob said.

Mitch looked askance at him. "They don't pay us big salaries, but we're still the ones who get shot at." He checked his watch. "Almost nine-thirty now. We'd better get going," he added and hefted the duffle bag onto one shoulder, lifting his carpetbag with the other hand.

"We can drop off our carpetbags at the rooming house, but I'll keep this one with us."

While their carpetbags held only clothing, it wouldn't do to have someone poking around the duffle. Not only had Mitch loaded it with weapons, but it contained experimental—and useful—scientific gear from a genius inventor at Tesla Westinghouse in New Pittsburgh. Some of the equipment was sanctioned by the Department. Other pieces were custom-made, off-the-books items that Mitch maintained were need-to-know only. And the Department, in Mitch's opinion, did not need to know.

Ruin Creek had one main street. Hastily erected wooden buildings lined both sides of the thoroughfare, with sidewalks made of rough-hewn planks. Half a dozen saloons, three bordellos, four rooming houses, a dance hall, and a dry goods store sustained the hard-working railroaders and those who had come West to help them spend their money. Behind the main street sat a blacksmith's forge, a stable, and a few dozen houses that were more like shanties.

"Looks like the townsfolk know how to have fun," Mitch observed drily. Faces peered from the windows as they walked the length of the main street. Jacob felt like he and Mitch were being paraded for the town to see, and his hand never strayed far from his gun. The hair on the back of his neck rose, though nothing presented a clear threat. The town was eerily silent except for the rustling of the wind.

"If it's like the other railroad towns we've been in, they're a long way from home doing a hard job, and they take their comfort where they can," Jacob replied.

Cline's Rooming House was a two-story clapboard home at the end of Main Street. Its weathered siding did not look as if it had ever been painted, and dust clouded the windows and covered the front porch. Mitch and Jacob climbed the stairs and gave a knock at the door. No one answered.

They looked at each other and shrugged. Just in case, Jacob drew his gun, but he kept it down at his side as Mitch pushed the door open.

The rooming house kitchen was unremarkable. A battered farmhouse table and chairs were in the center of the room, while a Hoosier cupboard sat along one wall and a cast-iron stove hunkered against the back wall.

"Looks like no one's home, so I guess we'll figure out where our room is later," Mitch said, as Jacob nosed into the parlor and found it empty. "Let's drop off the bags and find someone who can tell us why we're here."

When they headed out a few moments later, a lone man stood on the porch, waiting for them. He had sharp features and tawny skin, and he wore a loose chambray shirt over worn denim pants and scuffed boots, along with a black reservation hat with a woven hat band. The stranger held up his hands. "I mean you no harm." He paused. "Are you from the Department? Thank you for coming."

Mitch wore the same expression he used for poker, flinty-eyed and unreadable. "Maybe. Who are you?"

"My name is Ahiga Sani. This is Navajo land, and I'm the local shaman. I came to greet you, and help you understand your task."

Mitch stepped forward to shake his hand. "Agent Mitch Storm, and this is my partner Jacob Drangosavich," he said, with a smile that didn't reach his eyes. Jacob noticed that before Mitch shook hands with the stranger, his left hand closed around a charm on his watch fob. It was a gift from an absinthe witch, a way to tell if the person being touched had magic. His expression gave nothing away, but Jacob knew his partner well enough to notice a slight flinch. *There's magic afoot,* Jacob thought. *But why?*

"What seems to be the trouble?" Jacob asked. "Contacting the Department means you're requesting a very specific type of help. We're not exactly the Texas Rangers."

"No, you're not," Sani replied. "Ruin Creek has a peculiar kind of trouble, and that requires a particular kind of help."

"We were invited by a man named Eli Bly," Mitch replied. "Have you seen him?"

Sani nodded. "I met Mr. Bly. But he is gone now. As for the reason for the telegram, you are correct about there being 'problems'. Strange airships have flown overhead. A silver ship crashed near here. Pieces of it scattered across the desert. They call to the *chindi,* the bad ghosts. They brought a skinwalker and an outlaw. Bly's message for you was to find the pieces, set the ghosts to rest, and release the spirits."

"Who's the outlaw?" Jacob probed. "And if an airship crashed, what do the pieces have to do with ghosts and monsters? Why would it cause problems for the town?"

"Some things aren't meant to be here," Sani said. "They give off bad energy. Strange power."

"Do you know where the pieces are?" Mitch asked. "Can you lead us to them?"

Sani shook his head. "No. Their power wars with my magic. But the railroad people disturbed the site after the crash, brought things to the surface that should have stayed asleep. No one can rest until it's put right."

That explains why Mitch reacted the way he did. Jacob thought. "So you think the pieces that caused the problem are near where the railroad construction was?" Jacob eyed the stranger warily. Something about the man made the hair on the back of his neck prickle.

"It wasn't a regular airship, was it?" Mitch asked.

Sani shook his head. "It was not meant to be here. What it left behind doesn't belong. Things won't be right until it's gone. You have to find it."

"We're not going to have any problems with the tribe, are we?" Mitch asked. "Because top people signed off on our clearance."

"The tribe is not the problem." Sani led them to where they could see the horizon west of town. "See that rise?" he asked, pointing. "Just over it is a valley. About six months ago, people started seeing strange lights in the sky from over that way. Bright lights that weren't stars, moving too fast to be anything natural. Odd noises, too. Scared off the animals — even the coyotes, and they don't scare easily," he said with a chuckle.

"Then folks saw airships in the sky, day and night, but they didn't look like regular airships," he said. "Too many lights on them, and too much metal."

"Maybe the Army is trying out new equipment," Mitch suggested.

"The Army denied ownership, remember?" Jacob said recalling one of the few pieces of information they were given. *Typical,* Jacob thought. *Try out a bunch of newfangled inventions, scare the locals half to death, and pretend it never happened.*

"There was a crash. Some people from the town disappeared," Sani continued. "Cattle died. Chickens quit laying eggs. Dogs barked at nothing."

Mitch and Jacob exchanged a look. *Now we're getting somewhere,* Jacob thought. *Strange airships and weird occurrences are right up our alley.*

"What about the railroad?" Jacob asked. "That's why the town is here. How much longer will the work last?" He looked around at the deserted streets. "And where is everyone?"

Sani shrugged. "They finished the bridge the townsfolk were here to build about six months ago, right after the crash. The work's dried up, and Ruin Creek dried up with it. But there were a few still doing clean up, moving the last of the supplies. The ones that didn't leave town after the crash, the skinwalker took. All that's left now are the dead, buried out yonder by that big tree," he said with a nod of his head. "But they don't rest easy."

"You never said how you knew about the Department." Mitch said it casually, but Jacob picked up on the caution in his partner's tone. "After all, we're not common knowledge."

"Eli Bly told me to expect you." Sani said. "Then he left."

"Where did he go?" Mitch asked.

Sani shrugged. "Don't know. But he wasn't the only stranger poking around. There's been another man looking around the ridge. Bly said he was an outlaw. He took a shot at me, when I got too close. The spirits don't like him, either."

"What did he look like?" Jacob raised an eyebrow, as a suspicion grew.

"Tall man, thin like a scarecrow. Sharp nose. Hair like straw. Shot his gun left-handed," Sani replied.

Mitch and Jacob exchanged a glance. "Peter Kasby?" Mitch said with a sigh. "He's trouble, all right."

"From what you've said, it makes sense he'd show up here," Jacob added. "Everyone calls him 'The Prospector' because he goes out to sites where there are problems and sees what he can steal."

"He's a dangerous man," Sani agreed. "Be careful. He may still be around."

"We've tangled with Kasby before," Mitch replied. "But thanks for the warning. Now, we need some horses and supplies if we're going to have a look over that ridge."

"You'll find your horses in the stable, ready to go, saddlebags packed with all the equipment you should need," Sani said. "Best you be back here by nightfall. There are worse things than coyotes in the dark. You'll find food in the cupboard for your meals and some to take with you when you ride out to look beyond the ridge. There's a well in the back to fill your canteens, and a few bottles of whiskey in the dry sink cabinet. You're the only guests at the rooming house."

"Sounds like you've taken care of everything," Mitch said. "So we'll get to work." He glanced at Sani. "Are you coming out to the ridge with us?"

Sani shook his head. "My magic will not permit me to enter the crater. The power of what the silver ship left behind wars with my abilities."

He dropped his voice. "I speak with the dead. The spirit of the captain of the silver ship came to me. He told me to find the metal boxes and turn them off so he and his people can finally rest."

"Metal boxes?" Jacob asked. "Equipment?"

Sani sighed. "I am a shaman. I speak with spirits. But sometimes, the spirits can't say plainly what they need. This spirit shared an image with me, of two metal boxes and a silvery oval. I assume they were the equipment he meant. I gathered they were damaged in the crash, and something about those boxes is raising hell. It got worse when someone started digging, bringing them closer to the surface. The sooner you can shut them down, the better." Sani gave them a tip of his hat in farewell and strode off down the street. Mitch and Jacob turned and walked toward the stable

"You believe him?" Jacob asked under his breath.

"Not completely," Mitch replied. "There's something weird about this place—but that's the point, I guess. The sooner we find out what it is and how to put it right, the faster we can get back to New Pittsburgh or somewhere else that's civilized."

"You think Bly just told him about the Department—and us?"

Mitch shrugged. "Maybe. We don't know how well he knew Sani, and what called him away. And the Department didn't bother to tell us. Typical."

"So is Bly really missing? Or just reassigned?"

"Maybe when we get to the bottom of this, we'll know," Mitch replied.

They found the horses saddled and tied up to the hitching post by the stable. Mitch and Jacob checked the saddlebags and found food, water, and survival equipment: a pickaxe and shovel, compass, tarpaulin, and a few other essentials. Mitch secured the duffel bag and the two men rode out toward the ridge.

"Ruin Creek isn't the first place to report strange airships," Jacob observed.

"Been a lot of reports this year," Mitch agreed. "Always in some god-forsaken corner of the desert where the people who might see something aren't likely to be taken seriously."

"Do you think Sani is telling the truth about Bly?" Jacob asked.

"Don't know what I think about that," Mitch replied. "Bly sent a request for backup. So where is he?"

"The West is a big place," Jacob said. "He could have gotten reassigned by one of the other managers. You know they don't talk to each other. We drew the short straw because we were handy. For all we know, Bly's up in the Yukon, looking for sasquatch."

"Are those hairy guys causing problems again? I thought we told them to keep it quiet and stay in the woods." They rode in silence for a while. Jacob kept looking over his shoulder, sure they were being watched, but he saw no one. Still, he made certain his duster was out of the way of his holster, in case he needed a fast draw.

"Well, will you look at that?" Mitch murmured as they reached the crest of the rise. Below them spread a wide crater with deep, sloping walls. "Holy Hell."

Jacob raised an eyebrow. "Whatever made a hole like that when it hit had to be big."

The desert stretched as far as the eye could see in every direction. They slipped and slid their way to the bottom of the basin. "Yeah, they were looking for something," Jacob observed. Dozens of holes pockmarked the bottom of the depression. They had clearly been shoveled out and the work looked recent.

"Sani's story doesn't explain why people disappeared or why there were problems with the livestock," Jacob replied.

"Could be coincidence. Something strange happens, and people blame everything that happens afterward on it, whether the two are related or not," Mitch said with a shrug. "Or maybe they got hit with the ship when it fell. Doesn't take much to set dogs to barking, and chickens go off laying for all kinds of reasons." He pulled out a black box with a silver metal probe connected by a cord and cranked it up, watching the dials and gauges as he swept the probe in an arc around him.

"I'm getting some very strange data," Mitch said. "The EMF readings are pegging the dials."

"Okay," Jacob replied, drawing out the syllables. "That could mean about a dozen or more things."

"Despite what I picked up from Sani, I don't think we're dealing with magic out here." Mitch tucked the meter away and drew out the charm he had been given by the absinthe witch. He held it by a thin silver chain, and to Jacob's eye, the charm did absolutely nothing. "See? It's not glowing or spinning."

"There's magic, and then there's the supernatural," Jacob said. "People call those hills the 'Superstition' Mountains, for a reason. We're on Navajo land. Maybe Renate's charm doesn't pick up on Navajo juju."

Mitch scowled at him and shoved the charm back in his pocket. "There's a new toy Farber built for me—a mineral detector. It's the funny-looking thing in the duffle bag that's not a gun. How about taking a look around with it?"

"What are you going to do?"

Mitch grinned. "Fiddle with the Maxwell box."

Jacob had plenty of experience with Adam Farber's experimental gadgets. The young man was a certifiable genius who impressed even Nikola Tesla with his designs. But often, the first-of-their-kind pieces of equipment Farber built for the Department caused unintended consequences. Jacob had learned to be cautious.

Jacob pulled out a metal contraption that looked like a pole with a few loops of steel tubing at the bottom, and plenty of wires and gauges along the sides. Powered by a Gassner battery, and embellished by Farber, the detector began beeping loudly as soon as Jacob turned it on.

"There's iron scattered all over this lake bed," Jacob said. "Lots of it. Some nickel, too."

Mitch kicked at the ground, then bent down to pick up a handful of blue-white crystals. "Bring that thing over here, will you?" Jacob rolled his eyes but complied.

Mitch flipped a switch on the detector, then ran the crystals beneath the scanner. "Look at this," he said. "Really strange quartz—not like anything I've ever seen before. Even the scanner is saying there's got to be an error."

"Maybe the airship crash did something to the rock, especially if there was a lot of heat," Jacob said.

"Maybe." Mitch pulled out a black box with knobs and gauges. "Let's see what kind of ghosts we can call up."

"I really wish you wouldn't," Jacob replied. "We don't have the usual protections."

Mitch made a dismissive gesture. "I'm not going to turn it on full blast. Let's start with the simple stuff."

"Only you would consider ghosts to be 'simple'."

Mitch glared at him. "All right. Just in case, grab one of the Ketchum grenades in the bag. And there's an icon in that red box from Father Matija."

Jacob grumbled under his breath, but he retrieved the items. Mitch turned the knob on the Maxwell box. They didn't have long to wait.

"Look!" Jacob said, pointing to the ridge. Light shimmered like heat waves coming off the desert all along the lip of the depression. In those shimmering waves, Jacob made out the faces and forms of people, though they were distorted by something that pulled them this way and that, like a column of smoke in a breeze.

"Something's interfering with the Maxwell box," Mitch said. "Something strong enough to repel the ghosts even though I've got the power turned up." He glanced at the gauges. "We're pegging the meter. Plenty of ghosts to go around, but for some reason, they can't pass the crest of the ridge."

"Let them go," Jacob urged. "Bad enough that they're dead. Now we know—this place has the spirits all stirred up, but they don't want to come into the basin."

Mitch nodded and turned down the knob on the Maxwell box. The shimmering line of ghosts winked out. "They're gone," he said, looking up at the now-deserted ridge.

"I still feel like we're being watched," Jacob replied. "You believe Sani about *chindi* and the skinwalker?" he asked as he replaced the grenade in the duffel bag and drew his revolver. The heavy, cold steel was a comfortable certitude.

"I believe that he believes in them," Mitch replied with a shrug. "But I'm intrigued about these 'missing pieces' and I really want to know why Kasby—if he's the one—is hanging around."

"Maybe someone else has a wunderkind like Farber coming up with secret inventions," Jacob said. "Only one of theirs didn't work so well. And maybe their 'silver bird' had other off-the-books gadgets onboard that got damaged in the crash and are going haywire." He shrugged. "Imagine an airship crashing with a Maxwell box onboard and having it get stuck turned on full blast."

Mitch repressed a shiver. "I'd rather not, if it's all the same to you."

"What now?" Jacob asked.

"We go looking for the pieces that Mr. Sani told us got dug up in the railroad construction. Find them, and we're closer to fixing the problem."

"There's a lot of nothing out here." Jacob kicked a rock and sent it tumbling through the dust. It was still mid-morning, cool by desert standards. Saguaro and mesquite stretched as far as the eye could see. "And so far, we've seen more rattlesnakes than pieces of strange airships."

"I think Sani was right," Mitch replied, ignoring his comments. "Somebody crashed an experimental ship with gear onboard. Either they couldn't find the missing pieces or no one filed the right paperwork for a recovery team, so it's still here, causing issues."

"You think it's one of ours?" Jacob asked, raising an eyebrow.

"We're pretty far south for it to be the Canadians," Mitch replied, walking a parallel course to the railroad tracks, running the metal detector back and forth. He frowned as the detector beeped, but all he found was the button from a man's jacket. He straightened and looked at the button in the light.

"What if it's other?" Jacob asked.

"European?"

"Farther than that."

Mitch shrugged. "Maybe. It's happened before. Those orbs over New Pittsburgh. Remember?"

Jacob remembered. The Department of Supernatural Investigation was not limited to problems with rogue magic. Sometimes, the threats came from far away—not just beyond the United States, but beyond Earth. "Yeah, I thought of that. But let's start with the simplest explanation. And that would be someone with enough resources to outfit an experimental airship with off-the-record bells and whistles. That's scary enough, considering the short list of who might be behind a project like that."

Mitch held out the button to Jacob. "What do you make of this?"

Jacob frowned as he examined the stamped brass. "Military issue. One of our folks. Doesn't look like it's been out in the elements too long."

Mitch nodded. "Might be a clue to confirm our hole-digger. Now let's see—treasure hunter, rogue agent, outlaw—sure sounds like someone we know."

Jacob swore. "Yeah, the Prospector. I was hoping it wasn't."

"Well, it all fits. I thought they'd finally locked him up in Fort Leavenworth," Mitch replied.

"Maybe he got out for good behavior. Or escaped. Or paid someone off," Jacob said.

"Think he had anything to do with Bly being here—or his sudden departure?" Mitch's tone made his own opinion clear.

"I think it's very possible. Even likely."

Mitch and Jacob were both on the lookout for danger as they climbed the sloping sides of the basin. Nothing but cactus and rock formations met their gaze as they peered over the rim before scrambling out.

"I set the Maxwell box to its lowest setting," Mitch said, glancing at the device. "Farber assured me that would just monitor whether ghosts were present, but not call them or drive them away."

"And?"

Mitch made a face as he stared at the readings. "There's a lot of activity around the basin. And some weird readings I can't explain."

Mitch gave the Maxwell box to Jacob and took the mineral detector for himself, hefting the duffel bag with their extra weapons over his shoulder. Then they led their horses by the reins over to the railway tracks.

The stretch of railroad tracks ran as far as the eye could see. They agreed to walk for two miles in either direction of the track closest to the crater, then switch sides. Out of the corner of his eye, Jacob glimpsed movement, but when he turned to look, no one was there. *On the other hand, my horse is skittish as a colt,* Jacob thought. *People say horses can see ghosts. So maybe I'm not crazy. I'm certain we're not alone, and I'm positive we're being watched.*

"I'm getting some strange readings," Jacob said.

"Me, too," Mitch agreed.

The toe of Jacob's boot caught an edge of something metallic. "I've got something!"

"What did you find?"

Jacob bent down, kicking at the dirt for a better look. "A bit of silvery metal—not the kind of thing I'd expect from the Atcheson-Topeka."

"Throw it in the bag," Mitch said. "We'll sort it out later."

"And you?'

"Lots of rocks," Mitch replied. "Bits of something my detector recognizes as metallic, but can't identify the composition. We may have to send them to the lab at HQ to get an analysis."

"We can send a telegraph from Ruin Creek," Jacob said.

"Yeah," Mitch replied. "I think that would be a good idea. Something about this whole mission gives me the creeps."

Jacob was glad Mitch admitted being uneasy. He had misgivings since they had been dispatched. The missing folks of Ruin Creek and the mysterious Navajo shaman only deepened his concerns.

"Now that's interesting," Jacob said, bending down for a better look. A smooth, oval-shaped metallic object caught the light. It was no bigger than his palm, and definitely not natural.

"What?"

Jacob let his hand hover over the object and felt a prickle of power. "I'll throw it in the bag," Jacob said. "You find anything?"

"Nothing bigger than a quarter," Mitch replied. "Makes me think our Navajo friend was right, but whatever it was didn't just crash — it exploded."

"Makes you wonder what they had onboard," Jacob said.

They heard the unmistakable crack of a rifle shot, and the bullet barely missed Jacob's shoulder. His horse shied. Mitch had his own rifle up and sighted before Jacob could calm his frightened horse, and returned fire, though there was no one in sight.

"Get to cover!" Mitch snapped, and Jacob pulled his mount into the only shelter close at hand, the shadow of three large saguaro cactus. Mitch swung partway up to the saddle, rifle at the ready, as he rode for the scant protection of a rock pile left behind by the railroad construction.

A second shot kicked up dirt just behind Mitch's horse. Jacob returned fire. He could not spot the sniper, but the only likely cover was another pile of dirt from the construction efforts, far enough away to make even a sharpshooter's aim iffy.

"Look!" Jacob called to Mitch, pointing toward a rising dust cloud behind a rapidly retreating man on horseback. "Do you think we can catch him?"

Mitch shook his head. "Too much of a chance he's leading us into an ambush. He'll be back."

"It's not like Kasby to miss," Jacob observed. Mitch was a sharp-shooter, and long ago, Kasby had been part of Mitch's rifle unit. A lot of bad blood separated then from now.

"He missed on purpose," Mitch replied, anger clear in his voice. "He's warning us away from 'his' find. To hell with that."

All of their hot, dry hours of work led to a bucketful of bits of odd metal, fused rock, and shiny objects. All the while, Jacob could not shake the feeling that they were being observed.

Movement off to one side caught Mitch's attention. "What was that?"

"I don't know," Jacob said warily. "Whatever it is, I don't like it."

Both Jacob and Mitch pulled their guns. This time Jacob caught movement out of the corner of his eye, something cutting them off on the right. "Let's get back to town," he murmured.

"Sounds good to me," Mitch agreed.

A strange, lonesome cry broke the desert silence. Both their mounts spooked at once, whinnying and prancing nervously. When Mitch and Jacob looked up again, a hunched, snaggle-toothed creature with red eyes and sharp fangs blocked the roadway.

"That's a skinwalker," Jacob said quietly. "When it's not wearing a borrowed skin. Saw a drawing in an old book. We're in trouble."

"Get out of the way," Mitch said, drawing his Peacemaker. "We mean you no harm."

The creature glared at him, a crafty, hungry look. It did not move to let them past.

"Stand aside," Jacob said, bringing up his revolver where he was sure the creature could see it.

In response, the creature snarled and lunged straight at them.

Jake and Mitch reined their horses in hard to keep them from bolting. Mitch fired a shot, but the bullet passed right through the skinwalker without harm.

"It's a ghost!" Mitch shouted.

"Yeah, but it's coming right at us!" They took off at a gallop. The ghost followed, snapping at their mounts.

"I have the feeling we're being herded," Mitch called over his shoulder, as he and Jacob tried to outrun the creature. Every time they tried to get back on the road, the ghost snapped and dove at them, driving them around the rim of the crater.

"Yeah. Me too," Jacob admitted. "The question is—why?"

By this time, they were on the opposite side of the huge depression from where they had entered. The ghost hunkered down just far enough away to keep the horses from bolting. Construction crews had dumped dirt and debris on this side of the basin, and windblown mounds stretched for a quarter mile.

Mitch swung down from his horse. "Maybe we're supposed to find something here Maybe that's the point."

"*Maybe* that shadow has friends, and they're going to eat us," Jacob replied. "Maybe *that's* the point." They were quiet for a few moments, keeping a careful eye on the skinwalker as they looked for debris.

"I think Sani knows more than he's saying."

"Yeah," Jacob said bending down to examine something that was half buried in the sandy soil. "I think you're right."

Mitch picked up on the change of tone. "What did you find?"

"Not sure," Jacob replied. "But it might be what Bly and Kasby were looking for."

By the time they returned to Ruin Creek, the moon had risen. The skinwalker shadowed them back to town but made no further move to attack.

They headed into the rooming house. Lanterns burned in the windows, but the kitchen was quiet. Dried sausage, cheese, dried fruit, and hard bread were in the cupboard just like Sani said, as was the whiskey. Jacob took a bucket and went out to the well, returning with fresh drinking water.

"I think it's time we got some back-up," Mitch said. "Let's get a telegram off to Agent Kennedy. I want to make sure she's going to have an airship out here to pick us up, and if she's got any intelligence on weird airship sightings, now's the time to sing out about it."

Jacob gave a curt nod. "Agreed. Right after we eat."

With a skinwalker and a hostile sharpshooter on the loose, Mitch and Jacob went together to send the telegram. Mitch took the duffel bag of weapons and the three most valuable items they had found at the crater with them, in case Kasby had tracked them to the rooming house.

Lights glowed in the windows of the houses, saloons, and brothels. Faint strains of music carried on the night air, and shadows moved behind the curtains.

"I thought Sani said everyone else was gone," Jacob said nervously. "Are you sure the Maxwell box is off?"

"Yeah, I'm sure," Mitch replied. "But I'm starting to wonder just what kind of trouble Bly's gotten us into."

"There's the railroad station, where the telegraph office should be," Jacob said, with a nod toward the small shed. Dust covered everything in the cramped office. Rumpled, yellowed papers lay scattered across a hard-used desk. Jacob rustled through the papers while Mitch stood guard. "Can't find anything dated more recently than six months ago," Jacob said. He reached for the telegraph key and began to tap out the Department security code. "Damn."

"What?"

"Telegraph isn't working," Jacob said, adding a few choice curse words in his native Croatian for emphasis.

Mitch kept his gun at the ready as he craned for a look out the window. "Well, that would explain why," he said, pointing. Jacob peered over his shoulder. The nearest telegraph pole was down, and it had pulled the wires right out of the wall of the station when it fell.

"Tomorrow, we'll nail down the truth from that shaman," Mitch said. "Let's get back to the rooming house. I don't know what's going on, but I definitely don't like it."

Both of them had their revolvers in hand as they walked back toward town. Their boot steps echoed on the plank sidewalks. Music still came from the saloons and bordellos, and they could see the silhouettes of townsfolk going about their evening routine behind the thin curtains.

The sound of a raucous player piano grew louder as they approached the Brass Pounder saloon, along with a woman's laughter and the muted rumble of men's voices. Mitch pushed open the door into the tavern and found a darkened, abandoned shell.

"Nobody's here," Jacob said.

Mitch glanced down at the Maxwell box. "Oh, they're here. The meter on the box is jumping like catfish on a hot summer day. Sani told us the truth, at least about the dead being restless." He looked up at the dirty mirror behind the dusty, ornate bar. "Isn't that right?"

The mirror cracked loudly enough that for a second, Jacob mistook it for a gunshot, fracturing from the center out, showing the ruined bar like a crazy carnival mirror. Glassware hurled itself off of the shelves, sending a spray of shards into the room. Jacob dug into the duffle and pulled out a strange long gun, like a shotgun wound with wires and tubes. He kept his revolver in one hand and the newfangled weapon in the other, as Mitch and he began to back toward the doorway, one of them facing in each direction.

Footsteps sounded on the stairs from the second floor. The piano music suddenly started up again, though the old upright along one wall was as swaybacked as a knacker's mare. A chair tipped over, as if its occupant stood suddenly, but the Brass Pounder's patrons were not visible to anyone but the Maxwell box.

Someone shoved Jacob, hard enough to make him take a step back. It was a move he would have expected from a belligerent drunk looking to start a fight. Out of nowhere, a tattered playing card wafted down in front of Mitch and landed at his feet.

"All bets are off," Mitch muttered. "Let's get the hell out of here."

Back on the sidewalk, some of the lights had gone out. The Brass Pounder's competition remained lit up, as did the brothels, and as soon as Mitch and Jacob started to walk away, the sound of distant music filled the night air once more.

Unsure who was watching them, Mitch and Jacob stayed to the shadows, moving with prudent speed toward the rooming house. As they passed the Rusty Spike, Jacob peered in through the doorway. What had appeared to be a busy tavern seconds before was as empty as the Brass Pounder.

"Hey!" Mitch shouted at a woman who emerged from a doorway up ahead of them. In the moonlight, Jacob could just make out the name over the door as The Parlor, and he could guess its type of business. He and Mitch ran to catch up with the woman.

"Miss! I'd like a word with you!" Mitch called. Just as they closed the distance, the woman turned. Her mouth moved but no sound followed. It couldn't have, not with the ear-to-ear slice across her throat.

The woman's figure winked out.

A low growl sounded behind them. Mitch and Jacob wheeled to see a huge, misshapen black dog with glowing red eyes standing in the middle of the street. Head down and hackles raised, it drew back its lips to expose sharp, white teeth. This time, the skinwalker was no ghost.

Mitch and Jacob shot simultaneously. Old danger and long practice meant they fought as a team. Mitch put a shot through the creature's forehead, and Jacob's bullet hit it in the chest, but the beast barely rocked on its feet. Two more shots each hit their target, to no effect.

"Get down!" Jacob cautioned, leveling the strange long gun. He braced himself and pulled the trigger. An invisible cone of energy burst from the muzzle, hitting the skinwalker and tossing the monster half a block down the street.

"Run!" Mitch said, and before the creature could gather its wits, they took off at top speed. As Mitch and Jacob ran past the general store, the lanterns in the shopkeeper's apartment overhead sputtered out. So did the lights in the Brass Pounder and the Parlor, the Rusty Spike and the Paris brothel. Ruin Creek was going dark.

Jacob looked up to see Eli Bly gesturing to them from an alleyway. He motioned them toward the rooming house. Before either of them could say a word, Bly ran past them at the skinwalker, which barreled in their direction. The skinwalker stopped in its tracks as Bly advanced on it, and then began to warily back away.

"How does an old guy with no gun scare something like a skin-walker?" Jacob panted.

"Got a theory, but you aren't going to like it," Mitch said as they jerked open the rooming house door and flung themselves inside.

When Jacob looked back, both Bly and the skinwalker were gone.

Jacob leaned against the locked door, trying to get his breath. Mitch dropped the duffel full of weapons where it was handy and went to dump out their bag of rocks from the crater on the kitchen table. "Ghost?" Jacob asked, meaning Bly.

"Alien?" Mitch replied. "Or maybe competing skinwalkers."

"Aren't you just a ray of sunshine."

"Someone isn't telling us the truth," Mitch said, anger clear in his voice.

"Before we sift through those rocks, I want to make sure no one's upstairs," Jacob said. "We haven't found the sniper. I want to make sure he didn't find us, first."

They lit two more lanterns from the kitchen and headed for the steps to the second floor. Four doors lined a short hallway. One door was open, and the twin beds were made up for company. "Guess that's our room," Jacob said.

Mitch opened the first door and held his lantern aloft. The bedroom was empty. A bed, washstand, and dresser were covered with dust. "Doesn't look like anyone's been in this room for a while," Mitch said, batting away a cobweb.

He opened the doors to the second and third rooms and found the same thing. The fourth room had an occupant. "There's someone in the bed," Jacob hissed. He brought his revolver and the force gun up to point at the figure beneath the covers.

Worn boots sat beside the door and a battered valise lay on a chest at the bottom of the bed. Objects were strewn across the top of the dresser. Mitch laid a hand on the figure's shoulder, turning it toward them, then flinched as the desiccated corpse fell onto its back.

"I think we've found Eli Bly. Let's see what we can find out from his stuff," Mitch said.

Jacob lit the bedside lantern. Mitch gave Bly's corpse a careful once-over. "He had a bad wound to his shoulder," Mitch mused. "Doesn't look like he had a doctor around to treat it, either." He looked up at Jacob. "Want to bet it's a bullet?"

"You think Kasby was cold enough to shoot him in his bed?

Mitch shrugged. "Doubtful. I'm betting he was nosing around that crater and Kasby winged him. Maybe Kasby didn't even mean to kill him; just scare him away. But at Bly's age, who knows?" Mitch said. "Came out here in the heat, poked around all day without enough water, and got shot—maybe his heart just gave out on him, or maybe the wound went sour."

"From the way he's all shriveled up, he didn't just die in the last few days," Jacob said. "Looks like a mummy I saw at the museum."

"Blame the dry air," Mitch replied. "But you're right—it takes time for a body to dry out like that. Long enough that there isn't even a smell left."

Jacob walked over to Bly's valise and looked inside. "Clothing, and a couple of notepads."

"Bring the notepads," Mitch said. He had moved over to look at a wooden crate by the window. "Looks like Bly was picking up rocks from the crater, too." He hefted the small crate. "Let's take this stuff downstairs. I'm pretty sure the answer is in here somewhere."

Jacob had locked the front and back doors before they headed upstairs. He peered from the window. "I'd bet you next week's pay there's something out there."

"Yeah, but is it the skinwalker or Kasby?" Mitch replied. "Or Sani?" He poured a finger of whiskey into each of their glasses. "You take a look at those notebooks. I've got a theory I want to test."

Outside, the wind caught at the screen door, and it thudded against its frame. Jacob heard a few bars of a piano playing saloon songs, and it sent a cold shiver down his spine. A wolf howled in the distance, and an unholy screech answered the wolf. Ghostly faces appeared in the windows, vanishing before Jacob could get a good look at them.

"Bly had terrible handwriting," Jacob said, skimming through the notebooks while Mitch tinkered with his equipment. "What are you doing with those wires?"

"You'll see," Mitch replied. "What's in the notes?"

Jacob scanned the pages. "Looks like Bly came out here on a hunch. He was interested in all the strange airship sightings, and he wanted to see what he could find out."

"More than he bargained for, apparently."

Jacob nodded. "Yeah." He riffled through pages again. "He spent a lot of time out at the crater, picking up pieces from the wreck." He nodded toward the largest item, a second featureless box. "He mentions finding the box and not being able to turn it on or open it up."

"That's because it's already on," Mitch said, wrestling his contraption to secure more wires. "Even if he didn't realize it. The trick is turning it off."

Mitch pointed toward the silvery object Jacob had found, and the heavy gray box they had unearthed that matched the one in Bly's room. "I think these are pieces of equipment from the ship."

"Difference engines?" Jacob said, raising an eyebrow.

Mitch shrugged. "Maybe. Now see what happens when I turn this on," Mitch said. He pulled out the EMF frequency meter. "I tinkered with the settings." He turned the meter on and suddenly, the room around them changed.

A matronly woman bustled around the stove. Two men sat at the table. The door opened, and Eli Bly walked in. He didn't look well. Jacob gathered that Bly was going up to his room to rest. A brown mutt begged scraps under the table.

Mitch turned the meter off. The images disappeared.

"What the hell was that?" Jacob asked, eyes wide.

Mitch grinned. "I can tell you what they weren't: ghosts or magic."

"So what were they?"

"Ever see a Theatre Optique?" Mitch asked. "Projects a series of still images onto a screen fast enough that your brain thinks the images are moving."

"Yeah, I saw one at the vaudeville theater last month."

"It's a machine that stores pictures and projects them to tell a story," Mitch said. "And I think that's just what one—or all—of these pieces of 'equipment' do."

Jacob frowned. "Why would an airship want equipment like that?"

Mitch shrugged. "Maybe it's an advanced camera. Or maybe it was damaged in the crash, and it's not working right." He pulled out the Maxwell box and the metal detector from underneath the table. "I'm going to fiddle with these and see what I can rig up." Mitch cleared away the silvery debris and fused rock into Bly's crate, leaving only the two gray boxes and the oval-shaped smooth metal object. He maneuvered his jury-rigged machine onto the table. "I've got a theory I want to test."

"God help us all," Jacob muttered.

"I'm connecting the Maxwell box and the EMF detector, and powering them up with the Gessner battery from the metal detector," Mitch said as he worked. "Crude as hell, but I want to see if I can get any of these pieces to show us more."

Jacob scooted his chair back from the table. Mitch flicked switches and turned dials, as the Gessner battery hummed. And in the blink of an eye, the kitchen of the boarding house disappeared and Jacob and Mitch found themselves on the bridge of the strangest airship they had ever seen.

"Where are we?" Jacob whispered.

"Right where we were before," Mitch replied. "Remember Theatre Optique? It's all just photographs. With some extra technological mojo."

Unlike the jerky projected images Jacob had seen at the vaudeville theatre, these images moved and looked like real people, three-dimensional, but not solid. "Technological ghosts," Jacob said.

"More like a record of a journey made by explorers who have a leg up on us when it comes to inventions," Mitch answered.

Jacob watched the crew of the strange airship bustle back and forth. They passed straight through him, and through the table and furnishings of the kitchen. The crew's uniforms were unlike those of any airship company or navy Jacob could call to mind, and the sleek, smooth bridge looked advanced beyond anything in the Department's fleet.

"Alien?"

"I'd bet money on it," Mitch said.

They watched the silent images react as something went wrong aboard the airship. The crew rushed back and forth, trying to save their ship as it pitched and then dropped out of the sky. A moment later, the figures of the crew disappeared. But before Mitch could turn off the connection, new images sprang to life. Mrs. Cline, moving around her comfortable kitchen. Eli and the other boarders eating dinner. They watched for several more minutes as the boxes showed the everyday routine, and then Mitch unplugged the equipment.

"What about the ghosts we saw out at the crater?" Jacob said. "The Maxwell box called them."

Mitch nodded. "And something about the crater pushed them away. If an alien airship crashed, there could be other bits of technology still puttering away over there—which would account for the weird EMF readings."

"But did we get what we were sent out to find?" Jacob asked. "After all, we still don't know who Sani really is, or what he needed us to do that he couldn't do for himself. And what about Kasby and the skinwalker?"

A rifle shot crashed through the window, barely missing Mitch's ear and lodging in the wall behind them. Mitch and Jacob dropped to the floor, guns ready. A second shot broke the lock on the door. Jacob and Mitch fired back. The door swung open to reveal an empty porch.

A dark form shattered the window on the opposite side of the kitchen, landed in a crouch and came up firing. Bullets shattered the plaster in the walls, broke the ceramic plates on the rack over the stove, and shot up the Hoosier cabinet. Kasby ducked behind the cast-iron stove, which gave him an angle that kept Mitch and Jacob pinned down.

"Fascinating theories," Kasby gloated. "Hope you don't mind me listening at the window. I'll take it from here. I've got buyers lined up for those boxes—and those crates of rock. They'll pay a lot more than the Department does."

Mitch rolled and shot, coming close enough to drive Kasby back behind the stove. "You killed Eli Bly?"

"Fortunate accident," Kasby replied. "The old man was poking around that crater. I got there first. Thanks to you, that junk is a lot more valuable now that it works."

Outside, a preternatural howl sent shivers down Jacob's spine. He glimpsed a dark shape in the moonlight, hunched and misshapen, though no less fleet of foot for its disfigurement.

"Did you mean to blow the doors open so the skinwalker could eat all of us, or was that just a bonus?" Jacob snapped.

"Not a bad way to get rid of your bodies," Kasby replied, swinging out to take a few more shots that were too close for comfort. "I didn't call it. The energy from the crash did, just like it energized the ghosts."

Eli Bly's ghost appeared at the bottom of the stairs and gave a soundless howl of rage. The ghost charged at Kasby. Mitch brought his rifle to his shoulder and squeezed off a shot that went right through Bly's translucent form. He hit Kasby square in the chest at the same time that the high-pitched whine from Jacob's force gun let rip and a wave of energy threw Kasby's bloody form out into the street. The skinwalker lunged, sinking its long fangs into Kasby's shoulder. Kasby screamed, thrashing and kicking to get loose, held tight in the monster's maw.

The ghosts of Ruin Creek woke up. Lights went on in every building in town. The music reached a crescendo like a traveling carnival, pianos playing several popular tunes all at once and out of key. The sidewalks filled with townspeople caught in the loop of their past, going about their errands, stopping to talk, just an ordinary day snatched from the collective memories of the dead.

Every pane of glass in the rooming house shook until it shattered, and the shutters banged as if they would rip from their hinges. A noise like claws being drawn across the siding boards raised primal fear deep in Jacob's gut. Corpse-pale faces stared through the windows. The skinwalker gave a high-pitched howl. All hell had broken loose on Saturday night in Ruin Creek.

Abruptly, everything fell silent.

"I think Mr. Sani has some explaining to do," Mitch said. That was when Jacob turned to find their patron standing in the boarding house doorway.

"You knew the boxes from the crash were out there, but your magic won't let you go into the crater or handle them yourself. Why?" Jacob demanded.

"Because somehow, you're connected to the aliens who crashed, aren't you?" Mitch supplied.

The Navajo shaman sighed. "Yes. But for my people to rest in peace, I need your help."

"Your people?" Jacob asked. "Somehow, I don't think you're just referring to the tribe."

Mitch gave Sani a measured glance. "How about you tell us what's really going on, and then we decide whether we help you or not."

"Fair enough."

"That was a real skinwalker that ate Kasby," Jacob said.

"I'm betting the strange equipment called it here," Mitch said with a nod toward the items he had assembled. "Just like it riled the ghosts."

"Yes, the skinwalker came shortly after the crash." Sani said. "What you saw at the crater was a projection from the airship commander to get you to look in the right places."

"What about the people we saw on our way into town?" Jacob asked stubbornly.

"They were either ghosts—real ghosts—or projections from the broken equipment," Sani said, and his expression was sad.

"You've played several parts for us," Mitch said. "The Navajo shaman. That first monster that looked like a skinwalker but wasn't. Who are you, really?"

Sani nodded. "I am a real Navajo shaman—and a spirit medium. When the silver ship crashed, I was one of the first to approach the crater after the skinwalker appeared. That's when the ghost of the airship commander spoke to me—and requested my help. I'd like to let him speak for himself," he said.

Sani was silent for a moment. He closed his eyes, and a subtle change came over him. His stance and expression shifted, and Jacob was certain that someone else was in control when Sani spoke once more. "I was the commander of the airship you saw." The voice came from Sani's lips, but the tone and cadence was different. "We came from very far away. When we crashed, my crew was killed, my ship was destroyed, and the equipment that survived was badly damaged—dangerously so."

He motioned toward the gray boxes. "We use those to record our missions, to play for our commanders when we come back. If things go wrong, they keep a record for the inquiry. That silver object, is a *psych-pod,* and held data about our crew," said the ghost of the commander. "Including the wavelength of our personal energies. It monitors and protects us on the long journey."

"You're a poltergeist," Mitch said, looking at the alien objects on the table. "When your ship crashed and your equipment got damaged, something mashed up what the gray boxes and the silver oval thing did, and you're stuck here."

Sani nodded. "So are my people. Our spirits are trapped, still tied to the devices that once protected us. And as you've seen, we disturbed the ghosts of the dead near here." He paused. "The energy that raised them also makes the spirits quick to strike out at anything in their path."

"The *chindi,*" Jacob said. "Vengeful ghosts."

"That's where I need your help," the commander's ghost said. "Because the equipment is causing my problem, I can't touch the pieces. And because the energy of the crash site is unstable, Shaman Sani cannot enter the crater or handle the boxes. But with your help, I think we can drain the power from the boxes and that should set us free." Sani smiled. "You now have everything we need pulled together—I just need your hands to do the work."

"You tried to connect with Bly," Jacob said.

"Yes. That other man injured Bly before he could help," the ghost brought an unmistakable change to Sani's manner, resigned yet in command. "He was one of the first to visit the crater and survive. I had not yet met the shaman, so I was less able to communicate. But I believe Bly suspected what was going on, which is why he telegraphed for help, even though he knew it would arrive too late to save his life."

"That was really Bly, out in the street waving us in," Mitch guessed. "And he's the one who charged at Kasby." Sani nodded.

"Come," the ghost said. "If you will be my hands, we can set this matter to rest. We share a desire to go home as quickly as possible."

Out in the town telegraph office, a collection of wire, metal clips, and other odds and ends lay scattered across a scarred wooden table. Jacob brought the silver object, and Mitch hauled the two metal boxes and his bastardized detectors along, just in case.

"I'll talk you through it," the alien commander said through Sani. He glanced at Jacob. "I saw you out here earlier. The telegraph pole outside is down, but the wires still carry current. You should be able to reconnect the equipment to signal your friends."

"Let's get started," Mitch said.

Though the components were scavenged and primitive, physics remained constant. It took half an hour for Mitch and Jacob to put the pieces together and wire the silver data recorder to the two boxes according to the ghost's instructions. "You know, after we turn this off, our bosses are going to want us to turn it back on again," Jacob said.

"That won't be possible," the ghost replied. "What you're about to do to disable the box will permanently destroy it. That's for the best. Our worlds are not yet ready to meet one another."

"Well," Mitch said when they had everything assembled. "Are you ready?"

Sani nodded. "Yes. And I'm grateful. Your world is very pleasant. But if I can't go back to my world, I would rather go... on."

"There are a lot of questions I'd like to ask you," Jacob said. "A lot of knowledge you could share."

Sani shook his head. "Less than you'd think," the ghostly commander said. "I'm just a shadow of my real self, part projection, part ghost. I've already begun to fade since the crash. I'm less and less who I used to be. My memories of before the crash have slipped away. A few more weeks, and I'd probably be like the rest of my crew — conscious, trapped, and unable to do anything about it."

Jacob shivered at the thought. "Then it's time to send you on your way."

Mitch flipped the switch. The makeshift mechanism hummed, and the silver device glowed with an internal light. Sani shuddered, and the ghost stepped away from him looking very real and solid. Then, Mitch reversed the current, draining the power. As the light dimmed, the ghost became translucent.

"Thank you." The last of the glow faded from the silver form, and the commander's ghost vanished. Seconds later, the equipment fell silent.

"You know that the Department will hang our asses out to dry for not bringing him in to be interrogated," Jacob said.

"Ghosts can't be interrogated," Mitch replied.

"And what about the horses? The ones we rode out to the crater? They were real. What happens to them if everyone else left town or died?"

"Forgive the deception," Sani said with a wan smile, back to being himself once more. "I borrowed the horses from the tribe, and have returned them to their owners."

"Then we'd better hope that I can get the telegraph working," Jacob said. "Because it's a long way back to Phoenix." He sighed. "Do you think this means we'll get sent up to the Yukon?"

Mitch shook his head. "For sasquatch? Nah. We've got a guy we call in now and again from Georgia for that kind of thing. Let him handle it. I'm ready to go home."

Agent Kennedy steered the airship into position just after noon the next day. That gave Mitch and Jacob time to bury Bly's body. Sani stayed to help, and said a blessing over the grave. They gathered up Bly's things along with the alien equipment and Bly's notes and put it all in a small crate, which they sent up to the airship with their carpet bags in a rope net while they climbed a dangling ladder.

"If anyone asks too many questions, we'll present them with the boxes and bargain our way back into their good graces," Mitch said as he and Jacob climbed.

"C'mon, c'mon. We don't have all day!" Agent Kennedy shouted down to them, clearly enjoying having the upper hand. Jacob suspected she would not let them live down needing to be 'rescued' for a long time.

"Thanks for coming to get us," Mitch said. The airship rose skyward, and the ghost town of Ruin Creek receded beneath them.

"Glad I was in the area," she replied. "What are friends for? But I still don't understand how you got all the way out here. I checked the schedules. Hasn't been a train out to Ruin Creek in six whole months."

VIA CON DIABLO

BRYAN C.P. STEELE

"…AND MAY GOD HAVE MERCY ON YOUR SOUL."

Those were the last words I heard before the floor dropped out from under me, the rope snapped tight, and the world went black. It wasn't so bad, gettin' hung, not really anyway. Yeah, there was a bright light, and I reckon it would've been nice to head on toward it, but that wasn't in the cards for me. No, there ain't no pearly gates for Johnny Hollow. That bright light lasted for a tick, then it was gone. Everything got real dark and real cold, real fast. I felt like I was drowning in ink. The world was black and I was treadin' darkness.

I went and got myself dead.

Sure, I lived hard. Hard as a ten penny, and I probably earned that rope. My trigger put nails in quite a few men's coffins, I bought half a dozen horses on stolen dollars, and I left my share of broken hearts around the frontier. My name was spat by every lawman within five days' ride from Cripple Creek, and my ugly mug was charcoaled on more than a few posters. A lot of folk might say I am…I *was*…a bad man.

Yeah, I wasn't goin' out and gettin' fit for a bright white hat or a nickel-slick badge, but I did what I had to. What I was good at. Bit of a welch, you know? A carpenter puts up a good house, a barman pours a good glass, a whore gives a good…*smile*, and an outlaw slings a good pistol. And I was one hell of an outlaw. I was just doin' what the Lord put me on this Earth to do, and it got me killed.

Anyway, back to that day...or days...or weeks. Who knows how long I was floatin' in that darkness. I felt nothin', saw nothin', heard nothin'. It was like that one old Greek fella once said, or somethin' like it, I was becomin' part of that darkness all around me. I was lost in it.

All of a sudden, like Momma's Good Book said, there was light. Blindin' light. Imagine that first stab of day hittin' your lids on a rye whiskey and loose saloon gals hangover. Now turn that feelin' up a few dozen times and stick hot hatpins in your face at the same time — that's how this light felt when it blazed on. All around me was hot, bright, and hurtin'. I went from nothin' to high noon in a flash.

The light was painful, but the voice was worse.

Johnathon...

All it said was my name, but it was like a trumpet in my head. It was a hundred of my sister's kid beatin' on two hundred kettle drums. It sent lightning through my brain, down to my toes and fingers, and then back up again. My whole body was on a rack from the inside out.

Then it stopped. The pain. The light. All of it. The only sensation I felt was the dusty wind on my cheeks, the hard packed clay under me, and something tuggin' at my boots.

I cracked an eye, and was greeted by the Colorado night sky. I was happy as a pig in shit to be alive. I didn't even care that some scruff-necked herdsman was tryin' to steal my brown beauties, so I laughed. Laughed like I heard the best joke any saloon had ever been home to. My laugh must've spooked my boot thief, because he jumped up like a jackrabbit.

"*Dios en el cielo!*" he shouted, letting go of my ankle and turnin' white as my bare ass. He said some other Mexican chatter as he ran off into the night, but I was too busy enjoyin' bein' alive to care where he went off to.

Once I got my wits back, I slowly got up. Every muscle in my body ached. My skin felt too tight. My mouth was drier than a weed. When I moved, my joints cracked and popped like kindling in a campfire. Something about me just felt off. I took that *pee oh tee* stuff once on a dare, wrecked me from the guts on out for days, and I felt like a stranger in my own body the whole time. This was different.

All that said, I couldn't stop grinning like an idiot — I was alive. Don't know how, don't know why, don't really even know if the whole damn hangin' was a bad dream. Yeah, had to be a bad dream. I rubbed my throat, remembering the rasp of that rope like it was still there, and found somethin' totally new.

A necklace. When the hell did I get a goddam necklace?

It was too small, tight like a dancer's choker, but made of lead wire all twisted together like a vine. I twisted it around to find the clasp, but there wasn't one. This damned thing was wound around itself fifty times over, so between the wire and my achy fingers I wasn't gettin' it off anytime soon without tinsnips, that's for sure. Frustration filled my pipes with heat, and I grabbed the necklace and gave it a hard yank. It did nothin' of course, just jabbed a jagged piece of the thing through my thumb.

Strange enough…it didn't hurt. Not like a "gettin' hit in the jaw by a drunk dandy" doesn't hurt, more like a "couldn't feel it at all" doesn't hurt. I looked down at my hand, saw the two tears in my thumb, but not even a drop of blood out of either. I even gave it a squeeze, and nothin'. I might have well been made of leather!

It was while I was lookin' down that I saw it—someone else's pistol tucked away in my holster. I skinned it, feeling how heavy a thing it was. Hardwood grip, dirty black metal like the kind you find in old church fencing, six-round cylinder, and a long barrel. The iron sight was sharp and the hammer thin; this was a one-shot, one-kill kind of sidearm, not for fannin' or spray gunnin'. Might have been kind of ugly, but it was a hell of a piece.

I dropped the cylinder out, looked to give it a spin, and found not a single round inside. What good is an empty pistol on the hip of a gunslinger, eh? I plucked a slug from the case on my belt, and brought the cylinder up to my eye line. I've done it a thousand times without lookin', maybe more, but this time somethin' felt different.

Inside the chamber I was about to load, inside all the chambers actually, were tiny slips of paper. I couldn't get my finger in to get them out, so I just dropped the bullet in, and the paper popped out the front of the cylinder. I snapped the pistol closed and holstered it, curiosity way stronger than my need to fully load it.

The paper was thick, more like the stock of a standard dollar, not newsprint. Rolled tight like a cigarette, it was only a few inches long when I unrolled it. On it was scrawled two words—*Martin Jenkins.*

As soon as those twelve letters hit my eyes everythin' changed.

The ink on the paper burst into blue flames, consumed it up in a puff of smoke that curled up into my nose against the blowin' of the plains breeze. It was like a match struck in my nostrils. Burnt sulfur, the sting of saltpeter, and a hint of seared flesh. It wasn't the smell that got me, not by a long shot. It was the way the world *changed* right before my eyes.

The darkness split, swirls of crimson light popped into being. Footprints of fire in mid-air, they seemed, that wandered off into the night. Well, I'm no hardened explorer or nothin', but I wasn't about to let this go unexplored. I shook the sand off my back, undid what little work ole Pedro did on my boot with a stomp to make it tight again, then followed the trail.

Like some Injun scout I wandered the wilderness in the dead of night, following flamin' red wisps floatin' two feet above the road. I walked for hours. So long that I knew that dawn was comin' soon. That fat, pink orb was about to give birth to a new day when the trail led me to a one-tent camp out in the middle of nowhere. No mules, no horses, no nothin' but the tent and some cold cookin' ashes. Herdsman, maybe? Fellow outlaw on the run? I had no idea, but the trail disappeared just a few paces in front of one of the moldy canvas one-man.

What the hell am I doin'? I thought as I approached what *had* to be a sleepin' fella's tent. What was I goin' to do? Just walk on up and ask for this Martin? Do I knock on a flap? Walk right in? I was goin' on instincts alone, even if it felt like those instincts weren't even mine to follow.

I took a deep breath, walked on up to where the last wisp hung in the air, and cleared my throat—which was oddly much harder with my mouth full of road dust. I'd walked all night, hadn't a single blister under my boots, and just realized I never even took a sip from a canteen that I didn't have anyway. Whatever was happenin' to me, it made me forget all my troubles on such a long wander, that's for sure.

"Mah…Marth…" I rasped. Talkin' was harder than I reckoned it'd be, dry gulched or not, "*Maahrtiin…*" I managed to croak it out, and I didn't sound a bit like myself anymore. "*Martin Jenkins…*"

"What the all hell?" someone said from inside the tent. I could hear 'im rustlin' around, too. "You goddam know what time it is? Sun's barely up, you idjit…"

"*Martin.*" I wanted to say my name, but all I could get out of that dusty trap of mine was this grumpin' fella's name. It was like my mouth was broke. I wanted to say a dozen different things while the stranger mucked about in his tent, rubbin' sleep out of his eyes while I tried to spit out even somethin' so simple as my damned *name*. "*Martin…*" My tongue was a stone in my mouth. No matter how hard I pushed my lips to make a sound while he grumped about gettin' ready to come out and greet me, all I had was his name at a stutter that sounded like I was garglin' shine all night.

"Alright, Jack," he said, yankin' the flaps back and comin' out in the brightenin' mornin'. He had tough guy writ all over, between the broke nose, the missin' teeth, and the buckshooter in his mitts, he came out ready for a tussle. "Who the hell are you?"

"*Maaartin Jeeeenkins…*"

"Are you touched, boy?" he laughed. Not like someone said somethin' funny, but that nervous thing a bad card player'll do when he's about to call on nines high. It wasn't quite light yet, but I could see every line in his face, every wrinkle and scar, and I couldn't figure out why he was squintin' so hard to see…I was only ten paces away, right in front of him. Must've had the fever a ways back, milked up his eyes or somethin'. Then, plain as a barkeep's smile, I knew he saw me — because his eyes went like shotglasses.

"Who…the…h-hell…are you?" he shouted. I knew that tone all too well, too. It was the scared shout of someone who thinks they're goin' to die. If you ever done killed a man, you know that sound. "What in G-God's name are you?"

Yeah, sure he was shocked, but I was too. This whole "follow a mystic fire trail to the tent of a person I don't even know" thing had me confused already, but what happened next downright made me question everythin'.

"*Martin Jenkins…*" I said it again, but I found my lungs fillin' up again to add, "*…may God have mercy on your soul.*"

That's when I noticed the weight in my hand again. Sometime between walkin' half the night across the plain and sayin' this scruffy stranger's name a dozen times…I'd skinned my new pistol and didn't even know it. Whenever it happened, it was tight in my grip now, and the whole world was slowin' down. Martin there was movin' like he was made from clay. I saw the first drop of sweat bead down off that whiskey-bulb nose. Watched his lip slowly curl as he shrugged the yella out of his spine and gave him the instinct to fight. Even with that instinct, he was just too damn slow. I could've brewed a pot of hot coffee and fried an egg for as long as it took him to get that shotgun up past his waist at me.

I don't know why someone with a draw that slow would ever want to go heels with anybody, let alone a hip hangin' gunslinger like me. That part of my brain that set me apart from a random cowpoke and made me a killer was in full control, and my muscles were doin' everythin' on their own it seemed. I leveled my barrel, and damn if it didn't feel good in my palm. The weight was solid, but even. That bladelike iron sight lined up right, and pudgy ole Jenkins there was an all-too-easy target. My trigger was smooth, tucked in the crease of my finger, and I knew it wouldn't take much to slide that back and let my bullet fly. I readied to squeeze…

Why am I killing this man? What did he do? I thought, giving a moment's hesitation.

It was stupid, a rookie greenie mistake. Even with as slow as he was movin', he yanked back on that single-barrel.

Dammit – that was the only thought that managed to cross my mind as his hammer slammed down into place.

The ten paces between us filled with smoke and flash. A cloud of buckshot came singin' out of that cloud like angry bees from a hive. A hundred pea-sized chunks of lead rippin' toward me as fast as powder'll make 'em should have made me turn my pants dark on both sides, but I didn't even flinch. Not a muscle. I just held board stiff and let them pass around – and through – me.

I've been shot before, I have, but like everything else today, this was different. Normally a bullet or a piece of shot hittin' you is like gettin' punched by the strongest child in town. You'd feel the pressure of it hittin' you first as a hot coal in the meat, then the cold ache of leakin' red creepin' from all around the wound. The throbbin' comes with every heartbeat, and if you don't get it patched up much after that you'll probably bleed out.

Bein' as familiar with what gettin' shot feels like, I was bamboozled when the heat didn't happen. I'm not sayin' that I didn't get hit… I absolutely did. I'm sayin' that the dozen or so places those little metal bastards ripped into me didn't get the hot, or the cold, or even the wetness of bleedin'.

It didn't even *hurt*.

All I felt was the impacts all over me; a few in the arms and legs, a couple in the gut, a handful under my collarbone, and one even stuck just under my right eye. I should've been dead. Should've been cryin' out to the good Lord above, but I was focused on just two things – the sound of the shot hitting me and that it didn't even make me budge. They sounded like pebbles being thrown hard into wet mud. That wet *smack-plop* that doesn't echo or carry at all, just hits your ears with about as much grace as the action deserves.

Even after gettin' peppered like that, my arm stayed up. Stayed ready. Stayed aimed. That iron sight hadn't moved an inch off Jenkins' middle.

"Devil's balls!" the lug shouted, fumblin' with his shotgun to get the spent shell out and shove a new one in. "No, no, no!"

Whether that pepper hurt or not, I wasn't about to give Marty here a chance to get another shot off. My finger squeezed back like it had so many times before, the hammer came down, and my new fancy pistol bucked like an unbroken mule in my hand. My one round, the one I loaded the night before, exploded out that thing with a flare as red as a Colorado sunset and smoke that smelled more like a pipe match than a gunshot's plume. It fit so perfect in that barrel that it sang, made that little chimey ringin' sound they sometimes do, when it came burstin' out.

The shot hit 'im straight in the guts. Less than a handspan above the belt buckle and left of where his momma tied him off at birth. Lookin' back, I should've aimed for a cleaner kill. Where I stood like a statue, that one shot folded him in half like a Mexican dinner roll and knocked him back through his campsite, down rollin' into his tent.

A belly hit is one of the worst, but Jenkins there was sure sellin' it. Rollin' around in the campsite, moanin' and groanin' like he was. It was kind of pathetic. He could last for hours, even days, bleedin' from a gut wound like that one. I reckoned I ought to put him out of his misery though. I've been a bad man, but I ain't *that* bad.

I walked over to where he was gettin' all caught up in his tent leathers and bedroll, stood over the ugly scene. He was bleedin' bad from his guts, which he kept wipin' all over everythin'. When he looked up and saw me standin' there, he started whimperin' — like dead men always do.

"N-no…you don' have to…no…please…"

I popped open my cylinder and plucked another bullet from my belt, but all his beggin' and squirmin' about must've got him all too worked up — 'cause he sighed out his last sigh and gave a few jackrabbit twitches, but that was all.

Well, that's what I thought…until Jenkins' eyes snapped open. Columns of light the same color as a full moon on the prairie, one from each dead-but-opened eye, shot up into the clouds. I looked up, followed to where they went, and that little church-goin' boy inside me whispered about 'Heaven' in my head. The lights flared for a moment before fading, leavin' me in the mornin' breeze once again. I just stood there, gun in one hand, bullet in the other, and tried to comprehend.

Am I still dreamin'?

Dream or not, I needed to move on. I went to load up again, and when I pushed that bullet into the next chamber, another little slip of paper fell out and dropped in the dust at my feet. I felt my dry skin crease with a wide smile.

Before I knew it, I scooped it up and was unrollin' it between my fingertips. This time it had three words on it.

Yep, you guessed it…another name.

"*David. Michael. Bennett.*"

The slip of paper burned to ash, and my flamin' trail lit the way toward the big city. I was about to snap the gun closed, but I paused and looked into the rest of the empty chambers.

Four more rolls of paper.

Here we go again, I thought as I holstered my reckoning and felt my legs takin' the first steps down the fire and brimstone path.

A path that I had a feelin' I would take four more times before this dream would be over.

If it ever ends at all…

RATTLER

R.S. BELCHER

THE PINKERTON MAN IN THE LOCK CAR DECIDED TO EARN HIS PAY. HE shot down the Captain and put two lead pills into Gurney before the Chaplain killed him. Now, the thieves were riding south with saddle bags stuffed full of stolen greenbacks, and Gurney dying slow from a gut wound.

The Arizona sun was a harsher punishment than any a judge could impose on them, and the desolate wastes they fled across felt like what waited for them on the other side of the hangman's noose.

Gurney and the woman Bill Hoxie had pulled out of the passenger car both looked like they couldn't ride any further. Both were tied to their mounts, and only their bonds were keeping them on the horses. The Chaplain signaled to stop, and the crew did. They paused in the massive shadow of a hunk of red stone that looked like a giant anvil if you squinted at it the right way.

"What's this shit?" Hoxie asked, climbing off his horse. Bill Hoxie was a beast of a man, towering over everyone else. His massive bulk was all hard muscle and ugly scars. Hoxie had been a road agent since the end of the war, and the Captain had recruited him when the crew had been passing through Nacogdoches. No one liked Hoxie, but he was good at killing and almost as good at stealing, so the Captain took him on and kept him under control. Now the Captain was dead, and Hoxie was already making noise like he planned to step up and lead the crew.

The Chaplain climbed off his horse and brought his canteen to the lady. "Josh, Isaiah, tend to Gurney."

Josh and Isaiah Doncaster were brothers. They had fought in the same unit as the Captain and the Chaplain during the war. Isaiah was the oldest of the two at nineteen. They had been farm boys in Virginia until the war, and they both still looked like children to the Chaplain— children with dead eyes. Josh carried his canteen to their wounded comrade. Gurney was a broad black man with graying hair. His eyes fluttered open as he drank, then closed again. His breathing was ragged.

"Don't give him but a little to swish in his mouth," the Chaplain said as he held his canteen up to the dry swollen lips of the woman. "Can't give him much until a sawbones opens him up and sees how bad that belly wound is." The woman's eyes fluttered open as she felt the cool, silver water wet her lips. She was pretty—even covered in trail dust— raven hair, blue eyes, and dressed in a simple skirt and buttoned jacket bodice, both of light gray.

"Thank you," she whispered through a throat of broken shale. She took the canteen with shaking hands and began to drink.

"Not too fast," The Chaplain said. "Too much, too quick will make you sick."

"Well ain't that just as sweet as fucking molasses," Hoxie said, as he walked up. He pushed his campaign hat back on his head and wiped the sweat from his brow with a filthy kerchief. "Don't be giving the whore too much of our water, Chap. We're going to need it."

The Chaplain turned to Hoxie. "Wouldn't have to be giving her any if you hadn't pulled her off that train and dragged her along with us," he said.

"Shit," Hoxie said, spitting dirt out of his mouth at the Chaplain's feet, "we'd all be as dead as the Captain and Gurney if'n I hadn't."

"Gurney ain't dead," the Chaplain said.

"Just a matter a time," Hoxie said. "He's slowing us down. We should leave him."

"Ain't leaving no one," the Chaplain said. "They're gonna chase us further, longer 'cause of her," he nodded in the direction of the woman. The Chaplain walked to his horse and unbuckled one of his saddlebags.

"I can fix that," Hoxie said, taking another gulp of water. "Y'all ride on a spell and leave her with me. I'll have a little fun and then plant her. Problem solved."

The Doncasters muttered between themselves and shook their heads, but they knew better than to go against Hoxie.

"Nobody touches that woman," the Chaplain said. He pulled a Bible out of his saddlebag. The book was black leather, old and worn. It fit easily in his large hand. He flipped it open, found a section that seemed to meet with his approval and tore the onionskin page out of it, neatly. He dropped it back in his bag and fished a small pouch of tobacco out.

"And who the fuck do you think you are to be giving orders?" Hoxie said. He snatched the canteen away from the woman and took a long draw off of it.

"Give the water back to her." The Chaplain said. He sprinkled a line of tobacco into the crease he folded in the Bible page, using his back and the flank of his horse to hold the hot dry wind at bay.

"And what do you intend to do if I don't?" Hoxie said, striding toward the Chaplain. The canteen was still in his hand, spilling water into the baked soil as he swaggered. The Chaplain still had his back to the red-faced outlaw. "You've thought you were some damn huckleberry above a persimmon ever since I joined up with this outfit," Hoxie said. "The only reason I didn't kill you cold as a wagon wheel a long time ago was I respected the Captain enough not to!"

The Chaplain licked the paper and rolled up his quirley as he felt Hoxie's ham-like hand grip his shoulder like a vice. The Doncasters were moving back, their hands on their pistols.

"I'm talking to you, you greyback son of a bitch!" Hoxie said, his free hand reaching to his holster.

"You remember to reload?" the Chaplain said softly as he slid the cigarette into the corner of his mouth. "All that shooting and fighting and running...you sure you remembered to reload, Bill?"

Hoxie paused for a second. The Chaplain's smile was a thin razor cut. He could almost smell the smoke coming out of Bill's ears as he tried to recall. The Chaplain turned, breaking Hoxie's grip on his shoulder firmly with one hand as he did. Smoothly, almost effortlessly, the Chaplain plucked the Colt out of Hoxie's holster, only inches from Hoxie's hovering hand, and chucked up on the barrel like it was a hammer. He drove the heavy butt of the revolver into Hoxie's head, and the stunned outlaw staggered back. The Chaplain followed and struck him again and again in the face and the head. Hoxie moaned and fell. He looked up from the desert floor, blood streaming down his forehead, into the barrel of his own gun. The Chaplain's face was hidden by sun and shadow, unknowable.

Hoxie heard the hammer of the pistol click as it fell. He opened his eyes. He was alive. His empty pistol landed in the dust at his feet. He heard the Chaplain's gun cocking and he looked up into another barrel.

"I didn't forget to reload," the Chaplain said. "You ever touch me again, I'll kill you. You ever point a gun at me, I'll kill you. You touch that woman, and I'll kill you. We square, Bill?" Hoxie nodded and rubbed his bleeding head. "Good," the Chaplain said. "Now, let me tell you how this is going to be — I'm running this crew until we get Gurney patched up, we split this take even, and we go our separate ways. Get your ass up, give that woman some water from your canteen, and get ready to ride."

The Chaplain walked over to join the Doncasters, holstering his gun as he did.

"You should o' ought to killed him, Chap," Josh said in a low voice. "First chance Hoxie gets, he's gonna put a bullet in your back."

"He's welcome to try," The Chaplain said, lighting his quirley with a wooden match. "How's Gurney?"

"Dying," Isaiah said, also talking low, "If he's gonna have any chance at all, we need to get him to a doctor 'fore nightfall."

"Closest town?" Chaplain asked.

Isaiah pulled a tattered map from a wooden tube and knelt in the red soil, brushing aside small rocks and pebbles to clear a surface. He laid the map down and weighted it against the wind with his pistol near its center.

"We're hereabouts," Isaiah said, jabbing a finger down on the map. "There is a main road that takes you to Tucson. We can connect up to that...here," he slid his finger a short distant as he spoke. "Be there by tonight."

"Along with every railroad dick and lawman in the territory," Hoxie said, coming to join the conversation. "We can't go anywhere near a major town. They'll have us swinging before sun-up."

The Doncasters looked to the Chaplain, who was squatting now and scanning the map.

"Bill's right," Chap said, puffing on his cigarette. "If I was hunting us, that's the place I'd expect us to head to. So we can't."

There was a grinding sound near the desert floor. The Chaplain looked to his left. About ten feet away, a Rock Rattlesnake was coiled, its tail shaking hypnotically.

"Shit!" Isaiah said, about to jump to his feet. Chap steadied him with a palm on his chest.

"Be still," the Chaplain said, his cigarette balanced on the edge of his lips. The Chaplain picked up a rock slowly and eyed the rattler. "Go on," he said, his voice oiled steel, "git." The snake's rattle stilled, and it glided away in the direction of a shady pile of rocks.

"Jesus," Josh said. "Where the fuck did that thing come from?"

"It's been sitting there since we got here," the Chaplain said. "We just riled it a bit." He looked back to the map. "What's this place? Here." He jabbed his finger down on a spot not very far from where they were. It was odd, but he could have sworn it wasn't on the map a moment ago.

"Black Fang?" Isaiah said. Chap could tell that the boy hadn't noticed it until now either. "I'll be damned. Sorry Chap, I didn't see it."

"Me either," Chap said. "Anyone ever heard of Black Fang before?" Heads shook "no". "Sounds perfect, then," Chap said, standing. "Let's ride."

As they approached the town, the bloated red sun was slowly being dragged down by the dark talons of the rocky horizon. The reason for Black Fang's name became obvious—two massive, jagged spires of stone, wrapped in the lengthening shadows, jutted behind the tiny town, like two razor-sharp incisors.

They passed a small graveyard on the horse trail they followed to the edge of town. Below, the town's few lights were burning. They rode down the main street, past several shacks, a barbershop and dentist, and a saloon called the Snakebite. They passed a boarding house and a simple stone building that was the town jail. At the end of the street was a quaint little chapel with a whitewashed steeple. In front of the church was a large stone well.

"Purty little town," Hoxie said through a mouth full of trail grit. "These folks won't give us a hooter of trouble."

"Just hope they have a doctor," Josh said.

The Chaplain brought his horse to a stop in front of the Snakebite and dismounted. The others followed. "Josh, arrange to get us some beds. Isaiah, see to the lady and to Gurney. Bill, you and me are going to find a sawbones."

Stepping into the Snakebite was like entering a parlor of ghosts. There was no music, no laughter, no conversation. Just thick, stifling silence. The barkeep was a fat, bald man with muttonchops and a green brocade waistcoat. He was leaning on his bar across from his only customer, a rail-thin man in a dark suit. The only other occupants of the Snakebite were an old man with a drooping handlebar mustache and a redheaded woman dressed scandalously in a chemise and thigh-high black stockings. The old man was nursing a mug of beer; the redhead's rump was resting on the edge of his table as she engaged him in whispered conversation. Hoxie grinned when he saw the woman. The Chaplain, however, noticed the tin star on the old man's coat. Both men at the bar regarded Chap and Hoxie as they entered through the swinging bat-wing doors.

"Evening," Chap said. The barkeep nodded

"Evening," he said. "What can I get you gentlemen?"

"Two beers," Chap said. The barkeep nodded and went about pouring the beers. They sat at the edge of the bar closest to the door. Chap took a long drag on his beer. He'd tasted better, but he couldn't recall when. Hoxie drained his mug in a single long chug, then burped.

"We just rode in," Chap said. "Don't suppose you folks have a doctor in these parts? One of our friends took ill on the ride."

"We got Earl Lynch," The slender man in black said. "He's not a paper-on-the-wall doc, but he does well by us. He has a place at the edge of the road. Want me to fetch him?"

"I'd be much obliged," the Chaplain said. "We're rooming at the boarding house..."

"Mr and Mrs.Whittcomb's," the bartender said, "They'll treat you right."

The slender man got up. "I'll make sure Earl comes a-calling on your friend over at the boarding house." He departed quickly. Hoxie's eyes were transfixed on the redhead, and she was now slipping coy glances to him whenever the old sheriff wasn't looking.

"Don't do anything stupid, Bill," the Chaplain said. "She's with the law. Let her be."

Hoxie ignored him, motioned to the barkeep to give him another round, and kept flirting with the redhead. Chap finished his beer and left.

Josh was waiting for the Chaplain by the parlor door in the boarding house. The Whittcombs—an old man and woman in their 60s, dressed farmer plain—greeted him at the door. Josh pulled him aside and they sat in the parlor, while Mrs. Whittcomb prepared them tea in the kitchen.

"Where's Hoxie?" Josh asked.

"Off doing something stupid," Chap said. "Where's Gurney and the lady?"

"Gurney's in his room, resting," Josh said. "The lady is resting. She gave me a little chin music when we were getting the rooms. I told her if she made a fuss, I'd kill her and the old folks too. She gentled down after that."

"Doc's on the way to see Gurney," the Chaplain said, heading up the stairs, his saddlebags over his shoulder. "Let me know when he's here."

"You okay, Chap?" Josh asked.

"No," the Chaplain said. "I don't like this place, don't trust it. We're riding out in the morning, if Gurney's able."

Chap knocked once on the door to the bath room and swung it open. The woman from the train was standing in the large steel tub, nude, soap running down her sleek body. Her hair was wet and falling down her shoulders and back. She tried to cover herself as best she could. The Chaplain looked away. "Sorry," he said, "I thought you were in your room."

"I couldn't lie down until I cleaned myself up," she said. Her voice held a remarkable amount of strength and confidence. She was startled and embarrassed by his entrance, but she had already recovered. "So much dirt from the ride. I expected you to be Mr. Hoxie, coming to make good on his threats."

"I won't let him harm you…Miss?"

"Anna," she said as she stepped out of the tub and grabbed a large towel and wrapped herself in it. "Anna McCutcheon. You can come in and shut the door. You're letting the heat out."

He did, leaning on a stool next to the door. "Pleased to make your acquaintance, Miss McCutcheon," he said.

"Just 'Anna''s fine," she said sitting at a vanity with a large oval mirror. "Last name's supposed to be changing pretty soon—the Miss part too. You'll forgive me if I don't say it's a pleasure to make your acquaintance. You're the first one of your associates to even ask my name. I assumed I was just gonna be 'her' or 'the whore'."

The Chaplain laughed and reached for his saddlebags, retrieving the battered Bible. "I apologize for my crew. They're not very good at much besides soldiering."

"Killing," Anna said. "Your men are killers, not soldiers. The war's over."

The Chaplain rested the Bible on his lap, opening it. "Getting hitched soon?" he asked.

"On my way to meet my fella in Contention City," she said as she began to brush her hair. "We're sweethearts since before the war. He came out here after, and he's got some prospects, so he sent for me."

"Congratulations," the Chaplain said, selecting a page and tearing it out of the battered book. He began to carefully measure out a line of tobacco in the strip of onionskin. "Well, Anna, you cooperate, don't do nothing reckless, and you'll make it to your beau."

She stopped brushing and turned to him. "May I ask you a question?"

He struck a match to the wall and lit his quirley with it. "Yes," he said.

"Why do they call you Chaplain?" she said. "Were you one in the war?"

"No," he said, exhaling a long stream of smoke. "No, my pappy was a preacher, though, back in South Carolina. He introduced me to the power and glory of the Lord — with a leather shaving strop and a zealous heart, and I believed — I wasn't given much of a choice in the matter.

"When the war came I thought I was fighting God's fight against infernal northern aggression." He took a long draw on the cigarette. "I was a fucking idiot. I thought God punished the wicked and spared the innocent. Then I saw 'the power and glory' of war. I saw it in places like Shiloh, Stones River, Antietam...saw men, hell, children, hacked and maimed, saw brother kill brother like Cain and Abel, saw creeks run red with blood, like the plagues of Egypt." He was silent for a moment, the red tip of his quirley flared. He exhaled.

"I know the war tested faiths," Anna said. "It was a nightmare that wouldn't end, that you couldn't wake up from. But surely in the heat of battle, when you were so close to so much death, you must have cried out to our savior for comfort, for protection, Mister...What is your given name, sir?"

"Doesn't matter," the Chaplain said. "Some days, even I don't recall. I saw the elephant plenty and it scared the hell out of me every time. A man is in that and he's not scared, he's already dead, just don't know it. I don't believe in a God anymore, Anna, or the Devil. Man's an animal, locked up in a dark, empty box. Alone, truly alone, in the darkness of that box...well, that would drive any poor creature mad, make them hallucinate gods and devils to keep them company. Me, I don't cotton much to company. "

"I've never heard such blasphemy," Anna said softly. "That's why you defame the good book so?"

"It was my pappy's," the Chaplain said, patting the worn leather. "Only thing he left me."

"But, if you are such a man as you claim, of such low morals," Anna said, "why did you stop Hoxie from..."

"I'm a criminal," the Chaplain said, sliding the battered Bible into the inside pocket of his coat. "I'm a professional criminal and I have a code I live by—that's what keeps me from being Bill Hoxie. It's a fine distinction, but it's all I got in my dark empty box to keep me company."

Anna stood and removed the towel. The Chaplain looked away. She slid on a chemise, and gathered up her combs and towel.

"I'll pray for you," she said, "If you don't mind."

"Thank you," he said.

There was a scream—a man. The Chaplain drew his Colt. "Stay here, until I get you," he said. Anna nodded. He slid open the door, scanned the hall, and then slipped out, shutting the door behind him.

Josh was lying in the hallway, shaking as if he were cold. His pistol lay near him.

"What the hell happened?" the Chaplain asked, kneeling by the boy.

"He...he bit Gurney," Josh muttered and then passed out. Mr.Whittcomb came up the stairs, huffing. He stopped when he saw the two men in the hall.

"Get downstairs," Chap growled. The old man nodded and hurried down the stairs. The Chaplain stood and pushed open the door to Gurney's room. It was cold. The window was wide open and the curtain fluttering. Gurney was on the bed shuddering, much as Josh had been. Gurney's sheets were soaked in blood. No one else was in the room.

"Gurney," Chap whispered in the wounded man's ear. Gurney groaned. There were two large, ugly-looking puncture wounds on Gurney's shoulder. The skin around them was swollen and discolored.

Chap noticed something by the window—it looked a little like a tangled blanket. He knelt by it. It was skin, smooth and dry. He lifted it, gingerly, and saw it was a human's skin, complete with hair on the head. The mouth of the hollow mask of flesh was torn and tattered, as if it had been stretched to the point of shredding. Chap shuddered and dropped the skin. He looked out the window and saw only the tree near the window and the dark, empty street below.

Isaiah crashed into the room, twin six-guns drawn. He lowered them when he saw only Gurney and Chap. "What's wrong with Josh?" Isaiah asked.

"Get him to bed," Chap said. He pointed to the wounds on Gurney's shoulder. "Look and see if he's got anything on him, like that. Stick with him and let me know if he wakes up or he gets worse."

Anna appeared at the open door. "What on Earth happened?"

"I thought I told you to stay put," Chap said as he closed and locked the window.

"I ignored you."

"Get to your rooms, lock the door and keep the windows shut," he said to Anna and Isaiah. "Don't open up for anyone but me, y'hear?"

Once the Chaplain was sure they were all locked in, he closed Gurney's door and walked downstairs to the parlor. The Whittcombs were standing at the edge of the landing watching him with expressionless eyes.

"The doctor?" Chap said. "Did Lynch show up?"

"Couldn't rightly say," Mr. Whittcomb said. "I didn't see him come in, young fella."

The Chaplain nodded and headed back upstairs. The old couple looked at each other and said nothing. Chap returned to Gurney's room, checked on his comrade who now seemed to be breathing well enough. He put fresh dressings on Gurney's stomach wound and on the odd punctures, locked the door, and sat in a chair next to the bed. He slept very little, and when he did his dreams were dark, squirming things that licked at the edges of his waking mind.

Dawn gave way to bright morning. The Chaplain woke with a start to Gurney's smiling face. "You look like shit," Gurney said.

"How you doing?" Chap said, sitting up and rubbing his eyes. "You were dying yesterday. You took one to the gut." Gurney sat up. He pulled the bloody bandage away and there was a discolored, puckered scar where the day before there had been an ugly, wet hole.

"What the hell?" the Chaplain muttered, looking closer at the bullet scar. "Gurney, this ain't possible."

"You sound upset I ain't dead, Chap," Gurney said, climbing out of bed. "Anything to eat hereabouts? I'm starved." Chap stood and looked at Gurney's shoulder as he swung to the edge of the bed. The punctures were gone. He glanced over at the pile of skin by the window, but all that remained of it was a pile of dust in the morning light.

"No, I'm glad to see you up and around," Chaplain said. "Just...didn't expect it."

Breakfast was a hearty affair. Mrs. Whittcomb laid out quite a spread for the crew. They were apparently the only boarders in the house. Gurney was starved, so was Josh, who had awoken in the morning feeling fine. Hoxie stomped into the house with a huge grin on his face, joined them at the table, and began shoveling food into his mouth.

"Where you been?" Isaiah asked, sipping his coffee.

"Off having a time with that redheaded adventuress from the saloon," Hoxie said dropping a pile of hoecakes onto his plate from the platter. "The things that whore did to me..."

"Language!" the Chaplain said. "Got ladies present." Anna blushed and looked at her plate. Hoxie looked and her and snorted.

"Shit," he said. "Pardon-fucking-me, your highness."

"Enough, Bill," the Chaplain said. "Or do you need another reminder like out in the desert?"

"Might not fall the same way it did last time, Chap," Hoxie said, grinning through the food in his mouth. He took his hat off and Chap noticed that the ugly bruises and cuts he had inflicted on Hoxie yesterday were all gone.

"Okay, everyone's good to ride," the Chaplain said, "I say we resupply and get the hell out of here. Head for Nogales and we divvy up there. I'll use part of my share to buy Anna, here, a ticket on a coach back to Contention City and we all go our separate ways. Agreed?"

Laughter erupted at the table from Hoxie, Josh, and Gurney. "I ain't in no hurry to leave," Josh said.

"What are you talking about?" Isaiah said.

"Same here," Gurney said. "Seems as nice a place to hole up a spell as any other, Chap. Better than most."

"So, looks like were staying put," Hoxie said. "'less you care to ride off minus your share," he said. "We ain't leaving yet, and neither's the money."

After breakfast the crew split up. Outside, Chap, Isaiah, and Anna walked along the warped boards set up on either side of the main street to act as sidewalks.

"What the hell happened to Josh?" the Chaplain said. "Did he say anything to you, Isaiah?"

The elder Doncaster shook his head. "Nothing much. He was all shivering last night and he had a great big old bite like the one Gurney had on his arm."

"Bite?" Anna said.

"Yes ma'am," Isaiah said. "Looked like a bad one and whatever gave it to him it was big. Josh woke up this morning all smiles and shines. He said he couldn't recall how he ended up on the floor or anything about him or Gurney getting bit. Matter of fact, when I looked at his arm this morning..."

"The bite was gone," Chap said. Isaiah nodded. "Same thing happened with Gurney's bite, and he seems in a damn fine mood for a fella we should be digging a hole for."

"What do we do, Chap?" Isaiah asked. "Josh ain't acting like Josh. I don't like it."

"Let's go pay a visit to this sawbones and see what he has to say about all this," Chap said.

The shack had a tar-paper roof and a small shingle hung by the door which said "*E. W. Lynch: Physician.*" Chap knocked while Isaiah and Anna looked around the edges of Main Street.

"Sun's well up and not a soul to be seen," Anna said.

There was no answer to the Chaplain's knock. He rapped harder on the door. "A lot of these houses look empty," he said, "unused." There was still no response to his knocking. Chap looked over to Isaiah. "We clear?" he asked the elder Doncaster. Isaiah's eyes scanned the street and then he nodded curtly as his hand fell to his holster.

"Clear?" Anna asked a second before the Chaplain kicked in the shack's door, its small lock flying across the room with a metallic 'ting'. Lynch sat up in his small wrought-iron bed as Chap and Isaiah entered. Lynch appeared to be naked except for the sheet covering him. Anna followed them and swung the damaged door closed.

"Morning, Doc," Chap said, standing at the end of the bed, and drawing his pistol. He pointed it at the wide-eyed, shivering Lynch. "Need your medical opinion on a few things, hope you don't mind we ain't got an appointment."

"Get the fuck out of here," Lynch said, "else I call the law on you!"

"How you gonna do that with a hole in your head?" Chap said, cocking the Colt. "You were supposed to come by and minister to our friend last night, recall that?"

Lynch glared at the Chaplain. Chap noticed that Lynch's skin seemed very pale, vaguely translucent, and it almost glistened as if he were covered in a sheen of sweat. His dark hair was slicked back from his face as if it were wet, or greasy, but Lynch was dry.

"You sick or something?" Isaiah asked. Lynch only glared.

"Did you see Gurney and Josh last night?" the Chaplain said. "I ain't going to ask you again, and you won't be able to answer anyway if you wanted to." He steadied the gun and Lynch threw up both arms in front of his face, as if it would stop the bullet.

"Yes, yes!" Lynch shouted. "Put that damn thing away!"

Isaiah crossed the room and pulled Lynch from the bed. The doctor was naked and his whole body had the same odd sheen. "What the hell did you do to my brother, you sumbitch!" Isaiah shouted. Anna looked away.

"Nothing," Lynch said, trying to cover himself, "not a damn thing! I swear!" Something caught the Chaplain's eye. There was a crumpled, dried mass peeking out from under Lynch's bed. "At least let me put my pants on, for god's sake," the frightened doctor said while Chap prodded at the mysterious mass gingerly with the toe of his boot. It made a dry hushing sound like dead leaves as it was kicked out from under the bed. It was a snakeskin, a big one. A dried rattle about the size of man's palm gave a hollow hiss as the skin was slid across the floor.

"Jesus, fuck," Isaiah said as Lynch fastened his canvas jeans. "That is a hell of a snake! What is that six, seven feet long?"

Something jagged tumbled in the Chaplain's mind—pieces that could not possibly fit together in a sane, rational universe run by a benevolent god. The snakeskin, the man skin... nope, it was crazy, but the world was too. His guts—the same instincts that had allowed him to survive hell on earth and everything after it—screamed at him to act. He raised his gun again and pointed it at Lynch. He recocked the hammer. "Isaiah, son, get away from him." he said.

Lynch hissed and opened his mouth wide, too wide for a man. He had large wicked, curved fangs, dripping something. Moving faster than humanly possible, he struck at Isaiah's shoulder. Anna was shouting something. Chaplain fired, and the Colt thundered in the small cabin. Stinging gun smoke filled the air, biting at the Chaplain's eyes. Lynch's shiny chest erupted as the .45 round ripped through it and continued on to blow a hole in the wall of the shack above the bed. Lynch's eyes were wide with pain and something else—a madness, an unreason that glazed them. The insane light dimmed and then departed his eyes as he stumbled back from Isaiah, bumped against the bed rail, and fell to the floor, dead.

"Sumbitch bit me!" Isaiah shouted, as he clutched the two deep punctures in his shoulder. Anna grabbed the corner of the sheet from the bed, tore it, and quickly worked to administer a bandage to the wound.

"Hold still," she admonished Isaiah as he winced in obvious pain. "What is he?" she asked the Chaplain, who was kneeling beside Lynch's body. A pool of black blood was gathering around his still form. "He's not human," she added as she had Isaiah sit on the edge of the bed. He did so reluctantly. "How can that even be?"

"I don't know," Chap said, poking the dead doctor's mouth with the barrel of his gun. The body suddenly convulsed and the mouth bit at the steel with the large fangs, dripping a slightly yellowish substance. Anna and Isaiah both jumped back.

"Reflex," Chap said, pulling the gun away, "just like a dead snake." He used a piece of the sheet to wipe the liquid from the fangs off his gun. "And venom," he said and looked to Isaiah. The boy was already starting to look waxy, and his eyes were looking weak.

"Am...am I gonna die, Chap?" Isaiah said, sounding more like the frightened boy he truly was. Chap patted him on the knee and stood up.

"Not if I can do anything about it," he said. "Anna, grab the doc's bag, and we're getting the others and getting out of this hell hole."

There was loud banging at the door. "Alright, we heard the shootin'," a dry, gravelly voice called out. "Open up and throw your irons out here now, or else we'll shoot all of ya down!"

"Who is this?" Chap shouted, as he stood by the side of the door and cocked his pistol. Isaiah drew his own pistol, but it fell to the floor as he winced in pain and fell back onto the bed, seemingly unconscious. Anna started to reach for it, but Chap shook his head. He pointed to a rickety wardrobe in the far corner of the room and mouthed "hide" to the woman.

"This is Sheriff Canebreak," the voice replied. "I know who you are, fella, so I recommend you come on out, nice and gentle."

Anna opened the wardrobe; it smelled of mothballs and old tobacco. She slid in-between the rows of coats and shirts and disappeared. Chap stepped over and closed the doors.

"Hang on," he shouted out to the sheriff. "I got a sick man in here. I'm coming out. Don't start shooting."

One more thing to do quickly. There was an ax near the small wood stove in southern corner of the shack. He hefted the ax and in one clean motion took Lynch's still-biting head clean off his shoulders. The head rolled across the floor and continued to mindlessly bite. Finally, it was still.

Chaplain looked at Isaiah's pale form. He could already feel the heat coming off of him. He tossed the ax away and picked up the boy's gun. He threw open the door, threw both pistols in the dust and raised his arms in the air.

Sure enough, Sheriff Canebreak was the old man from the Snakebite saloon the night before. He had a white mane of hair and a prominent handlebar mustache. His star reflected the desert sunlight. His .44 pistol was leveled at Chap's chest. There were three men with him. All were armed and looked ready to kill him at the slightest twitch. Chap didn't twitch.

"Not looking for any trouble here," the Chaplain said. "Got one of my crew in there been bit by a snake," he looked at the sheriff's dead, dark eyes. "A big one."

Only Canebreak's lips moved, "Hank, Artie, go see to the doc." Two of the men went inside cautiously, passing Chap, guns at the ready.

"What the hell is he?" Chap asked the lawman. "I've seen some damn queer things. I saw a giant winged bird the Sioux say serves the Great Spirit; I've seen strange airships lit up like gas street lights, burning bright and silent in the sky. Saw a white spirit buffalo. Once I even saw a dead man rise up on the battlefield, no soul left in his eyes, but I've never seen anything like that."

"Stop jawin'," Canebreak said and spit a line of tobacco juice onto the thirsty dust. One of the gunmen stepped out of Lynch's shack, his gun holstered.

"Doc's dead, Sheriff," he said. "Boy's in there. Looks like he's been bit."

"Take the boy to the church," Canebreak said, "and take this son of a bitch to the jail. Lock him up."

"The church?" the Chaplain said. "Why the hell..."

The Chaplain never saw the blow from behind coming—a gun butt most likely. There was a flash of white light behind his eyes and then darkness. His last thought was that he deserved the darkness to never go away.

Chap opened his eyes and was greeted by a dull pain behind them. He tried to stand but only made it to his hands and knees. He was in jail. He'd been in enough to know what they sounded like, smelled like. It was dark out. The place was illuminated in the grimy, shivering light of an oil lamp hanging on a post near a desk and a few chairs. He coughed and struggled up onto the hard bunk that was chained to the cinder block wall. He looked around. To his left was an empty cell, separated from his by a wall of bars. To the right was another cell, but this one was occupied. The man was an Indian, most likely a Zuni from his ornate turquoise-and-shell necklace and bracelet. The Indian wore a simple headband and his silver hair fell to his shoulders. He wore a buckskin tunic and simple denim work trousers, like cowboys favored. His face was weathered and calm. He looked at Chap and nodded.

"How are you feeling?" the Indian asked in decent English.

"Like someone used my head as a chamber pot," Chap replied in broken Zuni. The old man's face lit up at the sound of his own language.

"You just told me you are a stinkhole," the Indian said. Both men laughed. "Where did you learn to slaughter my language?"

"I almost married one of your girls," Chap said. The smile slid off his face. "It...It didn't work out. She died."

"I'm sorry," the old man said. "My name is Lonan."

"People call me Chaplain," Chap said. "Nice to meet you," he said, looking at the bars that separated them, "given the circumstances."

"This is a very bad place," Lonan said. "I imagine you are here for the same reason I am—you are a danger to them. I discovered this town through dreams—it draws bad men to it. I came here and was soon taken prisoner once they learned I knew their true face."

"True face?" Chap said. "You know what's going on here?"

Lonan nodded. "I came here to stop it," he said.

"Stop what, exactly?" the Chaplain asked.

The old Indian leaned back against the wall, sighed, and closed his eyes. "There is a very old story among the first people about where the rattlesnake comes from," Lonan began. "The world was to be wiped clean in a great rain. Situlili, the spirit, tried to warn a group of haughty, evil humans the rain was coming. They laughed at him and taunted him. He tried again to warn them, but they took their gourd rattles and they danced and mocked the snake spirit even more.

"As the rain fell and the lightning crashed, the dancers were transformed one by one into snakes, each with a rattle at the end of their tail to warn others of their evil and their foolishness, for all time."

"So, Lynch is one of these snake people?" Chap said, rubbing his aching head.

Lonan shook his head. "He is related to them," the Indian said, "cursed to wander this world full of the venom of evil. If one of these creatures bites a man, the man either becomes one of them or dies a painful death."

"What determines which end they meet?" the Chaplain said, leaning forward on his bunk.

"The goodness in their heart," the old man said softly.

The Chaplain chuckled; it was a dry thing, like dead leaves spun on the wind. "So if you're a bad person, you change, and if you're good..."

"You die," Lonan said. "It is a mercy, truly. Life for these things is a torture. Why did you laugh?"

"Because, my friend, I am a very, very bad man," Chap said.

"You do not seem so," Lonan said.

The Chaplain shrugged. "I am. A few days back I shot my friend. He was called the Captain. We served in the war together. We endured that madness and survived it, and when I had a dark second to myself, for no one to see, I shot him dead and blamed it on a Pinkerton agent."

"Why did you kill your friend?" Lonan asked, his face still calm.

"One less share to split of the money we stole," Chap said looking past the bars to a terrible place inside himself. "He saved my life a few times. We'd laughed and cried together. He was my brother, my friend. Truth is, I couldn't say why I killed him. I pretend I live by some imaginary code, but scrub that off, and all that's left is bad."

Both men were quiet for a time. Finally, Lonan stood and stretched. He turned to Chap. "The Cherokee have a story," Lonan began. "They say there are two wolves living inside each of us. One wolf is good — compassion, joy, love, hope, and sacrifice. The other is evil — greed, anger, guilt, arrogance, and false pride. The two wolves war constantly inside each of us."

Chap looked up from the floor at the old man. "Which one wins?" he asked.

"The one you feed," Lonan said.

The iron door of the jail opened with a groan. Sheriff Canebreak entered with one of the men who had been with him at Lynch's place. Gurney was with him too, looking much better, smiling, in fact. The sheriff nodded to the two men and they drew their guns. Gurney's revolver was pointed right at the Chaplain's heart.

"Okay, you two," Canebreak said, unlocking the cell, "walk out nice and gentle. You try anything these two fellas will lay you low. You have an appointment at the church."

The Chaplain looked at Gurney, at his gun. "What the hell you doing, Gurney?"

"You'll understand," Gurney said, gesturing with his gun, "real soon, Chap. Hell, they'll probably make you damn mayor around here."

Lonan stepped out of the cell and the Sheriff moved away from him. "It's the well for this here damn injun sorcerer and that bitch you brought into town with you," Canebreak said. "They both smell too damn bad, or good—depending on how you look at it—to bite, but they'll feed the little ones down in the well. They've been ornery since hatching time, hungry little fuckers. Yeah, your crew rounded up the bitch after that boy, Isaiah, came around."

Chap looked at Gurney. "This all there is to it?" Chap said. "I save your life and you turn into one of these damn things, go along, pretty as you please. I thought you had more sand than that."

Gurney's eyes changed, they became dead black. His tongue, now forked, shot out between his lips and retreated to his mouth. "You might just want to shut your damn mouth there, Chap," Gurney said. "Else I decide to throw you in with the old Indian, and the girl. I've seen that well. You don't want to go down there. Makes hell look like a whore's parlor."

"Settle down, now," Canebreak said. "We got plans for him, he's a joiner for our little community, that he is. Now come on."

Gurney had always been hard to rile, but this Gurney wasn't. Chap gave his old friend a sideways look, and Gurney raised his gun to pistol-whip his former friend. In that instant, the gun wasn't pointed at Chap, and he grabbed the burning lantern off the post and smashed it into Gurney's face. The hot oil ignited, and Gurney screamed. There was a gunshot, and Canebreak was screaming something. Chap pried Gurney's pistol free of his spasming hands. Gurney was flailing about, and Chap kicked him toward Canebreak. Chap heard the sheriff cuss and then scream as Chap spun and fired at the other gunman, his pistol smoking in his hand as he turned to fire again at Chap. Chap fanned the Colt and three bullets howled to the other man's one. The gunman hit the floor, bleeding, choking, as Chap began to smell smoke and burning meat.

He looked back to Lonan. The old man was hit in the arm and was struggling to his feet. Chap helped him. There were no more screams— both Gurney and Canebreak were dead, their bodies blackening and curling up on themselves as if they were made of paper, not flesh and blood. Chap looked at the old Zuni.

"Fire purifies," Lonan said. Chap handed him Gurney's pistol and grabbed a Winchester and a bandoleer of bullets from behind the desk. The wooden post and the furniture were already catching and black smoke was gathering everywhere.

"Let's get out of here before it purifies us," Chap said, heading for the door.

Outside the desert night was deep, cold, and slumbering. The town seemed empty, just like when they had rode in, but far down the street was the sound of voices, singing a tuneless hymn Chap did not recognize and didn't want to.

"That arm okay?" Chap asked. Lonan nodded. "Good. I want you to get us horses and water, and get my crew's saddlebags from the boarding house. Then you start purifying this whole goddamned town, you hear me.

Lonan nodded, smiling. "Yes. And you?"

"I'm getting Anna," he said. "Only reason she's in any of this mess is on account of me and mine. I'll meet you at the edge of town."

The old man nodded and then was gone into the darkness. The Chaplain loaded the rifle carefully as he walked down Main Street toward the old church with the well in front of it.

A crowd had gathered in front of the church, about fifty people all told. Most were armed. The Chaplain had a bag slung over his shoulder, and he cradled the rifle in his other hand. A cigar he had picked up at the Snakebite hung at the corner of his mouth. It burned cherry red at the tip. He stopped about twenty feet from the edge of the crowd, who had all turned silently to regard him. He scanned the faces: all were black dead eyes, like Gurney's and Lynch's, inhuman eyes.

"Not looking for trouble here," the Chaplain said, "Just give me the girl and we'll be on our way."

"Don't work that way here, Chap," Hoxie said, stepping to the front of the crowd. His pistol was stuffed in his belt, an easy draw for him. "You either join the nest, or you feed the nest."

"I ain't never been much of a joiner," Chap said. "Most of the folks I see here don't look like they have too much experience with a shooting iron. I figure they don't want this to turn ugly."

"We do," Josh said, stepping beside Hoxie. Isaiah joined him on the other side of Bill. "There's three of us and we know all your tricks, Chap. Why not just join up?"

"It's ain't that bad," Isaiah said. "Part of you dies, but all the stuff you wanted to do, but were scared to...it wakes up—wide awake. You'll love it."

"Where's the girl?" Chap asked.

"In the well," Hoxie said. "Feeding the little ones."

"Well, then," Chap said, "let's get to it." He brought the Winchester up fast, but Hoxie already had a shot. He fired at Bill and saw his head explode about the same time he felt the hot nail hammered into his chest. He gasped, cocked the rifle and fired again, this time at Josh—the better shot. Josh's bullet hit him in the upper leg, but he managed to stay on his feet. Josh fell. Isaiah's bullet missed Chap, and he pivoted on this good leg and put a bullet into the last of his crew. All three were still. Chap could feel the hot bullet sizzling in his chest. He coughed blood and reached into the bag.

The townspeople were changing before him—eyes dark voids, jaws opening wide, fangs appearing, dripping. Chap watched as their skin began to stretch, and then split at the mouths. Their bodies fell to the dust like great circus tents, collapsing. Massive rattlesnakes slithered from the mouths of the loose, empty, human skin. The air buzzed with the sound of their fist-sized rattles.

Chap used the fancy cigar to light the rag in the neck of one of the liquor bottles he had also taken from the empty saloon. Hurled it and tried not to pass out from the pain. It exploded in the middle of the crowd, and they hissed. Those who hadn't completely changed yet screamed in terror. He threw another as a few bullets whined in his direction, but none hit. More fire, more of the locals screaming. The third bottle hit the pretty little church, and it erupted into flame. The creatures scattered to the quivering shadows thrown by the fire. This side of Black Fang was burning. He took Hoxie's pistol and limped to the well. It was deep darkness below. He heard Anna scream. There was a rope tied to the stone edge of the well. He looped it about his waist and slid into the darkness with a dead man's gun in one hand, a burning bottle of whiskey in the other.

The chamber at the bottom of the well smelled of fear and the dry breath of reptiles. There were bones everywhere, and hundreds of rattlesnakes slithered and coiled among the dry remains of the dead. Anna was perched on a pile of broken rib cages. She screamed as she saw him descend.

"Hang on," he said as he threw the whiskey bottle into a nest of dozens of too-large snake eggs. The whole side of the chamber exploded in fire, and it spread quickly. Screams came from the eggs—a horrible gurgling sound like colicky babies drowning in phlegm. He landed on the sand floor. Anna jumped into his arms. The Chaplain winced in pain and then began to pull them up. A large rattler launched itself at Anna. Chap blew its head off with a clean shot from the pistol. The nest chamber roared with hungry flames. Snakes sizzled and popped as the flames devoured them. They reached the mouth of the well to be greeted by more flames. Black Fang was burning. Anna helped him walk as they headed for the other side of town.

"You didn't get bit did you?" he asked her.

"No," she said. "But I was about to. Thank you, bless you."

Lonan was waiting for them with horses and saddle bags stuffed with money. They rode hard out of the inferno that was Black Fang. The fires from the town illuminated the indigo tatters of the final gasp of night. None of them looked back.

The sun was high and merciless when Chap called to stop. He fell from his horse. Anna started to dismount.

"Stay away," Chap said. "Stay on the horse."

"What's wrong?" she asked. The Chaplain pulled up his trouser leg to show the dark bruises and swelling around two deep punctures. He slumped back onto a large rock and hacked up some more blood.

"We got to get you to a town," Anna said, "to a doctor!"

"No," Chap said. He was pale and sweating. "There's a chance I'll turn into one of those damn things and...no. No, I'm not letting that happen."

"We can't just leave you," she said.

"Yes, you can," Chap said. "Take this money, Anna—do good with it. Call it a wedding present. Lonan will get you to a town. Go on. Find your fella, Anna."

"If you begin to change..." Lonan said. The Chaplain patted the revolver next to him.

"I'll take care of it," he said.

"What if it was just a normal rattler," Anna said. "You could die out here for nothing."

"I'll keep my horse," Chap said. "If I think I'm safe I'll come along after you. Don't you fret." He looked from the woman to the old man. The Zuni nodded.

"So which one is going to win in me?" The Chaplain asked. Thunder boomed, and heat lighting danced across the sky.

"The one you fed the most," Lonan replied and glanced at Anna. "The fight's never lost, or won."

"Come," Lonan said to Anna.

"I'll pray for your soul," Anna said.

"Put in a good word for me," the Chaplain replied with a smile. "Take care, Anna."

They rode away, Anna looking back. Soon, they were dark specks at the edge of the endless wastes, then they were gone.

He was alone. He pulled out his bag of tobacco and his father's bible and flipped to a random page. The words caught his eye. *"They will pick up serpents with their hands; and if they drink any deadly poison, it will not hurt them; they will lay their hands on the sick, and they will recover."* The Chaplain laughed, and made his cigarette.

They were many miles away when Anna heard it. A single rumble echoing through the canyons and mesas, across the wasteland. Till the day she died, she never knew if it was a gunshot, or the sound of futile thunder.

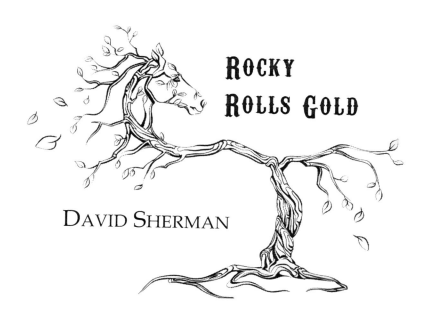

ROCKY ROLLS GOLD

DAVID SHERMAN

VLANCH ROLLED HIS SHOULDERS IN A NOT-QUITE SHRUG; IT SOUNDED like boulders grinding together. "What can we do?" he asked in a gravel-pit voice that somehow managed to sound plaintive.

Grubble shook her head, a boulder pinging down a rocky slope. "You claim you're the smart one," she said in a voice not as gravel-pitty as Vlanch's, more like a shaken sack of pebbles. "You tell me what we can do."

He blinked at her; if the lids that scraped across his eyeballs had been steel, they would have struck sparks. "You heard the Dwarf. If we go back there, it will not go well for us." He raised his left arm to display the light streak where a blow from the pick wielded by the Dwarf leader had gouged his side. He knew the Dwarf had meant to only scratch him that time.

"But you promised me gold and gems!" Grubble squealed, a granite spike scraping down a sheet of slate.

"And I will get you gold for your birthday, and gems for our anniversary," he rumbled. Then, in a voice like sand sliding on a gentle grade, "Just not from the Dwarves." He looked down the mountainside, past the green band where trees girded its loins, to the red gash in the ground just above where the mountain turned to plain. A red line where Men had recently finished constructing one of their aboveground caves, a place that was quickly vanishing as Men planted greenery and laid out roads and walkways.

Another line of barren ground, angling down the mountainside until it passed nearly a mile north of the hotel, was the trackway of an avalanche, dotted by boulders, large, medium, but mostly small, and kept clear of new trees and shrubs by the passage of an occasional freshly tumbling boulder.

Vlanch ignored the copse of thin, mirrored towers that rose offset to one side of the structure, which he knew stood very nearly atop the Dwarven gold mine they'd been forced from. Instead, he looked at the swath of forest that backed against the hotel, and the rock-strewn ground above the trees. A plan began to form in his mind.

Vlanch and Grubble squatted in that trackway, looking like nothing so much as two piles of boulders, one slightly larger than the other. A casual viewer looking in their direction might wonder at boulders piled thusly. But nobody looked that way.

A green-eyed woman with an ivory complexion and ruby lips stood at the check-in desk of the Glittering Nugget Hotel; two traveling trunks and a carpetbag sat on the floor at her side. She was in obvious disagreement with the clerk who opposed her from the far side of the counter.

"You cannot deny a woman a room simply because she is traveling unaccompanied," she stated firmly. "Especially not when she has wired ahead to reserve a room. I have been *so* looking forward to this holiday, too much so to allow an impertinent clerk to disturb it."

"Madam," the clerk said haughtily, "the Glittering Nugget Hotel has its reputation to consider. Unaccompanied women checking into a hotel are often…well, I don't wish to be indelicate. But I cannot let you have a room. I'm certain you can find suitable quarters elsewhere, perhaps in the workers' lodging." A smirk graced his visage.

Danger flared in the woman's green eyes, and she parted her lips to verbally lash the impertinent clerk when a man in a newly cleaned frock coat stepped to the counter and spoke to her.

"Miss Kitty Belle!" he said with clear delight, and raised fingers to his brow, as though touching the brim of a hat.

She turned her face to him. "Why, so I am, Mister Cheyenne Walker," she said, with a slight nod of her head.

"Is Mister Reghaster causing you distress about your registration?" Walker asked.

"Not as much distress as I shall cause *him* if he doesn't promptly honor my reservation!"

Walker slowly shook his head. "I'd rather you didn't. It's so hard to find clerks proficient in the operation of the Babbage Analytical Engine."

"This hotel has a Babbage Analytical Engine?" she asked, with obvious surprise. When Walker replied in the affirmative, she turned to the clerk. "I want to see it in operation," she demanded.

"But—" he said uncertainly, and looked to Walker. Walker simply smiled softly.

"And what might your position be here? Surely you're not the manager," she asked Walker while observing the clerk clack fingertip levers to make a punch card.

A sound like teapot-whistle emitted from beneath the counter. "Are you brewing chai?" she demanded of Reghaster.

"That is the engine that provides the motive power for the Babbage," the clerk replied haughtily.

Walker ignored the byplay and answered her original question. "I have a table in the salon, and share my winnings with the hotel."

"And how often are you challenged?"

Walker laughed. "Never! Ever since the incident on the Samuel Clemens, I remove my coat and pull up my shirtsleeves before I game. None can claim I slip hidden cards into my hand." Miss Kitty well recalled their sojourn on the paddlewheeler and could not fault him his caution.

"Miss?" Reghaster interrupted them. "This," he held up the card he'd just punched, "will show whether you have a reservation." He inserted the card into an orifice in the machine, clacked a lever, and stepped back. "Now we wait for a moment." He sounded like he thought finding a reservation wouldn't change matters. The teapot whistle increased in volume.

A new clacking sounded from within the machine, and another punched card poked out of a different orifice. Reghaster removed the new card to another machine, inserted it, and again stepped back. The second machine began teapot-whistling and clacking with slender arms that slapped out of a well in its center onto a sheet of paper.

"That looks ever so much like one of those typing machines on which Mister Twain writes his humorous books!" Miss Kitty Belle exclaimed.

"Yes, it's been modified for automatic writing," Reghaster said with a sniff. The clacking stopped and he whipped the sheet of paper from the machine and looked it over. His expression of superiority quickly vanished as he read, and he ran a finger around the inside of his collar.

"Miss, this says your registration was made by Mister Pinkerton himself." He cleared his throat. "Would that be *the* Mister Pinkerton?"

She smiled at him.

"Oh, dear." He read farther and said again, "Oh, dear. There is a note appended to the reservation, a note from Colonel Gimble, to accord you every courtesy."

"Colonel Gimble owns the Glittering Nugget, along with other establishments in the territory," Cheyenne Walker said in answer to Kitty Belle's eloquently raised brow.

After confirming the reservation — and again reading the note from his employer — Reghister's fingers veritably danced over the levers of the Babbage Analytical Engine, causing the teapot-whistle to sing merrily. After a moment — somewhat longer than the one it had taken to discover Miss Kitty Belle's reservation — a card poked out of the same orifice as the reservation had.

"Ah, Miss Belle, I do wish to apologize for the misunderstanding earlier, and to make amends," Reghaster said. "To that end, I can," his eyes skimmed the card, "I can put you in a suite. Not, of course, the bridal suite —" he blushed at that mention, "but certainly a suite superior to the simple bed-sitting room your reservation requires." He shot an embarrassed glance at Cheyenne Walker. "That is, naturally, at no additional charge to either you or to your employer." He briskly tapped the bellhop's bell, and turned to fetch the key to the suite he was assigning to her.

Cheyenne Walker accompanied Miss Kitty Belle as she followed the bellhop. Her luggage was in the bellhop's care.

"Mister Walker, the whistling of the Babbage Analytical Machine," she asked, "is it steam-operated, as were the great wheels on the *Samuel Clemens*?"

"It is indeed. As were the fans that propelled the *Argus*, and as is the Otis that will convey you to the ninth floor."

"The ninth floor." She shook her head in wonder. Such a tall building would barely be possible were it not for Mister Otis and his marvelous lifting apparatus.

"Ah, but the Glittering Nugget has *twelve* floors." Walker sounded so pleased with twelve floors that a casual over hearer might be forgiven for assuming that he was the proprietor.

An elevating room was waiting when they reached its lobby, where Cheyenne Walker and Miss Kitty Belle parted company.

He gave the Pinkerton agent a slight bow and asked, "Might I have the pleasure of your company at dinner this evening?"

"I would be displeased if you didn't desire it, Mr. Walker," she answered with a smile and a dip of her head.

"Will six o'clock suffice?"

"Let us make it half past."

"Half past six it is. Until then."

Vlanch kept a cautious eye toward the immediate environs of the Glittering Nugget, watching for any who might see him and Grubble as they slowly made their way toward the bordering trees. He knew that their forms would look to a Man like nothing so much as two jumbles of rocks: a careful observer might notice that their parts maintained their relative positions, or that they were moving in defiance of Galileo's gravity law, that they didn't move toward the center of the Earth, but rather sideways, toward the edge of the trackway. And even a bit uphill.

But he saw no one looking their way, not even with the most casual of glances, much less the lingering look required to see their non-Galilean movement.

And he knew that the Men in the aboveground cave possessed gold and gems. If the cave were shattered, he could get into it and find that gold and those gems, keeping his promise to his mate.

They kept up their cautious movement.

Half past six found Cheyenne Walker ensconced at a table that gave him a clear view of the entrance to Placer's Poke, the Glittering Nugget's dining salon. His wait for Miss Kitty Belle wasn't excessively long, merely long enough to pique his appetite for her company.

When she arrived, the *maitre'd* bowed her in like visiting royalty; he seemed nearly overwhelmed by her glory.

Walker stood as if physically drawn to his feet. "You look spectacular, Miss Kitty Belle," he said, his gaze traveling appreciatively over her brocaded skirt of crimson arabesques on a field of ebony. He liked that there was no bustle, and the way her jacket was patterned in reverse of the skirt's coloring. It hung open down the front framing the pale pink of a ruffled blouse. The jaunty angle of the hat cocked on her crown teased a smile from Walker's lips. Brilliant feathers cascaded from one side of the hat, and the opposing, higher, brim was speckled with seashells. He added his bow to that of the *maitre'd*.

"And you, Cheyenne Walker," she said as she eased onto the chair drawn back for her by a waiter, taking in Walker's freshly brushed frock coat, ruffled shirt, and string tie held beneath his chin by an onyx clip, "look quite dashing yourself."

On the *maitre'd's* recommendation, she had quail in puff pastry, and Walker ordered pheasant with figs. They shared a bottle of sauvignon blanc.

Once sated, they engaged in small talk over coffee. Until she said casually, "I heard a rumor that an engineer on a routine inspection of the steam works vanished. Have you heard about that?"

Walker cocked his head. "I thought you were on holiday."

"I am. But a detective can't help but overhear things and wonder about them."

He shrugged. "I also have heard that rumor. I've also heard that the engineer, by name of Hyram Scott, was later seen in the Yellowstone territory spending gold and attempting to sell diamonds. And I heard he was doing the same at the same time in Dodge City, Kansas."

"Well! And where might he have found gold and diamonds?"

"Not from any of the guests here. At least, none have reported such a theft. Neither was the security of the hotel's safe breached."

Miss Kitty looked out the window, at the climbing face of the Front Range behind the hotel. "Gold has been found in many places in Colorado. It could be that there is gold near here."

"And a Dwarven gold mine?"

Her eyes went unfocused for a moment, then she said, "I've long been fascinated by the workings of steam. Do you think I could visit the steam room?"

"Certainly. I'm sure the hotel's manager will allow us to examine the basement." Although he did wonder about her sudden change of topic.

"Sir." An attendant interrupted, leaning in to whisper into Walker's ear.

"Thank you. I'll be right there." Walker rose to his feet and essayed a bow to his dinner companion. "I fear duty calls, Miss Kitty. My table awaits me, along with gamblers who wish to attempt to divest me of my money. Shall we meet again for breakfast, and then hence to the sub-levels?"

She tipped her head and graced him with a smile. "I'm sure you will be able to pay for both our breakfasts."

The din of the steamworks grew from almost inaudible to nearly deafening as Cheyenne Walker and Miss Kitty Belle descended a long flight of stairs tucked away behind the accounting office. There were whistles and clanks and pings and pops; all the sounds of metal expanding and contracting as it heated and cooled, containing the steaming-hot water it directed from boilers to destinations through pipes. All of which pipes had welded valves joints that sometimes, Walker knew and Kitty Belle suspected, sprang leaks.

Chief Engineer James Bankey, who had been alerted by the manager to expect visitors, met them in a small, gas-lit anteroom at the foot of the stairs. Conversation was possible so long as one spoke in a loud voice.

"Mr. Walker, Miss Belle," Bankey said, giving them a satisfied look. So often visitors came clad in their holiday finery, such clothing destined to be ruined by the oil and dirt and steam beyond the anteroom. These two, at least, wouldn't complain about the state of their clothes after they left: Walker wore a canvas overcoat and trousers, and Kitty Belle a well-worn denim skirt and matching jacket, much more suitable clothing for their visit. "I've been instructed to accord you every consideration," he said as though delivering a rote presentation. "So I can, for a short time, spare Thomas, one of our apprentices, to escort you about and answer your questions — to the best of his necessarily limited ability, him being only an apprentice." He indicated a sturdy young man standing at his left shoulder. "Is this satisfactory?"

"It is more than satisfactory, Mr. Bankey," Walker said. "We had thought we might have to stumble through your environs unguided and be abjectly ignorant of what we looked on," he jibed, suspecting Bankey would rather visitors wandered unattended provided they didn't touch anything.

Bankey snorted. "Not likely I'd allow civilians to traipse about my workings and get into who knows what mischief.

"But since I must," he grudgingly added, "you had best wear these." He reached into a pocket of his grease-stained overalls and drew out two sets of ear mufflers. "Without these, it might be hours after leaving here before you can hear normally again." After adjusting the mufflers on Walker and Kitty Belle, he resumed his own, as did the apprentice.

"Now, Thomas," he said in an even louder voice, one that sounded through the mufflers as from a distance, or penetrating a dense fog, "take good care of our guests."

Beyond the foyer, the din was so great that the mufflers hardly seemed to reduce the noise. Walker quickly saw that some of the sunlight funneling into the cavernous space was deflected to an array of mirrors on the ceiling, reflecting it to bathe the space with light.

"How do we not hear this inside the hotel?" Miss Kitty shouted, leaning close to Cheyenne Walker's ear.

He leaned close to her ear and shouted, "It's not directly under the hotel. It's under the sun-towers."

She didn't strain her voice replying, merely nodded as she recalled the group of parabolic-mirrored towers such as she'd seen in other locations — only not so many together. Indeed, they stood at a slight distance from the hotel. The earth would absorb the sound and vibrations of the steamworks. She remembered that the mirrors captured the rays of the sun, and focused them to heating mirrors under the boilers. One tower for each boiler, she assumed.

While there was space around each boiler to allow easy access for the engineers who tended them, elsewhere passages were tight, and people moving from one place to another sometimes brushed against hot pipes, scorching their clothing or smearing grease on them. Cheyenne Walker and Miss Kitty Belle were no exception. It wasn't long before she looked at her sleeves and skirt and decided she'd likely have to discard the garments after this expedition. A penetrating glance told her that though Walker's coat and trousers suffered more than her clothing, they were of a sturdier material than hers, and would more likely survive the steamworks to be worn another day.

Thomas didn't attempt to talk to them, but rather contented himself with gestures, and tracing patterns in the air. Probably describing the inner working of the steam in the pipes.

The wending path the apprentice led them on eventually reached a wall, where the constant din was less. Walker drew him close and asked about the stony nature of the wall.

Still signing rather than strain his voice, Thomas indicated that the basement was dug into bedrock. Nodding his understanding, Walker then asked if Thomas had known Hyram Scott. When the apprentice nodded, Walker asked if he knew what had happened to the man. Thomas spread his hands in an I-don't-know gesture.

"Where was he last seen?" Kitty Belle shouted.

Thomas looked into the distance, then waved a "follow-me." He led them to another section of the bedrock wall, where he again spread his hands, this time with a shrug.

Before either of them could ask who had been the last person to see Scott, a whistle, far louder than any they'd heard before, blasted through the steamworks. Thomas' eyes and mouth popped wide, and he signed them to stay put, then dashed off.

"I think we should find our way out," Walker mouthed, but Miss Kitty wasn't looking at him. Instead, she was staring at the wall they stood next to. Walker's eyes followed her gaze.

The bedrock here had been disturbed.

There was a filigree of cracks in the face of the rock. In a couple of places, flakes had chipped off, so the cracks seemed to be wider under the surface than on it.

Walker drew a folding knife from a pocket of his coat and used its blade to pry a flake from one of the cracks. Not only was the crack wider under the surface, there was what looked to be a foreign, whitish substance inside it, bulging toward the surface. He used the point of his blade to scrape off a little of the substance and touched it to his tongue.

He leaned close to Miss Kitty and said loudly, "Lime." Someone had used cement to seal the cracks — from the inside!

Walker removed the muffler from his right ear and pressed it against the cracked surface. Miss Kitty did the same. They exchanged astonished looks.

While they were considering the cemented cracks that widened beneath the surface, and the sounds they'd heard from beyond it, Thomas reappeared and waved at them to follow him. In a few moments he had them back at the entrance to the cellar.

Inside it, the apprentice said his first words to them. "Mr. Bankey hopes you enjoyed your visit. Now it's time for you to leave." He held out his hands to receive the mufflers they'd worn. As soon as he had them, he left the two with nothing to do but climb the long flight back to the ground floor of the Glittering Nugget.

Upon gaining the ground floor, they retired to their own rooms to refresh and change into clean clothes, agreeing to meet again in the Placer's Poke. They were shown to a table in an alcove, where they were unlikely to be overheard by other diners. They waited until the bread and cheese plate they ordered was served before they began talking about what they'd seen—and heard.

"Ladies first. What did you hear?" Walker said, daubing mustard on bread for a chunk of cheese.

"It didn't sound like the sea in my ear, like a conch shell makes," she said. "There was a faint two-tone beat, a sort of high-low, repeated in different registers." She shook her head at the memory.

"Punctuated by faint *clinks*, as a pick might make striking stone," Walker said.

She nodded. "Most peculiar," she agreed.

"Did you notice the patterning of the cracks?"

She poked her fork at chunks of cheese while remembering the face of the wall. "Again odd. It was as though the wall had been reassembled."

"After having been broken through from the other side." He peered unfocused into a never-never for a long moment, before slowly saying, "There are old legends of Dwarves mining for gold and gems in the front range. But the legends always put them in remote locations where hardly anybody ever goes. Certainly no place where a white man ever stumbles across them. I wonder if it's possible that Dwarves are mining here."

Miss Kitty Belle looked at Cheyenne Walker and nodded sagely. "I suspect that on the other side of that repaired wall, there just might be a Dwarven mine."

"Do you think that's even remotely possible?" he asked, surprised.

She shrugged. "I don't advise opening that wall to find out. The little I've heard of Dwarves, they seem disinclined to welcome visitors to their mines."

Vlanch and Grubble, still slowly moving, had at length penetrated the forest at the edge of the avalanche trackway and were working their way to a spot directly above the Glittering Nugget Hotel. They increased their speed and headed uphill, aiming for a field of boulders above the trees. Particularly for a giant boulder that perched just above the beginning of a knife-edge ridge that plunged a short distance down the slope.

On the morrow, Miss Kitty Belle and Cheyenne Walker joined an expedition of hotel guests for a picnic high on the slope above the hotel.

On preparing to leave his room, Walker had glanced at his Gladstone bag, in which his Buntline Special revolver was stored. A second's consideration told him neither grizzly bear nor mountain lion would attack a sizable party, so he had no need of it.

The group consisted of some ten vacationers, led by a mountain guide named Beavertrap Jackson, and accompanied by a small coterie of hotel staff bearing food, drink, dinnerware, and silver, as well as tablecloths on which to lay out the provisions. It was cool under the trees. Not bracingly, but cool enough that there was little perspiration dripping off the group of mostly flat-landers. The slow amble at which they climbed aided in keeping them relatively dry. After a walk of close to an hour and a half, they reached a patch of nearly level ground where rustic tables and benches had been erected to receive the cloths and provisions.

"So much for roughing it," someone in the group quipped, which elicited relieved laughter from most of the group.

"This hike has been roughing enough for me," another offered.

The porters, who made this trek weekly, set about covering the tables and benches with the blankets, and laying out the picnic. The meal was cold cuts on bread, salads, with sarsaparilla as beverage. The picnickers made short work of it.

Someone had brought a ball, and after the meal the men tossed it around while the women clustered together to chat.

When it came time to head back downhill, Cheyenne Walker and Miss Kitty Belle decided to stay behind and explore farther up the mountainside. They needed to talk more about what they'd discovered — or thought they'd discovered — in the hotel's steamworks. If there actually was a Dwarvish gold mine, they might be able to find its entrance. Although what they'd do if they found it, they didn't know.

Half a mile up they came across...

"How strange," Walker said. "Strange that two piles of small boulders would be within the trees without a trackway to show how they came to this place; and strange that they roughly resemble human forms."

"Someone must have put them there," Kitty Belle said brightly. "But let's not tarry." She grasped his arm and continued rapidly uphill.

He looked at her curiously, but went without protest.

⌒ " ⌒

"Do you think they recognized us?" Grubble asked.

"How could they," Vlanch replied. "They never saw us before.

Grubble playfully punched his shoulder, sending a cascade of sand down his arm. "Not *us*, silly. I mean our kind."

"They said nothing."

"That means nothing."

"We should have killed them?"

"We still should kill them."

"Then let us follow them."

They resumed their slow, upward trundle.

A quarter mile beyond, Miss Kitty Belle stopped and peered at their backtrail. Speaking softly, hardly more than a whisper, she said, "I think those were rock trolls. Let's keep going."

"Rock trolls?" Walker asked. "I've never heard of them."

"They are trolls that appear to be made of rock. They are slow moving, but are nonetheless very strong, and can be extremely violent. Let us be sure to avoid them on our return."

They walked more briskly, and soon came to the high treeline at the peak of the knife-edge ridge.

Walker said, "They might have something extremely violent in mind, if they're what you say." All thoughts of finding the entrance to the Dwarven mine were driven from his mind by the approaching threat. "If they can move that big one, and send it down the ridge rather than sliding off its side, I think they might be able to start an avalanche that would smash directly into the hotel. But why would they do that?"

"They would," a harsh voice said, "because they're thieves, an' they wants gold."

Walker and Miss Kitty spun toward the voice.

"Who's there!" Walker demanded when he saw no one. His hand reached for the side of his coat before he remembered that he left his Buntline Special locked in his room. "You also, I see," Miss Kitty murmured. Her Colt Peacemaker was likewise locked securely in her room.

A stout man, only chest-high to Walker, stepped from behind a boulder the size of a cottage. A bushy beard covered his face below a bulbous nose, and eyebrows so thick they nearly hid his eyes. A red, tasseled stocking cap lounged atop his head. A green, homespun jerkin was belted with a length of leather, and brown homespun trousers on his bandy legs were tucked into scuffed boots with steel caps on their toes.

"The rock trolls," the apparition said, "already tried to steal from us and we sent them off. But why would they want t' destroy yon hotel?"

"Maybe to get to the hotel's safe," Walker said uncertainly.

"'Tis of no mind to us if they do. But ye, ye *are* of a mind to us. We saw ye looking at the place where poor Hyram Scott found the break into arr mine shaft afore we could repair it. Then he had the misfortune t' enter the mine." The Dwarf shook his head sadly. "He's been slavin' fer us ever since. Ye would'na be thinking o' following him, would ye?"

"I think that would be highly unwise of us," Walker said to the Dwarf. In an aside to Miss Kitty, he added, "So Scott is in neither the Yellowstone nor Dodge city."

"That 'tis good thinking on yer part. Ye would'na want t' join Mr. Scott in slavin' fer us, now. That would be a most uncomfortable fate to suffer. I'll be taking me leave o' ye now." He doffed his cap and turned to go.

"A moment, Mister Dwarf," Miss Kitty called. "It might be of mind to you if the rock trolls destroy the hotel."

"Oh? An' why might that be?" the Dwarf asked, turning to face her.

"Because if the hotel is destroyed, there will certainly be an investigation. That investigation will most assuredly find your mine shaft."

"Ye think so, do ye? An' why would that be?"

"I am a Pinkerton. You know what that is, don't you?"

He screwed up his face and peered at her. "A Pinkerton, eh? Can ye prove it?"

She reached into a pocket and withdrew a leather wallet, which flipped open to show her badge.

"Well, well. So ye are, it appears. An' ye would know about an investigation? An' what if ye were killed in the avalanche, an' could'na tell any about the mine?"

"In that case, the Pinkertons would be most anxious to investigate — and avenge if needed — the death of one of their agents. And be assured, they would find your mine."

"So ye say, so ye say. Hmmm." The Dwarf twined his fingers into his beard, tugging on it, lost in thought.

After a moment that ended before it became long enough to grow uncomfortable, the Dwarf peered up at them through his bushy brows. "So ye say t'would be to arr advantage t' prevent the trolls from raining boulders down 'pon the hotel."

"Yes, it would be highly advantageous to you," she said, pressing her edge.

"I'll gi' help." The Dwarf spun about and disappeared with a *pop* of displaced air.

"It would be an interesting job to catch him," Walker said after a few seconds.

"T'would be interesting to *try*, anyway." Miss Kitty said. "Although I'm not sure we could, given his ability to vanish."

"What's that?" Walker suddenly snapped, twisting to look downslope.

"Oh, no," Miss Kitty exclaimed. "Could it be the rock trolls already?"

It could and it was.

Fifty yards away, they saw a slender tree crash to the ground, its trunk smashed by a blow from one of the stony creatures.

"Oh my," Kitty Belle said.

A rumbling came from downslope, noise like boulders grinding together, and a gravel pit stirred by a gigantic ladle. They saw indistinct gray forms moving through the foliage and shadows, and heard more crashes as the trolls in their haste knocked down more trees.

"Run!" Walker shouted, grabbing Miss Kitty's hand, he stepped to the right, and immediately turned to step to the left.

"What way do we go?" Miss Kitty shouted.

The ridge was so narrow between its precipitous sides they'd have to brush past at least one of the nearing rock trolls to get past them, or risk plummeting over the edge.

"Uphill!" Walker shouted at the same time Miss Kitty cried out, "Climb!"

They scrambled, increasing the distance between themselves and the trolls, who were now climbing at the speed of a walking man. Past the large boulder they paused to consider their next move.

Miss Kitty looked at the ground ahead of them, and at her boots. The otherwise barren ground was speckled too thickly with small rocks ranging from baseball-size to fine gravel, to leave open spaces for her to step securely. The soles of her boots were narrow, and her heels were a full inch and a half in height. Her boots were fine for walking on the leaf-litter under the trees, but her footing here would be very treacherous.

Walker saw, and looked at the huge boulder. It rose vertically nearly fifteen feet above the ground. He said, "Up. I doubt that they can mount this boulder."

"I think you're right," Miss Kitty said, looking at the side of the knobs and indentations on the rocky face. "But the first handholds are too high for me to reach."

"Here," he said, lowering a knee and offering his hands as a stirrup.

"Yes!" She stepped into his hands and straightened as he did likewise. She stretched. "Not quite, I need a couple more inches."

He let go of her foot with one hand, placed it where she wasn't wearing a bustle, and pushed.

"Sir, your hand!" she yelped. But that gave her the extra height she needed to grasp a knob to pull herself farther. "I can make it from here. But what about you?"

"Keep climbing." He backed away and anxiously watched as she clambered upward. When she was far enough, he sprinted forward and jumped, planting one foot on the face of the rock, to vault high enough to grasp the first protuberance. He pulled up, and soon clambered high enough that his face was next to her ankle.

In seconds more, just as the rock trolls reached its base, they were atop the bulging peak of the cottage-size boulder.

"Now what do we do? They are too high for us to reach," Grubble wailed.

Vlanch considered the situation for a moment, then said, "You stay here in case they try to come down. I'm going around to the other side and dig out in front of it. Then we will push, and make this rock roll. And this stone will tumble down to smash into the Man-cave so we can get to the gold it hides — and crush the two Men on top of it as it rolls."

"You are so smart, Vlanch!"

Miss Kitty flung herself down on the boulder's top, head downslope. "Hold my ankles," she ordered, and slithered forward so she could see what the noise was she heard from the downhill direction. "This wasn't a good idea," she said when she saw the rock troll shoveling its stony hands into the earth at the foot of the boulder. "He's digging it out on that side so it'll roll."

"The other one is guarding the back side," Walker said. He stood and looked around, seeking a way to the ground that would avoid the two rock trolls. The only way he saw, to one side, risked a twisted ankle, or worse. "We're trapped," he shouted.

And no sooner had he said that than a wild *harroo* sounded from many voices, and a flurry of small, stocky men in homespun boiled out of…of…of somewhere, and attacked the two rock trolls.

The Dwarves were armed with picks and sledges, mauls and chisels, rakes and shovels, hammers and drills. One had an oyster rake, of all things, and Walker couldn't imagine what another intended to do with the broom and coal scuttle he bandied about.

The Dwarves hopped and leaped and skittered about the two rock trolls, distracting them from their fronts and striking them from behind, mostly skipping just out of reach when the trolls turned about to get at their tormentors. Here and there, now and then, one of the trolls' flailing arms connected with a Dwarf, sending it flying, broken and spraying blood.

All the while the Dwarves kept up a frightful *harroo* and skirl, even in the absence of pipes. Each time they connected, sparks flew from the trolls, and pebbles and sand were flung off their sides or fronts, or wherever they were hammered.

The rock trolls shouted, the roars of twin avalanches. They swung their mighty arms, digging divots in the hard earth and stone of the rock-strewn ground. They backhanded the boulder with flesh-and-bone-crushing blows. With every strike of pick, sledge, maul, chisel, hammer, drill, every flinging of pebbles and sand, the rock trolls shrank in size.

And they shrank and shrank, and grew smaller by the stroke.

The rock trolls were backed against the boulder, and their mighty — though diminishing — arms flew side to side with greater urgency, always seeking a Dwarvish target which was never there when their granite hands reached their targets. But often their swinging fists struck the boulder hard enough that had it been metal, it would have rung like a Gothic cathedral's entire bell tower of bells. Which caused the boulder to twitch and tremble and threaten to topple.

At length, the rock trolls were beaten so they were no larger than the Dwarfs, at which point the maul and chisel-armed Dwarves closed on them and sundered their limbs, hand from forearm, forearm from shoulder, foot from ankle, shin from thigh, head from neck, neck from chest, chest from belly. Others grasped the pieces and flung them over the sides of the narrow ridge, where they tumbled down, cracking and splitting as they fell.

The Dwarf who had first appeared to Cheyenne Walker and Miss Kitty Belle looked over one side and briskly brushed his hands against each other. "I told ye, ye'd come to no good end if ye again tried to take arr gold."

"Ah, some help here, if you please?" Cheyenne Walker called down from the now-swaying boulder top.

The Dwarf leader looked at the two people, his eyes metronomically following their movement. Then his look shifted to the boulder itself, and he realized the movement was in the stone, not the people — and the swaying was increasing. He shouted a rapid command to his companions, and they scrambled to his side. Then to Walker and Miss Kitty. "Jump, we'll catch you!"

Walker looked at the mass of little people. He thought he could probably make the jump uninjured without their help, and sufficiently break Miss Kitty's fall. But if the Dwarves could be trusted to catch them, both of them would be safe.

Miss Kitty made the decision. "Ready, I'm coming!" she shouted and dove, arms spread, and body parallel to the ground. Eager arms reached out to cradle her and stop her fall before she hit the ground.

"Your turn," she called to Walker as soon as she gained her feet.

He manfully followed her example, and the sturdy arms of ten Dwarves reached out and held as he plopped into them.

With both on their feet and unharmed, the head Dwarf stood before them, arms akimbo.

"Ye recall what I said about poor Hyram Scott, and the consequences of following him?"

"Yes, we do," Walker said. "We will not follow him."

"And the Pinkertons now have no need to investigate," Miss Kitty added.

"Ver' good." He turned to his troop. "Let's be off, high-low!"

There was a sudden rumble, and the earth shook as the boulder finally rocked too far, and began to roll downhill, heading straight for the Glittering Nugget Hotel!

"No-no!" Walker shouted. He jumped to the side of the huge boulder and pushed.

The boulder ignored him, and continued on the route that would send it crashing into the hotel.

"Ach! Push it aside, lads!" the Dwarf leader bellowed.

The Dwarves scrambled madly, seemingly in all directions at the same time, miraculously not bumping into each other or tripping one over the other. In seconds, they were at the side of the boulder, pushing.

In a moment they altered its track enough that it headed for the edge of the ridge, and tumbled over on a trajectory that would take it wide of the Glittering Nugget.

Brushing his hands after looking to assure himself the boulder would miss the hotel, the chief Dwarf said to Walker and Miss Kitty. "No need for an investigation."

"No need," Miss Kitty said.

"None indeed," Walker agreed.

In a trice, the Dwarves all vanished, carrying their casualties with them.

"Well," Walker said, wondering where the Dwarves had disappeared to and how they had so quickly vanished, "I think now we can safely return to the hotel."

"Yes, before our erstwhile picnic companions start inventing reasons for our absence," Miss Kitty said.

Partway down the hill, during which they didn't speak of what had just happened, she suddenly said, "Some would say that where you put your hand was inappropriate."

"But you needed to go higher, and that was the most expedient way to boost you."

"Um hum. And in another time and another place..." Miss Kitty Belle picked up her pace and walked with a sway to her hips that hadn't been there before.

Smiling, Cheyenne Walker slowed down, and enjoyed the view.

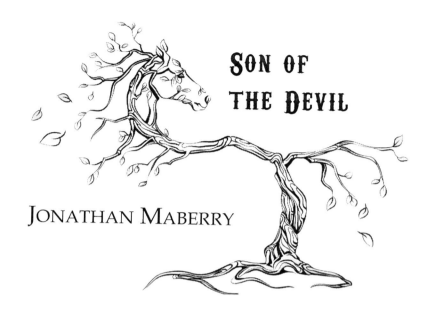

SON OF THE DEVIL

JONATHAN MABERRY

I

His name was Nebuchadnezzar, but everyone called him Neb.

When they were being nice, which was only when his Pa was around. People were always polite if they thought Big Tom Howard was in earshot. Or any kind of shot, for that matter. That was the thing. That's what everyone was afraid of.

But Big Tom wasn't always around.

Then the kids had other names for Neb. Most of them weren't really names, they were words that Neb knew they hadn't learned in church or school. What Mrs. Carter from the next farm over called 'barnyard words'. The kind of words that would have earned every one of those kids a solid beating if they'd used them around the house or in front of grown folks. The kind of words Neb never used at all, even when he was alone and had to clean up the whole house by himself.

Well, that wasn't entirely true. He used one of those words—a really bad one—the day the sheriff and his men came out to arrest Neb's Pa. All eleven of those men had come busting into the house with their ropes and chains and guns and fell on his Pa while he was still sleeping off a drunk. They'd have never come out when Big Tom was even half sober. No sir.

Neb ran after the men when they rode off with his Pa slung like a sack of beans over the bare back of a packhorse. He'd chased them all the way to the row of trees that separated the Howard spread from the

Carter place, but by then Neb knew he wasn't going to catch them. And he knew there wasn't a blessed thing he could have done if he did. They were grown men and he was twelve. There were a dozen of them and he was all alone. They had guns and badges and all he had was his fear and his anger.

So he yelled at their retreating backs.

"God damn you all to burning Hell."

It wasn't obscene, but it was blasphemous.

That was not the really bad word Neb used. That was still percolating in his chest.

Mrs. Carter came running out and threatened to cuff those words right out of him. She said it was the Devil himself speaking out of him like that, and she raised that little Bible she always carried as if it was the hand of God ready to strike him down.

"But they took my Pa," he protested, trying not to sound like a little boy. Trying to sound like he was Big Tom's only son.

His plea hadn't softened Mrs. Carter much. She lowered her Bible, though, and gave him a pitying look.

"And the Devil's been in his soul since he was your age, young Neb," she said in a voice of iron. "Now I hear the word of Satan falling from your lips." She shook her head and pressed the leather-bound book to her skinny breast.

"They *took* him, ma'am," said Neb, and the tears were in his voice if not yet in his eyes. "They had no right to take him."

Saying that did something to Mrs. Carter. She lowered the Bible and walked up to him, standing face to face with him. Although she was a full-grown woman and Neb was young, he was two inches taller. Somehow, though, he felt much smaller, and she seemed to tower over him. A thin scarecrow of a woman with sticks for arms and eyes the color of dust. Straw-dry hair pulled back into a bun that looked so tight it had to hurt, and a black dress with a white apron that flapped and snapped in the east wind.

"Listen to me, Nebuchadnezzar Howard," she said in a voice that was only slightly louder than the whisper of the breeze over the tall grass, "it's not your fault that you were born to such a family. A whore for a mother and a lawless devil of a father."

"Don't say that," he said, but his voice was nothing, too small to be heard.

"We are all sinners," she said. "We are born with the sins of Adam and Eve painted on our hearts. They betrayed the trust of God, and therefore we are all born in the shadow of that crime. All we can ever hope for is to find acceptance in the Lord and to beg for him to rescue us from the Pit."

"N-no…"

Mrs. Carter raised the hand holding the Bible and pointed with one bony finger at the group of riders that had dwindled down to specks.

"Evil is born unto evil as sin is born out of sin. Your father is a monster. A killer of men who has known the inside of every whorehouse west of Laramie. He has blood on his hands, oh yes he does. And as Adam's sins were passed down to his children, so are the sins of Thomas Howard passed unto you. Your soul must bear that weight, and it is up to you to find a way to expunge this guilt." She bent close and he could smell apples and bread yeast on her breath. "You stand at the very brink of Hell, Neb. Take one step and you will burn, like your mother burns now, and like your father will surely burn when they slip that noose around his neck. Mark me, child. Mark what I say."

"You're crazy," said Neb. "Ma used to say you were, and Pa said it all the time. You're crazy as a barn owl and twice as ugly."

Mrs. Carter's eyes flared as wide as an owl's right about then.

And before Neb could say another word of sass, she slapped him across the face. Not with her hand, but with the black leather-bound holy book she always carried. She was as skinny as a hickory pitchfork handle, but she was as tough as one, too. The blow caught Neb square on the side of the face, and it sent him crashing against the post rail. He rebounded and dropped to his knees in front of her like a sinner in church.

That's when Neb said the bad word. The barnyard word.

"Fuck you!" he screamed.

The words seemed to roll away from his mouth, blow past Mrs. Carter like a hot wind, tumble all the way to the distant line of mountains and come echoing back. And as they did his shouted words sounded like they were in his father's voice and not Neb's own.

Mrs. Carter stared at him with eyes as wide as saucers, and as he watched, Neb saw a strange expression come over her. Or, a series of them that pulled onto her face and then moved on, like cars in a locomotive. First there was blank shock, and then horror, then righteous indignation, and finally a smile crept onto her mouth. It was one of the ugliest smiles Neb had ever seen. Cruel and triumphant and delighted, as if she had waited all her life for just this moment, and now that it was here, with the proof of his sinful corruption still burning in her ears, her life's mission was complete. She seemed so incredibly pleased to have her certainties confirmed. Mrs. Carter pointed the Bible at him the same way his Pa would point at someone with his gun.

"You are going straight to Hell," she said in a tight whisper. "You will burn in eternal hellfire where you belong."

Neb Howard got slowly to his feet. His cheek hurt and his face burned and tears stung his eyes. He wanted to break down and sob, and he knew there would be time for that, but he would die first rather than give her that kind of satisfaction.

"You're always telling people that they're going to Hell," he said. "I heard you say that to half the people in town. You think everybody's going to Hell. Or maybe you think they all deserve to go there 'cept you." He took a step toward her and there must have been something in his voice or in his face, Neb couldn't be sure, but Mrs. Carter flinched backward half a step. "If everybody you ever told to go to Hell ever did, then it would be full to busting. All the people down there and you up here. You'd like that, wouldn't you?"

She straightened and tried to reclaim her power. "It would be the fitting justice of the Lord. I pray for all you sinners every day."

"Well, I'll tell you this much," said Neb, "maybe you'd better pray real good because it'd be my guess that Hell's going to get mighty full. And all them sinners down there will be remembering who sent 'em down to burn."

He took another step.

"And I wonder what'll happen with there's no more room in Hell, Mrs. Carter." He smiled and Neb knew it was a bad smile. It hurt his face to smile like that. "What do you think will happen then?"

She held the Bible out between them as if it could protect her from him and his sinful words.

Neb looked from the book to her and back down at the book. Then he hocked phlegm from deep in his throat and spat at the Bible she held. It was a big green glop that struck the black leather and splashed on her bony fingers.

The woman screeched like a crow and immediately wiped the spittle off on her apron, then pawed at the leather to insure that it was clean. She made small mewling sounds as she did so. Neb stood there and slowly dragged the back of his hand across his mouth. He studied the glistening wetness for a moment, then he looked up at her again.

"It's getting dark," he said. "You better run home now."

It was still early in the day. The darkness, he knew, was in her soul and in his heart.

Mrs. Carter backed up all the way to the road, then she turned and ran home. Only when she was halfway up the footpath to her own front door did she turn and shake the Bible at him and shout something. But Neb turned away, shutting out the sight of her and anything she had to say.

2

It was a long, bad day.

For a long time Neb sat on a hard wooden chair in the kitchen, surrounded by the silence of an empty house, and waited for something to happen. A thought, an idea, a plan. A hope.

Nothing.

His heart hurt and his head felt like it was full of hornets. His thoughts buzzed and stung him.

Ten different times he got up to head outside to saddle his horse, Dunders, and once even had the saddle on and the straps buckled. But then he unsaddled the old horse and trudged back to the house, knowing that his presence in town wouldn't do his father any good. There were a lot of stories about Big Tom and though many of them were wild, Neb suspected that most of them were true. Even if half of them were lies and the other half exaggerated it still meant that his Pa was a bad man.

A sinner.

Neb thought of this as he sat in the house, wrapped in shadows that rose up, towered over him, and fell crashing down as the sun moved through the sky and threw light in through the windows. The truth was a hard thing to know. Knowing it made it hard for Neb to breathe sometimes. Not just then, but at nights in his bed when he heard Big Tom downstairs weeping or yelling, raving drunk. Telling bad truths to the night and whispering into his whiskey bottle.

Neb knew that it was what happened to Ma that turned his father bad. Ruined him. That was probably the better way to think about it. Mrs. Carter and the ladies at church had a lot to do with that. With what happened to Ma and what Pa turned into.

It was on account of the baby.

Neb's little sister, Hannah, had only lived long enough to cry once and then she stopped crying, stopped wriggling around, stopped breathing. Neb had been eight when it happened. He'd seen stillbirths before, it happened a lot on a farm. And there were birthing deaths in town, too. The Pederson twins both died, and Mrs. Sykes died along with her sixth kid. It happens, and even as young as he was Neb Howard was old enough to know that life was hard and life was fragile. Dying came easy out here. Maybe it was different in the big cities back East, but not out here. There was sickness and there were all sorts of dangers. Fires and ranch accidents, flash floods and all sorts of things. Death walked everywhere and there was no one who didn't know the sound of the Reaper's voice.

But with Ma it had been bad.

She'd been sickly for a long time, having never really recovered from a sickness that cut through this whole region. The influenza Neb thought it was called. That was the word people used, though Mr. Flambeau who owned the livery called it the *grippe* It gripped all right, Neb knew. It grappled hold of people from Sadler's Fork to Indian Pass, and by the time that winter passed there were probably a thousand new graves dug in the soil in the shade of these mountains. Ma had almost been one of them, but even though she lingered there on the edge she came back. It was Pa who brought her back. Sitting by her side every night, holding her hand, praying to God and to her for her to come back, come back, come back to him. That's what he said, and Neb was sure he heard his father say those words ten thousand times.

Come back. Come Back. Come back to me.

And even though she'd looked like death lying there with sweat-soaked hair and gray skin and hardly no breath at all, Ma came back. Slowly. Maybe reluctantly. But when Pa called her she came back.

She was never the same after that, though.

Neb once heard Mr. Flambeau say to his wife that 'Meg Howard looked like death warmed up.' And Mrs. Schusterman over at the general store said that she looked like a ghost.

Neb thought she looked like an angel, and sometimes at night he wondered if maybe Ma HAD died and it was her angel that had come back. Ma was so gentle, so soft, so quiet after the sickness. And she was always fragile as butterfly wings. She rarely went out in the bright sun and could not abide loud noises. She left the heavy farm work to Neb and his Pa.

Neb missed the old Ma. He missed her laughter and her energy. He missed the Ma who could bake a dozen pies at Christmas and decorate the house and the big tree in the yard and do it all with a smile. After the sickness he never saw that Ma again. Instead it was the angel.

Then she got pregnant. Even as a kid Neb understood about that. This was a farm after all. She got pregnant and every day, the bigger she got the sicker she looked. It was as if the baby growing in her belly was draining all the life force from her. Like a tick sucking on blood.

Neb grew to hate the baby.

At first, anyway.

Later he realized that he was just afraid of what the baby was going to do to Ma by the time she came to term.

Then that night came, and it was as if the doors of Hell had been cracked open. The midwife came and so did some of the ladies from town. Even Mrs. Carter came over, drawn by the sound of Ma's terrible screams.

Neb tried to hide from those screams. First in his room, then in the barn. The horses were spooked by the sound, and they screamed, too.

It lasted all through the night and only around dawn did the screaming stop.

Neb, exhausted from a night of hiding and crying and praying for it all to end, heard the silence. That's how he remembered it. He *heard* the silence.

He crawled out from beneath the pile of hay he'd pulled over him, and crept out of the barn and stood looking at the house. He knew something was wrong. He knew that just looking at the house. It stood wrong against the dawn light. It seemed tighter, threatening. The gables and windows and everything seemed to be clutched into a fist. Ready to punch him. Ready to hurt him.

The silence was awful.

So awful.

Neb came up onto the porch and saw that the door stood open. It was never left open.

The living room was empty and messy. That was wrong, too. Ma always kept the house neat as a pin. Everything dusted, everything in its place. Neat and tidy and snug and comfortable.

Now chairs were in the wrong place and the hall rug was rumpled and there was a whiskey bottle standing nearly empty on the table. No glass. As if Pa had been drinking from the bottle itself. *Was that the haystack pa hid under*, he thought. It was a thought too old for a kid, but he thought it anyway and knew it to be the truth.

Climbing the stairs was the hardest thing Neb ever did. So hard and it took forever. The effort of lifting his leg to place the flat of his shoe on each riser was harder than lifting fence rails.

Then he was upstairs, down the hall, standing at the open door to his parents' room. It was as far as he would go. It was as far as he could make himself go. He stood with his hands on the doorframe and stared into a scene from Hell itself.

The town ladies standing around, each of them looking sad or shocked or horrified. All of them looking worn down. Ma was on the bed, but the bed was wrong. So wrong. It was painted in red. Splashed in red. Drenched in red.

Pa stood holding something. A tiny form whose legs and arms drooped down from the edges of his palms. It, too, was red.

Ma lifted a pale, blood-spattered hand toward the thing that Pa held. "My baby…," she said in a ghost of a voice. "Give me my baby."

Pa did not move.

Ma pulled at the neck of her sodden dressing gown, tearing it down, exposing one breast. "I have to feed my baby. Give her to me. Can't you hear how hungry she is?"

Mrs. Carter said, "You should have called Brother Taylor when I told you to, Tom Howard."

Pa lifted his head and Neb saw that there was no trace of comprehension in his red-rimmed eyes. "W-what…?"

"I told you that this would happen," said Mrs. Carter. "I told you that you needed the parson to come out here and baptize the child before…"

She let her words trail off, the meaning clear.

"Where's my baby?" cried Ma.

"Only those baptized in the blood of the lamb can ever hope to go to Heaven," said Mrs. Carter. "Only those blessed by the Lord can hope to escape the fires of Hell."

Pa clutched the still form to his chest and sank slowly down to his knees, broken as much by what had happened as by those dreadful words.

"Give me my baby," said Ma. "Little Hannah is so hungry."

He bent forward and laid the infant on the bed, let Ma take her, watched as Ma pressed the slack mouth to her nipple. Saw the smile on Ma's face.

"There she is," said Ma. "See how hungry she is?"

Those words beat Pa further down. He buried his face in the bloody sheets and wrapped his arms over his head. That's when Neb heard those words again.

"Come back," whispered Pa. "Come back. Come back to me."

But Hannah hadn't come back.

And as Neb stood there he saw Ma's eyes close and her smile slowly fade. It did not go away completely. Not even when she stopped breathing. Not even when Pa began to scream.

That was how Pa went wrong. Neb knew it for sure.

The preacher came out at noon, but Mrs. Carter met him on the porch and she had the same triumph in her eyes that day as she had this morning.

"I told Tom Howard to send for you while there was still time," she said. "Now look what he's done. That poor baby is lost for good and all."

Neb stood holding his Pa's hand, and he felt his father's grip tighten and tighten as they waited for the parson to refute those words, to say different, to say that Hannah was going to Heaven. To say that it didn't matter than she hadn't been baptized.

But the preacher only took Mrs. Carter's hand and patted it. "I'll say a prayer."

That was all he said and it wasn't enough. It wasn't near enough by a country mile.

Pa nearly broke Neb's hand by squeezing it so hard. If it had been a day later, Neb was sure Pa would have gone charging off the porch and punched them both. It if had been a month later he'd have taken a horsewhip to them.

If it had been this year, Pa would have shot them both sure as God made green apples.

Now Pa was gone. Dragged out of bed, beaten and slung across the back of a horse. Now he was in jail. And maybe he was going to wherever Ma and little Hannah had gone. Into the ground. Up to Heaven? Or, if Mrs. Carter and the parson were right, then down to Hell.

Neb huddled inside the rough blanket of his own hurt and wondered what to do.

3

He summoned the courage to ride into town that afternoon. The sun was tumbling behind the hills, throwing long purple shadows in his path. Dunders, who was an old and trailwise horse, seemed uneasy by the coming twilight and Neb had to yank on the reins and kick him a few times to keep the horse headed to town. Though in his head Neb understood and even sympathized.

"I don't want to go, either," he told the horse when they were halfway there. "But we gotta find out what's happening to Pa."

Dunders blew out a breath that was almost a sigh of resignation and plodded on. It was nearly full dark by the time they reached the outskirts of town, and Neb knew at once that something was wrong. Bad wrong. There were lights everywhere. Torches and lanterns. He could hear voices shouting and even some gunshots popping. Mrs. Carter's rickety old dogcart with her rickety old horse, Ahab, was tied to a post. He saw the parson's half-breed Appaloosa tethered next to it.

Neb almost turned around.

Almost.

Dunders stopped at the edge of town and Neb sat heavily in the saddle, knowing that nothing good was ever going to come of riding on. Nothing, no-how.

He rode on.

At a hesitant walk at first, then an unsteady cantor, and finally a full gallop.

Knowing what he would see. The crowd clustered around the jail, swelling as more people ran in. He saw the fists shaking in the air, heard the guns fire into the night sky, saw the big tree in the center of town lit by torches. Saw the rope.

He knew all about lynch mobs. Who didn't?

Dunders caught his desperate terror and ran harder than ever all the way up the length of Main Street.

Just in time to see.

There were so many things to see.

The sheriff sitting on the wooden plank walkway outside of the jail, his left eye swollen shut, three townsmen holding his arms. Torchlight struck sparks off of the sheriff's badge, and off the badges of the men restraining him.

The faces of the people in town. People he knew. Mr. Flambeau, Mr. and Mrs. Schusterman, the milliner, the man from the hat shop, the two sons of the farrier, the parents of his friends. He knew those faces and didn't know them. He knew them as people in town, people he knew or kind of knew, ordinary people whose faces he saw at church or at the town fair or clustered together in front of the general store on every other Tuesday when the mail coach came rumbling in. The faces of the people in his life.

Except now they were different. Now they were screaming and yelling. Now their features were twisted into strange masks by the flickering torches. Now they were like the faces of monsters. Not human at all.

Monster faces.

So many monsters.

Neb saw those faces and didn't know any of them anymore.

The only face he knew — the only face that he recognized now — was that of his own Pa.

Sitting on a horse. No hat. Face bruised and bloody.

Shirt torn and filthy, hair mussed and hanging loose over his brow. Hands tied behind his back.

A thick loop of rope around his neck. The air was torn apart by the yells of the gathered monsters. They shouted his Pa's name. They screamed aloud for the three burly men standing by the horse's head to do something bad. Something impossible.

"No," breathed Neb, though his voice was too small, too weak to be heard over the shouts.

He saw Mrs. Carter. She stood on a stump, shrieking as she shook her Bible at Pa. The parson was there, too, standing beside the stump, hands clasped together. For a moment — just one clear, sweet moment — Neb thought the preacher was calling for the crowd to stop, to step back, to not do this.

But then Neb saw the smile. A curl of his mouth that was too much like the triumphant smile on the twisted face of Mrs. Carter. That's when Neb knew it was all going to fall apart, that the hinges of his life had split from the frame and were falling off. He knew that as sure as he knew anything else in his life.

"No..." he said, smaller than before. Faint even to his own ears.

And then it bubbled up from the bottom of his soul, boiling up past his breaking heart and tearing its way from his throat.

"Noooooooooooo!"

It was so loud that it stilled the crowd. It froze the moment. Everyone turned toward him, every face, every eye. Even the horse on which his father sat. They all turned to Neb Howard, but all Neb could do was look into the eyes of his father.

"No," he said again. Once more small and faint.

His Pa said, "Neb, for God's sake, go home."

He was crying as he said it. Neb hadn't seen his Pa cry since that red day in his parents' bedroom. He'd heard him weeping in the night, but he'd never seen those drunken tears. Now, though, they ran down his cheeks like lines of molten silver. It burned Neb to see them. It stabbed him through and through.

As the moment stretched Neb saw how his presence began to change the faces of those monsters that used to be the people in town. Some of them looked angry that he was there. Others looked down or away, anywhere but at him. Some cut looks at Mrs. Carter, the sheriff, the rope, as if calculating how far this was taking them away from the people they were supposed to be.

And in that moment, Neb thought—wondered, hoped, prayed—that they were going to step back, cut him down, release the sheriff, not do this. They should. He knew it and they knew it, because this was a line that no one should cross. Not like this. Not when hate has turned them into monsters.

It was Mrs. Carter—of course it was her—who broke the fragile tension of that moment.

She yelled, "Damn you to Hell, Tom Howard. Your family is waiting for you in the Pit."

Neb heard the gasps from the people. Even the preacher recoiled slightly from her, his smile dimming.

Mrs. Carter stared down at them, looking around, disappointment and disapproval etched by firelight and shadows onto her face. And her face had never stopped being the mask of a monster.

"No, please," begged Neb. "For the love of God…"

Mrs. Carter spat toward him and then she threw her Bible at the horse. The leather struck the animal's hip with a sound like a gunshot. The horse screamed as if scalded. It reared back, breaking loose from the men who held it, then it lurched forward, crashed into the people who were too slow and too shocked to move out of the way in time. The horse raced past Neb and ran down Main Street, the sound of its thudding hooves chopping into the air.

There was no rider on that horse.

Of course there wasn't.

No one watched the horse go.

They stood like silent statues and stared at the thing that swung slowly back and forth on the end of the rope. No one made a move to cut Big Tom down. There was no reason to hurry. Not with a neck bent and stretched like that.

The parson was the only living person who moved. He walked five paces and squatted down to pick up the Bible. He brushed it off on his black frock coat and then held it out to Mrs. Carter. She stared at him, at the book, and up at the man she'd killed for a long time, then she stepped down and took the book from him, smiling all the while, and giving a small HMPH as she pressed it to her chest. When she walked away, no one said a word, no one tried to stop her.

Mrs. Carter paused for a moment in front of Dunders. She used her free hand to caress the horse's long nose.

"All sinners go to Hell, Nebuchadnezzar," she said. "And you will burn alongside the rest of your kin."

Then she walked away. She never stopped smiling.

No one could look at Neb. Not even the parson.

He sat there and felt his heart turn to cold stone in his chest. He could feel the weight of it as it tore loose from its moorings. It fell and fell, landing in a much lower place. Far too low.

He knew that even then.

4

They buried his Pa the next day. Four men brought his body out on the back of a cart and they set to digging in the front yard. They buried him next to Ma and little Hannah. The parson came out and tried to read some words over the grave, but Neb grabbed a pitchfork and brandished it at the parson.

"You take your lying words and that damn book and you git!" he snarled.

The parson was appalled. So were the gravediggers. "I am here to say a prayer over your *father*."

Neb took a step forward, the tines of the pitchfork held at heart level. "Will your prayers keep my Pa out of Hell?"

"You have to understand, son," said the preacher, "your father was a murderer. He gunned a man down in—"

"I know what he did. I hear people talking. But he was supposed to have a trial so the judge could hear both sides of the story. What happened to that? Did you speak up to protect my Pa from those crazy people and their damned rope?"

"I—"

Neb sneered. "Where were your prayers last night? What did you do to stop Mrs. Carter? What did you do to stop all those people?"

"You must understand…that was a mob. They were all whipped up and—"

"And what? Ain't you preachers supposed to stand up for what's right? No, don't answer 'cause I know you'd just lie."

"You ought to watch your tongue, boy," said one of the gravediggers.

Neb pointed the pitchfork at him. "And maybe you ought to hold yours," he warned. "This ain't about you. This is between my folks and his asshole of a god."

"By the Almighty," cried the parson. "Do you hear what you're saying? Do you not fear God's wrath?"

Neb nearly ran at him with the pitchfork. "Fear God's wrath? That's all I know of God. He took my ma and he took my little sister and you told me that she's burning in Hell because she died 'fore she was baptized. That's what your God does. And my Pa may not have been the best man but he deserved to have a trial and he deserved justice, but last night I saw you standing right there when Mrs. Carter threw her Bible at that horse. Wasn't that the wrath of God? She stood there and said it was GOD'S justice, and I didn't hear you speak out against that."

Neb moved forward, the pitchfork's tines gleaming like claws. All of the men, the parson and the gravediggers, moved away. Neb stopped at the foot of the half-filled in grave.

"You people ain't never done nothing but hate on my family. If you had even a shred of decency, you'd have told us that Hannah would go to Heaven with all the angels. My ma, too."

"God's truth is God's truth. I'm a man of God," said the preacher.

Neb didn't want to cry, but the tears came anyway. Hot as boiled water. "You could have had mercy," said the boy. "You could have lied to us. What you said, what Mrs. Carter said, that's what broke something in my Pa's head. It's what turned him mean as a snake. He wasn't evil... he was heartbroke. You're always preaching about saving souls—it wouldn't have taken much to save his."

The preacher said nothing.

"Go on and get off my farm," said Neb, his voice cold even to his own ears. "You're not welcome here. Not you and not your God. Now *git*."

He jabbed the pitchfork toward the preacher and again toward the gravediggers. One of the men started to take a threatening step toward Neb, but the crew foreman caught his arm.

"Leave 'im be," said the foreman. "This here's his land now. He wants us gone, then we best be gone."

The other gravedigger pointed at the grave. The corpse of Big Tom Howard was only partly covered, and there was a considerable pile of dirt standing in a humped mound. "You want us gone, kid, then you best finish this your own self. But bury him deep, 'cause he's already starting to stink."

He turned away, laughing, and followed his companions back to where they'd left their cart. The preacher lingered a moment, looking like he wanted to say something else. It was the kind of expression people had when they wanted to have the last word in an argument. But the pitchfork had the last word, and both he and Neb knew it.

The preacher backed away, then turned and hurried to catch the gravediggers.

That left Neb all alone with the half-buried body of his father. They'd wrapped him in white linen and someone had tied some rope crisscrossed from neck to ankles. Neb figured it was the rope they'd hung him with. People did that so they wouldn't have to use a bad luck rope.

Neb jabbed the pitchfork down into the ground at the foot of the grave and pulled the small hunting knife he wore in a leather sheath on his belt. With tears flowing down his cheeks he stepped down into the shallow grave.

"I'm sorry, Pa," he said, sniffing to keep from choking on the words. He bent down and sawed through the ropes. It was a horrible thing to have to do. His father's body was rigid with death stiffness. Neb knew that this would wear off after a couple of days; he'd seen that with animals he'd hunted and livestock here on the farm. Knowing that his father would go through that process — that he was stiff as a board now — reinforced the fact that Neb was alone. That Pa was dead. That everyone he cared about was dead. He sawed and sawed. It was a task assigned in Hell, and he labored at it with the diligence of the insane. He knew it. He could feel parts of his mind cracking loose and sliding away into darkness.

He stopped abruptly, his face and body bathed in cold sweat, most of the ropes cut, his chest heaving. He felt as if someone was watching him. There was an itch between his shoulder blades. Neb straightened and looked around.

The house was still and silent. The horses in the corral stood with barely a flick of the ear or swish of the tail.

But he saw two things.

One chilled him and the other set fire to something in his soul.

Above the yard, kettling high in dry air, were buzzards. A baker's dozen of them, swirling around and around. Here to feast on the dead. Neb wished that there was something like them that feasted on the living. Something he could sic on the parson and everyone who was there at the tree last night.

The sight of those birds chilled him.

But the thing that held a burning match to the cracked timbers of his soul was the person who stood watching him. She stood like a specter at the end of the road, her feet on her side but the weight of her stare reaching all the way to the grave.

Mrs. Carter.

And she was smiling.

5

It rained that night.

He saw the storm clouds coming over the mountain. Big, ugly things, dark as bruises, veined with red lightning. The storm growled low in its throat. It sounded like laughter of the wrong kind. The bad kind.

Neb stood by his father's grave and watched the storm gather.

And he was smiling.

6

Neb filled in the grave with his hands. He didn't bother to go get a shovel.

The raindrops began falling as he patted it down over his father.

"I love you, Pa," he told the dirt.

Lightning forked the sky and he looked up, gasping, as thunder boomed above him. The shock of it drove Neb down to his knees at the foot of the grave. He reached up to catch himself on the upright handle of the pitchfork, but his knees buckled and he slid down. He held onto the hickory handle, though, and laid his head against it, eyes closed as the rain fell.

"Come back," he whispered.

Come back.

He heard his Pa's voice echo in his memory. There, kneeling much like this at the side of Ma's bed, holding out the little dead thing and Ma taking it, too far gone to accept that Hannah was dead. Too mad with her own dying to know that the babe she put to her breast was not hungry. Would never be hungry.

"Come back," said Neb. He was hungry. Not for food. Not for comfort. Not for peace.

He wanted to hurt them all. Mrs. Carter. The parson. All of them. Everyone who'd held a torch or raised a fist. All of them.

"Come back, Pa," begged Neb. "You don't belong down there."

He did not know if he meant that his father did not belong in the ground or in the Hell that everyone said he was bound for.

The rain began to fall in earnest. Big, cold drops that hammered down on him and pinged on the leaves of the oak tree, and peppered the shingles on the slanted roof. Thunder rumbled and rumbled under a sky torn by lightning.

"Come back to me," cried Neb Howard. "You don't belong down there and I need you here."

The hurt in his heart was so big, so deep, so unbearable that he could not even kneel there without caving over. He fell onto his chest, onto his face. He beat the ground as the rain turned the dirt to mud.

The storm kept getting bigger. Louder. Darker.

The clouds swirled and changed from purple to gray to a black so pervasive that it swallowed everything. Only the lightning carved edges and curves onto the things around him, trimming everything with cold fire.

The world seemed to be so huge and so dark and so empty of everything important. No love, no heat.

"Come back, come back, come back," he wailed. "*Please*, Pa, don't leave me alone. Come back."

A light flared in the darkness and Neb stared at it. It was the Carter place, and Mrs. Carter was lighting her lamps against the darkness. He watched with hateful eyes as the house seemed to open its eyes, but then the woman began closing the shutters. The effect was like wide eyes narrowing to suspicious, accusing slits.

Neb did not even realize that he had clutched two handfuls of mud until the muck ran from between his fingers. He looked down at the mess. It was so soaked with rain that it ran like black blood down his wrists.

"Come back," he said. Then he pointed to the distant house with one muddy finger. "If you can't come back for me, Pa, then come back for *her*."

As he said it, the lightning struck directly above him, bathing him in so brilliant a light that it stabbed through his eyes and into his brain. Neb cried out and fell backward, flinging an arm across his face, screaming at the storm, hurling his rage, his curses, his damnation at the sky and all who lived under it. Hating Mrs. Carter and everyone in this damned town with a purity and intensity that was every bit as hot and bright as that lightning.

"Please," he whispered as he lay there. The rain fell like hammers, like nails. "Please come back to me."

Neb Howard lay in the cold mud and prayed his dark prayers as the heavens wept and the thunder laughed.

1

He did not remember falling asleep.

He did not know how long he slept.

Neb became aware of being cold. Of hurting from the cold.

It took him a long time to wake up.

When he did, the world was wrong.

He wasn't in the front yard anymore.

He was covered in mud, cold and sore, still dressed in filthy clothes, shoes and all. But he wasn't outside. He was in the house. Upstairs.

On the bed where his mother died. Where his sister never even got to live.

Laid out on the bed, but he knew he hadn't walked up here. He never came into this room. Never. He knew that he would never have gone to bed wearing muddy clothes. Never would have lain down with his shoes on.

Never.

Neb sat up very slowly. It took a lot to do it, his muscles hurt that bad. So did his head. As soon as he sat up, a cough took him and wouldn't let him go for five long minutes. It was a bad cough. Deep and grating, and when he was done coughing there were drops of blood on the hand he'd used to cover his mouth.

Sunlight slanted through the window, and outside he could hear the morning birds. A couple of cows mooed out in the field, needing to be milked. Dunders whinnied in the corral.

Neb got out of bed, moving carefully, afraid of that cough coming back. His feet were unsteady, and his body kept wanting to fall. He stayed up, though. And he got all the way to the top of the stairs before something occurred to him. He turned and looked the way he'd come. He saw the faint dried-mud smudges of his shoes on the floorboards, but they were coming out of the room. There were none of his footprints going in. There should have been, and his feet were covered in mud.

Not that there weren't footprints, though. It's just that they were too big. A man's shoes.

Like all the boys his age he knew how to hunt and how to track. He knew how to tell one set of footprints from another, animal or not. The shoes that made those prints were shoes he recognized.

"No," he told the morning.

No.

The prints remained, however.

Frightened, Neb hurried downstairs, clutching the bannister for support. The front door was open and there was a pool of water in the living room. There was a line of muddy prints leading in through the open door, through that puddle, and on up the steps.

"No," he said again.

Neb walked wide of the footprints and had to step over them to get out of the door.

He walked across the front yard to the little family cemetery. The muddy mound over his father's grave was torn up and sunken in.

Neb backed away from it.

He stood halfway between the house and the corral, looking everywhere for answers, needing to find some that did not match the pictures in his head. The cough came again. Worse this time. So deep. So bad.

When it finally passed the whole yard seemed to tilt and slide sideways. It took forever for Neb to saddle his horse. Dunders kept shying away from him and he kept dropping things. The blanket, the saddle, the reins.

Finally he managed to climb up onto the horse's back.

They rode away from the house.

The way to town took him past the Carter place. Neb stopped by the gate and studied the house. Their door was open, too. He could see faint light inside, as if no one had bothered to turn down the night lanterns.

"No," he said one more time.

He turned the horse and walked Dunders up the lane to the Carters' porch steps. He could see how it was. The doorframe was splintered, the lock torn clean out of the wood. The porch rocker lay on its side. There was a muddy handprint on the door.

But Neb knew it wasn't mud. Blood turns chocolate brown when it dries.

He slid from the saddle and staggered up the steps. There was mud on the porch. Footprints in that familiar shape. Going in. Coming out. They were the only footprints on the porch.

Neb stepped over them and went in without knocking.

He stood for a long time looking at the living room. Seeing it yanked him out of that moment and took him back to his Ma's room and how it seemed to have been painted red. This room was painted red, too.

Mrs. Carter sat on the sofa.

Some of her did, anyway.

The rest of her…

Well it was gone. Even from ten feet away Neb could tell it wasn't a knife that did this. Nor a wood axe either. He'd seen animals in the wood that had been set upon and half eaten. He knew how that looked.

He knew what he was seeing.

Once more the world tried to tilt under his feet.

Neb hurried outside and vomited over the porch rail. Half of the vomit was red with his own blood. He gagged, coughed, gagged.

Dunders nickered and tossed his head, his big dark eyes rolling, alarmed at the smell of sickness and of death.

Neb shambled down from the porch and climbed into the saddle. He went back out to the road. Along the way, there in the center of the road, he saw those same footprints. One set of tracks coming here to the Carter place. Another set coming out and then turning, turning, not heading home. Heading to town. There were dark splotches of dried blood mixed in with the mud.

Neb sat on the horse as more of that awful coughing tore at him. He knew he was sick. Laying out there in the cold and the storm…that had been bad. There was something burning inside his chest. In his lungs.

He sat astride Dunders, feeling lost, feeling sick, feeling like he was already falling into darkness. The footsteps went on ahead and vanished into the distance.

Neb did not follow them into town.

He knew what he would find there.

"No," he said one last time. But this time he knew that he meant 'yes'.

He turned Dunders around and let the horse take him home.

Once he was there he removed the saddle and bridle and let the horse go. Not into the corral. Just go.

Then Neb walked up the few steps to his porch and sat down on the chair.

And waited for his Pa to come home from town.

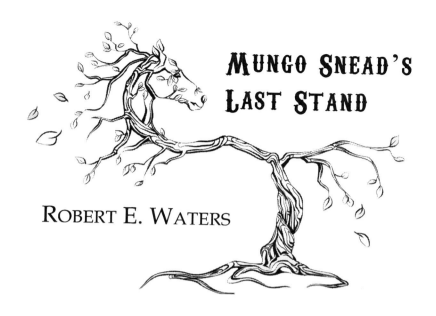

Mungo Snead's Last Stand

Robert E. Waters

June 18, 1885, Fort Henderson,
South Platte River, Colorado Territory

Captain Remington Alexander "Mungo" Snead peered through his binoculars toward the amassing Killajunkur horde. There was no other way to describe it, set against the backdrop of a rising orange sun and steam floating off the surrounding valley grass. To him the Killajunkur appeared as tiny specks, a jumble of blue and green and red Scalies preparing for war. Behind him, Corporal Seamus Johns cursed their bad luck and stabbed scorpions with an antique Highland dirk.

"This is what I'm going to do to them sons of bitches if they get close, Captain," the corporal said, slicing through the creature's tough, black carapace with a swift crunching sound.

"You better have something more than a knife, Corporal," Mungo said, adjusting the intensity of his binoculars to get a better view of the tall Scalie inspecting the enemy ranks. "The Killajunkur wear armour."

Corporal Johns huffed. "As if that'll keep them safe from a blaster."

"Aye." Mungo nodded. "But we don't have many; only two crates. And they have more...many, many more."

The corporal laughed, something he did regularly. This time, though, he sounded afraid. *He should be.*

"Don't you fret, Captain. The major will keep us safe from that murderous alien beast. And the 10th Royal Guard is still out there somewhere."

The "murderous beast" Corporal Johns spoke of towered over the ranks of his Scalie spearmen by a good two feet. Mungo adjusted the right lens of his binoculars and focused in on the scores of eagle and hawk feathers that hung proudly from Arjukadembo's prominent horns running from the crest of his skull to the small of his back. One feather for every victory against Her Majesty's Royal North American Legion. Which one represented the Pawnee Creek Massacre, he wondered. From this distance, he could not distinguish one feather from another. And did that feather carry the blood of the innocent women and children left slaughtered and face down in the red water?

Mungo let go of his binoculars, left them hanging from his neck on a thin cord of buffalo hide, knelt, and prayed. He prayed silently, for he could not let the men see his fear. Men and a few women serving the hospital, a handful of survivors from Pawnee Creek, a dozen missionaries who foolishly entered the territory with no survival plan save for their faith and Bibles, elements from the 7th British Expeditionary Force, and Fort Henderson's own small garrison. Maybe a hundred and sixty, a hundred seventy souls. Barely a fighting force. Corporal Johns' words rang in Mungo's mind. *The Major will keep us safe from those…*

"Captain!"

Mungo turned and saw Sergeant Williams saluting. The young man's tortured face told the captain everything he needed to know. "The Major will see you now, sir."

Mungo nodded and followed the sergeant off the ramparts and into the tiny building where Major John Willoughby lay dying on a bloody, sweat-soaked cot.

"Come here, you bastard," Quick-Shot Willoughby said, through gooey phlegm and the smoke of a blunt cigar wedged between his crooked teeth. The doctor had tried to keep tobacco away from the grumpy fool, but no one dared tell the major not to smoke.

Mungo respectfully removed his helmet and knelt beside the bed. The major placed his shaking hand on Mungo's shoulder. "Tell me one thing, Captain. Did I do good?"

Once word of Pawnee Creek had reached Fort Henderson, the major had decided to scout the enemy advance on his own, despite Mungo's stern objection. He managed to return with a few of his men, though barely, receiving a point-blank gut shot from a Killajunkur blaster. He'd lost too much blood. He was severely dehydrated, and the wound was infected beyond medicine and God.

Mungo nodded. "Yes, major. You brought two blaster cases back. Primed and ready."

"Very well." The old man coughed. A trickle of blood ran down his mouth. "You have to promise me, Captain. No retreat. Promise me that."

"Sir." Mungo leaned in to whisper his next words so that those standing nearby could not hear. "The Scalies number in the thousands. Arjukadembo is leading the attack. We have but a handful of trained fighting men. We *cannot* stand. We must abandon this post, fall back, and—"

"No!" Major Willoughby's eyes were bloodshot and violent, peering through a crust of yellow gore from the creeping blaster wound that had left him nearly blind. His breath was stagnant, his breathing hectic. He grabbed Mungo's brass-buttoned red lapel and pulled him closer. "If you fall back, Arjukadembo will sweep down the South Platte, destroying every outpost, every town, from here to Denver. Her Majesty's empire in America will crumble. You cannot retreat. Promise me that you will stand...and fight."

Mungo could do nothing but nod.

A withered grin crept across the Major's ruined face. He laid his head back into the dirty pillow, let out a final sigh, and died.

Mungo left the room, followed closely by Corporal Johns.

"Are you in charge now, Captain?"

Mungo nodded to the corporal. "It would seem so."

"What are you going to do?"

Before Mungo could answer, a low, howling whistle climbed through the mist. Mungo looked up and saw a flash of green-and-red energy, like a lightning bolt, arc into the morning sky from the Killajunkur position. For a moment, it reminded him of the streaming fireworks he used to enjoy as a child in the streets of London. But this was no pleasant object of celebration. This was an energy spear, tossed into the air from a powerful Scalie arm with a leather atlatl throwing sling, and its message was clear.

He watched it bend through the sky, over the outer wall of Fort Henderson, and strike a wagon in the covered center of the yard. Half the wagon shattered in a cloud of smoke, broken iron, and wood. The other half burned.

When the dust and shock of the strike settled, Mungo approached the spear cautiously. Along its compound steel structure, ropes of green-and-red electricity popped. He waited until its kinetic energy waned.

When it did, a small white flag unfurled out of its base and fluttered in the warm breeze.

"What is it, Captain?" Corporal Johns asked.

Mungo tried reading the charcoal scratches on the white flag. Alien words. Killajunkur words.

"He wishes to meet."

"Who?"

"Arjukadembo."

The corporal paused, then said, "What are you going to do?"

Mungo Snead turned and looked back up into the sky, and followed the spear's contrail down until it disappeared behind the fort's wall. Major Willoughby's words raced through his mind—*No retreat. Promise me that you will stand...*—and the foolish promise that he had made to a dying man.

Mungo turned to Corporal Johns and tried sounding brave. "I will go and face the enemy."

They met halfway between Fort Henderson and the Killajunkur horde. Captain Snead and Corporal Johns stood together in front of Arjukadembo. The alien chief towered over them, a seven-foot-tall cord of muscle and confidence. His red and green and black scales ran in narrow stripes down his chest and trunk and faded to dark red legs. Mungo was close enough now to see the majesty of his horn line and the long feathers that swung from them. He was impressive. Mungo could understand why the Killajunkur had made him a chief.

The Arapaho translator at his side worked his mouth furiously to give human voice to the screechy, raspy alien tongue. "I am honored to be in your presence, Captain Snead."

"Really?" He was genuinely surprised by the statement. "I was not aware that you knew of me, sir."

Arjukadembo nodded curtly. "Your reputation, as your people say, precedes you. The defense of Nine Pines. The counter-attack at Fordham Lodge. The retreat from Camp Smith. All impressive actions."

Mungo repaid the compliment. "And your military campaigns are equally impressive, Great One. The attack at Fort Laramie. The rout on the Kansas plains. The massacre at Pawnee Creek."

Arjukadembo took that last one for the insult intended. His powerful cheek muscles twitched beneath thick scales shifting black. "Is it a massacre when one is merely retaliating for the scores of dead women and children that my translator's people have endured? The rapes, the murders that the Pawnee have endured? The killing that the Killajunkur have endured?"

"Do not forget, Arjukadembo," Mungo said, "that it was your people that began this great war. Your starships dropped out of the clouds and dispersed your armies around the world. You've burned and pillaged for hundreds of miles, and you maintained that campaign unfettered until your ships disappeared. Will they come back? One wonders. Now that you have been abandoned and are running low on blaster fuel, with no refit coming, you've taken up allies in the hopes of surviving. Your decision to rely on armed conflict once again will not succeed. Your armies will—"

"This land is no more yours than it was the Americans," Arjukadembo said, interrupting, "no more than Louisiana belongs to the French, no more than California belongs to the Spanish. Your American allies could not defeat us alone, so they sold their souls and their country to Europe just to survive. Colorado is ours, Captain Snead. The South Platte is our river, and we will take it back.

"My message to you is simple. Leave Fort Henderson. Leave it by sundown, and I give you my word of honor that no one will be harmed."

"Why does my fort concern you so much?" Mungo asked, looking beyond the Scalie chief to the long line of skink riders waiting in multiple ranks. "Your army is so great, you can simply go around us and push up the South Platte unfettered."

Arjukadembo flashed a tortured smile. "General Davenport's 10th Royal Guard is out there somewhere. Without Fort Henderson to give it succor, support, they will be cut off. And then they can be routed."

Mungo was impressed and more than a little concerned that Arjukadembo understood the strategic situation so well. Then again, he lacked the prehensile tail that the rank and file in his army possessed: a sign of high intelligence among Killajunkur. Despite their outward appearance, their horrific reptilian visage, Scalies were neither brainless animals nor cold-blooded lizards, despite what some in Parliament might say. What they were specifically, he did not know. But they were not stupid. And their infamous war chief was the least stupid among them.

"Let's discuss peace," Mungo said, taking a chance with open arms, palms spread and empty. "I invite you and your translator to dinner tonight. By parliamentary decree, I have the right, as an officer of Her Majesty's empire, to negotiate peace terms and present agreements in writing to my superior officer, General Davenport, who then has the discretionary authority to approve such a deal. Let's talk, eat, and drink like civilized men, Great One. We could end this bloody affair tonight."

Arjukadembo laughed, his massive forked tongue flashing pink. "The matter has gone beyond breaking bread and drinking wine, Captain Snead. There is a saying among the Killajunkur: The mountain is only as tall as your fear. I have no fear today. How tall is your mountain, Captain? Judging by the man who sweats beside you, it must scrape the clouds."

Corporal Johns' face was a pale matte of cold sweat. He looked as if he were going to burst into tears. Instead, he pulled his dirk and rushed the Scalie chief. "You son of a bitch. You killed the major. You killed my wife! You—"

Before he could finish, the Arapaho translator pulled his own knife and struck Corporal Johns in the face with the bone hilt, shattering his nose and leaving him screaming on the ground. Mungo stepped in front of his corporal, shielding him from any further blows. A skink rider pulled from the ranks and raised his spear. Arjukadembo waved him off. "Halt! We will not spill further blood, nor will we waste a spear on this half a man, this coward that lies bleeding at my feet, who strikes at us under flag of truce. Take him, Captain Snead. Take your man back to your fort and consider my offer. Leave by sunset, and you will survive. Refuse, and you will die."

Arjukadembo turned and fell to all fours, then slithered back to his army. They greeted their great chief with a solid war cry that echoed through the valley. Mungo could barely hear himself think as he pulled the corporal to his feet, and they walked together back toward Fort Henderson.

"I'm sorry, Captain," he said, spitting blood from his mouth. "I just got so mad. I..."

Mungo stared him down. Under normal circumstances, a court martial would be in order. But this was not a normal circumstance, and although the Corporal's suicidal actions could have backfired, if he *had* struck with the knife, this whole matter could have been settled before it started.

"Don't fret it. You almost had the bastard."

Corporal Johns smiled, dribbled out a loose tooth, but stood taller. "You aren't seriously going to retreat, are you, Captain?"

Mungo shook his head. "Of course not. He knows that too. There is no alternative now, Seamus. We will stand and fight."

Even as Mungo said the words, the mountain of his fear grew taller and taller.

"Arjukadembo is strong, intelligent," Mungo said to the gathered officers, "but arrogant. He hasn't suffered enough defeat to make him respectful of determined defenders behind emplaced positions." He spread a map of the complex out on the table and pointed to the front gate. "He'll make a frontal assault first, thinking that his numbers will simply overwhelm us like the ocean tide."

"Will they?" Lieutenant Bolton asked, his expression a confusion of anxiety and attempted boldness.

"No," Mungo said, hoping he was right. "The wall is strongest there. It's made of mortar and solid rock. Fifteen feet high. It'll hold, so long as we stack them up quickly and pile bodies in front of the rear ranks. It'll take them time to clear their dead and keep moving." Mungo offered a smile, remembering his history. "It'll be like the French cavalry at Agincourt."

"But they don't have heavily armoured knights, Captain," Sergeant Williams said. "They have skinks that can climb walls."

Mungo nodded. "That's the only question mark remaining in my mind. By my quick survey of his lines, he has two hundred, maybe three hundred. That seems like a lot, but as we saw in Kansas, once a skink is dropped, its rider is a fair soldier at best. They fight like Napoleonic cavalry. They can scale the wall, yes, but I don't think he'll use them on the initial assault. He'll hold back, assess as he goes, and then deploy them, which I assume will be in rear assaults with his Arapaho and Pawnee allies. It's what I would do, anyway."

"Last time I looked, Captain," Corporal Johns said, winking his good eye through caked blood. "You ain't no Scalie alien."

That drew a few muffled chuckles around the table. "No, I'm not, Corporal. If Arjukadembo has learned anything from his time here on Earth, he should respect and appreciate general tactics of warfare.

"I want all able-bodied men, women, and children on the walls," Mungo continued, "especially the rear gate. It's the weakest and requires more attention. I want wagons, crates, barrels, rocks, whatever you can find, piled high to the ramparts, behind the gates. Find every seam in our walls and choke it with debris. Leave room for gun barrels, of course.

And hand out blasters every third or fourth man. I want blaster coverage around the entire complex, interspersed with carbines, percussion caps, and any personal sidearms. Use the blasters sparingly. We've got plenty of regular ammunition, but when the plasma runs out, they're gone. That applies to his force as well, I'm assuming, but I don't think they'll hold back. They'll hit us with everything they've got. The first two waves will be the hardest."

The silence among his officers was nerve-wracking. Mungo studied their faces. He wished he could give them all personal assurances that everything would be all right. They wouldn't believe him if he did. They were all veteran soldiers with experience against the Scalies; they knew what awaited them.

Mungo looked around the room one last time. He smiled and nodded his appreciation. "Okay, you all know what to do. Dismissed!"

Mungo squeezed the blaster trigger, feeling its powerful recoil through his whole body. The shot struck true, its high velocity magnesium bullet and plasma tearing through the skink rider as it tried scaling the wall. He fired again at the skink itself, for it too needed to be put down; its bite was poisonous and painful. He fired at another, and another, heedless of his own advice to conserve blaster rounds. The alien weapon was too lethal not to find comfort behind it. Good sense finally came to him, however, and he holstered the piece, drew his 1860 Army Colt, aimed carefully again, and sent a conventional round into the soft underbelly of another skink, putting it flat on its back to be crushed beneath the incessant charge of its companions.

As predicted, Arjukadembo ordered a frontal attack shortly after midnight. Three rounds of spear fire, followed by wave after wave of Scalie soldiers hitting the walls, and breaching at least in one place.

Mungo ducked a spear. It roared past his head, struck the door on the fort stable, and set it aflame. All the spears that had struck had set something on fire, some more ablaze than others, all choking the air with black smoke and soot. He could see that it was difficult for his defenders to breathe, but all they had to do was hold out; hold out long enough to force Arjukadembo and his mighty horde to realize their own mortality.

It wasn't going well.

Another breach was announced a hundred feet from his position, down the right side of the wall, toward the roof of the hospital. Pawnees, taking advantage of the massive Killajunkur assault against the main gate itself. Mungo turned his attention to the breach, pulling his sword and firing his Colt into the mass of natives pouring over the wall. For a moment, he was rather happy to be fighting an enemy he understood. He fired again and took out another Pawnee, then checked himself as his own men came into view, firing and slashing and punching their way toward the breach.

They were led by Corporal Johns, looking no worse for wear, his face bandage ripped from his nose and dangling on a loose thread. There was rage in his eyes as he struck foe after foe with his Highland dirk, driving the blade deep, cursing obscenities that would make an agnostic blush. Mungo joined him and drove the hilt of his pistol into the face of a Pawnee, feeling the crack of bone, the slime of spit. The man fell down the wall, striking an Arapaho ascending as he tumbled.

A horn echoed through the dark. Three loud bleats that caught everyone's attention. The Pawnee who had breached the wall fell back. A general retreat began around the entire fort.

"Cease fire!" Mungo ordered. "Hold!"

They watched as the last of the attackers melted away into the darkness. There was quiet, save for the death howls of the wounded Killajunkur and Indians writhing on the bloody ground below the gate. Corporal Johns pulled his pistol and was about to fire at one. Mungo stayed his hand.

"Don't waste the ammo!" he said.

"Sir!" Corporal Johns' face was a contortion of mixed emotions. "Blast that, Captain. We can't keep them down there moaning all night. Besides, a wounded Scalie is dangerous. You know that…sir!"

Mungo had watched a Scalie that seemed dead rise up and deliver a death blow to one of the Queen's finest generals back in '82. But no quarter? Had it come to that so quickly? And could they afford such savagery right now? They were still badly outnumbered. What would happen to human prisoners if and when Arjukadembo overran this fort? Mungo learned long ago that it was always best in the game of war to allow the enemy to refuse quarter first, thereby allowing your own decision to do the same to come from a more moral, dignified position. But was that policy correct in this situation?

Mungo shook his head. "Very well, Seamus. Find a sharpshooter to take them out. One at a time. True shots. Don't waste ammo, and don't take long. For they're coming back. As sure as I'm standing here, they'll be back."

The spear that had struck the stable door had burned the building to the ground. No amount of water would douse the flame. The fire rose higher and higher into the night sky until there was nothing left of the wood but smoldering ash. A few other spears thrown in the first wave caused damage as well, but the stable was the worst of it, taking the lives of two soldiers trying to rescue the horses inside. In the end, two soldiers died of burns, one soldier died of smoke inhalation, and ten horses died. Mungo nearly retched at the smell of burnt horse hair, hide, and meat. The first wave saw the death of an additional five soldiers. Mungo considered that fortunate.

"We won't be so lucky again," he said, helping ladle out a cup of water to a wounded boy. He put his hand on the boy's shaking head and smiled. "The first wave was a probe. The next will be a full assault."

"We'll be ready, Captain," Lieutenant Bolton said, hefting a Killajunkur spear with his bare hands.

"Have the Scalie bodies been piled against the front gate?"

"Yes, sir."

"When the next wave is fully ensconced against the wall, you set them alight. Understood?"

"Sir, I — I'm not sure about this."

Mungo had struggled with such a deplorable act at first as well, but the smell of those horses and the sight of his soldiers charred black from spear fire, made up his mind right quick. "If they like fire, we'll give it to them."

"But sir, the flames might ignite the front gate."

Mungo nodded. "We have to shock them. Try at least. Force them to recoil, thus giving us time to plug holes elsewhere. We'll worry about the gate when and if the time comes. Did you set the cannon like I instructed?"

"Yes, sir. They're ready."

Mungo dropped the ladle into the bucket and stood. His legs hurt, his arms hurt. His shoulders too. Every muscle in his body yearned for rest.

"Take your position."

This time, Mungo manned the rear gate, which comprised mostly survivors from the Pawnee Massacre. The few children capable of manning the wall were not given blasters; the recoil was too great for their small bodies. A few held pistols, a few carbines. The expression on

Molly Dupree's face told Mungo that she was not pleased.

"Children with guns!" She shot Mungo a nasty look. "You should be ashamed of yourself, *Captain*."

Dupree was the head nurse and about as stubborn and opinionated as one could be. A useful disposition to have on the frontier, but not now. Not in the midst of war. "I don't like it any more than you do, Molly. But what's the alternative?"

"We could have left," she said, checking her own rifle. "Like others have been saying. A deal was offered by that alien monster. Do you deny it? You should have taken it."

Mungo nodded. "And this fort would have been overrun, and the entire South Platte river valley would be burning right now. At least if we stand, we have a chance to give General Davenport and his 10th Royals time."

"We have no time, Mungo! None. Whether we stay or go, it won't amount to—"

"Enough! I've given you a choice, Molly. Either man a weapon or serve the hospital. Choose...now!"

He could see the muscles in her jaw tense. He knew she wanted to reach out and slap him, and he would allow it if necessary to guarantee her peace, but she would make her choice, one way or another.

She held her anger, cocked her carbine, and leaned over the wall. "April can handle the hospital. No one's gonna call me a coward."

Less than an hour later, the Killajunkur attacked the front and rear gates, this time trying to penetrate them both with spear attack. But the gates had been reinforced with overlapping iron bands and a lattice-work of high carbon filament taken from pieces of one of the alien starships back in '83. The wood would burn, but it would take more than a few knocks from spears to bring it down.

Blaster fire erupted along the walls, dropping attackers two, three at a time. They fired back, forcing those manning the walls to pin, wait, then shoot unaimed shots just to recover their positions.

Mungo grabbed up a spear and thrust it deep into the heart of an Arapaho warrior who had made it past a little boy cowering in fear on the rampart. The tip broke off into the man's ribcage. He yelped, clutched his pierced chest, then fell dead beside the boy. Mungo scooped the boy up and set him back down beside a ladder, saying, "Get to the chapel, son. Hide there."

The boy was so terrified he didn't move. Mungo popped him gently on the head with an open palm. "Did you hear what I said? Go!"

The boy finally found his courage and ran down the ladder, across the yard, and into the chapel.

A Killajunkur warrior attacked Mungo before he could return to the wall.

It seemed to appear out of nowhere, suddenly in his face, slashing with its large blue-black prehensile tail, trying to knock him from the ramparts. Mungo held tightly to a post, taking the tail blows to his shoulders. The pain was excruciating. He felt as if his shoulder blades would give out. His helmet was tossed aside, its broken strap flying one direction, the helmet in another. The tail struck his face, and he almost blacked out. His hand found his blaster, aimed it carefully beneath the relentless blows of the tail, and pulled the trigger.

The beast fell back, half a leg missing, its screech penetrating the roar of the battle. Another shot rang out, this time from a carbine. Mungo saw Molly Dupree standing her ground before the crippled Scalie, pumping round after round into its chest. Tears streamed down her face, and she screamed as she emptied her ammunition into an already dead alien.

Mungo gained his feet and stopped her, hugging her tight and bringing her down to sit below the protection of the sturdy stone wall. "Enough! It's over. It's dead."

She didn't seem to notice his voice, or his face. Then she softened in his arms, smiled through tears, and nodded.

When he was satisfied that she was okay, Mungo looked across the yard to the front gate and shouted, "Lieutenant Bolton! Give me fire!"

He said it twice to ensure the order was received, and then the Lieutenant barked back, relaying the order to three sharpshooters waiting along the wall. They fired flaming arrows into the pile of dead Pawnee and Scalies that smothered the front gate.

Flames burst outside the long wall. Blue-and-green flames as dead Scalie muck-sacks popped inside their necks from the heat and poured bile into the fire. The smell was overwhelming. Mungo could see men manning the ramparts near the flames bend in disgust, empty their stomachs, and fall into the fort yard.

It had the effect Mungo wanted. Those attackers who had been scaling the wall and trying to attack the gate were devoured in the flame. Some fell into the yard, screaming and burning, where they were quickly gunned down. The second wave fell back, and Mungo took a moment to breathe.

Sergeant Williams was, again, the bearer of bad news. "It's Seamus, sir, he...he..."

Mungo pushed past him and ran to the hospital. Wounded were lying all around the entryway, some serious, some walking. He found his corporal lying on a stretcher, gut shot.

"Thank heaven it wasn't a blaster," Seamus said, coughing through the pain.

"Yes, thank heaven," Mungo said. "Didn't duck fast enough, eh?"

The corporal managed a smile, nodded. "That was the problem, Captain. If I had stayed upright, it'd've hit me in the legs. Well, no matter. Just tell me...did we stop the bastards?"

"We sure did. And we'll stop them again too, I promise."

With the last of his strength, Seamus reached to his side and pulled his dirk from its scabbard. He handed it over with a bloody hand. "Take this, my friend. I know you'll put it to good use."

Mungo hesitated at first, then accepted the blade with a nod. "Thank you, Corporal. I will indeed."

He shoved it inside his boot, and watched Corporal Seamus Johns die.

Mungo stood, wiped sweat and blood from his face, then asked the sergeant, "What's our status?"

"As best as I can tell, Captain, we're in trouble. The blasters are near empty. We still have ammunition for our conventional weapons, but it won't last beyond another assault. I don't know the exact numbers on casualties, sir, but as you can see, they're piling up."

Mungo looked around the room. More seemed dead than alive. None of these people could be expected to man the walls again.

A private stepped through the door. "Sirs," he said, winded, in shock, and clearly not wanting to utter the next words. "They're coming."

The third wave hit in much the same fashion as the second, but with a double envelopment that threatened the left and right walls. Mungo had to shift everything around, including the guns, which sat waiting in the yard. Cries were made to bring them up closer to the ramparts, but he refused. "Turn the barrels," he said, "four left, four right. And wait for my signal."

He fought alongside Molly Dupree again. They shared the same crook in the wall, one firing while the other loaded. Their blasters were spent during the first ten minutes. Mungo used his empty blaster once to crack open the skull of a Scalie that threatened to split Molly open from belly to brains. The weapon shattered on contact with the thick skull of the alien. Mungo quickly grabbed up the alien's discarded spear, took out three more, than tossed it aside to regain the wall and fire his pistol again.

All along the line, men and boys and women fired and fired into the swell of Scalie bodies writhing up the walls, and one after another, they fell dead or dying onto the hard ground, only to be trampled beneath the next wave. Just like Agincourt, Mungo thought, only these were not arrogant French knights, nor was this a vast field of France. This was America, Colorado territory. Everyone wanted it, and everyone was fighting and dying for it.

Why?

As he filled his revolver with the last of his bullets, and emptied chamber after chamber into tooth-snarled blue-and-green Scalie faces, Mungo wondered why. There were other places, other territories that the Scalies had shown no interest in occupying. Why not fall back, pull out entirely and leave it to them? He again remembered his history. It had always been that way with conquerors to their conquered. 'We promise to stop here,' they'd say, and the oppressed would retreat, and for a time, peace would ensue. And the conquerors would return, saying, 'Now we want this land too, and this land, and this…" On and on it would go, until there was no place left for the oppressed, except some dry, untenable desert swath that held no life or promise for anyone. Is that the fate that lay before them? For humans? Were the Scalies now the masters, having turned the tables on a millennium of Earth history? In the midst of this chaos, it seemed so.

Lieutenant Bolton sounded a breech along the far left wall. Mungo turned and saw the line of Scalies and their Arapaho allies filing into the yard.

"To the guns!" Mungo yelled, pitching his dry, raspy voice above the din of battle. "To the guns!"

Everyone who could move now did as they had been ordered, abandoning the walls and retreating to the line of guns in the center of the yard. They had been placed almost in semi-circle, with crews ready and waiting. Mungo personally helped the wounded find their feet and make it past the barrels as the Scalie horde crested the walls.

When everyone was set, Mungo raised his hand, brought it down, and shouted, "Fire!"

All eight barrels roared with double-canister. Massive, bloody holes were ripped through the Scalie lines. Armour and scaled flesh, bone and carapace flew into the air like a shower of confetti, as gun crews filled their barrels again with canister and fired a second time as the Scalies tried recouping and attacking once more. The amount of damage was so severe that Mungo had to close his eyes to it. But he kept ordering to fire, again and again, until the screams of the Killajunkur subsided, the roar of their allies waned, and silence fell across the yard.

Mungo opened his eyes and saw the last of the Scalies that had survived jump the wall and disappear. His last remaining men were huddled nearby nursing wounds, shaking, exhausted. Molly Dupree lay at his feet, a blaster wound having ripped open her chest and arms. Sergeant Williams stood nearby.

"Sir," he said, in a whisper so no one else could hear. "We're done. We've no more canister. We've no more ammunition. If they attack again, there'll be no stopping them."

Rage filled Mungo's mind. He pulled the dirk from his boot, looked around the yard, and found a Scalie writhing in pain. He pushed away the dead bodies lying on top of it and held the knife to its throat. He was about to slash the beast's throat when Corporal Johns' words about the knife came to him. *I know you'll put it to good use.*

He paused and looked into the terrified, opal-colored eyes of the Scalie. He tucked the knife away. "Lieutenant, a piece of paper please, and a pencil."

The lieutenant found these items in the chapel and handed them over. Mungo spread the paper over the chest armour of the Scalie and scribbled a note. He wrote as legibly as he could, as well as his frayed nerves could hold the pencil steady and write. Then he folded it up and shoved it into the clawed hand of the Scalie.

"You cannot understand what I am saying to you," he said, his face mere inches from the Scalie face, "but you *will* understand this. Go...and take this note to Arjukadembo. It is my flag of truce. Give it to him, and tell him that Captain Mungo Snead wishes to meet when the sun rises in the East. Tell him that I will come, and I will discuss with him our terms of surrender."

The alien looked at him and flickered its blue forked tongue as if acknowledging his words. Mungo grabbed its left arm; Lieutenant Williams its right. They dragged the Scalie to the front gate and opened it. They let it go, and at first, the beast just lay there, staring into the early morning sky. Then it flipped over and scampered away through the burnt bodies and scorched buffalo grass.

"Are we really going to surrender?" Lieutenant Williams asked.

"What other choice is there?"

"What if he refuses to meet? Now that he is in a position of advantage, why would he?"

Mungo stared at his lieutenant with careful eyes. "Because Arjukadembo thinks himself an honorable creature…and so do I. Two honorable souls meeting to discuss peace." He smiled through a blinding headache, a heavy heart. "He will see my supplication as a sign of his superior strength and intellect. How could he refuse?"

They met like before, in nearly the same spot, as the sun began to rise. This time Mungo went alone, much to the chagrin of his officers who begged him to take an armed guard. He refused. The show of an armed escort would not garner the result that he sought, and the only kind of long-lasting peace that he could envision. He walked out Fort Henderson's ruined front gate, three hundred yards down the dirt road, and halted before the Great One.

"You have fought valiantly, Captain Snead," Arjukadembo said through his translator. "You have defended your fort far better than I would have imagined. You have killed many brave Killajunkur warriors today."

"Don't forget your Arapaho and Pawnee allies," Mungo said. *Or they might forget you in time.* "They are brave warriors as well."

The Great One flashed a smile, nodding to his translator. "Of course. But now it is time to rest, to put down your arms and surrender. Do you agree?"

Mungo nodded slowly. "You have won, Arjukadembo. We cannot hold out any longer. I am here to beg for the lives of my people. Will you allow us to gather ourselves and leave the fort in good order?"

Arjukadembo considered in silence, his thick scales showing brilliant red and green along his length, the muck-sack in his throat bobbing happily. Mungo could see the joy (and perhaps relief?) in the Scalie's amber eyes. Finally, he smiled again and nodded.

"Very well. You have leave to gather your dead and wounded and depart. We will give you two hours to do so, and no more."

"Thank you, Great One."

Mungo offered his hand. At first, Arjukadembo was reluctant to respond, the custom not practiced by the Killajunkur. Their scales shifted colors to denote pleasure or displeasure in agreements. The thought of touching a human was unsavory to them, Mungo knew, unless it was to kill. He thrust his hand forward and waited patiently.

"You are welcome, Captain Snead." Arjukadembo leaned forward and shook Mungo's hand.

Tears began to run down Mungo's face. He didn't even have to force it. Exhaustion, coupled with the sinking feeling of defeat, finally let his emotions overwhelm him. He fell to his knees and cried.

"Rise," Arjukadembo said, leaning forward even more to place his large clawed hands on Mungo's shoulders. "Do not cry. You are an honorable man, and an honorable man does not cry in the sight of an ene—"

Before Arjukadembo could finish, Mungo reached into his boot and pulled out the Highland dirk, thrust it forward and up, into the seam between the breast plates of the Scalie's armour. He struck the location he knew would do the most damage. The long, thick, sharp point of the dirk ripped through scales and bone and punctured the Great One's chest, and dark red blood poured from the wound.

Arjukadembo fell back, in shock, but lashed out with his claws and drove them across Mungo's face, leaving savage cuts. Mungo fell back as well, clutching his bleeding face, knowing that his left eye had been sliced. The Arapaho translator tried responding, but Mungo had prepared for it. Through his pain, through his half-sight, he pulled another smaller blade from beneath his belt and thrust it into the man's throat, leaving him writhing and bleeding on the ground.

Arjukadembo staggered back, gasping for air. "You—you have failed me," he said, trying to pull the blade free. "You have no honor."

"You're right, Great One," Mungo said through streams of blood. "I have no honor. This is war, and I did my duty today."

"My death is meaningless, Captain. My army will attack, and continue to attack until everyone in your fort is dead."

Mungo shook his head. "No, your death *does* matter. You're one of those rare creatures, Great One, that comes along once in a generation, once in a lifetime. With you gone, the Killajunkur will have to figure it all out on their own, figure out how to live together with all of us on this small rock revolving around the sun. And they may not be so brilliant as you, so confident, so able to make the right choices."

Arjukadembo fell to the ground. "Another will rise, Captain. To take my place."

"I'm playing for time, Great One. Time is the only thing we have anymore."

Arjukadembo did not speak again. Instead, with the last of his strength, he motioned his army forward. Then he fell and stilled forever, as the long line of skink riders moved forward, toward where their chief and Mungo lay.

With the last of his strength, Mungo rose up on feeble knees and flashed the small bloody blade he still held in his hand. *My last stand*, he thought as he waited for the first wave of Killajunkur to hit. *My last and greatest stand.*

As the first skink rider struck him, and as the rest trampled him into the soft ground, Mungo couldn't help but smile. For in the distance, he could hear the long, persistent note of a cavalryman's bugle.

General Davenport's 10th Royal Guard had finally arrived.

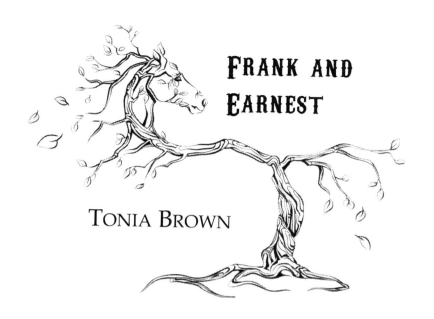

FRANK AND EARNEST

TONIA BROWN

FRANK POPPED THE SHUTTER OPEN AS QUIETLY AS HE COULD, FOLDING it back against the wall with a soft click. Thank goodness there wasn't an actual glass window to contend with, just a fine screen between them and the office beyond. Frank pulled a blade from his boot and set to cutting the edges of the screen.

"Good thing there's no glass," Earnest said.

"I know," Frank whispered over his shoulder.

"Cause it would be a lot harder with glass in the way." Earnest seemed to think about this a moment, then added, "And noisier."

Frank snorted at his cousin. "Yeah, and it's noisy enough as it is."

"Oh, sorry," Earnest whispered, and went quiet.

Frank got back to work cutting the screen away. Of course, he'd have to climb through and let Earnest inside. There was no way his younger, much larger cousin could fit through the tiny opening. Frank was so scrawny, he could've gotten through a window half the size. Heck, a quarter of the size if his life depended on it. His ma once said Frank could squeeze through the eye of a needle if it meant escaping the fires of Hell. And considering that Frank and Earnest often faced the possibility of going to Hell, for performing deeds such as the one they were performing now, Frank reckoned he had to agree.

Once Frank had the screen off, he slipped through the window and into the office. He then motioned to his cousin, waving the man toward the backdoor. Earnest held a thumb up, then lumbered off in that direction. Frank felt his way through the room and found the backdoor with little trouble. There, he popped the catch and opened the door wide for his cousin to pass through. Earnest blundered inside, unable to execute even the simplest of movements without evoking the spirit of a drunken ox.

"Thanks," Earnest said. The big man covered his mouth as his eyes flew wide in the moonlit room.

"You can talk now," Frank said. "I reckon it's safe enough in here. Just keep your voice down."

"Good thinkin', Frank."

Frank lit a small lantern, keeping the flame as low as possible. Holding the light up, he scanned the room. There didn't seem to be much worth taking. Frank stepped over a stack of dusty books and began rifling through the papers strewn across the untidy desk.

"Who you think lives here?" Earnest said.

"No one lives here," Frank said. "It's an office. Someone works out of here."

"Whatcha lookin' for?"

"Anything valuable."

"I don't think there is anything like that here." Earnest glanced across the sparsely decorated office. "This feller ain't got nothin' I want. It's kinda like other folks left stuff they didn't want either."

It was hard for Frank to disagree with that. The office was furnished with half rotten chairs and crumbling end tables and a musty old desk. Papers filled most of the corners, while crates of empty whiskey bottles lined the back wall. Someone liked to drink a whole heck of a lot of rotgut. Frank liked whiskey too, though not that much. Usually he and Earnest would steal a quart or two when they could, and try to make it last as long as possible between them. They did the same with food. And clothes. And money.

Thus was the life of an outlaw in the west.

Frank didn't really want to be an outlaw, and he certainly didn't want his impressionable younger cousin in the criminal way. Yet there wasn't much else they could do to scratch out a meager living in the harsh world of this new frontier. Ranch work was hard. Damned hard. Frank learned that after a month of shoveling poop and brushing down sweaty animals and getting kicked in the head every time he turned around. And the kicking thing was just the manager being a hard ass; sometimes a horse would kick him in the head too.

A fistful of blisters and two concussions later, Earnest and Frank decided honest work wasn't for the likes of them, despite what their respective mamas named them. Aside from hard work, there was little else to feed a pair of grown men in the wild frontier, so they turned to a life of crime. Trouble was, they weren't very good at a life of crime either, but at least they didn't get a face full of horseshoe or boot, or end up smelling like manure. Well, not much like manure. It was a hell of a life too, for the frontier did not suffer fools gladly. Or smart folks, for that matter. Pretty much anyone with a pulse was not suffered gladly by the harsh, open west.

"I guess so," Frank said, shaking his head. "I thought this place would have something worth taking. I heard this feller made good money as a private lawman."

Earnest gasped. "A lawman? Frank, we can't steal from a lawman. They got guns and bullets and badges that let them do stuff us normal folks ain't allowed to do."

"Don't worry, he's not a real lawman. He don't work for the government or nothin'."

"Really? Who does he work for then?"

"Anyone that'll hire him I reckon."

Earnest looked around again and wrinkled his nose. "From the looks of this place, not many folks wanna hire him, whatever he does."

Before Frank could think much more about it, there came a knock at the front door. He pressed his finger to his lips, warning his cousin to keep quiet, then pointed to a stack of whiskey crates. Earnest nodded and ducked behind the stacks.

The door slowly creaked open.

Frank blew out the lantern, crouched behind the long desk, and wondered what kind of idiot lawman went away and left their front door unlocked with so many criminals wandering about these days. He also wondered what kind of idiot criminal didn't check the damned front door first before cutting a hole in the window screen. As Frank contemplated these truths, a small halo of light drifted into the room, followed by soft footfalls on the hardwood floor.

"Mr. Jackson?" a timid voice said.

Narrowing his eyes, Frank pondered that voice. It sounded a lot like a child's voice. What in the heck was a kid doing out at this hour, much less pounding on the door of a gun for hire?

"Mr. Jackson," the kid said again.

The cousins waited in silence.

"I know you're there," the child said. "I can see your hat."

Frank reached up slowly and slipped the hat from his head.

"I can still see your head," the kid said. "You sure do have an awful lot of gray hair, Mr. Jackson."

"Go away," Frank grumbled softly. "I'm busy."

"I can't, sir. I know you don't like no one botherin' you or nothin', but I need help real bad. You're the only one that can help me, Mr. Jackson."

Cursing under his breath, and knowing the jig was up, Frank stood to his full height. A little blonde-haired girl waited on the other side of the desk. She lifted her lantern and raised her face to take him in. After a few moments, the girl blinked, then furrowed her brow.

"You ain't Mr. Jackson," she said.

"Ya don't say," Frank said.

The furrowed brow shifted to narrowed eyes as curiosity slid into suspicion. "Who are you?"

Frank scrambled for an explanation. "Mr. Jackson had to go away on a trip. I'm watching his place while he's gone."

"We," Earnest said.

"We?" the little girl asked, looking beyond Frank.

"Hello there," Earnest said. "My name is Earnest and this is Frank. It's real nice to meet you."

Frank groaned. Trust his cousin to introduce himself during a robbery.

"Shut up," he said over his shoulder before Earnest had a chance to say something even more stupid. Frank looked back to the kid. "What do you want?"

"You're working for Mr. Jackson?" the kid said.

"Sure. Whatever. Let's go with that."

The girl visibly relaxed at this, which was good. No need to have some anxious brat waking up the whole town.

"Now we got that settled," Frank said, "who are you and what do you want?"

"My name is Sally Tilson," the kid said. "I need help real bad. Victoria is gone and no one has seen her. I hear Mr. Jackson helps folks find lost stuff all the time. I was gonna wait 'til the mornin' to come and talk to him, but I can't sleep knowing Victoria is out there all alone. Anything can happen to her, mister. Anything."

"Victoria?" Frank said. Maybe an older sibling. Or younger? Some poor child lost in the unforgiving wilderness surrounding the small town. Frank didn't like the sound of that. "How long has she been gone?"

"Almost two days."

"Two days?" Frank scratched his chin stubble. "What yer folks got to say about it? Ain't they worried?"

Sally gave a little pout, poking out her lower lip. "Ain't got no ma. And pa says it's just one less mouth to feed."

Ouch. A harsh truth, but the man had a point. One less kid did mean one less mouth to feed. And considering how hard it was to feed your own mouth out here, trying to feed a bunch of little mouths too was a burden in and of itself. Still, a missing kid and a worried sibling was awful hard for even Frank's hardened heart to ignore. Not to mention the fact that if they found the girl, there might be some kind of reward. Maybe not from the dad, but perhaps someone would care enough to pay for her.

"How old is your sister?" Frank said.

The kid blinked in silent surprise. Then she grinned just a bit and said, "Victoria ain't my sister. She's my kitty cat."

Frank felt his mouth fall open a bit as Earnest gasped loudly behind him. All this fuss and tears for a lousy cat. What kind of garbage were folks teaching their kids these days? Frank went through plenty of cats and dogs growing up. When they got gone, you just forgot them and went onto the next one. Of course, Frank always was careful what he told Earnest.

"A cat?" Frank said.

"Yessir," the kid said.

"A cat."

"A kitten." Sally held up one hand and spread out her little fingers. "Five months old."

Frank rolled his eyes, looking to the ceiling for help he knew wasn't coming. "For the love of..." He glanced down at the girl with a frown. "Look, we'd love to help you but—"

"You will?" the kid said. She smiled wide as she rushed around the desk and hugged his leg. "Oh thank you, sir. Thank you."

Frank tried to wiggle out of her grip. It took a moment or two to pry the little crumb snatcher off of him.

"Wait up now," Frank said, holding her at arm's length by the collar of her nightdress. "I didn't say we would help you. I said we would like to, but we can't."

Sally stared up at him with a long look of sorrow. Then the waterworks started. The little girl's eyes welled with tears as her voice hitched on very word. "But you gotta help. I'm so worried, mister. I'm so worried."

"No," Frank said firmly. "We don't have time to go running around lookin'—"

"She's worried, Frank," Earnest said.

Closing his eyes, Frank groaned again. He didn't need to turn around to know his cousin was weeping as well. Frank could hear the blubbering from where he stood.

"She's out there all alone," Earnest said between sobs.

"All alone," Sally echoed.

Frank rubbed at his tired eyes and silently wished the girl would just disappear, taking his annoying cousin with her. Instead of the sound of them poofing into oblivion, there came the muffled clink of metal on wood. A familiar sensation crept over Frank. He knew that sound. There were two sounds in the world Frank was intimately familiar with. That particular sound was the drop of a coin onto a wooden table. Frank peered down at the desk between his fingers.

Sure enough, there on the worn wood lay a silver dollar coin.

A whole dollar.

"I got this dollar from my mawmaw," Sally said. "I was saving it for when we go to the city next month. I was gonna buy a new dress and shoes and a book and maybe some candy with the leftovers. But then I was gonna give it to Mr. Jackson to find Victoria for me. It's yours, if you help me."

Frank stared at that dollar. That unprotected, just sitting there for the taking dollar. He could just pick it up, shove the kid into the whiskey crates, and walk on out of here. That would teach the little one an important lesson on trust. Never pay for a service not yet rendered. On the other hand, could he rob from a child? Stealing from full grown adults was one thing. Did he have it in him to steal money from a little girl who was weeping an ocean of tears over losing her five-month-old kitty cat?

He thought on this troubling question. Invested carefully, a whole dollar would feed Earnest and him for a good long while. They could even afford a few nights in a cheap hotel.

Maybe not.

But maybe.

And all it took was that maybe to change his mind. Innocence be damned, Frank reached out and snapped up the silver dollar. Not only did he have it in him to steal the money, he was gonna lie about it too.

"Kid," Frank said, "you got yourself a deal."

Sally clapped for joy before she hugged Frank's leg again. "I just know you'll find Victoria for me."

"We sure will," Earnest said. "We promise."

Frank pocketed the silver dollar and pushed the kid off of him. "Go on then. Get out of here so we can get to work."

"Wait," Earnest said. "What does Victoria look like?"

Sally took on a dreamy look as she said, "Pa says she looks like a powder puff, she's so fluffy. She has tiny gray paws and a floofy silver tail and bright blue eyes and a cute button nose."

Frank did his best to ignore these adorable particulars as he rubbed at the coin in his pocket.

"Cute button nose," Earnest echoed as if committing the details to memory. "Oh, and you gotta tell us where we can find you once we get your cat back."

The little girl described a small farm house less than a half mile north of town. "When you bring her back, don't tell Pa I paid you the money. He'd be awful sore if he knew I spent my specials on Victoria."

"Don't worry," Frank said. "I don't plan on telling your pa nothin'." He smiled at this clever truth.

"Good," Sally said. With that, the little one turned and skipped out of the front door, taking the light with her, and leaving the pair of cousins alone in the moonlit office.

Earnest bright smile all but glowed in the shadows. "Aw, Frank, this is gonna be great. A whole dollar just for finding a kitty cat. Where are we gonna start looking first?"

"We ain't," Frank said. He took the dollar out and held it up to a beam of moonlight. It gleamed in his palm. A shining beacon of sudden wealth. His mouth began to water at all the things he could buy with a whole dollar.

"What do you mean we ain't?"

Frank pocketed the dollar again and felt his way to the backdoor in the darkness. "That cat's long gone." He opened the back door and was nearly through when he heard his cousin behind him.

"Frank?" Earnest said.

"What?" Frank said, and turned to face the man.

In a thin beam of moonlight, Earnest stared at Frank with a pitiful look of worry. "We are gonna find her kitty cat, ain't we? I mean, she did pay us a whole dollar and all."

"I said there ain't no use. Gone two days? Thing's probably starved to death. Or got eaten by something else."

"But we don't know that. Her kitty could be out there. And we promised her, Frank. We can't just take her money and not even try."

"You promised." Frank snorted. "I didn't promise crap."

Earnest whimpered as his eyes silently begged Frank for some sign of compassion.

Frank dug deep. He dug deep and he dug hard and he came up with…nothing. Sure, he had the nerve to rob a little girl blind. Yet he didn't have it in him to disappoint his cousin.

"All right," Frank said. "You got one day. If we can't find it by tomorrow night, then we move on. And we keep the dollar. Deal?"

"Deal." Earnest smiled wide again in the moonlight, baring nearly every tooth he still owned in his head. Which, considering his easy living and usually neglected hygiene, consisted of a surprising amount.

After bedding down in a nearby barn for the night, the cousins began their investigations bright and early the next morning. Frank led Earnest to the local inn for a spot of breakfast and some light interrogations. Then they went to the general store, where Frank bought a few provisions and a new canvas bag to carry them in, while Earnest asked if anyone had seen Victoria. It wasn't until midafternoon, as they bellied up to the bar to spend their last few pennies that Earnest began to see the way of things.

"We ain't never gonna find her, are we?" Earnest said.

"Sorry," Frank said. "But you can't say we didn't try."

Earnest slumped on the bar stool, folded under the weight of his failure.

Frank hated to see his cousin so down, but sometimes the truth was a hard thing to take. He patted the man's shoulder. "We still have a few cents left. Let's grab a beer or two and see if we can drink her off your mind." He waved the barkeep down.

"I couldn't help but overhear your story," the bartender said as he made his way to the end of the bar with two mugs of beer. He slid the beers across to the cousins. "You lost someone close?"

"Not close to me," Earnest said. "But she sure is important to someone."

The bartender shot Frank a curious glance.

"He's been looking for a little gray kitten with blue eyes," Frank said, for lack of a better thing to say.

The bartender rubbed at his well shorn chin. "A kitten you say? You know, if you're really in the market for a cat, you might want to talk to Professor Von Moose."

"It's not just any gray cat with blue eyes," Earnest said between gulps of beer. "She's a special cat. Her name is Victoria."

"Victoria. Victor. Vicky. Vixen. Hell, I bet the man has one of each by now."

Frank cocked his head at that. "One of each?"

"Sure," the barkeep said. "The man's been going around town snatching up all the stray animals. Cats, dogs, rabbits. Anything furry and four legged and can fit in his traps. God only knows what he wants with them."

Earnest looked to Frank, his eyes alight with joy. Frank was really hoping he would get out of here without having to actually track down the kitten. But now he didn't have a choice. Thanks to one mouthy barkeep, Frank was once again in the thick of it.

Earnest smiled wide.

"Where can we find this Professor Von Moose?" Frank said.

The barkeep sketched out a quick map that took the men about a mile south of town, down into the shadows of a gulley half hidden by a series of boulders and scrim and rocks. Frank never would've guessed that the mouth of a cave rested at the base of the gulley, just under an overhang of rock and dry grass. An excellent hideout if he had ever seen one.

"You reckon Victoria's in there?" Earnest said.

"Maybe," Frank said. "That barkeep claimed this professor person lives here."

"But why would a professor live in a cave? Don't they live in book palaces?"

"You mean lye-berries, and no. Not all the time. Sometimes they live in proper houses and have wives and such."

"You're pullin' my leg."

"No. I've seen it with my own eyes." Frank looked back to the mouth of the cavern. "But I ain't never seen one live in a hole in the ground like some kind of mole."

Earnest peered into the dark opening. "Whatcha think he gets up to in there?"

Frank leaned into the opening. A faint flicker of light lapped at the distant edge of the darkness. Frank couldn't be certain, but he thought he heard a soft chuffing sound escape the cave. "I guess there's just one way to find out." He held his hand out to Earnest. "You first."

"Why me?"

"Because you don't wanna disappoint that little girl." Frank gave his cousin a shove into the cave. "Go on then, get on in there."

Earnest stumbled into the opening and Frank followed. After they shuffled past a few feet of tightly grouped rocks, the cousins found themselves in a narrow tunnel. As they followed the passage, the flickering light flared into a soft glow in the distance. The chuffing sound increased too, a slow huff, huff, huff somewhere at the end of the tunnel.

"Whatcha think's makin' that sound?" Earnest said after a few minutes of walking along.

"I don't know," Frank said.

They continued to follow the tunnel toward the light and sound, not sure what they were in for, and Frank began to second guess the whole venture. Damn Earnest and his soft spot for cute, furry animals. It was gonna get the pair of them killed one day. Maybe that day would be this day? Not if Frank could help it. He cast a glance back over his shoulder, to the pinpoint of light that was the cave opening. Frank tugged on Earnest's sleeve, ready to drag the man back to civilization and away from that loathsome noise where they could forget this whole thing even happened.

"Come on," Frank said. "Let's get out of here."

"Wait," Earnest said, pulling away from Frank.

Frank grabbed Earnest's shoulder and tried to steer him in the other direction. "I think we should go. Something doesn't feel right here."

"No, wait. Don't you hear that?"

"Hear what?"

"Listen."

Frank paused in his retreat and turned his attention to the tunnel sounds. At first he only heard the strange, rhythmic chuffing noise. Just under it there drifted the faint strains of other animals; mewling and growling and yipping and meowing.

"It's the missing animals," Earnest said, and took off in a jog down the remainder of the tunnel.

"Wait a minute," Frank shouted as he ran after his cousin. "We don't know that. They could be the man's...own...livestock..." Frank's words trailed off as the pair of men reached the end of the tunnel.

And spilled into the enormous chamber waiting beyond.

The cousins stared in wonder at the huge cavern buried several hundred feet under the town above. The place was lit by a series of small bubbles mounted to the walls and ceiling, each casting an unearthly glow. The rocks and soil were much darker than the dry earth on the surface, and sported a deep sheen of crimson. One corner of the cavern contained all the amenities of someone's living quarters. A small cot, a wash basin, a rack from which clothes hung, a piss pot, and even a small bureau and mirror. Beside this there rested a long, chest-high table with an accompanying set of stools. The table lay covered in all manner of instruments; some looked like things made for doctoring folks, while others looked the opposite.

The majority of the chamber was taken up by a sizable as well as strange device—an egg-shaped metal and wooden construct probably a good twelve feet high. It was covered in levers and gears and flywheels, almost all of which moved in some manner. Parts of the machine spun while others rocked side to side and yet others bobbed up and down. The machine huffed and chuffed to the rhythm of these movements, explaining where the eerie noise came from. A gaping hole at least three feet wide rested in the middle of the thing, the edge of which was lined in series of fabric cover flaps. The empty space crackled, softly flickering as blue fingers of miniature lightning raced back and forth along from flap to flap.

Frank stared in genuine awe at the machine. He had no idea what it did, but he wanted to see the thing do it anyway.

"Frank!" Earnest shouted. "Look!"

Frank managed to wrench his attention away from the fantastic machine and toward his cousin's voice. Earnest stood before a wall of pens and cages stretching from floor to roof. Most of the pens were empty, as far as Frank could tell. The others held a wide variety of small, furry animals. Cats and dogs and rabbits, just like the barkeep said. In the middle of it all, Earnest stood cradling a gray kitten to his chest. A gray kitten with beautiful blue eyes that gleamed in the halo of flickering electric light.

"Well, I'll be," Frank said under the huff of the weird machine.

Earnest motioned to the other pens and said in a raised voice, "We should free the others too."

The furry beasts yipped and meowed as one, begging to be freed.

"No," Frank shouted over them. "We didn't come here for the others. Just the one."

"But Frank—"

"Don't but Frank me. We aren't carting a dozen damned cats back to town. Ya got your precious kitten, let's go."

Before they could argue further, or leave, the machine came to a sudden halt. The bobbing settled down. The spinning stopped. The rocking slowed. The chuffing and huffing died out in a soft echo. Even the animals stopped their griping, leaving a thick silence behind.

"What did you touch?" Frank asked.

"Nothin'," Earnest said.

"Gentlemen," a new voice said.

The pair of them turned about to find an older man standing beside the now-quiet machine. For a cave-bound man, he dressed awful fancy, sporting a dark suit pants and vest combo topped by a knee-length off white coat. His graying hair stuck out in all directions, nearly as wild as the bush of beard that had laid claim to the bottom half of his face. Through this beard there peeked a wide, peculiar smile. A pair of spectacles framed a set of wild eyes that stared at the cousins with undisclosed glee.

All of the animals let out a low whimper, including Victoria.

"May I assist you with something?" the man said.

"Professor Von Moose?" Frank said.

"Why, yes." The man cocked his head to one side. "I'm afraid you have the better of me."

"We're Frank and Earnest," Earnest said without hesitation.

Frank groaned.

"Are you?" the man said.

This seemed to confuse Earnest. "Yes?"

The man gave a soft laugh. "No, I mean do you live up to your name? Are you indeed frank and earnest?"

"We do our best," Frank said.

"I'm sure you do," the professor said. "Am I to understand this is a professional visit?"

"Um…"

"I mean I take it you're here for me?"

"No, sir," Earnest said. "We're here for Victoria." He held up the kitten's paw and waved it at the professor.

The kitten meowed.

Von Moose smiled wider, a feat Frank wasn't sure possible, yet happened. "Victoria? Yes. She is very useful. Very useful indeed. As are all of the animals."

"Useful?" Frank said.

"Of course," the professor said. He looked longingly at the egg-shaped machine as he patted the side of it. "They provide the spark that powers my little project here." The professor looked back to Frank again. "Are you sure you aren't here for me? I have been expecting someone to find me for a while now."

"No. We really are just here for the kitten."

"The kitten." Von Moose sighed and petted his machine as though it were a living thing. "Don't you even want to know what it does?"

Frank nodded. "Well, yea, sort of."

"Excellent." The professor rubbed his hands together with excitement and paced around the machine. "Gentlemen, may I introduce you to the Static Transfer and Halting Progression machine. Or as I call her, the STaHP machine. You see, I place one of the subject animals there in the center." He paused and pointed to the fabric-covered flaps that lined the hollow center. "The furrier the better. This hairy beast rubs against the machine, to which the velvet flaps transfer static electricity from the animal's fur into the heart of the STaHP via these wires here." The man waved at a series of complicated gadgets on the machine. "The electricity is compounded by the flywheels and gears, which in turn powers the main generator there." He pointed to the far end of the thing. "When directed to the core of our Lady Terra Firma, this heightened static electricity will slow her gesticulations. Ideally, it will halt her gyrations entirely." He stopped speaking and stared at Frank and Earnest, as if gauging their reaction.

Frank waited for more. There didn't seem to be anything else coming, so he asked, "What does it do then?"

"That's it."

"What's it?"

Von Moose's smile faltered. "Don't you understand? It's a doomsday device."

"A what?" Earnest said.

"A doomsday device," the professor said.

Frank had no idea who this Lady Terror Firmer was, or what a doomsday device was, nor did he want to know. From the way this professor man was leering and grinning and going on about using the machine on some poor woman's gesticulars, the whole thing probably meant something very private and embarrassing. And while Frank sometimes enjoyed a peep show now and again, he sure didn't want to witness this one.

"Ah, yeah," Frank said. "Well. As interesting as that is, we really are here for the cat. Do you mind if we, just, you know…"

"Frank," Earnest said.

"Take her and leave?" the professor said.

"Frank," Earnest said.

"If you don't mind," Frank said.

"Certainly not," the professor said.

"Frank," Earnest said again.

"Shut up, Earnest," Frank said. He nodded to Von Moose. "Thank you, sir. Sorry we troubled you."

"No trouble at all," the professor said.

"Frank," Earnest said.

"What?" Frank snapped.

"What about the other animals?" Earnest said.

"What about them?" Frank looked to the pens. "They all seem clean and warm enough. They all got plenty of food and water. He looks like he's taking fairly good care of them."

"Oh I am," the professor said. "I provide proper care and nutrition for each and every one. I need them in top shape for my needs."

"There you go," Franks said. He tipped his fingers to his hat and nodded once more to the professor man. "Good luck on your, um, machine."

"Thank you," Von Moose said. Just as Frank and Earnest neared the exit, with Victoria in tow, the professor added, "I just wished they didn't explode every single time I employed the machine."

Earnest gave a soft gasp. The kitten in his arms mewed. Frank stopped in place and closed his eyes, praying that he didn't hear what he thought he just heard.

"Explode?" Earnest asked.

"Yes," Von Moose said. "I can't manage to get it to reach full capacity without the excess static directing a jolt of feedback into the animals themselves. They explode under the pressure, you see. It causes quite a mess. As you can imagine."

Frank opened his eyes, turned on his heel and glanced about at the dark red soil and rocks. The *blood*-soaked soil and rocks. How many little Victorias had the man already exploded?

"Frank," Earnest said.

"I know," Frank said. "I heard him."

Victoria meowed.

Frank took a few steps toward the professor. "Sir, isn't there a way you can maybe not blow up animals? See, my cousin Earnest here has quite a soft spot for furry little creatures, and he won't leave here if he thinks they're gonna get hurt."

"That shouldn't be a problem," the professor said.

This was followed by a soft click.

"I don't think you'll be leaving," the professor added. "Not today. Not ever."

There were two sounds in the world Frank was intimately familiar with. One was the sound of money, or rather the noise of a coin dropped on a wooden table. The other was the sound of trouble, or rather the metallic click of a hammer being set on a pistol. He glanced down to greet the weapon now aimed at him and his cousin.

Frank raised his hands.

Earnest raised one hand, the other still clinging to the small kitten in his arms. "He's got a gun, Frank."

"I can see that, Earnest," Frank said.

"Why don't we have a gun?"

"Because they're expensive. And besides, you'd just shoot your fool head off."

"I think I could handle a gun."

"You can't handle your personals when you gotta pee. What makes you think you can aim a gun the right way when you soak your trousers half the—"

"Gentlemen," the professor said over their untimely argument. "I would like to thank you for stumbling on my little den of iniquity. I was hoping for a face-off against a worthy opponent, but I can see you're just a mild distraction. Never mind, I have plans for you. Both of you."

The professor flipped a switch on the machine, sending it into crackling, huffing, and whirling life. Blue lighting raced back and forth across the middle gap.

Frank wasn't certain, but he thought he heard Victoria growl.

A chorus of growls rose from the back of the cave.

"You should know," Von Moose said, "I hadn't really given human beings much thought when it came to the STaHP machine." One hand still holding the gun, Von Moose used his free hand to push a little cloth-covered trolley across the cave. "I always assumed animal fur was the perfect conductor for my needs. But now, ah, now I am forced to rethink my original plans. I must thank you gentlemen for this opportunity. Perhaps animal fur isn't what I needed all along. Perhaps human hair is the answer to my conundrum."

"Frank," Earnest said. "Frank. Frank. He's gonna put us in the machine, Frank. He's gonna put us in the machine."

"He's not gonna put us in the machine," Frank said.

"*Au contraire*," the professor said. "Your cousin is quite correct. I am going to put you into the machine."

"How?" Frank said. He waved a raised palm at the STaHP machine, or more specifically the gap. "That hole is far too small for either of us to fit."

The professor yanked the cloth away from the trolley. A fair number of blades and saws and other nasty as well as blood-soaked instruments were strewn across the cart. Von Moose held up a saw blade the length of his arm and coated in crimson. "You will fit. I can make certain of that."

It didn't take a professor to understand what that meant.

Frank and Earnest screamed together, and at the sound of their collected shrieks Victoria pounced on the professor. One moment the kitten was growling in Earnest's arms, and the next she was clawing and biting at the professor's face. Von Moose dropped the gun and the saw blade and hollered in agony as the kitten laid into the man, giving the crazy bastard all she had. The pair of them careened backward as the professor stumbled toward his creation in his efforts to free himself of the kitten. They slowly lurched toward the crackling, huffing, and whirling machine.

Frank scrambled forward and snatched up the gun.

"Victoria!" Earnest cried. "Look out!"

The kitten leapt away from the professor, her parting momentum providing a last push which delivered the man into the heart of the STaHP machine. Professor Von Moose's head landed square in the center of the gap, his neck coming to rest on the edge of the velvet pads. Tendrils of blue lightning reached out and stroked his face. For a brief moment the man smiled peacefully, his hair rising on end and his eyes lighting with wonder and joy.

"It's so beautiful," he said almost too softly for Frank to hear.

That beautiful moment passed quickly, replaced by a loud pop as the man's head exploded in a puff of crimson. The stump of his neck poured with blood, a shower of red that painted the adjacent walls and floor while his body kicked and writhed alongside the machine. Frank and Earnest and Victoria took a few quick steps backward to avoid the rushing stream of crimson until at last the body fell still.

The machine then began to chug instead of chuff, and give off an unpleasant odor of smoke that told Frank something wasn't right. Well, something more than the fact that a man's head had just exploded inside of the thing. Frank rushed forward, taking care not to slip in the pooling blood, and flipped the switch to what he hoped was the off position. The machine fell silent, until all that remained was the steady drip of life still draining from the professor.

"Frank?" Earnest said.

"Yeah?" Frank asked as he stared at the disaster.

"You reckon he's dead?"

"I don't think a man can survive a thing like that." Frank turned away and swallowed the bile rising to his throat.

"I don't guess so either. What are we gonna do about that dooms-deedoddle thing?"

"Leave it here I guess."

Earnest stooped to scoop up the gray kitten. "You suppose we should let the other animals go now?"

Frank nodded. "Yeah, I reckon we should since they got no one to care for them now. But be careful, they look pretty spooked." And Frank couldn't blame 'em. He was pretty spooked too. Hell, he was downright disturbed. It wasn't every day you got to watch a man's head blow up like that. Well, not often at least.

It only took a few minutes to release the two dozen or so animals penned up in the cave. Most of them took off in a run for the exit once their cage was opened, but more than a few remained behind. Frank knew it was their inexplicable love for his cousin. It seemed that small animals were drawn to the man. It was like he knew what they were thinking. Like he could whisper to them or something. Shame they couldn't profit from it.

Earnest began gathering the animals up, talking all the while.

"And I'm gonna call you Buzz. And you Mee-ko. And you Jewel, on account you got that pretty spot on your face. And you Fiona. And you Bustyr. And you Little Bustyr, cause you look like Bustyr, only smaller.

And you Kasey. And you Kizzy." He paused as he stuffed an adorably fluffy orange cat into his jacket pocket. "And I'm gonna call you Mr. Wiggums."

"Come on," Frank said. "Grab your furry friends and let's get the hell out of here before anyone finds us. I don't think we can explain this one without looking bad."

"We could just tell the truth."

"Would you believe us?"

Earnest grunted for a few seconds, then said, "No. I guess not."

As Frank led his cousin and the passel of animals back outside, he wondered what they would do next. He reckoned, aside from watching a grown man's head explode, they had just done a fairly wonderful thing. Sure they may have only rescued a bunch of animals, but that was the most good they had ever done in their whole, rotten lives.

"Frank," Earnest said.

"Yeah," Frank said.

"I kinda liked making money doing something good."

"Yeah, I sorta did too."

"You think when we give Victoria back we can find another nice job to do?"

"I would like that. Yeah."

And so it went. Frank decided that maybe this wide frontier had enough outlaws. Maybe what it needed were a couple of good guys.

Good guys for hire, of course.

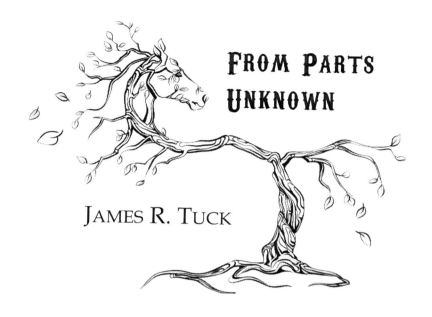

From Parts Unknown

James R. Tuck

TRUETT MCCALL LOOKED AT THE PEOPLE GATHERED ON THE SIDE STREET between the Velvet Tiger whorehouse and the Church Of The Tribulation chapel. The two buildings sat side by side but their entrances faced opposite ends so that any crossover patronage had the furthest walk possible. On one end of the alley formed by the two buildings high walls twittering churchgoers stood in dresses and hats and suits cobbled together to be presentable. They whispered amongst themselves behind the ratty rope strung up by the town constable to mark off the crime scene.

At the other end stood ten or so working girls, soiled doves, held back by another piece of ratty security rope. They gossiped every bit as much as the church folks, they simply did it around cigarettes that dangled from rouged lips and without any edge of hysterics. This far out into the Flats even the swift, sure hand of Magda didn't protect them. The town of Modest was a little shithole far from Lost Vegas, a scrap of survival carved out of the wasteland and built off the back of a decent strip of slag to mine. These girls had seen plenty. The dead body covered by a worn wool blanket wouldn't be the first for most of them.

Damn sure wasn't the first for him.

The constable shuffled his feet. "Sure you want to see this? I wish to hell I hadn't."

Truett spit a long stream of tobacco juice and looked at the short man with the bent tin star through a squinted eye, hand resting on the worn wood handle of the six-gun on his hip. The notch of the hammer rubbed the crease between two thick stripes of scar tissue. "You trying to be funny?"

The constable looked down at the six-gun, his eyes sliding sideways once there to stare at the dark-bladed hook-knife that hung beside it. "No, not at all. I was just..." he leaned toward Truett, his voice dropping to a whisper, "ah, hell, I'm spooked. This is a terrible, terrible thing and I've seen my share of terrible things."

"I'm sure you got me beat." Truett spit again. "Now pull that god-dam blanket back and get this shit over with."

The constable lifted the blanket slowly, looking away as he did.

The churchgoers gasped.

The whores quit talking.

The blanket stuck to the thing laying underneath it, some liquid that was never meant to be outside a body drying into the fibers. The constable had to shake and jerk to get it free.

Most of a woman lay there.

Her arms and legs were there, bent at wrong angles and splayed unnaturally, but there and attached to a torso that had been hollowed out, scooped clean of any type of organ or viscera. The ribs had been popped free of their nodules on the sternum and pushed open, spread like a bowl. The skin had been peeled back, ripped along the sides and tossed out of the way of whatever had disemboweled the woman. It lay across her left shoulder. Across the ground like a discarded shawl made of thin leather. The edges of it curled in the heat of the day.

An awful sight.

Her face made the entire thing worse.

It was untouched, serene save for a smear of dried blood across her pert little chin. Her wide mouth was slightly parted, not enough to see tongue or teeth, but the slackness of it very much as he would imagine her sleeping. It softened features that held a cruel beauty, features that could become harsh in anger, but in death lay like a masterful painting on a pillow of coarse reddish-brown curls.

"Who was she?"

"Only ever knew her as Lucille. Kept to one of the rooms under the Church here and worked what she could at the purification plant at the slag mine."

"Kin?"

"None that I know of. Nobody lived with her."

Truett squatted, looking closer. Something was wrong with her eyes. They were closed but they didn't look right. He poked one with a blunt-tipped finger and the lid sunk in. It was spongy underneath. He flipped one back with his thumb and found what he'd suspected. The eyeball was gone, leaving nothing but a socket full of congealed blood and aqueous fluid.

The constable jerked back. "Oh my fucking God!"

Truett ignored him, shifting on the balls of his feet and looking closely at the giant wound that took Lucille from crotch to throat. She was empty. Only bone and meat and cartilage left in the hollow. Everything soft had been completely removed. He studied the flap of skin tossed aside, his mind running over what he knew of the insides of corpses. The skin had no fat on it. No subcutaneous membrane. Even the woman's breasts had been scooped free of fat and mammary glands and left like tiny puckered purses in the center of the skin shawl.

The skin on her legs and hands had tiny circle wounds that dotted along their length, all of them the same circumference and depth. From the look of them he could stick his finger in to the second knuckle.

Almost to the third.

He wasn't going to stick his finger in a dead woman's wounds. She'd suffered enough indignity.

He flexed his left arm, feeling the double row of circle scars that ran around his bicep and onto his chest pull tight. They were souvenirs from a run in with one of Crowley's leftovers, a tentacled beast stuck in a partially collapsed gateway between its hellish dimension and a community of gypsies. The damn wildbloods had been feeding it settlers that encroached on their land. He'd been sent by Ann to put a stop to it. He'd done it, but it got him good with the suckers that ran underneath one of its flailing appendages, clipping the skin away in two trails of circles. The circle wounds on the body...Lucille...were similar, but random, no symmetry to them like his had.

It told him a lot. He didn't know what without some sorting, but all the information his eyes had taken in began to shuffle in his mind, finding its place next to what he already knew.

"Cover her up."

The constable pulled the blanket back in place. "You need her for later?"

"Save a chunk of hair, skin, and nail but bury the rest of her in hallowed ground." He turned to go. "I'd get to it a'fore sundown just in case."

"Where are you goin'?"

"Just do yer job and stay the hell outta my way."

"I don't think I should let your kind in here."

Truett looked at the man in the roman collar. "Open the goddamn door."

The preacher blinked at him.

There was a sore on the corner of the man's eye that cracked with each flutter of the lids, weeping thin yellow lymphatic fluid that trickled over skeletal cheekbones, drying in a broken crust along his jaw. Under his black suit the preacher was knobby, lumped over with tumors you could see in clusters. A pattern of sunken scars traced his slick brow, up over his cranium, and over one ear. He was a slag miner found religion.

Found spreading that religion was a helluva lot easier than digging radioactive ore from the leavings of Wormwood.

From the look of the sores and the tumors that distorted the fit of his clothes he found it too late.

"This is a house of the Lord of Light. We don't recognize the authority of spellslingers."

Truett hitched his shoulders, settling his coat around them. "I ain't here for your lord or your bullshit. I'm going inside this room to see if there's a reason something ate one a' your tenants innards. You ain't gotta like it, you just gotta open the door."

The preacher looked up at him, trying to read his eyes. Down the hall one of the other doors opened and a young man looked out. He saw Truett and pulled back inside, shutting the door with a slam. The sound of locks being turned clicked and clacked down the hall toward them.

The preacher stuck the key in the lock and turned it. He opened the door a crack, turned, and walked back toward the stairs they'd both come down, leaving Truett alone in the hallway of doors.

The spellslinger pushed the door open and stepped inside.

He wasn't alone.

He could feel someone else with him the moment he crossed the threshold. The dim light from the hallway streamed around him, breaking apart against the solid dark of the windowless room. The shadows were impenetrable.

Truett's hand was on his six-gun.

A match flared.

The small guttering of yellow light cut a giant of a man from the darkness.

Truett's hand slid off the pistol, closing on the handle of the hook-knife. The man in the dark's brow jutted forward over a nose like a fist, jaw spreading beneath like a shovel. Truett couldn't see his eyes, in the almost-nothing light they were just pits of black set deep in the overhang of that forehead. A scar ran down one side of his jaw and onto his neck, thin and delicate like it had been drawn there by a deft hand. When he spoke his voice was rich and deep, the voice of a politician or even a preacher.

"Shut the door. We should talk."

The lamp on the bedside table brightened the room. The fuel was some weird gray brack, probably some form of run-off from the slag mine nearby. It burned hard orange and sputtered soot in black swirls that drifted around the room, dimming the air to near dark again, but Truett could see the giant in front of him.

"You shoulda known Lucille. She was the air and the light."

"Why'd she get dead then?"

The man looked as if he'd been slapped. "She didn't deserve it if that's what you're implying."

"Sometimes there's no reason someone gets hit by the supernatural. Most times there is, inadvertent or not." He leaned forward. "What the hell are you?"

"What..."

"Don't lie. I ain't new at this and you ain't normal."

"I'm just...big."

"Bullshit. You ain't human, quit playing like you are."

The man shifted on the bed. His size and weight made it groan, wood slats grinding along wood rails. One of them broke with a sharp CRACK! but he didn't notice.

"I'm human, every part of me. My father gave me the best of everything, including life. When I wasn't everything he'd dreamed he abandoned me, left me to my own devices. Things got...dark. I did things I never meant to. Things that would have put me in your path at the time."

"Did you kill Lucille?"

"No!" the big man cried, face twisting at the horror of the thought. "I loved her. In my time on this earth I have loved exactly two women and she was one of them."

Truett weighed the man's words. Studying his face. The anguish there was raw, an open wound.

"What's your name?"

"Adam. Just Adam."

"Truett McCall." He stuck his hand out, the dull lamplight flickered over the dozens of thin scar strips across the back.

Slowly, Adam reached out, his palm bigger than Truett's entire hand. Wide knuckles closed iron fingers. The moment their skin touched Truett dug deep into a hangnail on the thumb of his other hand. The thin strip of skin tore downward in a raw little jolt of pain. He didn't feel it start to bleed but he felt the magick inside him kick to life at the sacrifice, just a small pop of the eldritch energy that lived coiled in his guts. Quick as lightning, it climbed his arm and crossed his chest. He pushed it down into the other hand, the one holding onto Adam's, and used his mind to turn the little jolt into something that could read Adam's intentions.

It bounced back into his skin, crackle-burning a blister there.

Adam looked him in the eye. "Magick has almost no effect on me."

Truett pulled his hand free and shook it, small droplets of energy rolling down his fingers and sputtering to nothing against the floor.

Adam sat up on the bed, another board broke, lowering him a few inches down in the mattress. "Certain spells and hexes hurt, and I can be knocked around by major arcana, but petty magicks roll off me like water."

"You're a null."

Adam nodded.

"Never met one before."

"Me either."

"Don't like it."

"Tough shit, cowboy."

Truett nodded. "Still got my six-gun."

Adam looked at his hands. "Never found one my fingers could fit."

Truett looked also. The hands hung on wrists the size of fence posts, each palm wide as his own face and slabbed with thick, hard muscle. The fingers were blunt, articulated with knuckles swollen like walnuts and edged with barnacles of callous that looked like horn. Raw destructive power radiated under the waxy yellow skin that covered the digits. They were blunt; indelicate and cumbersome.

Adam pulled them into his lap. "What?"

"Those hands couldn't have done to Lucille what was done to her."

"I wouldn't have hurt her at all."

"Did you see her last night?"

"No. She'd worked that day. She never wanted company those nights. The work at that damn plant was too much for her, the chemicals and radiation and all take their toll. We parted ways after our shift."

"You work there?"

"It's where we met. The slag run-off don't bother me."

"So she was fine when you parted ways."

"She planned to read the night away. She'd been paid in this oil," a giant hand swung toward the lamp on the nightstand, "and had borrowed this book from Dietrich, the man that runs the purification plant." He pulled a small canvas-wrapped square from under the stand. He held it out toward Truett. "He's a little sweet on Lucille."

Truett didn't correct Adam on the tense. His fingers tingled as they closed on the book.

"Damnation." he muttered.

"What?"

Truett didn't answer, just carefully began flipping through the book. The pages were thin as onionskin, sewn together, and covered with black scrawl. It appeared to be an old story about a woman and man looking for each other. A story writ' from the memory of someone from when books were plentiful, before Crowley broke the fucking world.

In the middle of the book he found what he knew would be there.

Stitched into the center was one folded piece of parchment, thicker than the others and made from some old pressed papyrus. The surface of the papyrus left his fingers coated in a thin oil that burned as it lay against his skin. One long sentence crossed the middle of that page. Written in a flame-script, it scrawled across, slanting and looping back on itself. He didn't know the language, something long dead and worth staying that way, but his mind read it the second it passed in front of his eyes.

From the outer darkness to the utter deep, I hunger.

The lamp sputtered out.

"What the hell did you do?"

The room had gone pitch black leaving Truett blind as a bat. The second the lamp had gone dark he'd jumped off the chair and crouched, leather coat pulled tight around him like a second skin, collar up, and his hat pulled low over his eyes. The bed cracked and crashed as Adam stood.

"Shut the hell up and be still," Truett hissed.

Adam stopped moving.

The air grew thick, hard to breathe.

A clacking sound started, a tiny sound, the enamel on enamel *click-click* of mandibles chewing, snapping and tapping as the sound grew and grew, filling the darkness.

Truett huddled lower in the protection of his coat, hands sunk deep in the pockets. The potential of something about to happen pressed against him.

Adam grunted and it sounded close, near his ear, loud enough to carry over the steadily growing clacks. He grunted again. After a second he cried, "Something's biting me!"

Something hit his coat like the fists of children, beating through the radiation-shedding leather. It climbed his body, battering at the coat as it did. He tensed, waiting, the edge of his collar touching the brim of his hat. When the battering was at his shoulder, he held his wrist out from under the coat.

Something bit deep, it was small, the size of the tip of his finger but it scissored into the scar tissue on the side of his wrist and snipped out a chunk like a plug of tobacco.

He jerked the wrist back into the coat.

The battering became a frenzy against the closed leather.

The bite throbbed, pulsing out a bead of blood that ran down his arm. He used it to kick his magick to life. It boiled inside him, churning as the blood trickled down his sleeve. The battering pushed him back, making him shift to stay upright. Adam growled a curse and Truett felt him move, his bulk displacing the air in the room. The edge of Truett's coat lifted from the floor.

The thing in the darkness rushed underneath.

Sharp pinches of pain through his pants as something swarmed toward his midsection. He stood and threw his coat open, ramming the magick in his guts out, shoving it in a focused blast.

He felt it strike the thing and shred through it. Felt it wash around Adam having no impact. Felt it strike the dead lamp and the weird liquid inside.

The lamp exploded in a ball of ectoplasm.

The dense liquid swirled in the air, tossing greenish light from floor to ceiling. In front of Truett hung a cloud of pure dark, broken by dozens of coin-sized mouths made of curved beaks like a swarm of cuttlefish, the edges of the bills gleamed like razored enamel. They snapped, clipping the air in front of him.

Looking into the dark, a chill soaked Truett to the bone. The hunger of it rolled across him and he knew this thing would devour every soft morsel inside him and when it finished it would *still* hunger and the loss of him would have no impact at all; the utter dark would move on seeking more flesh for consumption.

As the ectoplasm burned itself out the darkness broke apart, shredding to thin tendrils that failed to hold the mouths aloft. One by one they tumbled to the rough plank floor, clattering like tossed dice.

The ectoplasm sputtered out, leaving the room dark again, but now the soft darkness of normalcy.

Adam struck a match. Dozens of small wounds dotted his exposed skin.

Truett swayed, energy crashing. He'd tapped too much magick without enough flesh given. He put his hand on the wall, steadying himself.

"Let's get out of here. I need a drink."

The whiskey was rotgut, so harsh it had the texture of goat hair as he swallowed, but when it hit the bottom of his stomach it spread quick, lubricating his nerves and smoothing him out. He leaned forward over the table, offering the bottle to Adam. The giant held up one wide hand to decline.

Out in the light Adam was even bigger than Truett originally thought. Nearly two feet taller than himself and wide as a barn door. He moved with a solid weight, moccasined feet sinking into the muddy street as they made their way to the saloon front of the Velvet Tiger.

"You okay, cowboy?"

Truett swallowed again. "I've seen a lot of fucked up shit in this line of work."

"I'd imagine."

"Not many things scare me."

"You're scared of tiny mouths?"

"You don't understand."

"Enlighten me."

"Ta hell with that." another swallow. "You sure that damned book came from the foreman of the slag mine?"

"Dietrich."

"Whatever."

"Every other book she borrowed has." Adam rubbed his face. "You think Dietrich did this?"

"That's my guess."

"Fucking hell." he reached for the bottle and drank it down. The bottle made a brittle sound in his hand, thin fractures shooting through the glass. "I'll kill him."

"Well, let's get to it then."

The purification plant loomed into the bruise-colored sky. It was tin-roofed over clapboard and gypsum block walls. A train rail ran into the side of the building, iron ore buckets pushed up against each other, full of strange colored rock shot through with iridescent threads. Some of them glowed with dull light and the air above them shimmered with radiation. The back of the building hung over a deep pool of gray, brackish water that churned as if alive. More of it ran out of a flume of pitted steel, tumbling into large wire-mesh strainers on swiveling poles. It ran out and dripped into the pool. The strainers collected bits of ore and once they were full they were pushed aside and replaced by sallow-faced workers. People moved around the building, pushing ore buckets, carrying bundles, all with the trudging determination of pack animals. A cold, thin wind pushed a smell of rotten paper, mildew, and mold that smelled somewhere between a planted field and a corpse.

"I do that." Adam pointed to the strainers. "I work the entire shift by myself."

Truett grunted. "What is that shit they're straining?"

"Run-off. They boil the slag inside then shoot it with pressurized water, knocking out the loose dirt and mud from impact and leaving behind the clean ore. Bits of it come off so we catch it and strain it to make sure all the good stuff is brought in."

"Hard job?"

Adam shrugged.

"Looks like it would suck almighty."

"The water stings me, burns the others." another shrug. "Stinks."

"I can smell that."

Adam pointed. "Not many people around on third shift, but Dietrich is always here. He'll be up in that room."

The wind changed direction, ruffling up the back of Truett's neck. He looked past Adam. "Dietrich a lanky fucker? Walks like he's been ridin' bareback over a hundred miles of bad trail?"

"Yeah, why?"

Truett nodded his head toward the source of the wind. In the middle of the whistling gale ambled a long, dark man. His feet kicked out with each step, the long toes of his boots pointing to the night sky, followed by the firm planting of the heel before the entire foot rolled down to the silica sanded earth, carrying the man forward. He walked up and nodded to the spellslinger and the giant.

"Evening. Help you two?" He craned his neck so he could look up at Adam. "I know you ain't on shift til dawn."

Adam moved, his body so tight with rage he vibrated in his stitched-together skin. Wide hands reached toward the foreman, fingers curled in anticipation of soft flesh and jointed vertebrae under them.

Dietrich didn't even blink.

Truett spoke. "Hold up, Adam..."

Before he could say *this don't feel right*, the wind turned cold as the devil's conscience, spiking into them as the salted hum of magick rose in the air.

Truett's hand was on the hook-knife at his belt when Dietrich opened his mouth and hacked, the loose skin of his jowls swaying as he clutched thin arms around himself and retched. The scrawny man dry-heaved, shoulders lurching with it.

A split-second passed. Adam was one lumbering step closer to Dietrich. The hook-knife hovered over the back of Truett's empty hand.

Dietrich staggered, coughing again and his body rolled, chest expanding as something came up his esophagus. The skin of his throat swelled like a frog's air bladder, stretching thin, hardened arteries and veins standing like mooring ropes. Truett heard the *pop!* of the man's jaw dislocating as something filled his mouth from out his guts.

Adam took another step, just a few strides away from his intended victim.

The hook-knife hovered still as Truett watched, trying to suss out what would happen next. His stomach had gone greasy slick with dread and he almost dropped the knife for the six-gun to just put a bullet in Dietrich's forehead.

Dietrich opened his mouth and let the thing inside it fall out.

A wet ball of spines landed on the ground in front of Adam. It lay in the irradiated sand, quivering and steaming. It was a knot of dark swirls, dozens of them all made from hundreds of thin strands. A word jolted in Truett's head.

Trichobezoar.

A hairball.

Dead human matter ingested by a sorcerer, lain in his belly for gods knew how long, soaking up bits of magick with every spell, every incantation, every ritual, every working, the strands of hair that made its mass acting as tiny razor wire, making thin incisions in the lining of Dietrich's stomach, letting slips of blood trickle in until it was infused with the very essence of black magick and blood sorcery.

Truett's slashed down with the hook-knife.

Adam took another step.

Dietrich looked up, smiled, and whispered something not meant for human lips to form.

The trichnobezoar shrilled like a tea kettle and exploded into a wall of spiky tendrils. It doubled, then tripled, growing exponentially in the blink of an eye. Adam took the brunt of it, the hair tentacles driving into him and lifting him off his feet. They held him up, struggling in the air, as the edge of the hook-knife parted the scar tissue on the back of Truett's hand.

They drove the giant into him like a battering ram before he could do anything with the magick that welled up from the cut.

Everything went away as five hundred pounds of reanimated flesh crushed him to the ground.

Everything burned.

His wrists, the ligaments along his arms, his shoulder sockets. The heat even radiated across his chest and down his sides. His chest felt like it was being squeezed in a vise, deoxygenated air like lead in his lungs.

He cracked one eye open.

He hung from bound wrists ten feet or so over a bubbling pit of slag run-off that smelled like a dead man.

Across from him hung Adam, strung up the same way except chain bound his wrists instead of rope. The giant's feet were much closer to the bubbling surface of the run-off and he stared at Truett with a doleful, lambent eye.

Both of them were naked.

Adam's voice came over the gurgling of the death pit below them. "I thought I had a lot of scars."

Truett studied the man hanging across from him, using the exercise to keep his mind from tilt-sliding into chaos. Muscle lay over muscle, sometimes in ways he'd never seen them do in nature, as if the groups had been jumbled together. Stitching scars traced along his skin, trailing around each joint and also breaking free to zig and zag across a well-formed chest, over thick slabs of lats and sleek obliques. One thicker scar swooped across his hip, curving along the bone and spilling onto a meaty thigh.

Adam's member hung in a thatch of blonde hair incongruent with the hair on his head. It drooped, a sleeping python as thick as Truett's own wrist.

Despite his pain, things low in Truett's body tightened.

Damn fool, it ain't been that long.

Adam kept staring at him, as if nothing else was going on and they were standing in a field on a spring day. Truett was aware of what Adam saw. His scars weren't neat, they weren't clean and precise. They lay on his skin in hard lines of knotted flesh and in slick patches where he'd used the magick inside him to try and make this shitty, broken world livable for the weaker and the helpless. The magick Ann had showed him how to use required sacrifice of a specific kind and he'd made them every time.

He looked up at the rope that held him. The knots around his wrists were tight, the hemp interlocked in a way that his weight kept them taut. He hung where the strainer had been earlier, swung out on a bar over the run-off pit. The cut on the back of his hand from earlier was now a wide flat burn.

A voice rose up to him. "I had that cauterized while you were unconscious."

He looked down and found Dietrich on the edge of the pool looking up at them. Cauterizing the wound...the man knew how his magick worked.

Dietrich held up Truett's hook-knife. "I also have your athame. You're helpless so no need to struggle."

Helpless?

Damn bastard wasn't so smart after all.

Adam growled. "I'm going to kill you for Lucille."

Truett wondered at the even tone the giant had. Adam's voice sounded almost normal. The muscles of his own chest and sides were jumping, spasming, and the pressure of his body's weight hanging made it near impossible to do anything more than sip the air. A lesser man, a man who hadn't suffered so much self-inflicted pain or faced down the damn, fucking horrors he had in his line of work, would have been in a full-blown panic by now.

Or dead.

Dietrich sighed, mouth turning down. "I really liked her. I wish it had been different."

"Liar," Adam growled.

"Truly." Dietrich shrugged. "You'll never believe me, but that doesn't make it less true. Not that it matters. You'll be following her soon enough."

"Worse than you have tried. Death isn't a threat to me. I'll drag myself out of hell and rip the guts from your corpse."

Truett pulled up on the ropes, dragging air into his lungs so he could speak. "Why'd you summon...that thing?"

"It broke free from a chunk of Wormwood brought in by some slag miners out in Starvation Flats, killed the whole crew on that shift, everybody except me." He threw his hands wide, the skin of his arms hung off the narrow bones, gently swaying under outstretched arms. "My mama had witch blood in her veins. The Hungry kept me as its *pet*. I feed it, keep it satiated and entertained. Without me it would've eaten every soul in Modest. You two will buy everybody else a few weeks."

Truett pulled up, dragging in more air. "Don't...play the...hero."

"I'm no villain!" Dietrich cried.

Adam's chains rattled as he swung slightly side to side. "Call your master, you sonnuvabitch. Get it here so I can shove it up your ass."

Dietrich's face twisted. He pointed the hook-knife at Adam. "The Hungry comes. From the outer dark and the utter deep it comes to devour."

Beneath them the water began to boil.

Adam looked over. "You got a plan, cowboy?"

Truett didn't speak, his lungs hurt too much. He jerked his head in a nod and began twisting his wrists in the ropes. Immediately the skin lit up like it had been set on fire and the knots squeezed, pulling deep into his joints. His fingers had been cold when he came to, now they set to tingling with electric jolts of pain.

The water in the pit churned beneath his feet, droplets of it splashing up on his soles and shins. The oily surface turned dark as something massive swam up from below.

Truett sawed his wrists faster.

The skin tore, rope fibers ripping scar tissue open. Truett yanked himself up a few inches, gasping for air, his movements sapping what little oxygen he had. The ropes grew wet with lymphatic fluid.

Bleed dammit.

The Hungry broke the surface of the pool, surging up from the depths of it in tendrils of inky darkness. Set inside the mass of it were hundreds of chitinous mouths in all sizes, razor-bill beaks snapping and seeking things to pulp and swallow. The thing in the room earlier was a tiny echo of this massive creature, a cuttlefish to a Kraken, almost nothing compared to the greater thing that now spread beneath them.

"Starting without you." Adam flexed, pulling his arms apart. The chains binding him ripped in a squeal of tortured metal, *chinging* as the links separated and flew into pieces. He dropped like a stone, falling onto the Hungry.

Truett used his whole body to twist in the ropes.

From the shore Dietrich screamed something he couldn't understand.

Adam landed on the Hungry, wide feet slipping on the oily surface. He dug into the darkness with crushing fingers as a dozen small mouths bit deep into his reanimated flesh.

The ropes around Truett's wrists blushed pink as he began to bleed.

The magick in his belly kicked to life, just a twitch, and he pushed it onto the ropes, turning his lymphatic fluid into acid. The ropes began to smoke.

He glanced down, still pushing his magick as hard as he could. Adam was coiled in a dozen tentacle-like strands of darkness. He tore at them with the viciousness of a lion, ripping free handfuls of the black and tearing the beaks off any mouths that came near his hands and tossing them away. He was doing damage but he was losing, inch by inch being enveloped by the darkness.

A rope broke, burned apart by the acid.

It started a chain reaction.

One by one the ropes separated and Truett slipped down a fraction of an inch with each until they simply gave out and he was falling.

The pressure on his body disappeared and he sucked in one glorious chest full of air before he slammed into the rubbery surface of the Hungry and it was driven right back out of him.

Get up you damn idjit!

He scrambled, trying to get his feet under him. The skin of the thing roiled, bouncing him around. On his stomach he slipped across the slick, oily surface. His hand fell into an open mouth the size of his head and he jerked his hand out just as the beak snapped shut, nearly losing his fingers, the edge of the beak skinned his knuckles.

A tendril of darkness wrapped his bicep, anchoring him in place. He didn't fight it, using it to keep from sliding as he pushed to his feet. The mouth on the end of the tendril swung down, latching onto the muscle of his shoulder. It sank deep into his muscle, cutting out a plug of flesh the size of his thumb. Blood geysered from the wound as the tendril yanked free. Truett grit his teeth against the jolt of pain that shot through his chest and latched onto the rush of magick under his skin, called out by the bleeding wound.

He dumped it into the darkness that held him turning it stone solid. The Hungry fought him, screaming against his magick but he still had enough firm dark to stand. He searched for Adam and found him nearly buried in liquid darkness.

A dozen mouth-filled tendrils swung toward him, unspooling over the solid dark, ready to tear him to pieces.

Reaching up, he snapped the end of the tendril around his arm off into a length of solid dark with a razor-sharp beak on the end.

Swinging it down, he drug the edge across his own thigh. The beak was sharper than his hook-knife and cut deep, parting the skin and slicing through muscle. The pain of it throbbed to life instantly, a drummer inside him, the magick growing with each beat. He didn't mean to cut so deep. This much blood loss and he wouldn't last long.

He took it, gathering it inside himself.

The mouths drew closer.

The magick swelled, pushed against his skin, compressed his organs, making his joints pop as his bones vibrated in their housings. He held on, shutting it in, letting it compound until it felt like he would burst apart.

Adam disappeared into the enveloping darkness.

The mouths snapped, inches from his flesh.

Truett let the magick go.

It roared out of him, rushing from his skin in a flashfire of heat. The darkness bubbled, rolling back under the onslaught. The tendrils flailed, losing mouths in a hailstorm of scorched enamel. He pushed, taking a step onto the sticky, melty aftermath of his magick, driving it further, washing it over the quivering lump of dark that was Adam cocooned. His magick ripped at the darkness, peeling it off the reanimated man. The Hungry heaved, trying to get away from the pain of the hex. As the dark melted off him, Adam tore his way free, unaffected by Truett's magick.

Exhausted, the spellslinger dropped to his knees.

The Hungry began to sink, sliding into the pool to lick its wound.

Adam crawled over. "You hurt it. A lot."

Truett hauled air into his lungs. "It ain't dead."

"Can you kill it?"

Truett shook his head. "There ain't enough cutting I can do for that."

Adam nodded. They both looked around. Grey water rose as the Hungry sank beneath them.

Adam stood, dragging Truett to his feet. "You can't survive the pool. It'll strip your skin off."

"What're you doing?"

The giant scooped Truett up in his arms. "Land loose, it'll hurt less."

Before he could say anything Adam began running over the surface of the Hungry, running toward the shore, giant feet slapping on the quivering dark. At the edge where the water rose he stopped and flung Truett as if he were a child.

The naked spellslinger flew through the air, crossing over the water as if he were dreaming.

Until he began to drop.

Then the ground rushed up and hit him like a giant fist. He rolled across the sand, the grit scrubbing his skin raw. His body turned into one giant ache, all the individual hurts combining into one. He got up out of sheer stubbornness, crawling through the fog of pain.

He looked over the water and saw Adam, waist deep in the sinking darkness of the Hungry. The giant had torn free one of the cuttle beaks the size of a wagon and was using it to dig his way into the creature. He lifted it over his head and drove it down. The Hungry heaved at the impact, roiling and bucking, sending water splashing up on the shore. Truett took several steps back as Adam disappeared, falling inside the creature.

He must've broke through.

The Hungry flopped in the pool, sinking completely beneath the brackish water.

Truett felt the air shift behind him and fell to the ground, rolling. Dietrich stumbled over him, arm outstretched and off balance where he's tried to slash Truett with the hook-knife. The gangly sorcerer landed beside Truett who rolled, throwing one leg over and sitting on him. Dietrich bucked, trying to throw him off.

Sand had packed into the wide cut on Truett's thigh, sealing it almost completely. There was still a trickle of blood that seeped, still a corner of the incision open. The blast of magick he'd used to free Adam had drained him, sapped him, but that trickle, that little opening gave him just enough magick to double his weight. He sank into Dietrich's midsection, cutting off his air. The man under him stopped kicking, unable to move his torso under Truett's hex-affected weight, Dietrich began gasping for air and pushing against Truett's hips. The spellslinger leaned over and snatched up his hook-knife where it had been dropped.

He eased up a bit, allowing the sorcerer to draw in just enough air to speak.

Tears ran down the man's face. "How did you do that? Why did you do that? When it comes back it'll make me pay for you hurting it."

Truett knew how monsters worked. Dietrich had called himself the Hungry's 'pet'. The implications of what that could mean sent a chill through him. "It'll be down for a bit. Where's my clothes? I gotta town to evacuate."

Dietrich's eyes went wide. "You can't take away its food!"

"I'm gonna send everybody packin', call in the cavalry to put this sumbitch down, and then we're stringing you up." Ann could have the other spellslingers here after sundown.

Dietrich opened his mouth. One strange syllable, a low gurgling noise, rolled from the back of his throat.

Truett hit him in the mouth, his fist full of hook-knife handle.

He felt the jawbone break under his knuckles.

"No more spells." He pointed the hook-knife in Dietrich's face. "Try it again and I'll gut you and toss you in that fucking pond with your master."

Something moved in the water, a dark shape.

Truett moved off Dietrich, watching Adam walk out of the pool. Oily water streamed off him as he walked onto the shore. His left arm bent at an odd angle, jutting away from his body in a way it was not designed to do. Once he stood on the sand he reached over and took the wrist in his other hand and yanked. The broken arm twisted around, bone sliding back into place with a brittle sound. Adam flexed the fingers of that hand and shook the arm. Satisfied that it was fixed, he walked over to them.

Truett stood. "That thing coming back?"

Adam shook his head. "I doubt it. Found a hole to a weird place. Stuffed it in there and dropped a rock on it."

Truett grunted. "Might work."

Adam looked down at Dietrich. The sorcerer had crawled to a sitting position and sat hugging his knees to his chest.

Truett pointed. "You still want him?"

Adam sighed. "I'm tired."

"Not an answer."

"He's got to pay for Lucille and the others."

"At my hands he'll get a necktie dance."

"Good enough."

Truett watched the last bit of life kick out of the dead sorcerer as he dangled over the pool of run-off. He felt nothing for the sight of it, only glad to have his clothes, his six-gun, and his coat back. His thigh throbbed under his pants, stitched up from his kit. It would heal.

Eventually.

And leave another damn big scar when it did.

Adam pulled his own shirt on over his head. "Didn't think you meant to hang him so soon."

Truett spit tobacco juice. "No need to wait around."

Adam nodded. "So that's that."

"Yep." Truett looked at the giant sideways. "Where you off to now?"

"Don't know."

"You should go to Lost Vegas. There might be a place for you where I work."

Before Adam could speak a lilting female voice came from behind them. "Don't you think I should be the one to make a job offer, McCall?"

They both turned to find a woman standing just a few feet behind them. Midnight hair and kohl-colored eyes stood in stark contrast to the gleaming white coat that wrapped her slender form.

"Ann," Truett said.

Adam remained silent. Considering what he was and the thing he'd just killed, a woman who appeared out of thin air was nothing to be alarmed at.

She stepped close, kissing Truett on his cheek. "Be a dear and introduce us."

"Adam, this is Ann, my boss." Ann stuck her hand out. "Ann, this is Adam," The giant took it as Truett continued, "he killed a..."

Ann yanked down on Adam's arm, pulling him to his knees on the ground. In a blink she was behind him, dainty hands under his jaw. Heavy-lidded eyes opened wide in surprise as her fingers curled in, puncturing the skin and wrapping around his jawbone. Leaning back and twisting, she tore Adam's head off his neck and tossed it over her shoulder. It sailed through the air hitting Dietrich's body, bouncing off and tumbling into the pool below.

Blood dark with age spurted from the torn stump of Adam's neck as Ann grabbed the body by the shoulders and hurled it into the oily water as if it were a sack of rags.

When she turned to Truett the blood had disappeared from her coat and it gleamed once more.

He spit tobacco juice. "Bit extreme, don't ya think?"

Ann shrugged. "He was unnatural."

"So're we."

"He was a null, darling."

"Seemed to help him 'gainst the shit we just faced. Probably woulda' helped agin other shit we deal with."

Ann patted the side of his face. "If he went bad, he'd have been too difficult to stop without our magick working on him."

"I liked him. Felt like a good man."

"I'll get you a partner."

"Didn't say I wanted one."

"You didn't have to, darling."

Truett settled his coat around his shoulders. "What's my next assignment?"

"I need you in Starvation Flats, by Vulture Ridge. You'll wait for a woman and a child."

"On it." He glanced at the pool, then turned away.

"I can get you there faster."

He threw his hand up. "I'll walk."

He didn't glance back.

SUNDOWN

LIZ COLTER

THE SOUND ALERTED FRANK JUST AS THE SUN DROPPED BELOW THE HORIZON, A drumming on the hard-packed earth. He'd never believed the stories of a black-masked bandit riding a hound as big as a horse, but he couldn't deny what he saw out his own window. He crossed the sitting room at a run and bolted out the front door in time to see the man scoop Emily from beneath the apple tree. Without slowing, the bandit slung the limp form of Frank's eight-year-old daughter across the giant dog he rode—a short-haired beast the silver of liquid mercury with eyes like milk.

In the two dozen strides it took Frank to reach the corral, the bandit was already halfway across the pasture. Frank threw the gate open and scrambled onto his piebald mare bareback; the hound had a good lead but the mare had heart. Tangling his fingers into her mane, he kicked her into a gallop through the rough field. He was gaining ground when the bandit jerked the dog's bridle hard right. Frank pushed his left knee into the horse's ribs, and she obediently cut to follow the hound.

The man he pursued looked back and Frank's blood chilled. The black bandana was molded to the bandit's face like skin and covered him to his hatband with no sign of eyeholes. The wanted posters labeled him "The Child-Napper" but folk all called him Sundown, saying he was seen most often right at sunset.

The gap between them had closed by more than half when what looked like solid ground suddenly gave way. The mare's forelegs sank into the collapsing hole and Frank launched over her head, landing hard

on one hip. The impact tore at the half-healed bullet wound in his left side, a parting gift from his last shootout in Layton. He rolled to his knees in time to see his daughter and her kidnapper disappear over a rise.

The mare thrashed out of the sinkhole, snorting and tossing her head, though nothing looked to be broken. Frank struggled to his feet, latched onto her mane and calmed her before she could run. He glanced down into the hole where she'd fallen. Leathery limbs and dried bones poked up through the dirt. It looked to be an old grave that Frank hadn't known existed. A mass grave of pioneers maybe, ambushed or stranded decades ago.

He re-mounted inelegantly, belly-flopping over the mare's back with a grunt. White-hot pain flared from his old bullet wound to the new hip strain. Angry with himself for not pausing to grab a gun, he turned the horse toward the house. June was waiting for him on the porch when he cantered up to the hitching rail outside the front door. Her lines were tense, seeing his urgency but not understanding the cause.

"Emily's been taken," he said, sliding off the mare's back. "That bandit they've been talking about." He yanked a bridle from the post and secured the horse.

"Sundown?" She gripped the banister. Her thoughts visibly leaped down same paths as Frank's had done: shock, quickly shifting to fear of things more horrific than a kidnapping. "Do you think the stories are true?" Her voice was tight but steady.

He thought of the man's eyeless face, the unnatural hound. "I don't know. I didn't before, but I got a good look at him. Now...I just don't know."

Frank didn't want to believe that the first boy to disappear from this town had been abducted for a month, and escaped by clawing his way out of a shallow grave. Or that Dawson's seven-year-old boy had also been gone for a month and said he didn't remember anything at all. His parents thought he'd been too traumatized by his experience to remember, though the boy seemed fine. Until now, Frank had suspected the whole thing was a local legend grown out of all proportion, the boys playing it up. He wouldn't have given the stories any credence at all except that Sam Holland's girl was missing. She'd disappeared just before Frank moved his family here. It would be a month tomorrow. Frank had warned his daughter to stay inside this time of day, just in case, but Emily had always been one to test her boundaries.

He met his wife's eyes, pulling her from visions of Emily he could imagine too well. "It'll be dark soon," he said quietly. "If I go into town and ask Bill to send out a posse, they won't get one going until morning."

He watched the play of emotions on June's face. He'd made her a promise and it was up to her to release him from it or not. Frank had turned his star over to his deputy a month ago. He'd left Layton, wounded and older than his thirty-eight years, to become a rancher for her sake.

She was quiet for the space of a breath, weighing. "You go on after Sundown, then. I'll ride into town to tell the sheriff."

June came down off the porch and gripped his forearm. "You were twice the lawman Bill Watley could ever hope to be, and a better tracker than anyone around here." The lines around her eyes were tight with the risk of losing her husband and only child both, just when she'd thought this part of their life was over. "You go find our girl."

"I'll need my Colt and my Winchester. Some water and jerky, too."

June hurried inside while Frank limped to the barn for a saddle. She returned quickly, hung the canteen on the saddle horn and slipped the rifle into the scabbard while Frank tightened the cinch. The revolver she handed to him over the saddle.

Frank tied the saddlebags on and June packed the venison jerky while he secured a blanket behind the saddle. She stepped back as he mounted and turned the mare. He didn't look back, but he could feel her watching him as he rode away.

The fickle shadows of twilight were the worst time of day to track, but Frank followed the enormous dog prints well enough through the sandy soil out into the arroyos and canyons to the east. He chaffed at the encroaching darkness. All it would take was one good windstorm and the tracks would be gone forever. He searched the hills to either side periodically, as if he might see Emily standing on some outcrop, just waiting for him to come and get her.

The dry wash he'd been following came to an end in a low embankment. He halted and dismounted, careful not to eradicate any tracks. The hip pain was easing slightly, but the dull ache in his side had worsened with riding. He studied the ground while his horse bumped the reins trying to gain an extra few inches to graze the sparse brush.

Whatever the beast that had made these prints, it had spent a fair bit of time around here lately. Tracks ran in all directions. Close inspection indicated they were freshest to the right. Frank looked up the rocky ridge. There was barely enough light left to see the marks in the deep sand at his feet; the hard-packed hillside would be impossible. He untied his bedroll from the saddle, trying not to think how the odds of finding Emily would decrease overnight. Ten years with June, and Emily was their only child to survive more than a year. She was everything to him. His fearless tomboy. His story-time cuddler.

At first light Frank rode up the hill. Near the top it turned to almost continuous rock. Even if June had galvanized the sheriff into action, a posse would never find him over this terrain. Dismounting, he led his horse, moving slowly and scanning for the slightest telltale signs: the light chalk-colored scratches from the beast's nails, a scuff in the sand that littered the rock, a fragment of a paw print in the dirt-filled spaces. Maybe one tracker in a hundred could track with any accuracy over rock, but Frank had once owned a reputation as one of them.

Focused on the ground, he flinched at a sudden fluttering above his head. A barn owl perched near the top of the juniper tree next to him had spooked. The nocturnal owl being out in full daylight surprised him until he noticed its eyes. Instead of sharp and black, they were milky-white. The blindness explained the bird's presence, but the similarity to Sundown's hound made his spine prickle.

Frank topped the ridge and started down the far side of the hill. He was about halfway down when the trail vanished entirely. Tying his horse to a scrubby bush, he returned to the last set of scratches he'd seen and dropped to his hands and knees. The scratch on the far left was deeper than the other two. A weight shift? The animal might have turned. Searching to his left, he found a depression at the sandy edge of a rock. More signs ahead led into a narrow gully. Leaving his horse tied, he pulled his rifle from the scabbard and eased down the eroded wash. The tracks disappeared around a boulder. Frank cocked his rifle as quietly as he could. He placed his back against the boulder and peered around the side.

The boulder stood nearly touching another large rock, like pillars of some giant doorway. Between the two boulders lay an entrance to a bowl of sand hemmed in by rocky walls on all sides. The giant hound was stretched out in the middle of the sand, asleep. Sundown was nowhere to be seen.

Frank controlled his fear enough to breathe again, though in quick, shallow pants. On the opposite side of the bowl lay a similar gap between two up-thrusts. Paw prints entered on Frank's side, but no boot prints came out. Knowing how little it took to bring his own cattle dog from sound sleep to full alert, he eased around gently, turning his chest to the rock. With little more than his left eye exposed, he settled in to watch the far cleft. Only one thing stirred during his vigil—a small lizard bumped into his left boot. It climbed quickly up and over, scurrying away, but not before Frank saw its opaque, blind eyes.

A pink and orange softness crept across the sky and the air took on the quiet of day ending. Frank's eyes stung with the strain of watching. He rubbed at them. When he looked again, Sundown was there. The hound looked up suddenly, adding to Frank's suspicion that the bandit had not come in by the cleft but had simply appeared.

The enormous dog pushed to its feet and nosed the man's shoulder. Sundown patted its muscular neck, then turned and squatted near the base of one of the rock walls. The hound watched with blind eyes as the masked bandit laid both hands reverently on a patch of sand.

Frank would never have a better opportunity than this. He lowered his rifle and aimed at the center of Sundown's back. "Freeze."

The man froze, but the hound did not. It turned with a snarl and crossed half the distance to Frank in one leap.

"Off!" Sundown commanded, in a voice as rough as rocks grinding together. The hound stopped. Sundown stood slowly and turned to face Frank, keeping his hands visible.

Frank locked his muscles to stop them trembling, and held the gun aimed at the center of Sundown's chest. He tried not to think about that eyeless mask and the blind hound snarling at the man's side.

"Where's my daughter?"

"She's here, safe," Sundown answered calmly, his hands still raised.

Frank scanned the small bowl as if he might have missed her. "Where?" He entered the circle of rock and walked toward the bandit. He'd ram the barrel of his rifle right down the son-of-a-bitch's throat if that's what it took to force the words out.

The sand where Sundown had been squatting a moment before suddenly stirred. Fingers broke the surface and a small hand pushed up out of the earth. Frank stared in dumb amazement as an arm followed the hand, reaching toward the sky. He felt dizzy, too far from what was normal and right in the world. His eyes locked on the roiling sand, afraid of what might follow the arm.

He tore away from the sight a heartbeat too late. Sundown had lunged. The gun jerked from Frank's hands as the bandit threw his weight onto it and rolled to the ground. Frank instinctively went for his pistol but, quick as he was, Sundown had the rifle leveled at him before Frank could draw.

"I need to help this girl so it goes easier on her," Sundown said, standing. His gruff voice was quiet and reasonable. "Toss your pistol over here."

He'd been a fool to take his eyes off the man. Frank eased his pistol from the holster and tossed it at Sundown's feet.

Sundown shoved the pistol under his belt and backed up. He took the small, pale fingers in his own. When he pulled, the head and torso of a young girl emerged. Frank had seen her likeness posted around town. It was Betty Holland, Sam Holland's twelve-year-old girl.

Sundown mumbled some words in an unusual cadence, almost like the words to a song or poem. He tugged on her arm a little harder and Betty came all the way out of the ground, sand cascading from her clothes. The girl stood quietly at his side. Her expression was blank, her eyes fixed on some far point, as if unaware of anyone or anything around her. Holding her hand, Sundown moved to a low boulder and sat, the rifle still leveled at Frank. The girl obediently sat next to him.

"I suppose you'd like to know what this is all about." A twist in his voice and his mask gave the impression that he smiled.

"I'd like to know where my daughter is, you sick son of a whore, and what you've been doing to these children."

"Betty here's been buried for the full month she's been gone, and I've done nothing to her but give her a second chance at life. You know she had the cholera?"

Frank nodded. He'd heard her mama was sleeping in a chair by her sick bed the night Betty disappeared.

"She died." Sundown said, "I felt the death and I came for her. If I can get them before sunrise, I can save them."

"Only God can raise the dead, and he chooses not to."

"Well, God and me see differently on that, I guess."

"I don't believe you."

"Most wouldn't," Sundown said conversationally with a shrug. "My own boy died two years ago. Mountain lion attack when we were hunting. It got my boy first and jumped me when I tried to help him. Broke my neck in one bite." Sundown's forearm flexed, as if he squeezed Betty's hand tighter as he spoke.

"Next thing I remember, I was in the dark with something brighter than daylight ahead of me. My wife, who'd passed from influenza the year before, called my name. I was walking toward her when I heard my boy moan. I couldn't leave him." He shifted the rifle braced against his hip, keeping it leveled at Frank as he spoke. "Getting out of there was like swimming quicksand. By the time I made it back, my boy was dead. And so was I, though I wouldn't admit it."

"So that's why you steal other folks' kids? 'Cause you lost your own?" He scanned the rocks and crevices again, looking for any sign of Emily. Clothing. Blood.

Sundown shook his head. "I save other people's children because too many die young." Sundown raised his and Betty's joined hands, presenting her as an example. "My connection with death makes me aware of the dying and the dead, so I use it. That's how I sensed that grave at your place."

The man had the relaxed posture and sincere tones of someone telling the truth. Frank would've believed none of it, except that an eyeless man with an unholy hound was telling the story and Betty, just come up out of the ground, was sitting by him in a trance. He'd dealt with outlaws his entire life, though, he knew better than to think of them as anything but a pack of liars. He needed to keep the man talking until he gave away some clue to where Emily was hidden.

"Why bury them?"

"Death can't see them when they're buried. If I keep them in the ground for a turn of the moon, he loses his hold over them altogether. It took me a while to get it right, but in the last year I've managed to save a dozen children."

"Seems if you're doing good, like you say, you'd do it in the open. Let people know you could help them."

Sundown laughed, a coarse, phlegmy sound. "Would you have trusted me if I'd knocked on your door and told you I was going to take your daughter?"

The coming evening was shading the hideout to light gray. Frank heard a gunshot and distant sounds of horses whinnying at the loud report. The posse must have followed the hound's old tracks. The men were hunting dinner, having made camp somewhere far to the north.

"What about Wallace and Mary Anderson's baby? They lost her to typhoid not two months ago."

"If it's in the daytime, I can't do anything about it. I'm in Death's lands between sunup and sunset."

"So why did you take Emily?" he asked, playing his final card, the one he was sure would reveal all Sundown's falsehood. "She was as healthy as I am."

"She was until she fell from that tree. Her neck broke as clean as my own."

"Prove it," Frank said unsteadily. "Show her to me." He searched the sandy circle, unwilling to imagine Emily lying somewhere beneath the surface.

"I can't," Sundown said. "If I bring her above ground, Death will find her." He stood, letting go of Betty and taking the rifle in both hands. "I know this is hard for you, but you need to go. You leave Emily in my care and you have my word I'll see her safely back to you a month from now."

Frank looked from the rifle in Sundown's hands to the hound still tensed to attack. "Will she be blind?" he asked, stalling. "Like you and the hound?" The owl. The lizard.

"No more than Betty here is. It's why I keep this mask on." Sundown walked toward Frank. "Things ain't supposed to look on living death, I guess. What sees me without my mask doesn't see anything ever again." He nodded to the giant hound. "Hank was Death's hound before I stole him. Being blind don't seem to bother him anymore than it does me."

"So I'm just free to go?"

"Not quite." Sundown was nearly toe to toe with Frank now. "I'll need your word on two things. Promise me you won't come back here until I've returned Emily and moved on, and that you won't seek me out where I go from here. You've been the only one to find me. I can't have you after me again."

Frank wanted to say the words, but he'd never been able to lie convincingly. And he'd never leave without his daughter. "I promise that if my daughter comes back, and there's no proof you're harming anyone, I'll leave you be." He hoped that would be enough.

Sundown slammed the stock of the rifle against Frank's head in one swift motion.

Frank opened his eyes. Twilight hadn't deepened perceptibly; he must have only been unconscious for a moment. Looking down, he saw the bandit squatting at his feet. Sundown's bandana was around his neck.

The man's face was a nightmare. Deep gouges ran from his forehead to his chin, across both eyes. The orbs were shredded but not shriveled or dry. The torn flesh and eyes were as fresh as if they had just been ravaged, though no blood came from the wounds. There were deep bite marks on the throat.

One moment Frank was looking at the horrific tableau and the next he saw nothing at all. In panic, he groped to his feet. His balance was unsteady in the sudden darkness that was blacker than any night he'd ever known. His stomach clenched as he pictured his eyes a milky white.

"I'll be taking Betty home now," Sundown's deep voice said. She won't remember any of this. I'll keep her from being aware until she's back with her parents, unlike that boy that woke while I was leading a posse away from me."

Frank heard footsteps in the sand. Sundown's trousers rubbing on Hank's hide followed by the rustle of Betty's skirts told him they'd mounted.

"It's too bad the way things worked out," Sundown said. "If those men weren't down there, I could have just shot you and buried you next to your daughter. You'd have been home safe one day after her." Hank's heavy tread crunched in the sand toward Frank. "And if I'd let you go, we both know you wouldn't have been able to stay away. Better your girl lives with a blind father than you destroy her chance to live again."

A sick queasiness wormed through Frank's belly. Had he been blind all along; not believing the stories in town, not believing Sundown, not believing the proof of Betty Holland in front of him? If he'd believed, maybe he would have made the promises asked of him; maybe he would have had both his sight and his daughter.

"I assume you have a horse nearby." Sundown's voice came from next to him. "Grab onto Hank's tail and we'll get you back to it. I'll lead your horse near town, so it heads for home instead of for those posse horses. We'll leave some good tracks while we're at it, to lead them away from here."

Blind and scared, Frank had no options but to reach out for the dog. He'd found Emily as June had told him to, but he be coming home without their daughter, and blind on top of it. She was a strong woman; he hoped she was strong enough for this. He touched the dog's flank and felt down the side of the beast to the tail. The hound moved forward and Frank followed.

He held as tightly to the dog's tail as he did to the only thing he had left; his hope that Sundown was a man of his word. Frank wouldn't be reading to Emily anymore, but maybe a month from now he would hold her in his arms again.

FIFTEEN SECONDS

SCOTT HUNGERFORD

WHEN THE CHUTE DOOR OPENS IN FRONT OF ME, I HEAD FORWARD LIKE A prizefighter, nimble steps, fists clenched tight, boot heels leaving tread in the hard-packed dirt. Up ahead the entire stadium is an off-key symphony of alien voices, thousands upon thousands of Scales wailing for the spectacle to begin. Amidst the strains of their sing-song language, I hear my name spoken aloud by the announcer, the hard syllables echoing through the stadium on the backs of a hundred loudspeakers.

The high walls of the chute lead to a concrete tunnel that descends into the main arena. All of the walls are filled with little hairline cracks like everything else in this city, given a good shake by the bombings that turned bigger places like Kansas City into wide sheets of scorched glass. Above me, perched every twenty feet along the top of the chute, stands a soldier Scale with an energy rifle. Too high to reach, dressed in the dust-color jumpsuits that goes for military uniforms, they watch me through slitted black eyes, knowing that I could leap up, drag them down, and kill any of them at any time. But I don't want these ones dead. If I'm going to go forward with the plan, if I'm going to kill tonight, it's going to be out there in the arena under the hot lights, not by a quick death in the shadows away from the roaring crowd.

They hate us, the Scales. I've lost count of the years since we lost the planet to them, since they poisoned our lands, burned our cities, and replanted every river basin with wide-leaved *varrim* plants. *Varrim* is like a drug to them, like tobacco was to us, one that is sold across the countless planets the Scales call home.

Within the endless fields, those of us that survived the purge use hooked *tomak* knives to cut the leaves from the fast growing plants in twelve-hour shifts. We raise the wide-pawed *vako* lizards that the Scales use both as meat and as mounts and try to avoid being eaten or trampled to death in the process. The most unfortunate of us serve the Scales at their dinner table. Not as the main course, as our flesh tastes foul and unpleasant to them. But our blood is praised as a condiment, hot and fresh and lightly spiced, poured from a silvery cup to add umami for their otherworldly palates.

I've been in a dozen arenas before this as I made my way up to this final fight. But this is my first time in a stadium this large. All of the other battles, all of the other Scales that I've beaten, humiliated, or torn apart with my bare hands, all of those coliseum nights are behind me now. There is only Blackhat, the reigning rider in the competition. Soon the final moment will come to see which one of us is stronger. Whether he will be able to ride me, to subjugate me with his telepathic power — or whether I will be able to fight through his web of control, tear him off his mount, and rip the arms off of his small, child-like body. In this final tournament, my height and mass make me a monster, one that is revered, feared, and bet upon by the Scales in the greatest spectacle they have.

My name is Dotti, with an I and not a Y. And you better believe me — I'm going to win.

I was that cute girl in the middle row in high school, the one with curly brunette hair in a cowboy town filled with cheerleader blondes. I got straight B's in high school, worked my ass off in 4H, and spent a year as the flag-rider at every major county event when I turned fourteen.

Because of my family, my chores, and the choices I made, I didn't have a lot of friends growing up. For me, boys were never a problem. I didn't have time for them, not with school and all my extracurriculars, not with a forty-acre cattle farm to take care of with my Mom, my Dad, and the hired hands. I did a little bit of everything on the farm on the weekends, from sunrise to sundown just like the rest of my family, and learned to spit on my blisters and keep going no matter what.

Every summer at the fair, the bull-riding events came around, which was just for the guys. For us girls, there was barrel racing, which I loved from the time I first got to ride my mom's Dasher around the Braxton arena. Barrel racing is a dangerous sport, looping three cans in a matter of a few seconds at breakneck speed. But compared to the guys that climb onto a bull's back and try to ride it one-handed for eight seconds with only the angels watching over them, I was only looking at a busted arm if I fell. The bull riders were in danger of getting stomped, their skulls bashed in, their spines torn apart if they couldn't pull a hard ride. It was thrilling to watch, and all I wanted to do from the first bull ride I ever saw was to try my hand at eight seconds to see if I could match up with the best.

My grandfather used to kid me about that. We went together to every event, ate popcorn side by side on the hard wooden risers as bull riders tried to defy the will of the thousand-pound, pissed-off beast beneath them. With one hand on the rope and one hand raised up over their shoulder, a successful eight-second ride was like watching an Olympics moment or the last lap of a NASCAR race, where life could utterly change for good or bad based on your skill, your strength of will, and an arbitrary roll of the dice.

After my grandfather died when I was a sophomore in high school, I still went to the events without him, but with him, eating popcorn, drinking orange soda, and imagining what he would say as riders won and fell. About how this one had his weight shifted wrong, or that one didn't listen to the bull when it was in the chute, or how a white bull named Dustwrecker always spun left when it smelled like rain. Bull riding is part science and part superstition and there's nothing else like it in the whole wide world.

In my senior year, just a few weeks before I was going to graduate, the world ended. The Scale's silver ships appeared over all of our major cities, raining down sheets of fire. Smaller ones crisscrossed the rest of the planet, spraying an ocean of poison, killing our crops, our herd animals, reducing our forests to dead tinder that burned with even a hint of lightning. For the first four months we didn't even see our enemies, as the dwindling armies of the world were never able to bring even one of their ships down. They just kept poisoning everything, changing the pH of the soil, the acidity of the oceans, and there wasn't a damned thing we could do about it.

When the Scales finally came to Earth, revealed themselves for what they were, there were only a few hundred thousand humans left. Some parts of the United States had been untouched by the poison and the survivors came here, to Braxton County, where we were ready to put up our last fight. For my Mom and Dad and I, we did our part to keep the herds alive, to make sure that people had food and water, and support the soldiers and volunteers that were taking the last of humanity in.

When the Scales came in their hovertrucks and their hoverbikes, wearing dust-colored jumpsuits that seemed right out of a science-fiction film, we couldn't believe what we were seeing. They were alien grays no more than three feet high with wide black eyes, with elongated skulls that were more football-shaped than round. They came along the roads in convoys seemingly unaware that there was going to be a fight.

In the end, there wasn't. When they got within a hundred yards of where one of our ambush groups lay hidden in the brush with a bunch of high-powered rifles, or got close to a house with a few refugees hidden inside, they used their mind powers to force them to drop their weapons and walk out like so many docile sheep. A few dozen of the Scales could control a hundred people easy, make them just get up out of their chairs and walk outside into the sunlight, just like my Mom and Dad did on a bright summer morning. The last I ever saw of my parents was from where I hid by the kitchen window, when they were loaded up into a hovertruck and taken away with the rest of the neighbors.

For two days I was alone. Too scared to light a fire, I slept cold and ate food out of cans. I prayed a lot, cried a lot, hoped for some sign, some answer that would make this whole nightmare just go away. I wondered why they didn't take me, when they took everyone else. The county seemed empty, with only the pets and livestock left behind. I slept with a loaded shotgun beside me on the bed, with empty cans tied to the door handles all around the house in case they came back for more.

They did, two days later, and this time they caught me. The Scales that came down the driveway had devices with them, devices that let them track me. How, I don't know, but they came right up to the house like they knew I was there. Knowing the jig was up, I came out on the front porch and watched them, waited for them to try to take over my brain.

The leader, different from the others by the shiny, powder-blue jumpsuit he wore, he stepped up and tried to yoke me, to control me, to force me to my knees with a burst of pure willpower. I was tempted to go down just to make the pain stop, but I fought against it, managed to keep my feet, managed to buck the rider off of my back.

When he stepped back, staggered by my resistance, holding his stupid head, the soldiers in his platoon nearly shot me with their rifles.

But one of the leaders watching from the back, maybe a female due to her thinner skull and wider hips, she barked at them with a guttural sound, staying the killing shot. Coming forward, just like she was trying to keep from spooking a horse, she carefully bound my hands with something that reminded me of a rope of snot. Then she guided me toward the hovertruck, gentle and cautious at every turn.

It was here I realized that I was important, a human that was able to resist their mind control. But was I going to be vivisected like some kind of science experiment? I was terrified as I got into the truck, but didn't offer any resistance, as it was probably her way or six feet under. In response, she opened a can of warm Coke with her finger pads and let me sip it, even as she very carefully tickled the edges of my memories, trying to see if there was a way in. I was a stubborn cuss, just like my Mom and Dad, so I bore down, sipped my Coke, and kept her out, keeping the secrets of my life to myself.

I tried to ask about my Mom and Dad, or about what was going to happen to the cattle back at the ranch, but she didn't have words. She seemed to understand what I was saying, but had no real way to communicate back, not even a yes or no. All she had was her flat, expressionless gaze without a trace of human emotion anywhere in it.

An hour later I arrived at the Braxton Fairgrounds, where I was moved out of the truck at rifle point. While there were a bunch of other people lined up by the arena fence, the Scales marched me right in past the lot of them. I tried to see if Mom or Dad was there, but they weren't. A couple of sophomores I knew from school waved at me, but I didn't wave back. I had a sense something bad was going to happen to me, and I didn't want some other kid to be guilty by association.

I was taken into the center arena where a bunch of Scales sat at a long plastic cafeteria table. As they marched me up, I noticed something odd. Standing over by one side of the table was a Scale not wearing a jumpsuit, but a kid's cowboy outfit. With a red-and-white-checked shirt, blue jeans, and leather boots, he had a battered black cowboy hat jammed onto his head to complete the look. It would have seemed silly except for the two guns he wore on his belt. One of them was a heavy revolver and the other was a space-age gun made of a black, silvery metal.

When he saw me, he made a guttural, barking command that made the soldiers around me jump. Striking and shoving at me with the butt of their rifles, the little aliens backed me up until I was about thirty paces from the table. Then Blackhat did an unbelievable thing—he tossed the revolver out into the dirt in front of him. He waited, like he was waiting for me to come get it. I stood there not moving, arms crossed. I wasn't stupid. I'd learned to shoot from my grandfather, enough to shoot a few tin cans off the railing by the barn. But not enough to beat this guy to the draw.

Then he took a stance like a gunfighter — and pushed into my mind, forcing me, using all of his telepathic strength to control me. Unwillingly, I took a step toward the gun, and then another. Even as the handful of Scales in the arena cheered in their weird ululating way, the people lined up on the rail shouted for me to fight it, to fight him. I took a third step and a fourth. I knew that I had to take the gun. I had to pick it up and try to shoot him. But I stopped, forced myself to resist him, kicked him out, shoved him out the suicide doors and drove him out of my mind.

It worked. He stood there, shocked, even as the people cheered and the aliens hissed with displeasure. So I walked right up to him, moving past the gun still laying in the dirt, getting close enough to swing. He tried his mind effects on me one more time, but I pushed past them, raised my arm and slapped him to the dirt. Weirdly enough, I felt brittle bones in his face break under my hand, as just the mere force of a humiliating blow was enough to cause serious harm. When the little alien scampered back up from the dirt spitting white blood, he screamed a command and I was at gunpoint once again. I was still his prisoner, but he was humiliated, beaten, and all the humans in the arena were cheering like I'd just done a set of barrels in ten seconds flat.

As I got marched outside, this time through the rear gate, I saw something that made me sick to my stomach. Over in the corner of one of the cattle pens there was a pile of dead bodies, maybe a dozen total. Men and women and a couple of teenagers, all shot through clean either the heart or forehead. I got the sense right there of what would have happened to me if I had reached for the gun. Blackhat would have drawn on me and put me down. But I didn't and I was still alive, at least for the moment. With my Mom and Dad not in the pile, it was possible they were still alive too.

After sitting and waiting in a holding pen until it got dark, a different transport took me to a farm in North Braxton, out past the railroad tracks in the middle of nowhere. When I first got marched into the old barn, converted into a kind of barracks for special people like me, there were maybe thirty folks inside, each with their own cots and boxes of rations. I could see them just for a moment, all staring at me in the dim light. Then when the Scale slammed the door, I was left in pitch-black darkness with them. Over the next few hours until I could finally sleep, I got to know Jan and Stacy, Julio and Big Mike just by the sounds of their voices, and their smooth or rough hands holding mine as we prayed together in a circle on the straw-strewn floor.

For the next few months until winter came, I was put to hard labor. Working on the family farm meant I was no stranger to hard work, but when the first crop of *varrim* shot up in the sowed fields, towering two feet over my head with a crown of wide, teal-green leaves, I got to experience field work for the first time. It was simple work that didn't require much finesse, but there was a method to it, of cutting down the leaves that we could reach, then sawing the pole and cutting off the tuft of fresh leaves at the top of the stalk one by one.

All around us, beyond the hovering pylon forcefield fences that surrounded our area, the Scales had built other work colonies. In these places there were almost no guards. Every group of human workers, about five to eight in number, had a single Scale watching over them. Compared to those of us within the high-security perimeter that had some level of resistance to the psychic push, the ones out in the other fields toiled like drones and worked until they dropped. Every evening at dusk when the hovertrucks moved in to suck up the day's cut leaves, we would get marched back single file at gunpoint to the barracks where we would get fed and watered. The other people, off in the distance, followed along behind their Scale like so many bobbing balloons as their master psychically moved them slowly from field to shed.

Those of us in the Null barracks, as we started to call them, we got along pretty well. Most of the people there were my parents' age. We ate together, slept in the same room on cots, and cried together when the Scales left us alone at night with only the rafter cameras to watch us plot and sleep. We shared everything we knew about the Scales, about the landscape and the terrain around the camp and tried to figure a way out. But at the end of it all, even if we did get away, there was nowhere to go, nowhere they couldn't track us with those devices of theirs.

In the late fall, snow fell, which was really unusual weather for our part of the country. But the *varrim* plants kept on growing, even under four inches of snow and beneath miles of thick cloud cover. Here is where the weak amongst us fell, the ones who couldn't take the continual labor out in the cold and the wet. Those few who refused to do their duties, who dropped the tomak knives and refused to work, they were shot without hesitation. Big Mike, he tried to take one of the Scales out with a spear he'd carved from a *varrim* stalk, but he didn't get much further than that. Thirty became nineteen, and nineteen became twelve, without any new nulls to replace those that had fallen.

For me, I did calisthenics. I ran everywhere, did laps around the field whenever I could to keep in shape. I practiced swinging the *tomak*, throwing it, using it to cut stalks into makeshift spears. The exercise didn't just make the cutting easier, as someday when I got out of here, when I got the chance to run, I wanted to make sure that I could run for miles and miles. I was going to get away from the Scales, but I just didn't know how.

It had to be sometime around Christmas when the Scale soldiers came and loaded up Julio and I into one of their trucks. I was hoping to see the female who had saved me, but there was no sign of her, just more soldiers in dust-colored uniforms. A half hour later the two of us were back at the Braxton Fairgrounds, herded out at gunpoint, then marched through the pens down the chute to the arena. An arena that was now made up to look like a farm site, complete with a couple of shacks, barrels filled with *varrim* stalks, and a couple of *tomak* sickles scattered here and there in the dirt. Before we could ask questions or get a better look, Julio and I were each shoved into our own metal cage, in a long line of eight cages lined up in a row.

As the crowd of Scales shrieked, ululated, and smoked their *varrim*, we tried to figure out what was going on. While the people in the other cages were freaking out, Julio and I, in cages next to one another, just hunkered down and got ready for whatever was going to come next. Was it gladiatorial games of some kind? Were we going to fight for our lives with the tools we'd trained with in the fields?

When a Scale came out of the far gate, riding a giant, gray-green lizard with padded feet, the small crowd went wild. Small as a child, dressed up in a shining red jumpsuit, he seemed mean even from twenty yards away. If this Scale was going to be our challenger, the one that we were going to fight, Julio and I were ready for him. We might be able to pull him down off that lizard and tear him up a bit, if we could just get close enough to connect.

A low, rumbling tone blared from somewhere in the stadium and the cage doors all swung open. I started to leap forward, but got arrested mid-step as my legs froze and my feet got tangled up in themselves. The psychic push wasn't enough to fully stop me, but it was enough to tumble me face-first into the dirt. As I struggled forward, crawling out of the cage while trying to break the compulsion, over the screaming crowd I could hear a sound like a ticking clock counting down in the arena.

At the eighth stroke Julio was clear of his box. At the tenth I was as well. But the farmhand with the straw-colored hair in the next cell over, he was rooted in the cage, frozen in place by the rider, unable to move. Right up to the point where the fifteenth tick sounded and the boy died as all eight of the cages lit up with blue lightning forking from every bar. While three of the other occupants were up and sprinting, going for tools and weapons, the farmhand and two others were reduced to unmoving, smoking hulks on the final stroke.

As the rider turned to focus on the other three runners, tripping them all down within a blink of an eye, his hold on my mind loosened. Without a moment of hesitation I ripped through what little grasp he had and was up and running, using all my might to charge the little brat, even as the alien announcer amped up the crowd with the play by play. Scooping up a *tomak*, I didn't wait to get close. Like I'd done in the fields, I took a couple of steps, lined it up, and hurled the hand sickle at the Scale with full strength. The weapon took him handle first right under the jaw, toppling him off his saddled-up lizard, which hissed and scampered away toward the far exit as fast as it could stride.

Julio got to him first and kneed the Scale down as he tried to get up. I got there next and kicked him hard, feeling the fragile bones inside his torso break from the strike. Struggling, the rider tried to reach for his fallen whip, so I grabbed his arm and yanked, intending to hurt him, to keep him from getting the weapon. But I was more than surprised when I tore his arm clean off, spraying gouts of white blood on top of the dirt.

Freaked out, I dropped the useless limb and moved away, astonished at what I'd done. All around us, the crowd was making a really unpleasant, droning noise, something that reminded me of mourning, of loss. But I didn't care. The Scale wasn't moving and he wasn't hurting my people anymore. As the other survivors gathered around us, soldiers entered the arena once again with rifles in hand, making to move us back toward the pens. They weren't shooting, so that was something.

When we finally ended up in a small concrete room in the back, the same room where I used to do 4H presentations about ozone and rabbits, we were given real food, human food, microwaved TV dinners, beer, and even ice cream. That's when I saw the female again. She had a little bit more of a human expression on her face now, had learned to make a little crooked smile that worked against her jaw.

"You win," she told me, poking me in the chest with her blunted fingertip. "You good."

"And if I didn't win?" I asked her.

"Then die." She smiled even wider now, as if enjoying some great cosmic truth. But even as the crowd roared in the background once again, and the beating of the fifteen-second clock marched down toward the stroke when the cages would alight anew, I realized that the arena game wasn't an isolated event. It was a sport the Scales played with all of their slaves, a game of life or death where the rider controlled their charges or died at their hand.

I saw my way out. Or up was a better way to put it. Maybe there was a way to get my Mom and Dad free of this as well, if I could even find out if they were alive. I figured the longer I could play this game, the longer I could hold out, and the better chances I had to have a life somewhere other than a cage.

There were no more matches for the rest of the snowy winter, and no real change in routine for those of us at the camp. We told the others about what had happened in detail and started doing our best to get everyone in shape. If the Scales took Julio and I at random, to act as a kind of tougher seed in the battles, then it might well happen to the others at a moment's notice. The Scales didn't seem to mind that we were all running, getting stronger, even training right in front of them at the end of our field shifts with sharpened stalk staffs and *tomak*. A few of them even seemed to enjoy watching it, though their fingers were never far from their rifle triggers.

Around the circle of portable heaters every night, huddled together in the converted barn, we talked it all through. We figured that a strong psychic like Blackhat might be able to hold a couple of us, but not all of us. Against people with no resistance, like the ones in the next field over, up to a dozen humans could be controlled, or at least harnessed so they didn't become a nuisance. We also figured that different Scales had different kinds of psychic powers. The one that I'd disarmed seemed to focus on disrupting muscular coordination with his powers, while Blackhat controlled what you did, forced you to do things you didn't want to do. While we couldn't predict how the others would come at us in the future, Julio had read enough Stephen King books to know that there could be all kinds of psychics — telekinetics, empaths, mind-controllers, pain-givers. We couldn't be ready for all of them, but it gave us an idea of what they could do.

But best of all, we knew now that the Scales could die. If I could tear one apart with so little force, then it was just a matter of getting in close, or getting a lucky strike with a thrown spear. I had to assume that the one that Julio and I had faced in the arena, he wasn't very good at his job. The battles would likely get harder as time went along, but we would be ready. If I was going to somehow earn enough leverage to save my family, I was going to have to beat the Scales at their own game.

When the snow melted and spring started to come around once more, then the Scales started taking us in pairs again. Julio and I didn't get to go for another three months and had nothing to do but fieldwork and training. But of the other ten, four pairs were chosen — and only two pairs came back alive.

One of the women who returned victorious, an older lady named Kary who used to work as a postal worker, she revealed a very interesting fact. That if any of the humans managed to make it the whole way down the field to the far gate, they were considered safe. She and the seven others the Scale had faced off against had conducted a mad sprint across the dirt. Five made it to the end zone, while the other three were run down by the rider with either his lightning whip, this whirling bolo, or shouldered to the ground and pinned down by the lizard's wide-spread sticky paws.

Two weeks later the trucks took me and Kary this time. I wanted to go with Julio, but at least Kary and I had trained together, so we were ready.

Back at the Braxton Fairgrounds, the moment we were in the cages with the doors locked up tight, we started yelling to everyone that they had to get out of the boxes or die. When one old lady froze up when the doors swung open, Kary and I drug her out just before the clock struck fifteen. The Scale tried to freeze us as well, numbing our legs and arms, making it hard to know which way was up from down. But he could only hold one of us nulls, and not both of us together. Before long we were using *varrim* stalks to jab at his mount's sensitive eyes and mouth. The Scale may have thought it was safe saddled up there, but when we managed to unhorse him by sticking a splintery length of stalk up the lizard's nose, we were able to beat the rider down and got everybody else get to safety.

This time, the crowd was different. More than a few of them were rooting for us, the humans, the ones being ridden rather than the ones trying to dominate us into place. When I took my hat off and saluted the crowd, hat held high, some of them even cheered, waving fat handfuls of purple currency.

Again, at the end of the run there was real food, as well as Scales taking pictures of us with something that looked like a spherical iPhone. Out on the battlefield we were utterly expendable; in here, as the victors we were a celebrated commodity. I watched over my people as they ate, acting fierce and ornery as I towered over the three-foot-high Scales. It was all for show, as the guards could have shot me full of holes anytime they wanted to. But the more I acted the unholy terror, the more attention we got.

That night, when we got back in the trucks to head home, we didn't. We headed north, up through the canyon, passing abandoned gas stations and burned-out houses along the road. There were more Scale farms along the way, but most of the landscape featured an endless tide of wild *varrim*, waving in the spring breeze, obscuring everything beneath a shroud of purple and green leaves.

By the outskirts of Houston, Kary and I stayed in an old Hilton, in rooms on the bottom floor. There was a gym and a pool, and servant Scales cooked our food and brought us our meals. There was one overseer there who seemed to be making sure that we were well fed and cared for. When I tried to ask him what would happen to the rest of the people back at the farm, he had no words, no answers. Instead he just gave us boxes of clothes and board games stolen from a local Wal-Mart. Neither Kary nor I had much desire to play Monopoly, but swimming in the pool, working out in the gym, and practicing sprints up and down the long hallway that led from the lobby to the conference room, that's how we passed the time.

A week later, we were taken to a county fairground just down the highway. It was a bigger competition, not just a few hundred Scales in the seats smoking *varrim* and eating popcorn, but thousands of them sitting hip to hip. When Kary and I were waiting in one of the old concrete prep rooms before the match, we could hear our names being blasted through the loudspeakers in the arena. Kay-ree and Dough-tee, over and over again, hard syllables tangled up in the middle of the alien babble.

I paced back and forth, trying to keep moving, trying to keep limber, while Kary read a magazine in the corner, turning the pages of an old People rag she'd found in one of the drawers, dating back to before the apocalypse. We didn't talk, as both of us were nervous as hell. The other people fighting for their lives in the arena outside, we'd started to learn what the crowd sounded like when they were excited, and when they were outraged.

At eight o'clock sharp we were led down the chute to our cages and locked in. The arena around us featured a bunch of farm buildings, and even tools like axes and shovels were dropped amongst the usual *tomak* and barrels of *varrim* poles. Six other cages were lined up next to ours, each with their own people. These folks, like us, looked ready and they knew what was going on. This was the next rung up in the tournament, so there were no strangers to violence here.

When the rider came onto the field in a green sparkling jumpsuit, riding his lizard tall and proud, the crowd went wild for him. He lined up his mount, tipped his hat, then pulled out his bolo and started whirring it over his head. When the cage doors cracked open and the first tick sounded—

None of us moved an inch. I was suddenly overwhelmed with fear, drowning in it. Visions of my Mom and Dad lying in the pile of bodies in the cattle stall. Images of the whirring nest of hornets I once stirred up with my .22 rifle when I was a kid. Pictures of our farmhouse burning down amidst a field of slaughtered cattle. For nine ticks I couldn't move a step, before I finally staggered forward, eyes tightly shut against the visions of horror the Scale was pushing through my brain.

As I cleared the cage, trying to find the strength to push the bastard out of my mind, I heard the clock tick its last—and the rest of the cells behind me lit up like Christmas. When the psychic effects abruptly cleared, I turned to see who else had made it out, and realized with horror I was the only one.

The crowd was cheering so loudly I didn't even hear the whistle-whine as the Scale's bolo took me around the throat, knocking me hard to the ground. Struggling, bruised, and battered, I managed to get the damned thing untied, undone, and tossed it aside, but only in time for the rider to move his lizard right up over me. He waited as I stood up, whip in hand, waiting for me to do something, to make a noise or move to attack him. But instead I just started to walk, not toward him but past him, heading for the exit gate one step at a time.

The nightmare assault came on hard again, the bastard doing his best to force me to the ground with just the power of his mind. But I had already seen the end of my world. My parents had been taken from me. He'd killed Kary, leaving me alone without another human soul to depend upon. So I just kept walking, pushing back the nightmare visions, setting aside the torrents of torture and violation.

Screaming challenge, he came up behind me and knocked me to the ground with a *varrim* stalk he'd picked up as a spear. But as I got up, I wrested the spear out of his hands, broke it over my knee, and then kept going. He was beneath me, a thing of no consequence that could neither hurt nor stop me. As I approached the line, the crowd went wild, on their feet, shouting me on with every step. When he rode his lizard into me from behind, knocking me down, I just got up again, punched the damned thing in the eye and kept on going.

When I crossed the line, I looked back and saw that he was sitting in the saddle, defeated, with the most emotion I'd ever seen displayed on a Scale's face. As the announcer called out my name, Dough-tee, over and over again, I gave the rider the finger like he was some foul-mouthed jock from Algebra class and walked through the gate like I owned the place.

After that, my world became a blur. Kary was gone, likely tossed on the dead pile with the rest after the day was done. I cried for her, cried for the others, cried for my parents, cried for the whole damned world that had just vanished. The Scale guards didn't know what to do with me, and even brought in one of their doctors to see if there was something that they could fix. But after trying to give me a checkup, instead he went and brought me a fifth of bourbon and a couple of six packs of Coke from the hotel bar. I spent a day losing myself in Top Gun and Chasing Amy videos from the lobby rental counter, drank the whole bottle, got sick and hung over for another day, and then never touched alcohol again.

Over the next year I got taken around to different cities throughout what was left of the grain belt and was put up against some of the best riders that the Scales had. I was their prize, their fighter, the one who could stand up to the invaders — but only to the limits of what the event organizers would allow.

Beyond that, I trained. I conditioned myself as best I could for each of the type of psychics I encountered. The Scale with the ability to light people on fire with his mind, that was the scariest one I saw out of all of them, as no mental resistance could keep your hair from going up like a torch with a single malevolent thought. But as the other people with me died, I figured out pretty quick he couldn't burn what he couldn't see. So I hid in the *varrim* patches and tore down a staff for a spear while he circled and set the outer ring alight. But when I chucked my stick right through his throat, I put an end to his danger in the blink of an eye.

We spent a year or more somewhere in snowy Canada, and a couple of years in the ruins of Vail. I was getting older, more scarred, more convinced that there was no way out. I had become a killer, able to kick and tear and rip my enemies apart in the arena. But in the endless string of suites I stayed in, I never really had the urge to kill my guardians. I figured I could escape at any time, but Rex and Juvie, the two guards that had been with me since the beginning, they didn't deserve to die any more than I did.

Instead, I taught the aliens to play poker, drank Coke, went for laps in the pool, watched bad videos, and wondered what it would have been like to have sex, to get married, to have kids, to have grandkids, and all the other normal dreams that got crushed the day the Scales came.

It was a spring day when a Scale in a purple jumpsuit came into my room, and along with him the female back from before. She was dressed in human clothes, kid's clothes off the rack from some boutique. As they sat down on the couch across from my chair, prim and proper as any human adults, she opened her mouth and spoke to me in English—the first words of my own people that I'd heard in as long, long time.

"You've done very well," she said. "Dotti. With an I."

"Thank you," I said back to her. I was astonished. I waited for the other one to get in on the act, but he wasn't talking. "This is important, isn't it?"

"Yes," she said. "The Master of Games here, he is very pleased, as you're one of the best...workers he has. But we are both worried that there are elements who want to see you..." She struggled for the word. "To see you removed. They wish to see you investigated, scientifically, to see if we can determine what gives you your unique resistance."

"So you can inoculate yourselves against it?"

She shook her head, then corrected herself, nodding, affirming. "They mean to dissect you. To remove the threat."

"So what do I do?" I'd expected for years to die on the field. But being cut up in some surgical lab? It wasn't right. I turned to the Master of Games, begging for my life. "I've fought for you people. I've given you everything you wanted. I've watched my friends die, killed the Scales that weren't strong enough to beat me, turned your sport into something bigger than all of us."

"Dough-tee, you must win one more time," she said with that peculiar smile. "You will see an old enemy in three night's time. You are the only one that ever beat him."

"Blackhat."

She shrugged a shoulder, not understanding the word. "The one who could not make you shoot."

"And if I defeat him?"

"Then the Master of Games will make sure you run free. You have made him very rich, where before he was nothing."

"That's it?"

"That's it." She stood, smoothing her skirt. "I will make the arrangements. You will have your freedom if you win. If you do not, then they will have their experiment."

"Thank you," I said. "But where the hell am I supposed to go?"

"I know a safe place," she said with that same peculiar smile. "You will like it there."

I exit the cracked concrete tunnel and stalk into the main arena, moving into a place dominated by bright lights and a thundering, screaming crowd. I don't know the city or the stadium, but the place looks big enough to hold the Superbowl. The entire arena is packed with hundreds of thousands of Scales. Every seat, every row, it's all full of aliens. As far as I can see, I'm the only human here.

Battle has happened on the field already, from the boot-heel scuffs in the dirt to the bloodstains spattered on one of the sides of the *varrim* stalk barrels. But this time there is just one cage. One cage for me and me alone. I take note of the six patches of plants that I could use to navigate my way downstream to the exit. There are more than enough tools lying on the ground for me to choose from, though these have silvery blades that reflect the light. The bright lights overhead are nearly blinding, and the loudspeakers thrum with the announcer's growling voice. He says my name, Dough-tee, and the crowd surges to its feet, the entire stadium a living wall of noise. I tip my hat, knowing my place, then get in the cage and pull the gate shut behind me with both hands.

On cue, Blackhat rides out of the far side of the arena, dressed in the same kinds of kid's cowboy clothes I saw him in last time. The crowd also goes wild for him; this must be a bout that is going to go down in history. While he has the standard lasso and bola, I can also see that he has his laser pistol holstered as well at his hip. On top of that, his mount doesn't have green scales, but white, a shocking pearly white that vividly stands out against the arena background. It has more horns and spurs than the others of its kind, and scuttles from side to side faster as Blackhat guides it with his knees.

He rides up to the start point, to the line just outside the makeshift village, with close-up shots of his expressionless face for all to see on the Jumbotron overhead. I can see that his cheek is kind of deformed; the slap I'd given him years ago never healed right, which gives me a perverse satisfaction.

Blackhat salutes me with a tip of the hat. I do the same, baring my flat, wide teeth in a way that I know will make the crowd crazy. His hand rests on his bola; my hands clench into fists, ready to move, ready to sprint, ready to fight through whatever the rider throws at me.

A tone plays, vibrating the stadium floor — and the gate swings open. I start to move, only to feel Blackhat's filthy psychic fingers slip into my brain. For a moment I'm afraid he's got me, as I can't move a muscle through the second tick. But then I force my way through it, letting my deadweight carry me forward so I stagger and belly flop to the dirt just outside of the gate, trying to get enough air to fill my frozen lungs.

When I get the ability to look up, Blackhat has already galloped his lizard right up in front of me, his mount covering the twenty yards in seconds. His bola is already swinging in hand and he isn't going to waste any time. I can smell the sharp urine stench from his mount up close; the lizard's flickering tongue is nearly close enough to reach up and grab.

But when Blackhat turns his mount to the side to get a better shot, for the moment when he can't see me through his lizard's head — I have control back, the magic spell broken. Raking up a big handful of dirt, I get up off my knees and hurl a cloud of dust at the Scale, blinding his wide, unblinking eyes.

Distracted, he screams and throws his bola wide — even as I punch his lizard in the nose, causing it to buck him off.

At the ninth tick he crashes to the dirt and I'm on him like a furious bucking bull, stomping him, kicking him, crushing him underfoot. The stadium is a riot of alien voices, noise like no human has ever heard before, part cheering, part horror, part bravado, part dismay.

When he fumbles for his holster, even as he tries to get his psychic hooks back into me again, I backhand him hard, knocking off his hat, disorienting him further. The back of my hand is covered in white blood; his face is probably ruined for good. I lift him up by his shirt collar, his little feet kicking off the ground. By the look in his eyes, he already knows what's coming next.

"Don't," he whispers in my language, but I'm too far gone to care. Spinning around, I chuck him like an oversized rag doll right through the cage door, where he racks up against the back bars. And just like that, the clock strikes fifteen.

The cage roars with lightning, right on cue, frying Blackhat to death right in front of the panicked crowd, symbolically burning the Scale champion alive in front of a universe of fans.

Now nobody is a fan of mine. The whole stadium wants me dead. Calmly, I brush the dust off of my jeans, then take his hat and put it on. It isn't a great fit, but it shows the message. I tip a brim to the silent stadium, then walk down the middle of the aisle and out the exit gate to where a squad of armed Scales waits for me. They don't wait for orders, but beat me to the ground with their rifle butts, hit me over and over again until one scores a lucky temple shot and puts me under.

When I come to, I'm with the female Scale in another vehicle. But this ship is flying, with blue skies outside of the windows. The doctor is there too, tending to my wounds, doing his best to mend my cuts and bruises. We don't speak, as there are other Scales there, official-looking ones in black jumpsuits. But occasionally the female looks at me sideways and nods, just a little bit, as if to let me know that it's just a little further. Just a little further still.

Two hours later we landed near the ruins of San Diego, the blue Pacific Ocean visible through the windows. From the hoverport they drove me down to Baha, through the now-abandoned border checkpoint at Tijuana. When we finally got to where we were going, down amongst the towering cliffs overlooking the beautiful blue sea, there was no trace of *varrim*. It was lush and warm and nothing was poisoned, with fruit trees and scuttling crabs on the beaches.

Just outside the front gates of a resort they dropped me off, sent me out into the bright sunlight, left me blinking against the glare.

"Where am I?" I asked her.

"Home," she said, and then gestured for me to go on, to head on up the road. Not knowing what else to say, I nodded thanks, then limped my way along the broken concrete. That's when I heard it. Laughter. A human child's laughter, bright and sparkling. When I came around the bend there were people, dozens of real people sitting around the swimming pool over by the cabana building. As they came up to me, welcoming me, happy to see that another human made it to paradise, I looked back behind me and see the female Scale. She waved as she climbed back into the hovertruck, smiling full on like a human without a trace of shame.

That was seven years ago. My husband, Michael, a handsome third-year med student back when the world ended, he keeps track of the date on homemade calendars, to make sure we always know when Christmas is, the Fourth of July, even April Fool's Day. We have to keep track of the small things up here, the last rituals we have left from before.

We have a house up on the edge of the hill, away from the crowded resort that seems to add another few people every month. Up here, in what was once a million-dollar paradise of sloping eaves and Spanish tile, we are alone with our five year-old daughter. Her name is Kary, named after my friend who fought beside me so long ago.

One night, as we all slept in the master bedroom, I had a very odd dream. I dreamt I was standing knee-deep in the ocean, the waters perfectly still, with the female Scale standing next to me. We were both looking out at the horizon, at the sun rising over the edge of the world. She turned to look at me, to say something, but then she saw what I was holding. I looked down at my hand, expecting to see smiling Kary, her hand folded into mine. But instead, I was holding a *tomak* blade, edges silvered in the early morning light.

"Soon..." the Scale said without speaking—and then I startle awake, soaked with sweat.

I spend the rest of the night pacing, thinking, and then deciding. The next morning, I draw a picture of a *tomak* in the dust with my finger for my daughter to see, beginning her training. Because when the Master of Games comes for her, she will be ready.

She is the one who is going to win.

REDEMPTION SONG

JOHN G. HARTNESS

TIME STOPPED WHEN THE MAN FIRST SHOWED UP IN THE GOLDEN GRIN Saloon. It was one of those between-the-raindrops moments, when everything fell silent for an instant, and everyone's attention landed on the same spot. Big Bob, the piano player who took an Ohlone arrow to the knee that ended his trapping days, finished one Stephen Foster tune and began leafing through a tattered Dan Rice songbook for another song to play. The man stood in the doorway, hat pulled down low over his eyes and a long leather duster hanging well past his knees. He looked like a man who had been rode hard and put away wet—thin almost to the point of gauntness, and so pale one could see the veins in the back of his hands if they let their eyes linger long enough, something not many were inclined to do.

He stood motionless, nothing about him even twitching except his eyes. Those chips of flint flickered back and forth across the room, taking in Leila and her dancing girls on the tiny stage in one corner near Bob, JR sitting at his faro table flipping cards and stacking chips, and Smilin' Bill behind the bar polishing a glass in his eternal battle against the grime of the street. The man held the gaze of every soul in the Grin for a long heartbeat, then he stepped forward, and with the jingle of his spur the spell was broken. Big Bob launched into an old minstrel tune that had the girls high-kicking, JR flipped over a Queen to top the bettor's nine and take his last chip, and Smilin' Bill set the glass down on the bar and poured a slug of whiskey into it.

The stranger put one foot onto the bar rail and leaned on the polished oak. Smilin' Bill gave him one of his trademarked grins, gold tooth sparkling on his lower jaw, and slid the whiskey into his hand. "First one's on the house, friend. You look thirsty," Bill said. "I'm Bill Evans, owner and proprietor of the Golden Grin Saloon, the finest drinking establishment for at least a hundred feet in any direction!" Bill laughed at his own joke, and a couple of the regulars at the bar joined him out of either manners or a hope for a free drink of their own.

"Thanks," the man said. He slammed back his whiskey and dropped a golden eagle to spin on the bar. "Another." His voice was more a rasp than speech, like the sound of two sheets of paper scraping across each other in the wind.

Bill poured another and slid two quarters across the wood. The man made a gesture to him, and Bill nodded his thanks as he slipped the four bits into his apron pocket. "Where you from, stranger?"

"East."

"Well, son, we're in San Francisco, 'bout everything's east of here!" Bill laughed, but not quite as loud as the first time. There was something a little off about this stranger. Something about the way he talked, or didn't talk, or maybe it was just those eyes, the way they never stopped moving. Either way, this fellow wasn't quite right somehow, and Bill hoped he wasn't planning on staying long.

Audrey Reese hadn't taken her eyes off the stranger since he appeared in the doorway. And that was the right word for it—*appeared.* No one heard his boot clomp up the steps. Not a hint of a spur jingling announced his coming. There was no creak of a swinging saloon door to herald his arrival. One minute the doorway was empty, the next he was standing there, alabaster skin looking like it was carved from marble, not flesh. His perfectly black pants and coat seemed to absorb all the light from around him, as if a young gunfighter like him could just step sideways into his own shadow and disappear.

Audrey shuddered on the lap of Rich Spence, her current beau and the man sitting behind the biggest pile of bills, coins, and chips at the poker table in the far corner of the Double G, as the locals called it. *Goose walked over my grave*, Audrey thought as she tried to adjust her bustle so her movements wouldn't distract Rich.

"You okay, darling?" Rich asked. His voice rumbled deep in his chest, like distant thunder. She liked to lay against him when he talked, feeling that thunder peal across her face as he talked aimlessly in his deep voice. But now that voice had an edge to it, and Audrey looked down at her man. He caught her gaze and jerked his chin at the stranger by the bar. "You know him?"

"No, baby. He just... looked like somebody I used to know for a minute. But I don't know him at all." *Do I? He looks... But that can't be...*

"Maybe you need to go on over there and see what he looks like instead of squirming around on my lap like some little brat. I'm trying to work here." Now Rich's voice was hard, his words grating on one another like granite, and Audrey felt the fear blossom in her chest.

"No, Rich, baby. He's nobody. I'll just sit here and watch you take all these nice people's money." She flashed a smile at the two miners and one trapper who shared the table with Spence. The trapper had already lost most of his winter stake, and the miners were down to one small bag of gold dust between them. The bigger one, that Audrey had heard called Jeremiah, was fingering a stack of papers in his jacket pocket, and she hoped against hope he wasn't about to wager his claim against Spence. Rich Spence was a good enough poker player to take most everything these men ever owned or ever would own without any help, but when he put Audrey to work distracting his opponents, he could cheat like an honest-to-God magician.

There was a flash of black in her vision, and when she looked up, the stranger was just *there*. She woulda sworn he hadn't walked across the saloon to stand in front of the table. One minute he was at the bar, leaning over a whiskey like a respectable human being, the next he was right in front of her, standing there with a handful of five-dollar gold coins.

"You got room for one more?" He asked, and that sandpaper voice crawled down Audrey's spine like a spider, sending another shiver through her.

Crack! Spence's palm slapped her on the butt, hard. "Woman, I told you to sit still or get gone. Now what's it going to be?"

Audrey shrank in on herself, becoming very small and still on Rich's lap. "I just want to sit here with you, Rich, baby. That's all. I'll be good, I promise."

Rich smiled, an oily grin that never reached his empty blue eyes. "You do that, honey, you be good and we won't have any problems. But you keep that tight little ass still or I'll have to teach you how to be still. Now you don't want any lessons tonight, do you, sweetheart?"

"No, Rich. I don't want any lessons, please. I'll sit still."

"Good." Rich turned his attention to the stranger, who stood motionless over the table, his hat obscuring his eyes and the upper part of his face from the table. "Now, stranger, you want to play some poker? I believe we might be able to accommodate you. What do you think, boys?" Rich unleashed a wide grin on the table that made him seem like the affable gambling buddy instead of the man who'd been cheating them out of their very livelihood for the past six hours.

The miners both nodded and scooted their chairs over, while the trapper stood up and said "You can have my seat, friend, but watch his hands when he deals." The trapper pushed past the stranger and headed for the door, his last few dollars clenched tight in his fist. The newcomer pulled Matthias' abandoned chair out from the table and sat, every motion smooth as glass, almost like he didn't have any bones in his body whatsoever.

"Matthias?" Spence called from his seat.

The trapper stopped. He slowly turned to face the gambler. "What, Spence?"

"Tip your hat to a lady when you leave the table, you mannerless cur." Spence's voice was cold and low, but it cut through the bustle and music of the bar like the crack of a whip.

The man called Matthias stiffened at the insult, but he nodded to Audrey and tipped his coonskin cap. She gave him a polite nod, and Matthias turned to go.

"Matthias?" Spence called again.

Matthias turned to find Spence standing beside his chair, Audrey staggering back from being dumped off the man's lap. Spence's coat was brushed back over his hip to show off the mother-of-pearl grips on his Peacemaker. Matthias looked down at the gun, and at Spence's hand dangling beside it.

"W-what you want now, Spence?" The trapper asked.

"It seems to me that you might have felt that I wasn't dealing fairly as we played cards. That hurts my feelings, Matthias, to think that you would accuse me of being a cheat. And to do so right here in the Grin, where I do most of my work. Why, that might be considered in some circles as downright insulting. And I don't appreciate being insulted."

"I didn't mean nothin' by it, Spence. I's just mad on account of I lost and now I got to go back up in the hills and git more pelts instead of spending some time with Miss Audrey's girls like I had planned to do this winter."

"But is that my fault, Matthias? Is it my fault you gambled with money you couldn't afford to lose? Is it my fault you aren't the poker player you thought you were? Is it my fault you are too stupid to quit before you are flat damn broke?" The gambler had taken a step forward with every sentence until he was right on top of Matthias.

The trapper looked up at the tall man, his eyes darting about for an exit. "No, Spence, that ain't your fault!" His words tumbled out quickly, like a stream babbling over stones and skipping over syllables.

"Then why in the world would you call me a cheat?" Spence's hand rested on the butt of his forty-five.

Matthias looked around the bar as if for help, but all the other patrons were very studiously not looking at him or Spence. Just as he drew a breath and steeled himself to clear leather on the gambler, a voice came from the table.

"You gonna play cards, or you gonna kill that man? Whatever it is, I wish you'd get on with it. I'm bored." The grating sound of the stranger's voice cut the silence like a bullet through flesh.

Spence cocked his head to one side and turned, very slowly, to face the stranger. His hand never left the butt of his gun. He looked at the stranger like a dog examining a bumblebee, trying to figure out where the noise was coming from. "Did you... say something, stranger?"

"I told you to get on with whatever you were about. I came here to play cards, not to watch a floor show. And if I'm going to watch a couple of jackasses dance around a saloon, I hope at least one of them has better tits than y'all."

Spence stared at the man, now seated at the table with a stack of gold coins in front of him. He stood there unmoving as a statue, eyes locked on the stranger's own grey orbs. Neither man blinked for a long time, then Spence threw back his head and laughed. It was a big laugh that broke the room free of its stillness. "God-*dammit* that is the funniest thing I've heard in a coon's age! Bill, you grinnin' idiot, bring us another bottle! We got a *gambler* in the house tonight!" He stomped back over to his seat at the table, swept his coat over the back of the chair with a flourish that both drew attention to his fine clothes and let him keep his gun swinging free, and sat down.

"Matthias!" Spence called, patting his knee for Audrey to sit.

The trapper turned. He was almost at the door and hadn't looked back since the stranger spoke. "Y-yeah, Spence?"

"You watch your goddamn mouth next time. You ever call me a cheat again and I'll shoot you right here at my poker table."

The trapper nodded, turned, and half stumbled, half ran out the swinging doors. Spence turned his attention to the new arrival.

"Well, howdy, stranger." Spence stuck out a hand. The pale man just stared at it and after a long moment Spence dropped his arm. "My name's Spence. Richard Spence. You got a name?"

"Yup."

"You care to share it with the table?"

"Let's play cards."

"Well, I like that!" Spence said, slapping his leg. "Come on over here, Audrey. Don't you like a man who gets right down to business?"

"I do, Rich. I like that." Audrey sat down on his leg, but her eyes never left the newcomer. She couldn't see his eyes under the wide brim of his black hat, but she thought that she could feel his gaze on her, measuring, judging somehow and finding her wanting. She didn't enjoy that feeling, that sense of not being quite good enough for this smooth-walking stranger with the gravelly voice, but she wasn't quite sure why it bothered her so.

"Let's play cards, he says." Rich grinned as he reached for the deck. "Let's play cards indeed."

The pale man's hand flashed out, quick as a blink, and he snatched the deck out from under Rich's grasp. "She deals," he said, never looking up.

"You don't trust my dealing, stranger?" Rich glared at him.

"I don't trust anybody," the man replied. "She deals, and she sits there." He pointed to a chair exactly between himself and Spence, a chair currently occupied by the smaller of the two miners, a man called Morris who fidgeted like his chair had bugs, or he did.

"Morris is sitting there," Spence said.

"Morris has lost enough for one night," the man said. "Right, Morris?"

Morris looked from Spence to the new man and back again. Audrey could almost see the moment when he decided his money had a better use somewhere else. He gathered up his last few gold nuggets and a couple of loose coins and shuffled off over to the bar, where he ordered a whiskey in a shaky voice and very quickly commenced to forgetting all about the pale man in the back corner.

Spence turned his attention to Jeremiah, the last remaining gambler from his original game. "What about you, Jer? You decided I've taken enough of your money for one night, or you gonna throw down the deed to that claim you been fiddling with for the last half hour?"

Jeremiah opened his mouth, but a ten-dollar golden eagle flew across the table and spun down in front of him. "Jeremiah is going to join his friend at the bar and drink until he's blind while we get down to business. Isn't he, Jeremiah?"

Jeremiah glared at the stranger and opened his mouth to speak, but then he caught sight of the man's eyes. The big miner blanched pale and grabbed the coin, along with three nuggets and a depleted sack of gold dust. He stood up, shoved his gold in his pockets, and tipped his hat to Audrey. "I think it's about time for a drink. You two have fun." He turned and headed over to the bar. Smilin' Bill set a shot glass down in front of him and filled it to the rim with amber liquid. After the fourth shot Jeremiah stopped seeing the pale man's eyes.

"Now we got that all settled, we can play cards," The pale man said.

"You ran all the easy money off the table, mister. How do you plan on making a profit now?" Spence grinned around a cigarette.

"Since you done took everything they got, I figure now I'll just take everything you got." A slow smile crept across the man's face as he slid the deck across the felt to Audrey.

"Stud poker, nothing wild. How's that grab you?" Spence asked, tossing a dollar coin into the center of the table. "Ante's a dollar."

The pale man didn't speak, just nodded to Audrey and tossed a dollar to clink against Spence's. Audrey dealt a card to each man facedown. Spence peeled up the corner to see his card, the ten of clubs. He looked across the table at the stranger, but there was nothing to see. The man gave nothing away, no hint of whether he had an ace or a three. Audrey dealt the first face-up card, a Jack of spades to Spence and an eight of diamonds to the stranger.

"Jack bets," Audrey said, with the calm manner of a woman who has sat at many card tables.

Spence threw out a dollar. "Just a dollar," he said. A little feeler bet, to see if the old boy liked his cards or was going to be pushed around. The stranger barely took time to breathe before he tossed a dollar back out, calling the bet.

Audrey dealt out the next card, a nine of spades to Spence and a five of hearts to the stranger. "Jack is still high," she said, motioning for

Spence to bet or check. He tapped the table, indicating he checked. The stranger checked behind, giving nothing away. Spence chewed the inside of his lip a little — this one wasn't going to make it easy on him. The fourth card came down, a ten of spades for Spence to show a possible straight and possible flush, but really giving him a pair of tens.

"Jack bets," Audrey said, motioning to Spence, who already had money in his outstretched hand.

"Five dollars," he said, dropping the coins onto the table one at a time with a *clink*.

"Call," said the other man, tossing a single coin into the pile. Spence studied his opponent but still saw nothing. He nodded to Audrey, who dealt the last card face-up. Spence showed the Queen of spades, filling the flush if he had a buried spade, filling the straight if he had a King or an eight underneath, but leaving him with just a pair of tens. The stranger caught a five to pair his board, and the action went to the high hand.

"Pair of fives bets," Audrey said, motioning to the newcomer.

The pale man tossed out another five-dollar coin, and Spence looked hard at him.

Spence stared at his unmoving opponent. What was he holding? There were a lot of hands that beat him here. A five in the hole made trips, but would he have stayed on every street fishing for trips? Did he catch two pair on the river to sink him? What did he have under there, and was it worth a call to find out? Spence's head went back to something his Granddaddy told him when he was a little boy learning the game at his knee. "The worst thing you can ever do, tadpole, is call a bet. You want to play poker, you bet or you raise. But men don't ever call."

Spence grabbed up five five-dollar coins and shoved them forward. "Gone cost you more than that to bluff me, stranger," Spence said with a grin as he leaned back in his chair.

"I never bluff," the stranger said as he slid four golden coins into the center of the table. He turned over a five of spades for trips and leaned forward, looking dead at Spence.

Spence took his cards, turned them all facedown, and flung them over to Audrey. "You got it, stranger. Good hand." He tapped the table in a show of respect and anted up a dollar for a new hand. The stranger raked in the pot and slid a dollar into the middle, then flung a dollar to Audrey.

"That's for you, dealer," he said, with one corner of his mouth tweaking up just a hair. Audrey caught the dollar in midair and slid it into the purse on her hip. She smiled and nodded at the stranger, then dealt the cards. The men played poker for hours, neither gaining a significant advantage over the other. Some hands the stranger would come out ahead, some hands Spence would find himself raking in double handfuls of golden dollars. They had long since foregone using chips to keep track of their bets, preferring the jingle of real currency and the pain of real loss on their opponent's face.

The sun was peeking over the low horizon when Smilin' Bill wandered over to the table. "You boys going to finish up anytime soon? I'm thinking I might shut her down for a few hours before we have to go again tonight."

"Bill Evans if you don't get away from this table right this second I swear to God I will shoot you in the face," Spence growled. "Can't you see we got us a pot here?" There was indeed a sizable pot building, and quite the run of cards. Spence had a three, four, and a five showing, with a deuce in the hole for an open-ended straight draw. The stranger had three spades up, with one of them the King for a high flush draw. The bet was on Spence, and his once-mighty stack of coins and bills had dwindled over the course of the night until he was sitting behind less than a hundred dollars in cash and the small sack of gold he took off Jeremiah so many hours before.

"I reckon I'm gonna bet it all, stranger," Spence said as he shoved the rest of his money and gold into the middle of the table.

Audrey took a minute to count it all out. "One hundred six dollars and three ounces of gold, comes to one hundred sixty-six dollars."

The stranger stacked his coins and slid them into the middle of the table. "That's one hundred fifty dollars," he said. Then he twisted the wedding band off his pale left hand and placed it atop the tallest stack of coins. "There's almost an ounce of gold in that ring, so if you'll agree, we can call that even."

Spence looked at the pile of coins and gold in the middle of the table, more money than he'd ever seen at one time, and nodded at the stranger. "That'll be good, partner. Audrey, deal the river."

Audrey flipped over the last card for each man and slid it to him. Spence's card was the Ace of spades, making his straight. The stranger's card was also a spade, this one an eight for a flush if he had a spade buried.

"Well, friend, it seems like this was not your lucky night," Spence said, flipping over his deuce to show the five-high straight.

"I reckon it wasn't at that, but it wasn't yours, either," the stranger said as he turned over his hole card. Spence's eyes went big and he flew out of his chair as he saw the card, the Ace of spades.

"What the hell is going on here, son?" Spence shouted. "How long you been cheating me?" He pointed to the table, where two Aces of spades lay next to each other.

"I ain't never cheated you, Richard Spence. Not like you've done so many men for so many years, but I ain't cheated you. I ain't the one dealin' the cards." He picked up the deck of cards and flipped them over one at a time. Ace, Ace, Ace, every card was an Ace of Spades. Every card was Death.

Spence turned to Audrey, who was on her feet and backing up. "What is this, Audrey? Is this some kinda trick? Who is this man? What are you playing at?"

"I swear I don't know, Spence! I ain't never seen him before..." Her voice trailed off as her own eyes went wide and all the blood drained from her face. She stood, staring at the stranger, who was on his feet and for the first time since he walked into the bar, not wearing his hat. His cold blue eyes were set deep in his brow, and his dark hair was cropped close to his head. But it was the scar that ran through his left eyebrow that held Audrey's eyes. The scar he got when...

"Ashley?" She whispered.

"It's me, darling," the stranger rasped.

"But they killed you," She said, her voice quavering.

"I got better," he replied. "You know me now, Richard Spence? You recognize the scar you gave me when you shot me? You recognize the man you cheated at cards, then murdered him and forced his wife to run with you and steal from these poor dumb bastards all over California?" He ran his fingers along the puckered line of flesh that crept through one eyebrow and arced back over his head to disappear into his hairline.

"What do you want?" Spence asked, his hand brushing the handle of his pistol. "I killed you once, you son of a bitch, I can do it again."

"This ain't about you, Spence. You can go to hell for all I care. I'm here for Audrey. It's time to go, darling."

"She don't go anywhere without me, and you don't go anywhere with my money, you cheating bastard!" Spence's hand dropped to his gun, but he staggered backward before it ever cleared leather. The stranger drew and fanned the hammer twice quicker than lightning.

Whitley 15

Liquid red roses bloomed across Spence's vest. He collapsed into the chair behind him, and stared up at the newcomer with dying eyes.

"Ashley!" Audrey ran to the pale man, who staggered as she wrapped her arms around him. "Are you all right?"

"I'm fine, honey, but you have to go now."

"What do you mean, go?" Audrey bit her lower lip and her jaw quivered a little. "Can't I stay here with you?"

"No, darling, because I'm not staying. Spence is gone, and this place is going soon. We have to go. Do you trust me?" His voice lost some of the rasp and when Audrey looked up into his eyes he was almost the man she married again.

"I trust you," she said, her eyes brimming with tears. "I'm so sorry, Ashley. I never…he tried to make me, but I wouldn't…I only ever loved you."

"And I only loved you, darling. Now go." He closed his eyes, placed a hand on her head, raised the other to heaven and chanted, "On behalf of this woman, who cannot speak, I beseech you clear her passage into heaven and allow her to ascend to sit beside her husband Ashley, who has waited patiently for many years. Glory, if you're listening, please cut the red tape for this one. She's a good lady and deserves a little help." His hand flared with white light, and when he opened his eyes again, Audrey was gone.

The pale man turned to Spence, who lay bleeding out in the chair. Spence looked up at him and laughed. "You ain't Ashley Reese. I killed that poor bastard."

"You're right, I'm not. I'm just a man who put on his wedding ring to do a job. And now his wife's spirit is free. And you? You can go to hell." With those words, the man's right hand flared with a red glow and power streaked from him. Crimson energy flooded the room, and Spence was gone. The pale man looked around, nodded to Smilin' Bill, and walked out the swinging doors into the sunrise.

"You okay, Harker?" The words jolted me the rest of the way back to my time, my reality, and my crappy little kitchen. The taste of the desert was still in my mouth, and the Charlotte humidity made it suddenly hard to breathe.

I jerked my hands off the table, and stared at the woman across from me. She was pretty, but not my type. I prefer them a little more broken, and with less baggage than me. Cassidy Kincaide missed on both fronts.

Besides, she hung out with some unsavory characters. But she was cute, though…

Perv, came the accusatory thought from somewhere outside my head. I rolled my eyes and told Detective Rebecca Gail Flynn, member of Charlotte's police department and sometimes hitchhiker in my head, *So screw off.* I blinked a couple times to get the last of the Old West out of my eyes, or my Sight at least, and pointed toward the fridge. Cassidy, a brilliant and talented woman, or at least a woman who'd spent more than five minutes with me, understood my universal signal for "beer" and grabbed a couple of Sam Adams seasonals out of the door. She popped the top on the edge of my counter, guaranteeing me another lecture from Ren when he came over to make sure I had food and toilet paper later, then she handed one beer to me and sat down across the table.

"How did it go?" she asked.

"I managed it. It wasn't easy, but I got it done. They're clean." I waved my hand at my scarred Formica kitchen table, where an antique Colt Peacemaker and a wedding band rested on a velvet cloth. "How did you know they were haunted?"

"I don't know that they were, until recently," Cassidy replied. I cocked an eyebrow at her and she laughed and went on. "I've had that wedding band for years, and it never showed any signs of any possession or even a particularly interesting history. Until recently."

"When the gun came in," I supplied.

"Exactly. Once the two pieces came in proximity to each other, strange things started happening."

"Makes sense," I said. "The woman tied to that ring had a serious hate on for the man who carried that gun. He murdered her husband and basically made her his slave until she caught him with his guard down one night and killed him in his bed."

"That sounds pretty justified to me," Cassidy said.

"Me too, but her ghost didn't see it that way. She felt like she'd betrayed her husband somehow, and only he could forgive her."

"So how did you get her to move on?"

"I forgave her."

"But you weren't her husband. Or were you?" Cassidy asked.

"I'm not that old, Kincaide. So no, I was never her husband. But she didn't know that." I drained half my beer in one long swallow, trying to get my voice back to normal.

"So you lied to her." I didn't have to look at her face to see the disapproval I knew was there. I just stayed focused on my beer. I'm used to disapproving looks from women, regardless of species.

"I lied to her, and now she's at peace. For me, that's worth it."

"I guess so. Anyway, thanks for this, I appreciate it." She gathered up the ring and the gun and put them into an oversize purse.

"No worries," I said, draining the last of my beer before I walked her to the door. "And Cassidy?" I asked as I opened the door.

"Yeah, Q?" She stopped at the top step and turned around.

"Tell that vampire buddy of yours he owes me one."

GRASPING RAINBOWS

DIANA PHARAOH FRANCIS

THE WOMAN KNOWN ONLY AS GRAY NEFF GATHERED EGGS FROM BEHIND her weathered log house. The chickens showed her the way, their hard blue eyes glistening like marbles, talons scraping furrows in the soil. They gave some of their bounty, and they saved some. For their generosity, Gray bartered neels, the yellow seeds she gathered from the twisted trees across the wall where no one in the settlement went. No one but her.

She set another of the brown-striped eggs in her basket. Each was the size of two fists together, the shell nubby as an orange rind and just as thick. Her fingers lingered on it, delighting in the bright warmth.

Cold and fog dawdled in her little hollow at the back corner of the settlement. The hulking trees of what the elders called the Baneful Forest crowded close, scraping at the protective boundaries the Wardmen had drawn around the Pride. A stone fence of piled rock marked the line between civilization and the wilds beyond. Gray liked the moss-furred trees with their strong, spreading branches and snaky roots. Often she sneaked over the wall to walk beneath the canopy, taking solace in their majestic silence. She liked the soft bed of plants and leaf mulch under her feet and the twitters and calls of the world beneath the canopy.

Her presence at the edge of the settlement softened the protections. Soon the Wardmen would come and strengthen the boundary spells as they did every month, all the while glaring at her from beneath the stern black crowns of their hats. As if she were to blame for eroding their spells. As if they didn't demand she live here, a bastion against magical attack.

Did they discover her forays into the forest, they would chain her to her stoop. They would say this proved the madness they suspected. Already an unnatural woman and recalcitrant neff, they would say she must be kept like an animal.

Gray shuddered as she thought of Denniel Proctor. Young, talented, charismatic — all the women of Wallaceton Pride fawned over the handsome sorcerer. He made Gray's skin crawl. His haughty arrogance was boundless, and he hated her. He hated that she did not lick his boots like the others; he hated that she didn't offer her body to his lust, as neff were obligated to do. After all, the magic had stripped her of her womanhood. Her womb a useless husk, she had no virtue worth protecting. There weren't enough women in the frontier, and single men had needs. It was an unwritten law of all the frontier settlements that neffs fulfill those needs. Gray had other ideas. She had no intention of becoming Proctor's whore or anyone else's. She no longer had a right to marry, nor could her womb catch seed, but that didn't mean she would be any man's pleasure doll.

Every day, Proctor grew more demanding. She did not think he would force her — his magic was useless against her, and the law protected her from rape. She was too valuable to the settlement. All the same, he was crafty as a snake. Thanks to him, fewer and fewer people of Wallaceton Pride came to her with their ailments. Fewer and fewer offered her food and goods that could be obtained only in town. She'd have gone and traded for herself, but she was bound to this place, to her job of protecting the settlement from hostile magic. Except for when the Pride sent trade wagons to the other settlements or to Boundary, she was tethered.

If not for her eggs, she might see no one but Proctor for weeks. Even Silla didn't come often. Her sister's husband, Elbi, had never liked Gray, but Proctor had stirred his dislike into hate. Now he kept his wife close, refusing to let her visit. Sometimes Silla sneaked away, but she didn't like deceiving Elbi. She didn't like having the lie on her conscience. It made her an unnatural woman. God might take his revenge on her, as he had on Gray, and turn her womb to dust.

A noise caught Gray's attention. At first she thought it was one of the jackdaws bringing treasures from the forest in exchange for a neel seed. They had a way of talking that she could almost understand. But no, this was a woman's voice, low and frightened. Silla.

Gray frowned and returned to her back porch. She went inside, setting the basket of eggs beside the others in the kitchen. It took up most of the house, except for a cozy bedroom. Three smooth plank tables ran the length of the east wall beneath a wide window. Rocks, plants, bark, and a variety of bottles, tinctures, grind stones, bowls, knives, and spoons littered the sill. Beneath was chock full of buckets and basket, all mounded with her harvests. Along the south wall were cupboards and shelves, a sink, and her massive iron stove. In the center of the room was a massive table that might have sat fifteen people around it, had Gray chairs enough. She had only four.

Shelves of crockery and preserves lined the walls on either side of the west-facing window. A doorway just past led off to the lean-to on the north side where Gray stored her garden tools and root vegetables, and aged her cheeses. In one corner was her privy. Up at the front of the house in the northwest corner was her bedroom, and beside it in her kitchen was her front door.

"Silla?"

Her sister had not come inside. Gray went to the front door and raised the bar. Foreboding itched in her chest and she picked up one of the loaded flintlock pistols she kept on the shelves just within. Swinging open the door, she eyed the open area in her front yard.

When Wallaceton Pride first was settled, the townspeople had picked where the neffs would live, built their houses, and then cleared the trees and rocks to give them space to grow things. They'd each been given breeding goats and chickens. In time, those had changed, as did most things on the edge of the settlements. Her chickens laid all through the year, and her goats gave milk even when the blizzards turned the world white.

It was spring now, and green sprouts pricked the tops of her carefully hoed rows. Grape leaves unfurled from bare vines along the arbor wall. Gray caught sight of Silla. She stood beneath the apple tree, screened from the road by the line of blood berry thicket. She waved frantically at Gray to join her.

Gray crossed the broad porch and strode through the open garden gate. The animals knew better than to go after its bounty. At the other side, she stepped up onto the stile.

"Hurry!" Silla called in a whisper.

Gray's sister had dressed in a brown poplin dress buttoned up under her chin. Her blonde hair was pinned firmly up on the back of her head and covered with a straw bonnet. She wrung her apron in her hands.

From her vantage point on the stile, Gray cast another look around her yard, and beyond to the road. The dirt was a pale scar through the greening of the land, disappearing over the brow of the hill. Pink-blooming plum trees ran along either side, blocking Gray's view of the fields beyond. Silla lived a mile west on the other side Heppler Hill. Elbi had a pretty piece of land close by the river. He grew potatoes, corn, turnips, and beans, and kept an acre or two of grapes to make wine. He ran a few head of cows and pigs for the meat, and had started breeding horses.

"I don't have much time," Silla called. "I don't want Elbi to miss me."

Gray's frown deepened, but she did as bid. Much as she resented Elbi's hold on her sister, she wouldn't risk anything that would keep Silla apart from her more than she already was.

"What's wrong?" she asked.

"I came as soon as I could," Silla said. "Elbi only told me last night."

Foreboding itched harder. "Told you what?"

"About the neffs they brought from Cromton Pride. They arrived last night."

"New neffs? What for? The town already resents the five of us." All told, Wallaceton had five neffs. Gray, Peach, Rose, White, and Red. The Elder board had assigned them names and homes, reminding the women they were a burden to be borne and only their immunity to magic made them valuable enough to keep on. They must now serve and be grateful for what they were given.

Of the five, Gray's protective immunity from magic was greatest. She was called to ride with the trade wagons when they went out. It would take two other neffs to match her.

"It was Deniell Proctor's doing," Silla said, and though she was angry, her voice softened on his name. She was no more immune to his charms than the rest of Wallaceton Pride. "The Elder board says you're more trouble than you're worth. They plan to have a tribunal to prove you aren't behaving proper. Elbi says they may banish you. Or bind you."

Gray grasped hold of her fury before it could explode. She swallowed it. "When?"

"Soon as can be. They put out the elder summoning, and sent for Wardmen from Agleyton Pride and Biston Pride. They come today.

Comton Pride sent Wardman Nevering along with the neffs. Elbi expects they'll meet tonight and call a settlement meeting in the morning. He says you won't even get to speak your piece. Gray, what're you going to do?"

Gray. Like everyone else, her sister never used her given name. They'd grown up together, come to the frontier with their parents as budding young women, close as fingers on the same hand. Within a few weeks they caught the frontier sickness. Everybody did. It made sorcerers of some men, witches of a few women, and some it made neffs. Most it left alone, except sometimes for giving some people scales or moss for hair. Those were killed. Same as the witches. Neffs were suffered, but not welcomed. Their parents had died within a year of settling their homestead. Mamma caught wet lung and Pa had got carried away by a spring flood. A year after that, Elbi took Silla to wife and took her homestead rights, too.

Silla clutched her sister's arm. "Gray? You've got to bend to them. You've got to show them you can be obedient. Dress in skirts instead of trousers. Speak softly. Be pliable like they want." At her sister's scowl, Silla pressed harder. "What if they send you out into the wild? Think what the savages would do to you." She shuddered, tears running down her cheeks.

To Silla, there was nothing worse. But she was wrong. Binding was worse. Chained, Gray's body would no longer her own. Men would paw her, driving their shafts into her, rutting like beasts. Whether Gray bent to the elders or not, she would have to spread her legs for any unmarried men who sought her out. Silla would prefer that to what the Elvim might do, should they capture Gray. Gray would rather risk the wild.

She blinked away the burn of tears. Denniel Proctor was behind this. Her teeth gritted together. She gave a nod, making a decision. "All right."

"All right, what? What are you going to do?" Silla whispered. "Gray, please! I can't lose you. You've *got to* bend."

"Silla, you know what will happen if I do. And you know Elbi would never let you see me if I became the settlement whore."

"He doesn't let me see you now." Silla slapped her hand over her mouth.

As if Gray didn't already know. She embraced her sister. "Don't worry. I can manage myself." Neither the elders nor Proctor could keep her out of Wallaceton Pride. She'd visit Silla whenever she wanted.

Loosening her arms, Gray gently pushed her sister away. "Best get back before Elbi knows you went missing."

Silla dashed at the tears running down her cheeks. "Marien—"

"No!" She said the word more sharply than she intended. She wasn't Marien anymore. For Silla to remind her now—it was cruel. She gentled her voice. "I'm Gray. It's all I'll ever be. Best not forget it. Now go on with you."

"But—"

"Before Elbi misses you," Gray reminded her. Elbi had been known to use a switch or the flat of his hand to lesson his wife in proper womanly conduct.

Silla closed her eyes a moment, then nodded. She grasped Gray's hand tightly. "Promise you'll take care of yourself."

Gray nodded, her throat knotting. If not for Silla, she'd have no one. Her sister pulled away and dashed off, picking up her skirts to run faster.

Returning to the house, Gray considered. If Silla was right, she had perhaps the rest of the day, possibly until morning, before they came for her. That gave her time enough to move what she needed into the forest. They'd come hunting her, she knew, but that troubled her little. She knew the forest and she wasn't afraid of it.

She started packing her things. She gathered clothing, bedding, and personal things. Not that she had many. When she almost had more than she could carry, she lifted the packs over her shoulders and headed through the back.

The stone wall marking the spell boundary dividing the settlement from the forest stood only five feet tall. Gray took the weathered wood ladder she kept hidden beneath a bush and leaned it against the wall. Stepping up, she dropped her packs over. She lifted the ladder to the other side. Best to hide her things out of easy sight.

A hundred yards or so into the forest was a ravine. A massive tree had fallen over within, leaving a shallow cave where its roots had been. Beneath the tree's stem, animals had hollowed out a den, then abandoned it. Gray clambered down and hid her packs within.

She was scrabbling back up over the top of the ravine when someone grasped her collar and flung her into the air. Her breath exploded from her as she landed. Her left arm made an ominous cracking sound and pain streaked through her. She gave a whimpering cry, rolling onto her back and clutching her arm against her chest.

"What do you here?"

Above her a man towered. No, not a man. Elvim. Even in the dimness of the sun-dappled shade, she could tell he was not human. He stood as tall and broad as Proctor, but that's where the sameness ended. His crow-wing hair was pulled up in a topknot and hung to his waist in thin braids. His pale skin was faintly blue like skimmed milk. He wore a scaled vest and close-fitting trousers that revealed every curve of his muscular body. Like his lips, his fingers were blue, fading to white as they met his palms. Beneath each pointed fingernail was a poison gland. Neffs were immune to it. Marring his austere looks were ugly purple-black boils that pocked his brow, scattered along his cheeks and chin, bunched around the corners of his lips, and fled down his neck.

"What do you do here?" The Elvim pushed on her hip with his boot as he repeated his question.

Gray sucked in a breath as pain speared her arm. She sat up, wishing she'd thought to bring a flintlock. Not that it would have done much good. Elvim didn't die easily and he'd caught her unawares.

That's when she saw the Elvim wasn't alone. Another, a boy by the looks of him, lay across the clearing. Boils bubbled thick over his skin from head to toe, most of them seeping black fluid. His chest jerked as he fought for breath. His mouth hung open, exposing white teeth. On each side of his upper jaw, he had a pair of dangerous fangs. The forward one grew straight and razor sharp. The one behind curved like a wolf's tooth.

Gray's attention returned to the man standing over her. He started to kick at her again.

"Stop that!" she snapped, slapping at his booted toes. She should have been afraid. Maybe she would have been, had the elders not been about to tear her life to shreds. Now she was merely angry.

He blinked. "What do you do here, *rocha*?" His lip curled into a sneer on the last word.

Rocha was the word Elvim used for settlers. Gray didn't know what it meant, but it wasn't anything good.

"What's the matter with you? Are you ill?" Stupid question, though perhaps they'd rubbed up against a poisonous plant. Some were known to cause such sores.

He scowled and sneered at the same time. "Do you answer my question. What do you do here beyond your walls?"

"I am not beholden to you," she retorted, struggling to her feet. "Your people don't claim the great forest. What I'm doing here is none of your business."

A smile curled his thin lips. Like her chickens, his eyes were a hard, marble blue, but he had slitted pupils. Fast as a snake, he gripped her neck, his talons pushing dents into her skin. A hair more pressure and he'd poison her. If his poison worked on neffs, which it didn't. It didn't matter. He had strength in his hands, enough to snap her neck if he chose.

"No one claims the great wild. It is not for your kind," he said, bending close to her and drawing a long breath through his nose. He licked her skin just above her collar.

Gray jerked away from the intimate touch, fury and embarrassment burning her cheeks. The Elvim allowed her to back away, touching the tip of his tongue to his top lip. She scrubbed the wet of his lick from her skin with her knuckles, eyeing him warily. She didn't want to be scared, but she was. More than with Proctor. With the Wardman, she knew what he wanted and his weak spots. She'd thought of ways to stop him. The Elvim was unknown, but his tongue on her neck demanded the things Proctor wanted and the way he'd effortlessly tossed her, she doubted if she could stop him. Fear quickened her breathing and quivered in her knees.

Something caught his attention. He flung his head up and twisted, listening. Gray heard nothing but the chirp of birds and the scuttle of critters through the trees. The Elvim's expression sharpened. Moving almost more quickly than she could see, he crossed the clearing and scooped the boy in his arms. He turned as if at a loss for which direction he should run. For he was running. Gray read that in the taut line of his body and the set of his shoulders. She saw her fear mirrored in him.

"Who is hunting you?"

He stiffened and flicked a glance at her and away, dismissing her.

Gray licked her lips. A reckless idea took her. She needed help — with her arm broken, and she was sure it was, she could not escape her house with her things. The Elvim could splint her bone and help with the fetching and carrying. He could hide in her house for a few hours or the night.

"If you help me, I'll help you. You can shelter in my house."

His jaw slackened and his eyes widened. Gray didn't wait for an answer. Instead she started back up the hill to the ward wall. She didn't hear him follow. She chewed her lower lip. What could she do now? One handed, she could do precious little to escape or defend herself from the binding.

Nonsense, she told herself. She'd carry what she could to the wall and push it over, then haul it to the tree. If the elders showed up before she was done, well didn't she have two good pistols already loaded? She wasn't going to bend for Silla or the men and she wasn't going to be chained.

She wrestled the ladder up against the wall with her good arm, pain in the other making her eyes burn with tears. She refused to let them fall. Sniffing, she lifted her chin and climbed up, trying not to jostle herself more than necessary.

"We cannot cross."

The Elvim's voice startled her. She jerked around, her heart thundering in her chest.

"The magic is strong. I cannot pierce it alone."

"Don't worry," Gray said. "You don't have to."

She leaned her hips against the wall, steadying herself with her good arm. She lifted her leg over and straddled the wall. Sweat rolled down her neck and she shuddered with a strange cold. Fear maybe, or pain. Didn't matter. She had work to do.

Her presence on the wall made a breach in the spell boundary. She wasn't sure how wide. Enough for her companions, she hoped. The Elvim scowled when she waved him up. He hesitated. The boy moaned and his breath rattled in his mouth. Abruptly the Elvim jumped up on the wall beside Gray.

"I'll need the ladder. Set the boy against me and I'll steady him for you."

He snarled as if the thought of her touch was contemptible, then squatted, resting the boy over his knees. With a liquid movement, he picked up the ladder and tossed it over. It cartwheeled all the way to the porch. Gray sighed. Jumping down was going to jolt her arm something fierce.

"Best get down before I do," she told him, resolving not to get angry. She needed his help. The Elvim obeyed and she swung her leg over and slid down to the ground. As expected, fiery pain roared up inside her. She leaned against the wall and cradled her arm to her stomach, breathing deep until it passed. Then she straightened and led the way into her house.

The chickens gathered around. Several pecked at the Elvim's booted calves and feet. He ignored them.

"You can put him in the bed up front, if you want," she said, stepping aside so the Elvim could enter.

He looked into her room and then laid the boy on the table. Gray pumped water into a bucket and scooped it up in a cup. She offered it to the Elvim. He took it and lifted the boy, helping him drink. More than half dribbled down his front. His tongue was swollen, and his mouth was full of the boils.

"What happened to you two?"

Fury swept the older Elvim. He grabbed the front of her coat in his fist and slammed her against the wall. "You know. You did this. You *rocha*." He spat the last word.

Pain turned the edges of Gray's vision black. She kicked at his stomach, then braced her feet on his shoulders and shoved. He didn't move. He was a boulder of muscle, stronger than any human man she'd ever seen.

"I don't know what you're talking about," she said, panting. Breathing hurt. "Looks like you both got the wrong way of a devil plant or ate something you shouldn't have. Maybe a sickness."

"A magic sickness," he said, eyes slitted with rage. "It attacks my people. Those it touches die. We are hunted to keep us from giving it around."

"By all that's holy," Gray whispered. She believed him that her kind had brought such an illness. The Wardmen had long chafed against the settlement limits. They wanted more lands — Elvim lands. But the Elvim outmatched the settlers in strength and numbers. The only way to fight them would be something like this.

"You have sorcerers. Surely they can cure you."

"They study, but we die before they find answers." Pain twisted his face and he abruptly let go, returning to the boy's side.

Gray crumpled to the floor, chest and throat on fire. The Elvim bent and spoke in the boy's ear, stroking his forehead with gentle fingers. He loved him. Was the boy his son?

She could help them. The moment he'd said it was a magical illness, she'd known what to do. Why should she? The Elvim had broken her arm and probably a few ribs. If he learned that swallowing her blood would cure the illness, he'd drag her back to his people. They'd chain her up and harvest her blood. If she survived, they'd use her in their war against the settlers. If not, they would know to steal the neffs. Her life would never be her own again.

Or she could let the Elvim die and become Proctor's whore.

Leaving was no longer possible. Maybe with a broken arm, but never with damaged ribs. She'd not survive the wild lands. She wasn't even sure she could get over the stone wall. She wasn't without an escape. She had herbs that would end her life. Death or servitude and torture. No matter what she chose, her life was over.

She wasn't willing to let Proctor have her. Was she ready yet to die? What did life have to offer her but pain and humiliation?

The Elvim would take her into the wild lands. She longed to see more, to go beyond where she'd explored. Her heart longed to see its vast strangeness. Was that reason enough to live?

She didn't know.

Gray scooted around onto her knees, leaning on her right hand. By the god of rainbows, she hurt. Taking a shallow breath, she rocked herself to get enough momentum to stand. She bit her lips against the pain. Then hands slipped under her arms from behind and the Elvim set her on her feet.

"Thank you," she said.

He studied her, his brow furrowed. "I did not mean to cause you hurt."

"Lucky for me you weren't trying, then," Gray said, taking another cup and dipping it full, wincing as she leaned her hip against the counter. "You did a fine job." She nodded her head toward the boy. "He's your boy?"

The Elvim's face hardened. "He is."

"How old?"

"Thirteen seasons."

"What about his Ma?"

He shrugged, then stepped toward Gray, raising his hands. Blue magic wreathed his fingers like smoke. "I can mend you."

It said a lot of his power that he could call that kind of magic so close to her. Proctor couldn't. Or maybe it was because she was wounded, and that weakened her immunity. She had no idea. Not that he could actually heal her up. She was neff.

Gray opened the drawer beside her and drew out a skinning knife. The Elvim halted, raising his brows.

"I mean not to hurt you."

She tipped her head, curious. "You already have. Besides, you hate me—my people."

It startled her when he looked down. His cheeks flushed with blue, then his sharp gaze met hers. "It was carelessly done, and you have shown kindness."

Selfish kindness. She remembered the girl she'd been before coming to the settlement. She'd been joyful. She'd taken pleasure in aiding others. As neff, she'd resented it. Resented the settlement's disgust of her, the way they demanded her sacrifices like they had a right to them.

She looked at the boy. She could do a true kindness. Be better than what the homesteaders thought her to be. Be better than she'd been for a long time. She could take pride in saving the Elvim. She could give herself freely to them.

Give herself, unowned, unchained. Her choice.

That was surely worth the price of her life.

She pushed away from the sink and limped over to the table. The boy shuddered and trembled. The Elvim man followed her, his eyes fixed on the knife. She had no doubt he could snatch it from her before she could do any harm to the boy. Not that she planned to harm him.

Gray held the knife out to the Elvim. He took it, his brow furrowing again.

"Cut me," she said, holding out her right thumb. "Deep enough for blood to flow."

He didn't move, didn't speak. His eyes narrowed as if he doubted her sanity.

"I can't do it cleanly with only one hand. Do you want to see your boy well?"

His body jerked. "Well?" he echoed.

Gray took advantage of his confusion to reach over and slide her thumb along the blade. Her skin parted, a larger cut than she'd wanted. She hardly noticed the pain. She held her thumb above the boy's mouth and dribbled her blood in his mouth.

The Elvim dropped the knife with a clatter and snatched her wrist. She fought him, but even whole and healthy, she was no match for his strength. He jerked her away from the table.

"What are you doing?" he demanded, grasping her shoulders and shaking her hard. "Answer me!"

Gray's head snapped back and forth. She sagged in his grip as the pain overwhelmed her. Before she could fall, he slid his arm around her waist and despite herself, she leaned against him.

"He won't die," she said. "Neither will you. Not if you take my blood."

He went still. "I don't understand."

"I am neff. Magic can't touch me. If you take my blood, it should stop the disease."

For a long moment, he was silent. All Gray could hear was the oddly patterned thud of his heartbeat, and the squawk of the chickens on the porch. Then slowly the Elvim lifted her hand and touched her thumb to his lips. His mouth closed over her flesh and his tongue stroked her skin. Gray trembled. No man—no one at all—had every touched her so intimately. It was terrifying and yet strangely wondrous. If the settlers could see her now, they'd stone her. Even Silla. He licked her again and sucked gently. Gray gasped, willing herself to hold still, though everything inside her told her to run, to hide.

Abruptly he pulled away, his chest rising and falling as if from great exertion.

"How long?" he rasped.

"I don't know."

His son shrieked and convulsed. The Elvim twisted away. He barked something that could have been the boy's name. He gathered the boy in his arms, murmuring and stroking his head. The boy keened like a wounded animal, shuddering and shaking, his heels beating the table.

The Elvim stiffened, his arms loosening as his back arched backward. His face contorted. He dropped to one knee, his son thudding back down to the table. Gray scooted around to the other side, holding the boy steady as best she could. Already she could see the boils shrinking. His breathing had deepened and the rattling had eased.

Across the table, the Elvim gouged his fingers deep into the wood, holding himself upright. Waves of pain rippled over his expression one after another, but he made no sound.

Gray started when a hand closed hotly around hers. She looked down and met the boy's wide-eyed gaze, then went further to their entwined hands. Blue and sun-browned skin. The boy's head turned and he caught sight of his father.

"Konal," he said, letting go of Gray to clasp his father. "Konal," he said more urgently, then said more, liquid sounds that made no sense to her.

She watched them a moment. The Elvim wasn't as sick as his son. He collected himself, a brilliant smile breaking across his face as he grabbed the boy in a tight hug. Gray smiled, too, her chest swelling. Tears pricked her eyes. No matter if the elders and Wardmen would call what she'd done betrayal or treason or even deviltry. She'd done a good thing. Her womb could not give life, but she'd managed all the same.

The cacophony of squawking chickens warned her. They didn't like the elders, but they especially didn't like Proctor. Out the window, she caught sight of him. He had turned off the road onto the path leading to her house. He was alone. Gray's jaw hardened. She went to the front door. She put one of the pistols under her hanging left arm and picked up the other, then opened the door, shutting it firmly behind her as she stepped out onto the porch.

Gray waited on the top step, watching Proctor's approach. Like the Elvim, he was tall and broad. His hat shadowed his eyes, but his mouth and square jaw were set and forbidding. In one hand he carried a chain.

The chickens swarmed him, pecking and flying at him, He whacked one out of the air and swore when another gripped his upper arm and flapped, shredding his sleeve. Two more knocked his hat askew. He swung the chain. It whistled, thudding against the black bodies. Feathers exploded in the air and chicken bodies rolled over the ground.

Proctor lifted his left hand and sketched arcane symbols in the air. They glowed a pale yellow. Gray's lip curled and she hurried down the stairs. He saw her and his hand worked faster. She broke into an awkward run, her broken ribs sending porcupine quills through her chest. She was ten feet away when the symbols faded to nothing. She grinned at the fury and fear that swept his expression. After all, what was he without his magic? Just a man. A mean, cruel, ambitious man who enjoyed hurting her.

The Wardman's hat had fallen, vanishing beneath the chickens. They'd tear it to bits and shit all over it. Gray's smile widened. He loved that hat.

"Call your animals off," he demanded.

"What do you want?"

"Silla didn't warn you?" he asked, brows rising. He shook his head. "Elbi was sure she'd run off to tell you. One last time." He smiled unpleasantly. "She's about to get lessoning on obeying her husband in all things."

Gray bit her tongue until it bled. She couldn't help Silla. Her sister would have to find her own way. She lifted her pistol, leveling at Proctor's chest. "I'm not going with you."

He laughed. "Shoot me and you'll be stoned to death. Is that it? Would you rather die?"

Before she could answer, he leaped forward and knocked her arm up. The pistol discharged and fell. He grabbed the other one and flung it away. His broad hand slammed against her breastbone. She stumbled backward. Her heel caught on a rock and she tumbled, landing hard. Pain seared her arm and ribs. She yelped once, then gritted her teeth to keep from showing any more weakness.

Proctor bent to pick up the chain he'd dropped and came to stand over her. At the ends of the links dangled two leg shackles. He bent, catching one of her feet. She kicked to no avail.

"I wasn't sure if I preferred that Silla would convince you to behave yourself or if I wanted you to keep fighting," he said, tugging on her boot. He dropped it on the ground along with her sock. He slid the shackle over her ankle. She kept struggling, making it difficult for him to close it. "I confess I look forward to making you bend to me." He smiled at her. "It will be my pleasure."

She didn't hear the Elvim. Neither did Proctor. A blue hand closed around his throat, lifting him and throwing him against the side of her house. He crumpled to the ground. The Elvim followed. The boy squatted beside Gray, his forehead furrowed as he gently touched her cheek. His skin was nearly clear now.

By now the Elvim had grasped Proctor by his collar. He held a knife in his other hand, the same one she'd used to cut herself with. Gray didn't try to stop him, but only watched as he drove the blade into Proctor's forehead. It was just, Gray thought. The Wardman was a cancer in the settlement. Killing him wouldn't cure anything, but it might help the other neffs. It might help Silla.

The Elvim came to help Gray stand. She listed to the side to ease the pain in her ribs. The Elvim scowled.

"Thank you," she said.

"Your people would chain you," he said, and she could hear the question in the statement.

"I'm a neff. They don't like me much," she said. "I... don't fit." Vague, but true enough. "Now that Proctor is dead..." She gave a lopsided smile. "Let's say they won't be wanting to chain me now." They'd stone her dead. "Anyway, I knew they were coming for me. That's why I was in the forest. I was trying to escape."

"You would live in the wild?" His brows rose.

"I like it," she said simply. She wouldn't say that she felt a vast presence there, one that welcomed her. He'd think her mad. Not that it mattered what he thought. "But I won't survive it like this." She gestured at her left arm and ribs.

The Elvim folded his arms over his chest and scowled at the sky. Gray gingerly bent to retrieve her sock and boot. The boy made an apologetic sound, snatching them up and handing them to her.

"Thank you," she said. She gripped them tightly in her good hand. She needed two hands to pull them on.

She didn't know how to suggest that they should leave soon. She didn't know how long before the elders and other Wardmen would come looking for her and Proctor.

The elder Elvim rattled something off to his son. The boy hesitated and glanced at Gray, then nodded and returned to the house, shutting the door behind him.

The Elvim looked down at her a long moment. Gray couldn't read anything about what he was thinking. Suddenly he dropped to his knees, taking her sock and gently pulling it up onto her foot. She set her good hand on his shoulder for balance, hissing at the sparks of pain the movement caused. A moment later he pulled the boot on. She stepped back, expecting him to stand. He did not.

Gray didn't know what to think. What did he mean? She fisted her good hand inside her pocket.

"You saved my son. For that alone, I would serve you forever." He closed his eyes and when he opened them again, they were full of regret and dreadful guilt. "I must take you back to my people. Many are ill." He shook his head. "I can never earn forgiveness for such betrayal of your gift to me, but I will —"

Gray held up her hand to stop him. "I knew you'd take me when I gave you my blood. You needn't feel bad. It only makes sense."

He flinched as if struck. "Feel *bad*?" he repeated hoarsely. "I damaged you. Then I steal you from your home, from your people, and demand you give your blood. For such evil I should be flayed and left for the animals to gnaw the flesh from my bones."

Oddly, Gray found she wanted to comfort him. "It's no different from my life here," she assured him. "They keep me because I'm useful to the settlement. I'd rather give blood than— Well, it's no different," she said again, not letting herself think of what Proctor had planned for her. "Better even."

If anything, her reassurance only infuriated him more. He spat out words she did not understand. Breathing deeply, he collected himself. When he looked at her again his eyes glowed faintly, like the blue flames inside a hot fire.

"I will not permit you to be harmed more than necessary," he vowed. "Though nothing I do will ever equal what you have already given me, I will spend my life repaying the debt."

Gray shook her head. "You don't owe me. But if you want to give me something, you could show me the wild. I'd like to see some of it."

He stared a moment and then laughed, the sound harsh. "You ask little enough. Hardly worth the life of my son."

"It's what I want," she said tartly, irritated at his laughter. "Besides, nothing's worth the life of family. I wouldn't put a price on it."

He sobered and nodded. "That is truly spoken."

"All right then. If it's settled, I'd like to gather a few more things. My arm needs a splint and we should probably bandage my ribs up tight."

He frowned again. "I would heal you if I could."

She shrugged. "Well, you can't, and that's that. If you could, I couldn't have helped you and your son, so no sense regretting it."

He stared at her for a long moment and finally nodded. He rose to his feet. Finally. Gray didn't like him on his knees, not in front of her. She wasn't due that kind of thing. After all, if the settlement had been a kinder place, if Proctor hadn't been so loathsome, she might not have helped the Elvim.

She glanced at the Wardman. His eyes stared blindly. Flies had already started to settle on his wound. The chickens ignored him, circling her and the Elvim, pecking the ground. It appeared they liked him well enough.

The Elvim followed her glance. "What are these creatures?"

"Chickens. Of a sort. They changed when we brought them to the settlement. Like me. I've got goats, too." She tipped her head at him. "I don't suppose I could take them along with me?"

"If you desire it."

He said it simply. Gray blinked at him. She'd expected refusal. He held out his hand.

"Come. Let me care for you."

She stared at his outstretched hand. Let him care for her? What a curious thought. She met his gaze and read kindness there. And... respect.

Hesitantly she put her hand in his, feeling like she was reaching for rainbows and half-expecting him to pull away or slide a chain around her wrist. Instead, he smiled at her. It wasn't arrogant or cruel or pitying or scared. It was friendly and warm. His fingers closed around hers.

"You may trust me. I will not hurt you again."

And even though she knew his people would cut her for blood, she believed him.

THE FAERY WRANGLER

MISTY MASSEY

MÉMÉ PULLED OUT THE CARDS BEFORE DURANGO FINISHED HER EVENING tea. She let her own cup go cold, paying all her attention to shuffling and laying out different spreads, commenting under her breath before shuffling the cards and doing it all over again. Durango lit the lanterns as the shadows of night filled the corners of their tiny home, and still Mémé concentrated on her *tarau* cards. The old woman turned a card and laid it on the table with a sharp snick. "Ah, *ma petite...*" She patted the chair next to her. "Come, sit."

"I'm sorry, Mémé. Tell me about it in the morning. There's work to be done," Durango said, strapping her leather belt tightly around her waist. If she didn't get out on the hunt soon, she'd miss the clouds of faeries that always gathered around the glowstones on Reedy Creek.

"This one, it spells your destiny," Mémé said, her dark eyes clouded with worry.

"Does it say my destiny will be to catch a dozen faeries tonight?" Rain the last two nights had put her behind on her agreement with Katy Holder, the woman who owned and ran the general store in town and sold the faeries she trapped. "How about if I promise to gather a basket of honeysuckle for you just before dawn? It'll be sweet with the morning dew, just the way you like it." Durango reached up to the low rafter where her ash wood hoop and faery cages hung. She dropped the hoop into her pack, and tied the cages to her belt with a strip of cotton. "Where are the candles for my sparkle wheel?"

The old woman shrugged her shoulders. "You leave your toys all which-a-ways and I should know?"

"It's not a toy," Durango grumbled. Although Mémé was right—it was a toy. It was a painted wheel as wide across as her open hand, with a dozen flat metal paddles affixed to the outer edge and a square of tinder paper attached to the long metal rod it hung from. When a lit candle was placed below it, the wheel would spin, and the paddles rubbing against the tinder paper created silver sparks. It was the kind of thing town boys would buy to celebrate whatever war they were most proud of their ancestors winning. She'd spent good money on it some months back in town. Katy claimed she'd gotten it from a Chinese sorcerer, and that it would bring good luck. Durango wasn't sure about the luck, but it definitely attracted faeries when she lit it. Digging in her rucksack, she located the candles. Only two left, but that would be enough for tonight.

Her tiny lantern was on the hearth where she'd left it, but Mémé stepped in front of her, waving a card in her face. "I beg you seat yourself and listen, *ma belle*. Or does you want to have an argument be the last words between us?"

Mémé reached out and took Durango's brown hand in her own, darker one. She always insisted that their parting words be loving and kind, in case they were the last they ever shared. Durango loved the old woman like she would her own grandmother. Mémé had been the first to arrive the night Durango's parents were murdered, holding Durango's father in her arms while he breathed his last. She'd made him a promise, to keep his child safe. She gave up a life of power and comfort in New Orleans in order to spirit the baby away from danger and into the frontier. In sixteen years, she'd never once complained about it. Durango sat down. "I can spare a few minutes for you, Mémé."

The card lay face-up on the table, waiting for her. Mémé's *tarau* were hand-painted and featured symbols that were personal to Mémé herself. This card displayed a long, delicate hand reaching out from the card, a purple-stone ring encircling the middle finger and the skin dark as night. Behind it ran a stream of bubbling water over an otherwise desolate wasteland. Mémé stroked the card, then tapped it three times.

"Someone, he offer you a choice. He likely don't let you know what you truly getting 'til the deed be done."

"He? A man, Mémé?" Durango rolled her eyes.

"This card, it don't speak of romance, *ma petite*. It's a warning. Beware the man you meet. Accept nothing from him, not his hand, not his belongings."

"I'm not afraid of a man, Mémé." She patted the knife she always carried strapped to her leg.

Mémé pushed herself up from the table, and walked to the pantry cupboard. Opening the door, she began rummaging in its depths, emerging moments later with a small bag. "Take this."

"What is it?"

"Sea salt. I brought it with us from New Orleans. You feel a trap closing around you tonight, you pour this on the ground, and come home to me."

"Pour perfectly good salt on the ground?"

"Do as I say, *ma petite.*"

Mémé had been a priestess and a practitioner of magic in New Orleans before the war, but she was cautious out here on the prairie. The war might be long over, but dark faces remained rare and suspect to the white settlers in town. Other than reading the cards, Mémé never did anything that couldn't be explained. That didn't stop her from telling Durango all sorts of fantastical tales. Sometimes she spoke of the *loa*, supernatural beings that granted their believers power. Other times, it was the fae, who lived under a mountain somewhere but took walks in the real world to entertain themselves with unwary humans. Mémé had more warnings about the fae than Durango could possibly remember. Not that she believed any of it. How would salt be able to rescue her from any sort of trap? If she chose to argue the point, she'd be even later getting out onto the prairie, and there were faeries to trap. She smiled, and took the bag, tucking it into her rucksack.

"I'll be home around dawn, Mémé. I'll take great caution around any gentlemen I might meet tonight. And when I come home, I'll have your honeysuckle with me."

The old woman threw her arms around Durango, embracing her with an unusual strength. "See that you do."

Durango hefted her sack onto her shoulder, lit the tiny lantern, and headed for the door.

"Remember what I said," Mémé called. Her voice was strangely shaky, as if she was holding back tears. Durango looked back and smiled.

"I'll remember."

The prairie was quiet under the stars. Some nights the wind tossed and blew, filling her ears with the rush of rustling grass and sending the faeries to ground, but tonight was peaceful and perfect. The stars shone in the cloudless dark above her. A sliver of quarter-moon offered just enough light that she hardly needed her lantern to find her way. If she hadn't waited too long, the faeries would be gathered around the glow stones that always fetched up on the banks of the creek. They only kept their shimmer for an hour or two after full dark, and the faeries loved to flock around them. If the glow had gone out by the time she reached the creek, she had her sparkle wheel to attract her prey.

The little creatures everyone called 'faeries' were about the size of moths and they shone bright with a light of their own. They had arms, legs, and faces like people, with delicate, lacy wings on their backs, and needle-sharp teeth that stung like a wasps' sting if a human hand came too close. Pretty though they might appear, they were dreadful pests. Faeries swarmed light sources, whether lantern flame or glowstones, their tiny voices chiming like faraway bells as they flitted around each other, shoving and pushing to get closer. They'd been known to stampede cattle herds when the cowhands' cookfires attracted them, and more than once they'd accidentally set barns blazing when a farmer left his lantern wick too tall. The townsfolk had learned to plant primroses in boxes below their windows or screen their doors with rowan leaves to keep the faeries from coming too close. It had been Mémé who suggested catching them in cages woven of ash wood, to provide light for their little cabin after the sun fell. As long as they were fed and cared for, they were no danger inside their cages.

Durango hadn't considered catching and selling them until one afternoon in the general store. Katy Holder had noticed she wasn't buying nearly as many candles or lantern oil, and demanded to know why not, so Durango explained. Katy had tossed her red-gold hair and walked away. But the next week, when Durango returned to town for supplies, she discovered that Katy had tried to catch a few faeries herself, unsuccessfully. She'd told some of her white customers, who wanted faeries of their own. Since Katy had caught nothing but a few nasty bites from the little creatures, she suggested a partnership with Durango.

They'd been in business together for almost a year now. It was a lucrative arrangement, and she'd nearly earned enough to purchase two train tickets to New Orleans. Mémé wasn't getting any younger, and whatever danger had threatened them so long ago, surely no one remembered now. With any luck, she'd be able to take them both away before another winter.

Off to the west, she caught sight of a dancing glimmer. Faeries. And right about where the creek bed ran, so she wouldn't need to light her wheel. Shuttering her lantern to protect the flame, she took to her heels, running softly through the knee-high grasses, slowing to a careful walk when she was a few feet away. She dropped to a crouch, setting her lantern to her side and letting the grasses hide her.

A soft glow illuminated the edge of the creek, and above it danced a cloud of faeries. There had to be forty of them, all whirling and spinning around each other. The water gurgled and the faeries chimed, in a natural music. She'd never seen such a flock and for an instant, wondered if this was the trap Mémé had spoken of. Faeries bit, but they had no venom, and the injuries they inflicted weren't usually more than an annoyance. This many, though...could they do enough damage to harm her? It was a risk she'd have to take. The likelihood of seeing this large a flock ever again was too low.

She reached into her pack and withdrew the ash hoop. All she had to do was sweep the hoop through the flock, gently enough not to strike any of them. For some reason, ash wood confused faeries. Close exposure to it sent them spinning in slow, tight spirals, as if they'd been surrounded by an invisible bubble. Moving slowly that way, she'd be able to open the top of the little ash cages and capture the addled faeries before they regained their senses. She'd catch as many as she could, and thank her good fortune while the rest flittered away. She licked her lip and took a breath.

Something knocked into her shoulder, sending her sprawling in the grass. She'd lost her grip on her hoop, but she couldn't look for it now. The faery flock rose in the air and zipped away from their fading glowstones. Twisting her legs under her, she scrabbled to her feet and dropped into a defensive crouch, letting her hand slip down to the knife on her thigh.

A man stood near her, breathing hard. He was taller than most of the men she knew in the town, thick-bodied and broad across his shoulders. His black hair was drawn up and stiffened into a scalp-lock that looked like a horn. Shadows blurred his features to her eyes, but the scalp-lock told her he was Pawnee. The biggest Pawnee she'd ever seen. He extended his hand to her. "Are you injured?"

"No," she said, keeping a cautious distance. "You speak English?"

He shrugged, and let his hand drop. "You speak Pawnee?"

Whitley 15

She shook her head. Brushing her hands against her britches, she stood straight. "Why'd you knock me over?"

"You were getting too close to the *ahki*. They bite."

"You saw me with cages and an ash hoop, and you still thought I was too witless to avoid being bitten?" She snorted. The glowstones that attracted the faeries had lost their light, and the faery flock was scattered. She'd have to set up her wheel, and there was no guarantee the faeries would even fly back this direction after such a scare. "You've saved me, now go away."

"I think I'll stay."

"I'm in no danger. Never was. And I have work to do."

He crossed his feet and sank gracefully to the ground. "What sort of work does a girl do, alone in the dark?"

A spark of anger flashed in her belly. Was he trying to imply that she was a whore? Just because she was a girl, or because she was darker-skinned than he was? She drew a breath, calming herself. "I'm a wrangler. I catch the *ahki* and sell them in town." She watched him, but his face betrayed no emotion. He was bigger than she by a huge margin, but she was quick, and she'd happily slice open a hole in his chest before he could kill her.

"I made a mistake, then."

"You did. I won't hold offense about it."

He didn't look like he was in any hurry to leave her. "I want to see what a wrangler does."

This couldn't be the man Mémé had worried about, could it? Somehow she'd imagined some white cowboy, on a drunken ramble over the prairie. But a Pawnee...A sparkle caught her vision, and she glanced past the man at the creek. Faeries. They must have found another glowstone. If she could light her wheel and draw them back, she might still have a successful hunt. She swung her pack off her shoulder, and pointed at the man on the ground. "Stay if you want, but be silent and don't move."

He nodded, not speaking.

She pulled the wheel out of the pack. Standing the main rod against the dirt, she pushed it down until the wheel stood, suspended. With her thumb she dug out a small hole for the candle to stand in, opened one of the shutters on her lantern and inserted the candle far enough for its wick to catch. She placed the candle in the hole under the wheel, and waited.

Slowly at first, then gaining speed, the paddles turned, scraping against the tinder paper with a soft snick. As they sped up, sparks popped from the paddles, tiny stars that burst and vanished before the eye could even focus on them.

"What does that do?" His voice was the barest whisper. She should have guessed he couldn't stay quiet.

"Attracts the faeries. The *akhi*, as you call them. Now be quiet."

A flash, then another, then a tiny cloud of them rose from the banks of the bubbling creek. The faeries had noticed. They'd be coming to investigate. Durango set a cage on the ground next to her, and gripped her ash hoop. Time seemed to stop as she tried to keep her eyes on the glimmering flock drawing near. They swooped and dove, approaching as if following a curving mountain path. The wheel spat sparks into the night. Just when Durango thought she'd go blind from staring, the faeries swarmed her wheel. Their delicate chiming voices filled the silence, and the faeries tried to fly round and round in time with the wheel. Now was her chance.

Durango rose from her knees, leaning forward and reaching out with the hoop. She swept it slowly past the flock, then turned it to draw them up. The tiny creatures slowed, spiraling together in a long chain leading up from the spinning wheel. Durango dropped the hoop, opened the cage and, turning it upside down, trapped the slowed faeries inside before securing the lid again. She raised it to her face, and smiled. Eight little faeries, with drunken smiles on their faces. Not the treasure haul she'd expected before, but it was a start.

"That is wrangling?"

She sighed, for a moment having forgotten the strange man sitting across from her. He didn't seem to intend any harm, but she'd had enough of him being around. Blowing out the candle, she tipped it to let the melted wax run off before packing it away again. The wheel stopped spinning, the sparks gone. She latched the cage back onto her belt and packed her wheel away before picking up her lantern. "Yes, that's wrangling. And now that you've seen it, you can go."

He stood up. "I'm Táraha'," he said, as if he hadn't understood her words. "Means 'buffalo'."

"Named for a buffalo, but stubborn as a mule," she muttered under her breath. "Nice to meet you, but I have to go."

"Aren't you going to tell me your name?"

"Durango," she said, moving toward the creek. If she was lucky, she could find the rest of that huge flock from before, but only if she could rid herself of the man.

"But that's not your real name, is it?"

She stopped, suddenly aware of her heart thudding behind her ribs. She'd chosen to call herself Durango after seeing the word in a dime novel Mémé used to teach her to read. Mémé always said never to share her real name, and no one in sixteen years had ever asked. Until now. Despite the knife at her side, Durango felt as vulnerable as a newborn kitten.

Táraha' was nearer than he had been, and now he was smiling. A predatory smile, one that sent chills through her. She took a step away, and he followed with one forward. "It's not only the ash that traps the akhi, you know," he said. "It's the wielder, her intent. Only someone with a certain innate ability can use ash that way. Did you never wonder how you came by the skill?" He reached out his hand, his fingers long and delicate, and stroked her cheek lightly. Glittering sparkles followed the path of his fingers. "You're born with it. It's a gift from your mother. And I can tell you who your parents are."

She shivered. Mémé had never told her their names. Too dangerous, she insisted, even now all these years after they'd died. "You can?" she whispered in a ragged hush.

The night was just as dark as it had been, but now that he stood so close to her, his features were clearer to her eyes. The scalp-lock had been a disguise—he wasn't Pawnee at all. He wasn't any tribe she could name. His face was sharply angled, and his eyes were the color of clouds before a storm. They seemed to glow in the dark, transfixing her.

"Do you want to know these things I can tell you?" He spoke as intimately as a lover might, and her body relaxed under the silk of his voice.

"I do."

As she said the words, she heard a whisper in the far reaches of her mind, urging her to stop looking at the man, to run home and lock the doors. It sounded like Mémé's voice, and for an instant she remembered Mémé warning her about something. She wasn't sure what the warning might have been, though, and the desire to know the truth about her parents spoke louder.

"I can answer questions you don't even know you want to ask yet. Your father and the old woman, they have kept you hidden from your birthright for too long."

"My father is dead," she said, and as the words left her, she knew they were wrong.

"Your mother is dead. Your father is not," Táraha' said. "He lives. He searches for you. Isn't that nice?"

Her father was alive. Had Mémé known? Surely she wouldn't have kept Durango from her father if she knew he was searching. Then again, she'd lived in the same place all her life. How could her father be searching for her all this time and not find her?

Táraha' reached behind his back, and brought out a small loaf of bread. He broke off a chunk, and offered it to Durango. The scent wafted toward her, warm and rich as if it had only just come out of the oven. A lick of steam rose from it, and her mouth watered.

"Share my bread with me, little one," the man said, "and I'll be able to tell you everything you've ever wanted to know."

His eyes glowed as if reflecting the fire of her sparkle wheel. She stepped forward, ready to take the bread he offered. His hand seemed surrounded by light, the same way her tiny trapped faeries did. But he was too big to be like them. Then again, a moment ago she'd believed he was a Pawnee man named Buffalo. What kind of people could trick the eye into seeing whatever they wanted?

The whisper in the back of her mind roared suddenly into her hearing. 'Accept nothing he offers' Mémé had said, her voice clear as if she was standing next to Durango now. Durango knocked the bread away. Instead of falling, it exploded into sparkles that floated away into the dark.

"You will come with me, girl," he snarled, grabbing at her with both long-fingered hands.

Durango danced back, swinging the pack off her shoulder and flipping it open. The bag of salt seemed to come to her hand as if bidden.

Táraha' jumped at her again, missing her by inches. "You're a child of great people, and you belong with them."

"I don't think my father agreed with you," she said, working the laces on the bag of salt. A fingernail caught in the laces and pulled loose, the pain making her hiss. She yanked on the lace and freed it at last. She pulled the bag open and flung the salt at him just as he leaped for her again.

He reared back, howling in surprise. Salt crusted his face, and he swiped his hand across his eyes to clear them. "You thought to stop me with—" he stopped, and looked down. "With salt—" he began again, and moaned. Slowly, he dropped to his knees, and began to pick up the impossibly small grains. "How could you know?" he said, his voice almost pitiful. Cupping one hand, he counted grains into it. He glanced up from his task, his cloud-colored eyes filled with rage. "When I finish counting these..." He dropped his head again, and returned to the task.

Durango backed away, reaching down for her pack as she watched the man scrabbling in the dark. He had to count the grains of salt, every single one, and he couldn't stop until he was done. She headed for home, walking backward and only turning away when she could no longer see his glow in the dark. Counting the salt would take him all night or longer. She'd caught a cageful of faeries, and that would be enough to please Katy Holder for a day. Most important of all, Durango's father lived, and others wanted to claim her before he could find her. She needed to learn more about the magic Mémé wielded.

But there was a patch of honeysuckle to harvest first. Mémé always did her best talking over a cup of her favorite tea.

HAVEN

KEN SCHRADER

"LOOK PA! A SHOOTING STAR."

Wyatt Porter hit the nail off-center, bending it sideways, and burying it in the roof of his house. He muffled a curse. "It's daylight, son. There can't be a shooting star."

"Wyatt?"

The note in his wife's voice made him look in her direction. Sarah stepped off the porch and walked to where their son was playing with his puppy. Both of them stared into the sky.

Wyatt turned and looked up. "What the hell?"

In the sky was a shooting star. Only it wasn't like any shooting star he'd ever seen. It looked like a ball of fire — and it was getting bigger.

Wyatt scrambled down the ladder. There was no mistaking it. Whatever was in the sky was coming closer. Sarah laid a hand on his shoulder. "What is it?"

"I don't know."

Sarah turned. "Little Wyatt, you go on inside."

"Yes, ma'am." The boy picked up his puppy and trudged into the house.

Smoke was coming off the tail end of the fireball, and there was a sound, like thunder, growing in intensity. Wyatt couldn't look away. The thought that it might crash down into his house flowed over him like a chill wind. Behind him, the horses in the barn snorted and stamped.

The sound of its passage grew to an ear-splitting roar that Wyatt felt in his chest. It streaked across the sky, something dark at the center of the flames. He covered his ears, shaking his head as if he could clear the sound away. Windows shattered and his horses whinnied in fear, kicking against their stalls.

The fireball headed in the direction of town and crashed down beyond his sight. He heard a hollow boom and a smoky-orange cloud billowed into the sky.

"Haven." Sarah's voice was barely a whisper.

Wyatt turned and ran into the house. Inside the door hung his gun belt and vest with his badge. He put them on. Sarah met him on the porch. "I'm not going to try and stop you from going, Wyatt Porter, just you remember to come back to me."

"I'll be fine." Wyatt kissed her, then leaped down the steps. "I'll see you when I get back."

"The hell you will. I'm headed to the Wheel. You'll be wanting a drink later."

Wyatt smiled, then ran to the barn.

Haven was in chaos.

Wyatt rode to the jail, townspeople battering him with questions from all sides as he hitched his horse. Jake McEvers, Wyatt's deputy, stood on the porch trying to calm the crowd. "Make way, folks." Wyatt climbed the steps and turned to face the town.

"Everyone calm down. I saw the same thing you all did." The crowd rumbled, but Wyatt raised his voice. "I don't know what it was either, but I aim to find out." He turned to Jake. "Saddle two horses." Jake nodded and disappeared into the jail.

Wyatt turned back to the crowd. "Whatever it was, looks like it hit ground around the Anderson farm." He scanned the crowd. "Doc, are you out there?"

"Here, Wyatt." A short, thin man threaded his way forward. Doctor Eliot Harper stood just a hair under five and a half feet tall which made him shorter than most of the folk in town.

Wyatt glanced in the direction of the farm. Thick, black smoke rose into the air. "Best grab your bag, Doc."

Doc Harper lifted a brown leather bag. "Way ahead of you."

Wyatt smiled. "Now, I'm going to need volunteers." Before he finished speaking, several men stepped forward. Andy Turner, owner of the general store, said, "I'll bring my wagon and as many buckets as I've got at the shop."

Wyatt nodded. "Thank you, Andy. Volunteers, help load up and meet us at the Anderson place." Jake returned with two horses. "The rest of you go on back home. We'll get to the bottom of this." The crowd dispersed leaving Wyatt, Doc, and Jake alone in the street.

Wyatt's eyes drifted to the rising smoke. "Did you see it?"

"I don't think anyone in town missed it," Doc said.

"What do you think it was?"

Doc crunched a piece of broken glass under his boot. "It was probably a rock from space. Broke into a thousand pieces when it hit."

"Maybe." Wyatt swung into the saddle. Doc and Jake got settled on their mounts.

Doc snorted. "You think we'll find something else?"

"Lord I hope not," Jake said.

Wyatt flicked the reins and they started toward the column of smoke rising steadily from the Anderson farm.

The smell of smoke filled Wyatt's nostrils. Behind him, Doc, and Jake rode in silence. When they got within sight of the Anderson farm, Wyatt stopped his horse. "Good Lord."

The barn had been knocked down like a toothpick house. Burning splinters of it were everywhere. John Anderson and his eldest boy, Matthew battled the flames.

"Jake, take the men and put out that fire. Doc, come with me." Wyatt kicked his horse into a gallop. At the house, he slid from the saddle and leaped onto to the porch.

"Mary? Are you in there?" He opened the door.

Mary Anderson ran into the room. Her face was covered in soot and streaked with tears. Two little girls trailed behind their mother. The smell of woodsmoke covered everything.

"Sheriff. Thank the good Lord. John and Matthew are — "

"I've got men helping them right now." Wyatt stepped aside. "Doc's here too. Are you or any of the little ones hurt?"

Doc slid past and into the room. "I'll take care of things here, Wyatt. They'll need you outside."

Wyatt walked across the yard to join the others, then stopped, staring. Beyond the barn, a great furrow dug into the ground. It was twice as wide as a wagon and it went on until the end vanished in smoke. He walked to the edge of the furrow and looked down its length. At the far end, he guessed that it had to be deeper than his six-foot height. Dirt had been thrown up and out for yards by the impact. He couldn't believe that a single rock could do this much damage.

Through a break in the smoke, Wyatt saw...something at the far end of the furrow. Before he could think better of it, he hopped in and walked forward.

Crumbling earth walls on either side of him rose up past his head. The smoke was denser here and he stumbled over rocks and roots. Eventually the smoke thinned and Wyatt stopped, his mouth gone dry. The thing at the end of the furrow was no rock.

"Damnation." Wyatt had never seen anything like what lay partially buried in the earth in front of him. His mind struggled to categorize it, to put some kind of meaning to the object before him. It was slick and streamlined. In places where the dirt had fallen away, gleaming metal showed.

What the hell is—

There was a loud hiss and a hatch opened in the side of the thing. Wyatt scrambled back as something long and sinuous pulled itself through the hatch and tumbled to the ground. It hit hard and lay still. Despite himself, Wyatt took a step forward, trying to get a better look.

The creature was covered in short russet fur broken by patches of blue skin. It staggered to its feet, leaning heavily against the metal. It was tall, taller than he was, with tiny ears, black eyes, and an elongated snout. It stood upright, thick legs flowing into an inhumanly long body. It reminded him of a weasel.

Wyatt fumbled his gun out and nearly dropped it. He pointed the shaking barrel at the creature. It shook its head, lost its balance, and dropped to one knee.

Wyatt lowered his gun. Whatever it was, it could barely stand on its own. It didn't look like it was armed either.

The creature raised its head. It reached out a single, long-fingered hand with three fingers that ended in short, sharp claws.

Wyatt felt a tingling in his head, then the creature uttered a single word. "Help."

It collapsed.

Wyatt holstered his gun and ran forward. "Jake!" He reached the creature and stopped, uncertain. Lord, it was big. And it had a tail? Wyatt had no idea what he was looking at, but it had clearly asked for help and he wasn't about to leave it lying in the dirt.

He heard footsteps overhead. Jake, Bill Cooke, and Bill's son, Jesse came into view.

"Mother of God!" Jake said.

"Go get Doc," Wyatt said. "Have Andy bring the wagon."

Jake gaped at the creature.

"What are you standing around for? Go!"

Wyatt looked at Bill. "I could use your help down here."

"What the hell is that thing, Wyatt?"

"I don't know, but we can't just leave it here."

Bill paused, looking uncertain.

"I'll help, Sheriff." Jesse slid down the side of the furrow. Bill frowned at his son then, grumbling, slid down and joined them.

It took four of them to get the creature up and onto the wagon. There was solid muscle beneath the soft fur. Wyatt's fingers brushed over the blue skin. It felt supple, like a snake's.

"Wyatt," Doc said as he approached. "John and Matthew have some burns that still need tending to. What's so blasted —" He made a choking noise and Wyatt turned.

"This might be more serious."

They covered the creature with a tarp and took it back to Haven. None of the men wanted to ride with it, and Andy didn't even want to drive the cart. Exasperated, Wyatt gave Andy his horse and drove the cart back himself. Townsfolk gathered as they rode into town. Jake and Doc waved them off, saying that the Anderson's were fine. Wyatt didn't slow, he wanted to get the creature into the jail before it woke up.

When they reached the jail, the three men half-dragged the creature inside and put it in a cell. Jake slapped a set of handcuffs on it and left the cell as quickly as he could. Wyatt turned to Jake. "Keep anyone from coming in here until I give the word."

"Yes, Sheriff."

Wyatt locked the cell door. He turned at the sound of his desk drawer sliding open. Doc bent over the side of the desk and came up with a bottle of whiskey. It rattled as he set it down.

Wyatt took the bottle from Doc's shaking hand. "It might need your help."

Doc looked at the creature. "Good God, Wyatt, what the hell is that thing?" He reached for the bottle.

Wyatt put the whiskey back in the drawer. "I don't know. But it asked for help and I aim to make sure that it gets some."

Doc's eyes grew wide. "It spoke to you?"

"Yes, it spoke to me." He'd never seen Doc this rattled before. "Now what do you think?"

Doc tried to compose himself and looked into the cell. "What do I think?" He turned back to Wyatt. "I think this is a creature from another planet. How can you be so calm about this?"

"Somebody has to be."

Doc scowled.

"You didn't see it, Doc." Wyatt turned to cell. "It couldn't even stand on its own. It looked right at me and asked for help. Then it collapsed." He turned back. "Do you think you can do anything for it?"

"I haven't the first idea how to treat it. I could very well do it more harm than good. I don't even know what *it* is."

"*It* is awake and can hear you."

Both men jumped.

Doc scrambled behind Wyatt's desk and put his back to the wall.

Wyatt turned to the cell. The creature watched him with those black eyes.

"Are you hurt?" Wyatt nodded toward Doc. "Doc's a bit startled is all, but he knows his stuff. If you need him, we'll get you patched up."

Wyatt felt a tingling in his head as the creature sat up.

"I don't need to be...patched up."

Doc took a step forward. "You speak English?"

Wyatt frowned. "Course it speaks English. You just heard it didn't you?"

The creature leaned forward. "I'm wearing a translator." It started to raise its arm and noticed the handcuffs. It cocked its head and sniffed the metal encircling its wrists. It spread its arms and the chain between the cuffs snapped with a loud metallic clink. Broken pieces of chain clattered on the floor.

Doc jumped back with a gasp. The creature raised its arm showing Wyatt a thin band nestled in the creature's fur. "You're hearing...what did you call it? English?"

"What is the tingling in my head?" Wyatt asked.

"What tingling?" Doc said. His voice rose in pitch. "Does that thing get into our minds?"

"The translator will request the definition of terms and phrases that do not directly translate."

"Oh God." Doc shook where he stood. "Oh good God."

Wyatt crossed the room. "Take it easy, Doc." He steered his friend toward the door. "Why don't you head on down to the Wheel, have a drink on me, and calm yourself down."

Doc swallowed once, nodded and left. The door rattled in its frame behind him.

Wyatt turned back to the cell. The creature was taking in its surroundings. "Where am I?"

Wyatt sat on the edge of his desk. "You're in Haven. My name is Wyatt Porter and I'm the sheriff here."

The creature furrowed its brow. "Sheriff..." There was a prolonged tingling in Wyatt's head. He wasn't sure if he was comfortable with that thing rummaging around up there.

"You are a peace-keeper."

Wyatt nodded. "That's part of it. I'm also the man to turn to when an alien crashes into town."

The creature's face fell. "Did anyone need to be patched up?"

"Nothing Doc couldn't handle."

Relief flooded its face.

"What about you?" Wyatt asked. "When you arrived, you couldn't even stand. You sure you don't need Doc to take a look at you?"

"I will be well. I just needed time to...recover."

Outside, Wyatt heard footsteps on the porch. A voice filtered into the room.

"Don't you stand in my way, Jake. I'm going in to see my husband and I will knock you down if I have to."

The door opened and Sarah swept in. "Wyatt, some of the boys said you found something strange out at—" She gasped, staring at the creature in the cell. Her hand went to her mouth and she took a step backward.

The creature bowed its head. "Ma'am."

Sarah straightened. She tore her eyes from the cell and looked at Wyatt.

Wyatt scrambled to say something that might make sense. "Sarah this is..." He trailed off, turning to the alien. "I'm sorry, but I never got your name."

"I am called Molidialamulus." The creature bowed its head again. "It is a pleasure to meet you, ma'am."

Wyatt blinked. "Molidia—"

"Moli," Sarah said.

Wyatt looked from the cell to his wife.

She smiled at him. "It'll be easier for you to remember." The smile vanished and she turned to the cell. "Ma'am is it?" She walked forward. "Moli, what are your intentions?"

He blinked. "Ma'am?"

She sighed. "Are you harboring any intentions to harm my Wyatt or Haven?"

Moli sat up straight and met Sarah's eyes. "No, ma'am."

She stared at him for several seconds, then nodded, reaching a decision. "Then I reckon we can get along. Welcome to Haven, Moli." She turned to Wyatt. "Come on down to the Wheel when you can. I'll have something warm waiting for you."

She kissed him soundly, then left. Wyatt watched the door close behind her in utter silence.

"I like her."

Moli sat with his teeth bared in what was probably a smile. "She reminds me of my mate. They have the same—" Another tingle. "Fire. You are a fortunate man, Wyatt Porter."

Wyatt glanced back at the door and smiled. He walked over to the wall and grabbed a ring of keys. Returning to the cell, he unlocked the door. "I reckon I don't need to keep you in here any longer." He paused. "Not that I think the cell would have held you considering what you did to the cuffs."

At Moli's puzzled look, Wyatt gestured to his wrists.

"Oh. Apologies for damaging—"

"It's all right." Wyatt fished a key out of his pocket and removed the handcuffs. He felt a surreal wave pass over him as he considered that he was standing in a jail cell with a creature from another planet towering over him.

Wyatt put the broken handcuffs on his desk. Moli flicked one of the iron bars with a nail and it rang.

"So what brings you to Haven?" Wyatt asked.

Moli cocked his head. "I thought you did."

Wyatt shook his head. "No, I mean what brought you here? To Earth."

Moli walked over to the rifle rack and sniffed it. "My ship was shot down by the Mor-Dalgar."

"The what?"

He ran a claw along the barrel of a rifle. "Mor-Dalgar." Wyatt's head tingled. "Organized criminals."

"You're a lawman?"

Moli nodded and Wyatt wondered if he put that bottle away too soon. "Are there more than your kind out there?"

Moli bared his teeth and walked to the desk. "The universe is teeming with life." He looked at the rifle racks and then at the cell. "Most of us are peaceful, but some are not."

Wyatt let out a shaky breath. "That doesn't sound much different than normal folk."

Moli laughed. "Exactly." The laugher faded. "And like your people, we have need of peace-keepers—sheriffs." He exhaled. "The Mor-Dalgar are dangerous and I fear that I may have led them to you."

Wyatt sat on the edge of his desk. Other aliens—dangerous aliens—might be coming to Haven. It was too much to process. Desperate, he latched onto what he could make sense of. There was another sheriff in town and he needed help. Wyatt could get behind that.

"We'll deal with them when the time comes." Wyatt stood. "How about we head on down to the Wheel and see what Sarah's got cooking for us?"

As the day drew on toward night, they headed back to Wyatt's house. Horses spooked whenever Moli got near one, but he was able to keep up on foot.

Little Wyatt was fascinated with the alien lawman, asking endless questions about his ship and the planet he'd come from. Moli endured the attention with good grace until Sarah and Wyatt shuffled the boy off to bed.

After that, the three of them each took a mug of beer out onto the porch. The night was warm and clear. Crickets chirped softly in the grass and stars filled the sky. The view always made Wyatt feel pleasantly small.

"How was your first day on Earth?"

Moli chuckled. "It didn't start out so well, but it ended with friends." He took a drink. "And this...what did you call it? Beer? And watching the night sky. A very good ending, indeed."

"Which one is yours?" Sarah leaned back in the rocker she shared with Wyatt.

Moli looked up. He hopped off the porch and walked backward. After a moment, he pointed. "There." Wyatt and Sarah came over to look. "See where those three stars line up? Look at the lowest one. There's a star just to the right."

"It's beautiful." Sarah's voice was filled with wonder.

"Looks like it's a long way off," Wyatt said.

Moli didn't speak for the space of a long breath. "Yes, a very long way off."

Wyatt reached up and put his hand on Moli's shoulder. "Will you be able to fix your ship?"

Moli paused. "Perhaps. With the right materials, it should only be a matter of..."

He trailed off. As they watched, a tiny ball of flame streaked across the sky. It disappeared over the horizon.

Twenty-four hours earlier, Wyatt would have called it a shooting star and forgotten it as soon as it passed. A lot had happened since then.

"That wasn't anyone looking for you, was it?"

"Impossible to say." Moli glanced at Wyatt. "I suppose we'll find out soon enough."

Early the next morning, Jake took Moli over to Turner's to help Andy move some heavy items. Wyatt was alone in the jail, sweeping. The front door was propped open and a warm breeze flowed through, mixing the smell of horses and dust with the fresher scent of grass and wildflowers.

Wyatt leaned the broom against the wall and stepped onto the porch. He inhaled deeply, enjoying the breeze. Then, he heard the sound of galloping horses.

John Anderson drove his wagon up the road at a breakneck speed. Matthew was up next to him and the rest of his family was huddled in the back. They raced into town preceded by a bad feeling that Wyatt felt deep in his guts.

Anderson hauled his team to a stop. His eyes were wild.

"There's more of them, Wyatt."

"Take it easy, John." Wyatt stepped off the porch. "Start at the beginning. What are you doing racing a wagon with your family in the back?"

He took a deep breath. "More spacemen. Come down this morning and landed in my fields." He looked over at Turner's. Moli and Jake were on the way back. "They weren't like him. They were tall and thin. Started poking around." He turned to Wyatt. "They was green." He made a visible effort to collect himself. "I didn't like the look of them, so I got the family and got the hell out of there." He paused. "Don't know if we'll be going back."

"Your family's had that farm for years," Wyatt said. "Come inside and Jake will see to the little ones. We'll talk this out."

"Sheriff." Jake pointed down the road.

Wyatt saw three figures moving toward the town. They were tall, half again as tall as he was and thick limbed.

"That's them!" Anderson snapped the reins and the horses took off. Wyatt took a hasty step back.

"Damnation." He scowled at the retreating wagon. The visitors were the light green of a new head of lettuce. They wore vests, exposing muscular arms, and dark green pants tucked into heavy boots.

Moli curled his lip in a snarl. "Mor-Dalgar."

Wyatt looked at him. "Get inside."

"Wyatt, you can't step into harm's way on my account. I—"

"You're not the law here. In." Wyatt steered Moli into the jail. Jake followed. When they returned, Jake had a rifle and Wyatt was buckling on his gun belt.

The street emptied as the Mor-Dalgar walked into town. They each carried a long, thin tube that reminded Wyatt of a rifle barrel.

Wyatt stepped off the porch and faced the three visitors, his hands hooked into the loops of his belt.

"Welcome to Haven."

The Mor-Dalgar stopped. One of them took a gigantic step forward. "We come for the Taareki."

Wyatt frowned. "And you are?"

"I am Sak-Ratam."

"My name is Wyatt Porter and I'm the sheriff of Haven. If Moli wants to go along with you, that's fine with me, but I will not allow you to take him against his will. If those are weapons you're holding, you and your boys need to put them away."

"Miserable creature, you dare to speak to your betters." The Mor-Dalgar behind Sak-Ratam raised its weapon.

Wyatt's hand flashed to his hip. He drew his gun and fired. The Mor-Dalgar let out a squawk, staggered backward, and fell. The weapon erupted with a roar, spitting an ugly red light. Heat washed over Wyatt and something behind him exploded. Screams ripped through the street.

The other Mor-Dalgar shifted, but Jake raised his rifle. "Don't."

Sak-Ratam took half a step backward and looked at his fallen companion for a long second.

Wyatt pointed his pistol at Sak-Ratam. "Jake, go inside and round up some folk. Grab the buckets from out back and see what you can do to help."

The alien on the ground shuddered, gasped, then struggled to its feet. It stood, hunched and clutching at its chest. Its red eyes bored into him. It was hurt, but Wyatt wouldn't bet that it was out of the fight if it came to that.

"Your weapons are useless," Sak-Ratam said.

"I beg to differ." Wyatt's eyes flashed to the injured alien's chest. Was it even bleeding?

"You can beg all you want. If you do not surrender the Taareki to us by the time your sun is highest again, we will take him and leave this place in ashes."

They turned and left the way they came. Wyatt watched them go until they were out of sight.

⌒‖⌒

The front of Turner's General Store was a blazing wreck. The blast from the alien weapon lit it like kindling.

Wyatt raced to the store. The heat from the flames grew too intense for him to get to the door. Around him, townsfolk rushed to battle the blaze. He tried to see through the smoke. "Andy! Jake! Moli!"

The front door was impassable. Wyatt had already started around to the back when Jake came from that direction.

"The fire's everywhere." Jake coughed. "I couldn't get in. Moli—"

"Wyatt!"

He turned. Sarah ran up the road toward them, her skirts bunched in her hands. "I sent Little Wyatt into Turner's!" she screamed.

"Lord, no." A side window shattered. Fire engulfed the entire first floor and flames crept up the sides of the building.

Wyatt strode toward the door, but Jake blocked him.

"Get out of the way, Jake, that's my boy in there."

Jake shook his head. "Sheriff, he's—"

A wall on the second floor exploded in a shower of broken timber. Wyatt grabbed Sarah and Jake and pulled them away as a large trunk tumbled end over end to shatter in the street.

Smoke billowed from the hole, then Moli emerged. His fur was black with soot. Andy Turner was draped over one shoulder like a sack of grain. In Moli's other arm, Little Wyatt looked out at the town with horrified eyes.

Their eyes locked and Wyatt stepped forward. How the hell were they going to get them out of there? Maybe a ladder—

Moli disappeared back into the smoke. An instant later, he leaped out through the hole. Little Wyatt shrieked as they sailed through the air, barely clearing the burning porch roof. Moli hit the ground hard. His leg buckled and he fell, twisting to protect Little Wyatt.

Sarah was there in an instant, snatching the boy away while Jake and Wyatt helped with Andy.

"Get them away from the fire!" Doc Harper rushed past Wyatt and helped Jake move Andy across the street.

Wyatt draped Moli's arm over his shoulder and helped him to stand. Up close, Wyatt saw several burnt patches of fur and ugly black streaks across Moli's skin. "Come on, let's get you away from here."

Moli coughed and nodded. He limped and Wyatt nearly stumbled under the weight of him. When they reached the jail porch, Moli sat with a groan and shook his head, eyes downcast. "I am so sorry for bringing—"

"Don't you dare apologize for saving my boy." Sarah walked to the porch, knelt, and hugged him tightly. "Thank you. Thank you so much." Moli moaned and she rocked back in alarm inspecting his burns.

"Good Lord in Heaven!"

"I will be well," Moli said. "How is Andy?"

"Thanks to you, he'll be alright." Doc Harper walked to the porch. His hands shook and there was a tremor in his voice. He looked at Sarah. "Little Wyatt?"

"He's inside. Not a mark on him."

Doc nodded. He glanced at Moli and quickly turned away.

"Doc?" Wyatt asked

Doc stopped, but never turned. "I've got some more burn salve at my place. You can pick it up there." He started walking again.

"Doc!" Wyatt stood.

"I can't, Wyatt. I'm sorry."

"Damn it, Doc. I thought better of you." Wyatt stepped off the porch, but Sarah laid a hand on his arm. "I'll get it." She and Wyatt helped Moli to stand. "Come on. Let's get you fixed up. Tomorrow's going to be a busy day."

The next day, when they got to the jail, Jake was already there, loading rifles. Wyatt hefted one, intending to show Moli how to load it when there was a knock on the door. Jesse stood on the porch.

"I'll probably catch hell from my Pa." Jesse met Wyatt's gaze. "But I'm here to help if you'll have me."

Wyatt smiled. "Thank you, son."

As it neared noon, Wyatt started to feel fidgety. If the Mor-Dalgar intended to cause a ruckus, Wyatt would put an end to it.

Moli had told them what he could about the Mor-Dalgar. What their weapons — Moli called them blasters — could do, and where they were vulnerable to Wyatt's guns. If Wyatt's aim had been lower, he'd have likely killed the alien he shot yesterday.

Wyatt shivered. If he had to shoot a man, he preferred a quick end to it. It could take days for a man to die from a gut shot, even with help, but it wasn't men that were threatening his town. Sak-Ratam would make good on his promise to burn Haven to the ground if Wyatt couldn't stop him.

Doc Harper opened the door and stepped inside. All four of them stopped to look at him. He paused, then shut the door behind him.

Doc removed his hat. "You have a moment, Sheriff?"

Wyatt nodded. "Jake, Jesse, keep an eye on the street. Moli, you can—"

Doc cleared his throat. "I've actually got something I'd like to say to him as well."

Wyatt cocked his head, but waited until Jake and Jesse had left.

Doc put his bag on the desk and looked from one of them to the other. "I want to apologize for my behavior last night. I was wrong." He looked at Moli. "You scare the hell out of me." He fidgeted with his hat. "But you risked your life for my best friend's son and I repaid that with cowardice. You are a better man than I will ever be." He swallowed, then reached out his hand. It shook, but he kept it out there. "I'm sorry."

"You are a brave man, Doc." Moli took his hand and shook it. He bowed his head. "And a skilled physician. I accept your apology."

Wyatt clapped a hand on their shoulders. "There's something I didn't think I'd see. Now—"

"Sheriff!" Jesse opened the door. "The Anderson place is burning."

Wyatt stepped outside, looking in the direction of the Anderson farm. Thick smoke rose into the sky. He scowled. The Mor-Dalgar were coming. He stepped off the porch and walked out into the center of the street, followed by Jake, Jesse, Moli, and Doc.

They rode...something. Not horses, but two-wheeled contraptions of some kind. They made a hell of a racket.

Moli snarled.

On Wyatt's left, Jesse took a step backward, his hands tightening on the rifle.

"Easy, son. I still intend to end this peaceable." Wyatt nodded toward the approaching trio. "But no one would think less of you if you'd had a change of heart."

"I would." Jesse stepped forward. "These are my folk too."

Wyatt watched him for a moment. If they got out of this all right, he was going to make Jesse an official deputy. "Just be sure and remember that if it comes to shooting, you move and keep moving, hear?"

Sak-Ratam and his Mor-Dalgar stopped some distance from Wyatt and his men, the roar of the machines lowering to a rumble.

Off in the distance, Haven's church bell began to ring.

Wyatt nodded. "Sak-Ratam."

The alien nodded. "Wyatt Porter. I take it that you are unwilling to hand the Taareki over to us?"

"That's right."

Sak-Ratam tossed a burnt tangle of wires at Wyatt's feet.

"Taareki, this is all that's left of your ship. Come with us or this place will share the fate of that primitive hovel you left behind."

Moli growled. "They had no part in this."

Wyatt stepped forward. "Sak-Ratam, you are under arrest for the destruction of John Anderson's property. You and your men lay down your arms and be bound."

Sak-Ratam laughed and raised his blaster, but Jesse was faster. His rifle thundered and the front of the machine erupted in a shower of sparks.

All hell broke loose.

Wyatt crouched and ran to his left. Behind him, the ground exploded. Sak-Ratam cursed and tracked Wyatt with his weapon. Wyatt shot the Mor-Dalgar, knocking him off his machine.

Jake opened fire on the alien closest to him. His shot blew out the machine's front wheel and it toppled to the side. The Mor-Dalgar hopped clear and Jake's second shot took him in the chest, spinning him to the ground.

Moli leaped right at the third Mor-Dalgar. The alien raised his blaster, but Doc shot him in the leg. He screeched and dropped his weapon. Moli tackled him and the two of them rolled across the street in a snarling cloud of dust.

Jesse levered another round and fired, moving to the right—directly into Wyatt's line of fire. Wyatt cursed and just barely avoided blowing a hole in the boy.

The Mor-Dalgar that Jake shot staggered to its feet. It fired at Jesse, who was heading for the shelter of a wagon. The shot went wide, tearing through the wagon. Jesse yelped, finding himself in a cloud of burning, splintered wood. He dropped his rifle and covered his face with his arms.

Wyatt cursed the unnaturalness of it all and aimed for the alien shooting at Jesse. The shot went low and buried itself in the creature's middle. The Mor-Dalgar let out a gurgling screech. It clutched at the wound and collapsed. It didn't move.

Sak-Ratam bellowed and fired, catching Jake head on. Jake didn't even have a chance to scream as the blast threw his blackened, twisted corpse up the street.

Sak-Ratam whirled to Jesse. Wyatt sprinted across the street, tackling Jesse as a blast ripped up the ground where the boy had been standing a moment ago.

Shaking the dirt out of his eyes, Wyatt was already moving. He emptied his pistol at Sak-Ratam. Some of the bullets found their mark, but none hit the Mor-Dalgar's vulnerable middle. Sak-Ratam staggered, but didn't fall. He raised his blaster.

A horrible shriek cut through the air. Wyatt and Sak-Ratam turned to find Moli standing over the torn body of the third alien.

Finding himself outnumbered, Sak-Ratam cursed and shot the fallen machine by Wyatt. It exploded in a brilliant ball of green fire. The blast knocked him onto his back. Wyatt covered his head. Pieces of metal rained down all around him. One of the machines roared and, when he looked up, Sak-Ratam was racing away.

Wyatt took a couple of staggering steps after him. "And stay the hell out of my town!" He turned to Jesse who hadn't moved from the spot where Wyatt tackled him. "You all right?" Jesse nodded.

"Wyatt!" Moli limped to the last machine and lifted it upright. He started the machine and climbed on. "Sak-Ratam will return with an army if he doesn't simply decide to turn Haven into a smoking crater from space. We must stop him."

Wyatt stared at the machine. It was nearly as tall as a horse and it had a saddle like he'd never seen before, but there was room enough for two.

"Put your feet there." Moli folded down pegs that jutted out from either side of the machine.

Wyatt climbed on. He could feel the rumbling of the engine through his entire body.

"Hang on." Moli shouted and the machine began to roll.

Wyatt wrapped his arms around Moli as the machine shot out of town. It was terrifying. They raced over the countryside. The wind howled past his face so fast that he had to squint his eyes nearly shut.

Wyatt dared a glance at the ground and instantly regretted it. Hard-packed dirt and scrub blurred past just inches from his boots and he knew that if he fell off, he'd never get up again.

"There." Moli shouted.

In the distance, Sak-Ratam streaked over the land, heading toward the ruin of the Anderson farm.

In the center of a burnt and ruined field was another ship. All hard angles and sharp edges, it squatted in the middle of the destruction like a spider at the center of its web.

Sak-Ratam slid to a halt at the base of the ship. Already a door was lowering in the side. He pointed his weapon at them.

Moli cursed and the machine jerked to the side. Wyatt nearly lost his grip and tumbled off. He shrieked and scrabbled to stay on as a blistering red flash passed by them. When Wyatt looked again, Sak-Ratam was scrambling up the ramp and into the ship. Almost immediately, the ramp began to rise.

Moli brought the machine to a skidding stop at the foot of the ship. He lifted Wyatt like he was no heavier than a sack of grain and tossed him through the door. Moli followed after, dropping over the edge a bare instant before the door clanged shut.

Wyatt expected Sak-Ratam to be waiting for them, but the room was empty. He stood on shaky legs inside something that had been built on another planet. Blue-green lights glowed on the walls and the floor was made of metal that stretched out in a tight lattice. Across the room, stairs led up to another level. The ship had an odd smell about it. Something musty and oily at the same time.

"Wyatt!" Moli hissed in his ear.

He jumped. Moli had been whispering to him and he hadn't heard.

"Are you well?"

Through the bottoms of his boots, he felt the floor vibrate. "What's happening?"

"We're taking off." Moli hefted one of the Mor-Dalgar blasters. "Once he's off the ground, Sak-Ratam can program the ship to leave the planet and join the rest of his fleet."

The vibration in the floor increased, then the entire room swayed under Wyatt's feet. He grabbed at the wall to steady himself.

"We've lifted off." Moli crept across the room and went up the stairs.

Wyatt followed, but the floor was unsteady beneath him even as it pressed up against his boots. He couldn't imagine how fast they were going. At the top of the stairs, Moli started forward, hugging one side of the wall. Wyatt followed behind, gun pointed at the floor.

The corridor was short and ended in a closed metal door. Moli wrapped his hand around the handle and looked back at Wyatt for confirmation.

Wyatt drew a breath to calm himself, then nodded. Moli threw open the door and burst into the room.

It was empty. Moli raced from one end of the bridge to the other, looking for Sak-Ratam. Wyatt stood in the doorway unable to do anything but stare out the window.

Instead of the Anderson farm or even the deep blue of the sky, Wyatt stared out into empty space. His pistol fell from his fingers and clattered on the floor. A wave of dizziness passed over him and he grabbed the doorframe.

"That's..." He couldn't get the word out. Taking up the bottom part of the window was what could only be the gentle curve of the Earth. His fingers tightened. Were they falling? How could they not be—

Moli turned, snarling. His eyes widened and he raised his blaster when something hit Wyatt in the back. He flew across the room before crashing and tumbling into a console. A flare of pain streaked up his spine.

Sak-Ratam struck Moli with the butt end of a blaster. He crashed into the wall, his own weapon dropping to the floor. Sak-Ratam rushed him, driving the barrel into his throat.

As the two thrashed and fought, Wyatt crawled forward and grabbed the blaster. He staggered to his feet, the muscles in his back stiffening. He edged around to get a shot at Sak-Ratam, but the alien noticed him and lashed out with a foot that caught Wyatt in the chest. The kick sent him backward, his head bouncing off the metal wall. Wyatt dropped to his knees, gasping for air.

Moli used the distraction to force the barrel from his throat. He bit down into Sak-Ratam's wrist. The Mor-Dalgar screamed and drove a fist into Moli's nose.

Moli shrieked and lost his grip. Sak-Ratam smashed his head into Moli's, then hurled the dazed Taareki across the bridge. Moli crashed into a control panel that erupted in a shower of sparks and the ship lurched.

The sudden movement nearly threw Wyatt to the floor, but he caught the doorframe and stood. He pointed his blaster at Sak-Ratam.

"Moli, down!"

Moli dropped to the floor. Wyatt pulled the trigger.

In the small room, the shot was deafening. Wyatt found himself blinking away spots of light as his vision cleared. He was on his back out in the corridor and his shoulder hurt like hell. He lifted his head and groaned, dropping his head back. A few feet away, the blaster lay on the floor. It shook, then slid away from him and Wyatt felt the floor tilt. Gritting his teeth, he rolled over and climbed to his feet. His entire upper body was one big knot of pain as he staggered back to the bridge.

Moli was in one of the seats, throwing switch after switch and struggling with the controls. Sak-Ratam's body lay on the floor.

Alarms tore through Wyatt's head. Everywhere he looked, purple and red lights flashed. The Earth grew larger until it took up the entire window.

Moli cursed and hauled on the controls. The Earth tilted and an orange haze covered everything outside.

Wyatt stumbled forward as the ship starting shaking.

"Reentry," Moli said between clenched teeth. He looked over his shoulder to Wyatt. "Strap in!"

Wyatt lurched toward the empty seat. The ship bucked. Wyatt smashed into a panel, his shoulder erupting in a white fire of pain that nearly dropped him.

The ship rocked. Wyatt was thrown sideways into the seat. He clutched at the straps with his good arm and tried to tie himself down.

Outside, the orange haze disappeared to be replaced with familiar blue sky.

"Hang on," Moli warned and the ship spun. A patchwork of dark and light green took up the entire window. It was getting closer.

Wyatt struggled to secure himself. He could see Haven and the Anderson farm and his own place. They were so small.

Moli snarled, wrestling with the controls. They were so close now that Wyatt could see individual people scattering from Haven's main street.

A roar split through his head and dust completely obscured the view outside. Wyatt closed his eyes as the ship tilted sharply. There was a horrible jolt and he was thrown from his seat, his hand ripped from the straps despite the death-grip he had on them. His last sight was the floor rushing up to meet him, then everything went black.

"Wyatt?"

The voice was a crack in the dark. Pain leaked in. Wyatt groaned and tried to go away again.

"Here."

Clawed fingers lifted his head and touched wonderfully cool liquid to his lips. Wyatt drank. Even his throat hurt. Warmth flowed across his entire body. It touched every source of pain. In most places, the pain vanished. In others, the pain faded into an uncomfortable tingling. Wyatt opened his eyes.

Moli smiled down at him. "Welcome home." He helped Wyatt sit and pressed a cloth against his head.

"Your shoulder is broken." Moli helped him into a seat. "So are some ribs. The nanobots are repairing the damage."

Wyatt reached up and took the cloth from his head. It came back bloody. Moli pressed it back against his head.

"Be still. You've got a powerful anesthetic in you as well. You could further damage yourself and not know it."

Wyatt looked out the window. He could see the top half of the Creaky Wheel. "We're back?"

Moli smiled. "Oh yes."

"In Haven?"

"In the middle of Main Street."

Wyatt closed his eyes. He pictured the ship landing in the middle of town and the uproar it would have caused. His chuckle turned into a cough.

"Do you think you can stand?"

Walking was tricky for the first few steps, but Wyatt got the hang of it again by the time they got to the stairs.

Moli opened the bay door, letting the dust and the smells of Haven into the ship. That, more than anything, kept Wyatt steady on his feet as he walked out into the sunshine.

The ship stood right in the middle of Main Street. A blackened circle stretched from one side of the street to the other. Buildings on either side had damage from the ship's protrusions and some bore scorch marks. Everything was covered by a thin layer of dust.

Townsfolk crowded around, their voices tinged with fear. He tried to focus, but it was nearly too much for him to bear.

Sarah shouldered her way through the crowd and caught him in a hug. He ran his hand through her hair, thinking it was the softest, sweetest thing in the world. She kissed him and the world faded away into a pleasant silence.

Wyatt slept the rest of the day and all through the next. When he finally woke up, he didn't hurt anywhere. Every time he moved, he expected blinding pain, but it never came.

Doc Harper looked him over and pronounced him fit as a fiddle, but Sarah wouldn't let her husband wander any further than the porch for another day. During that time, he'd asked Moli about nanobots. Moli said something about tiny machines inside of him that fixed him up from the inside. At Wyatt's horrified look, Moli laughed and told him that, now that he was well, they'd probably work out of his system in a day or so.

That night, Moli moved the ship.

Wyatt watched, wincing as the surrounding buildings took more damage, yet completely awestruck as the ship drifted to the edge of town and landed gently as a thistle seed.

For the next week, Sarah didn't let Wyatt out of her sight. He officially deputized Jesse and organized repair crews. The entire town came together and, slowly, Haven began to heal.

Moli did the work of four people. He worked alongside the townsfolk during the day and drank with them at the Creaky Wheel at night. As the days flowed into weeks, the folk of Haven gradually adopted him. One month after he came to Haven, Moli announced that he was leaving.

The entire town was caught off guard except for Wyatt. The night before, he'd woken up to find Moli standing outside, staring up at the night sky, and knew the time was coming.

The next morning, all of the folk of Haven stood around the base of the ship. Moli and Wyatt shook hands, and embraced.

"You take care of yourself," Wyatt said.

"You as well." He turned to Sarah. "Both of you."

Sarah ran up and hugged him tightly, eyes wet. "You come back any time you want and you'll be welcome, hear?"

Moli smiled sadly. "I would love that." He blinked quickly. "For your sake, I will make sure that this planet remains unnoticed for as long as possible." He looked at Wyatt, then past him at the gathered townsfolk. "I will always keep you in my memories, friends. Thank you. For everything."

Sarah hugged him one last time, then stood next to Wyatt. Moli turned and stepped on the ramp and was about to enter the ship when Wyatt whistled.

He turned and Wyatt tossed something small and round to him. It flashed in the morning sun. He flipped it over to examine the face. "Deputy Sheriff, Haven" was spelled out around the edge of the tin star.

"Now it's official," Wyatt said.

Moli nodded once, then turned and went into the ship, raising the ramp behind him.

Wyatt and Sarah backed away. Softly at first, then with rising intensity, the ship's engines woke. Dust blew, forcing Wyatt to shield his eyes as the engines lit up, lifting the ship into the air.

It spun once, and rose into the sky, looking like a shooting star rising up into the heavens.

EIGHTEEN SIXTY

FAITH HUNTER

A spin-off short-short story from the world of Jane Yellowrock
Author's Note: This short story takes place in 1860.

THE YUNEGA WITH THE HAIRY FACE WAS FEEDING DRY PALO VERDE
sticks to the fire. The snap and spit of fresh wood was lost to the distance,
but the smoke rose and carried on the scant breeze, smelling hot and
tangy to Ayatas' cat-nose. The cowboys he had been following had
stopped early for the night, making camp at a watering hole to rest the
horses and let the cattle drink and graze. The watering hole and the small
crick that carried the spring water into the desert were muddy now with
the deep prints of cattle and filthy with cow and horse droppings, and
man piss. *Ama*—the water—was no longer drinkable.

Yunega always ruined *ama*. It was part of what they were, like a wolf
howled and bison grazed, white man ruined water. Always. *Lisi*, his
grandmother, told him, "Never live downstream of a *yunega*. You will
drink their shit." And the old woman had laughed. He wondered if *Lisi*
still laughed today. He hadn't seen her since the dreams sent him into
the sunset, to find the wildfire wind he saw in his visions.

His stomach cramped with hunger, and he pressed down on it with
his mind. His people were accustomed to hunger. They did not allow it
rule them, no matter how strong it became. He pressed his paws into the
stone ledge and his claws came out, white and pointed and sharper than
the claws of the panther that his father had most often shifted into. Jaguar

claws were better for what he had planned this night. Jaguar speed and strength, jaguar jaws and killing teeth. Jaguar scent that the horses and cattle would recognize and fear. Jaguar that was stronger in every way than the puma of his father's clan. That panther that had failed his father at the last and allowed him to die.

Down below, the small fire had caught, the flames a tight blaze in a ring of rocks. The white men were making biscuits in a tin pan, and heating beans that smelled sour. White men ate bad food and were often sick. It was beyond his understanding how a people who were so stupid had lived so long and conquered his own people, the *Tsalagi*, the Cherokee. *Lisi* said it was because his own people had been unwise and let them share the land. If his ancestors had simply killed them all, their lives would have been much better today, and they would still have their tribal lands in the green mountains.

The black cowboys, *gvnagei*, took care of the horses and piled the saddles around the fire. They put the horses' legs into twisted rope hobbles, so that they could graze without getting away. This would make his job much easier. He chuffed with pleasure, the sound too soft to carry. His scent was downwind of them, and the grazing prey did not know they were stalked.

The day darkened and the cattle lowed, the sound plaintive and lonely. The sunset was a red smear on the western sky. The scarlet light was hard to see in his cat-form—it was much easier to see greens and blues and the silver of gray—but he knew it was there. The western sky was always bloody here in the barren hills of the place yunega called Arizona.

He had been following the cowboys and their cattle for seven days now, and they were far enough into the desert to be at a good place for his ambush. They set a watch, a *gvnagei* on a hillock, but he was young and never looked into the hills around him. This was stupid, as Apache were known to raid here. Apache and Ayatas.

The men below him laughed and talked, the strange sounds carried on the nearly still air. Black men and white men, in two small groups, working the cattle but not working them together. Divided by tribe and skin color and *yunega* false superiority. *Lisi* had said the white man would eventually stumble and fall on his pride, but Ayatas had not seen signs of that, at all. He had believed her when he was a child, but *lisi* had gotten foolish in her old age.

Whitley
15

Back then, when he was a boy, living with her, he had been called *Nvdayeli Tlivdatsi*, or, as the white man would say, Nantahala Panther, but the Nantahala River was a thing of memory, lost to his people since the *yunega* sent them from their tribal lands in to the territories. Panther had been his clan name and his father's beast. But the panthers had been hunted by the *yunega* until they were no more, in the mountains of their first home, and *Tsalagi* had been driven away, in broken treaty, by lie-speakers of the *yunega* government. His childhood names were words of sadness and grief, and he had changed them after his spirit walk. He now called himself *Ayatas Nvgitsvle* or Fire Wind, for the raging fires he saw in his dreams. He had left *lisi's* house and searched for the winds for years, but still had not found them.

Instead, he had been chased and shot at by *yunega* and by many of the tribes he had come across. The Apaches were the worst, and the best. They were fierce and they might stop the white men. If they killed him and yet destroyed the white man, he could die happy.

But on his search, he had found a dead jaguar, shot by a *yunega*, beheaded and skinned, for sale to fur traders. The carcass had been three days old and stinking. But Ayatas had defleshed the feet bones and boiled them clean, and added the toe bones to his bone necklace. Now he could become jaguar any time he wanted, anytime he could bear the pain and hunger of shifting and walking in the skin of the beast.

Along the tops of the hills, the wind picked up, the tingle of magic brushing along his spotted pelt. He chuffed, his whiskers moving as he scented the magic in the air, his ear tabs flitting. The woman was right on time. That was another thing he had found, the white woman with hair the color of the sunset. She called herself Everhart, which he had translated into Forever Heart, or *Igohidv Adonvdo*. Or perhaps she had meant Forever Deer, which would be *Igohidv Awi*, but sounded stupid. Deer were prey. The woman was not. The woman had magic, though different from his, and different from the magic of the shaman of his clan. She called herself a witch. She did things that she called workings. And she was his. His *lisi* would have wanted him to find a girl of the *Tsalagi*, but he had *Igohidv*, his Forever woman. This was much better.

As the magics grew, the wind picked up and whirled, making the leaves of the tree whisper, making the white man's fire dance. On the hillside, the *gvnagei* lookout stood up and stared out over the open space. His eyes tracked the wind, moving back and forth, as if he too felt the magic. But Ayatas knew that humans could not feel the magic of his

Forever woman, and that no men of her tribe had magic. The *gvnagei* shielded his eyes from the last of the dying sunlight and focused in on the ledge where Ayatas lay. But perhaps he was wrong. This man might have different, dangerous magic.

The wind shifted and the smoke whirled and swept into the cowboy's eyes. Sparks flew and swirled among the leaves in the tree. It was drought season and any small sparks were a danger. He saw the tree catch fire; even from so far away, he could hear the *whoosh* as it caught and blazed. The men screamed and began to pick up camp, moving away. Ayatas chuffed with laughter. The smoke swirled again and careened among the horses, carrying sparks that bit and stung. They were too small to do real harm, but the pinprick fires hurt like a cowboy's spiked rowels and the horses threw up their heads and snorted, lashing their tails. One whinnied, its eyes rolling white. The others picked up its fear. One began to buck and lost its footing in the twisted ropes. It fell and screamed.

The wind whirled faster, up along the ledge where Ayatas lay, picking up his scent before whirling down into the gulch. The smell of jaguar and fire reached the cattle and the mindless beasts stomped and lowered their head, rolled their eyes, seeking out the dangers.

The *gvnagei* lookout pulled his gun, a six-shooter, and stared right at Ayatas' ledge. But the man was too far away for a reasonable shot. He would have done better to have a rifle like the one that Ayatas had taken from the dead body of an Apache who had challenged him to combat.

Ayatas pushed up to a sitting position, certain that he was now hidden in the shadows of the falling sunset. Below him, in the growing darkness, the white men were fighting to keep the horses calm. The cattle stomped. A mother was nudged away from her calf and she bellowed a warning. She raced up a short rise and lowered her head. With one horn, she gored a steer in the back. Two other steers jumped and hopped on four feet, bouncing in fear at the confrontation. Dust rose and added to the shadows. He growled, the sound coming from deep in his chest.

The cattle started bucking, the delicious scent of their fear growing fast.

They split, one group galloping into the sunset. The other beginning a constricted, spiraling race that grew tighter and tighter as the panicking cattle followed the circling female, frantically searching for her calf. Ayatas raised his head and called, the vibration sending the cattle into a frenzy, stomping hooves and goring horns. The smell of blood and panic rose on the woman's magic wind. Ayatas licked his jaws in hunger.

He called again and raced down the cliff, his spots hiding his movement. A gunshot sounded. Men screamed. Horses screamed. On the wind, Ayatas heard his woman's laughter.

He leaped down twenty feet, as *yunega* would calculate it, and landed with his front paws together, pushing off with his back paws as they touched down. He leaped on a young steer, his weight driving it to its knees. He caught its windpipe between his fangs and clamped down. Instantly the steer's back legs buckled and it fell. Ayatas dragged him into the small cave he had prepared before the white men arrived. Concealed behind brush, it had remained hidden. The steer struggled feebly and tried to get up. Ayatas held tight, and the steer flopped over. He held the killing bite for longer, to make certain that his dinner was dead. Then he ripped out its throat and gulped down its blood, his hunger, carefully held in check, instantly freed. He gorged on the soft tissue and blood, eating until the pain he had been fighting dissipated. He needed to eat more, much more, but his woman's magic called to him and he raced out of the small depression in the rock.

In the gathering dark and confusion, he saw horses break their hobbles and race into the night. A larger group raced after the cattle. The white men would follow the larger group first. Ayatas followed the two horses and though his cat-brain did not understand how to do it, the man part of him herded the horses toward his woman.

When the moon was full overhead, throwing black and white shadows, he chased the horses into the small arroyo where they had camped. His woman caught them with her song. She gentled them, as she had him. And she led them all to water.

Later, he followed his own trail back to the small cavern and pulled his kill out of the bushes and deeper into the desert. He ate. In the morning, he would carry the carcass back to the woman and shift back to human. Together, they would butcher the rest of the meat and then they would ride on, looking for the wildfire winds of his dreams.

ABOUT THE AUTHORS

Frances Rowat lives with her husband, their dog, and a not-quite-startling number of cats. She spends most of her time at a keyboard, and is fond of earrings, jigsaws, and post-apocalyptic fiction. Her short stories have been published in *The Sockdolager* and *Betwixt Magazine*, and one has been accepted to appear in *On Spec*.

She would like to thank her writing group for Sundays, her extremely patient family for support, and coffee for simply *being*.

Wendy N. Wagner is the author of *Skinwalkers*, a Pathfinder Tales novel inspired by Viking lore. She's published more than thirty short stories in anthologies like *Cthulhu Fhtagn!*, *Armored*, and *The Way of the Wizard*, and magazines like *Beneath Ceaseless Skies* and *Farrago's Wainscot*. She serves as the Managing/Associate Editor of *Lightspeed* and *Nightmare* magazines. She is also the non-fiction editor of *Women Destroy Science Fiction!*, which was named one of NPR's Best Books of 2014, and the guest editor of *Queers Destroy Horror!* She lives in Oregon with her very understanding family. Keep up with her at *winniewoohoo.com*.

Gail Z. Martin is the author of the upcoming novel *Vendetta: A Deadly Curiosities Novel* in her urban fantasy series set in Charleston, SC (Dec. 2015, Solaris Books) as well as the epic fantasy novel *Shadow and Flame* (March, 2016 Orbit Books) which is the fourth and final book in the Ascendant Kingdoms Saga. *The Shadowed Path*, an anthology of Jonmarc Vahanian short stories set in the world of *The Summoner*, debuts from Solaris Books in June, 2016.

Other books including *Iron & Blood: The Jake Desmet Adventures* a new Steampunk series (Solaris Books) co-authored with Larry N. Martin as well as *Ice Forged*, *Reign of Ash* and *War of Shadows* in The Ascendant Kingdoms Saga, The Chronicles of The Necromancer series (*The Summoner, The Blood King, Dark Haven, Dark Lady's Chosen*) from Solaris Books and The Fallen Kings Cycle (*The Sworn, The Dread*) from Orbit Books and the urban fantasy novel *Deadly Curiosities* from Solaris Books.

Gail writes four series of ebook short stories: *The Jonmarc Vahanian Adventures, The Deadly Curiosities Adventures, The King's Convicts* series, and together with Larry N. Martin, *The Storm and Fury Adventures*. Her work has appeared in over 20 US/UK anthologies. Newest anthologies include: *The Big Bad 2, Athena's Daughters, Realms of Imagination, Heroes,*

With Great Power, and (co-authored with Larry N. Martin) *Space, Contact Light, The Weird Wild West, The Side of Good/The Side of Evil, Alien Artifacts, Clockwork Universe: Steampunk vs. Aliens.*

Larry N. Martin is the co-author of the new Steampunk series *Iron & Blood: The Jake Desmet Adventures* and a series of short stories: *The Storm & Fury Adventures* set in the Jake Desmet universe. These short stories also appear in the anthologies *Clockwork Universe: Steampunk vs. Aliens, The Weird Wild West, The Side of Good/The Side of Evil and Alien Artifacts*, with more to come. Larry and Gail also have science fiction short stories in the *Space* and *Contact Light* anthologies and a new novella, *Grave Voices*.

Born in northern Indiana just months after the original Star Wars, **Bryan C.P. Steele** grew up with a powerful imagination — something that has since fueled nearly two million published words, countless plotlines, game designs and more. He grew up with his nose in comics and role-playing books, often turning the pages with an action figure or little lead miniature. Never reined by the banality of the world around us, Bryan defined himself through creativity.

Working on award-winning projects with a number of different publishers over the years, he has had input on several fan favorite games such as the Iron Kingdoms, Traveller, Shadowrun and RuneQuest. Bryan has also been fortunate enough to work with such fantastic settings as Conan, Babylon 5, Starship Troopers and Judge Dredd over the years. His work was even featured as a bonus in Lauren Beukes' amazing Zoo City (English-speaking release).

Bryan is the proud father to his young son Conor and soon-to-be stepdaughter Nori, who will soon be playing some of daddy's games and reading daddy's stories. With his beautiful partner in crime, Natalie, at his side, Bryan wants to make the world a more enjoyable place one page turned at a time.

R.S. (Rod) Belcher is an award-winning newspaper and magazine editor and reporter.

Rod has been a private investigator, a DJ, a comic book store owner and has degrees in criminal law, psychology and justice and risk administration, from Virginia Commonwealth University. He's done Masters work in Forensic Science at The George Washington University, and worked with the Occult Crime Taskforce for the Virginia General Assembly.

The Grand Prize winner of the *Star Trek: Strange New Worlds* Anthology contest, Rod's short story "Orphans" was published in *Star Trek: Strange New Worlds 9* by Simon and Schuster in 2006.

Rod's first novel, *The Six-Gun Tarot*, was published by Tor Books in 2013. The sequel, *The Shotgun Arcana*, was published in October 2014. His third novel, *Nightwise*, was released in August 2015, and his latest novel, *The Brotherhood of the Wheel* is scheduled to be published in March of 2016.

He lives in Roanoke Virginia with his children, Jonathan and Emily.

After a long career of writing mostly novels, mostly military, mostly science fiction, **David Sherman** is now concentrating on short fiction. "Rocky Rolls Gold" is his third story about Gambling Man Clint Walker and Pinkerton Agent Extraordinaire Miss Kitty Belle.

For more about his novels and other short fiction, please visit his website: www.novelier.com.

Jonathan Maberry is a NY Times bestselling author, four-time Bram Stoker Award winner, and comic book writer. He writes horror, thrillers, mystery, fantasy, science fiction and suspense for adults and teens. His novels include *Predator One, Code Zero, Rot & Ruin, Fall of Night, Ghost Road Blues, Patient Zero*, and many others. Several of Jonathan's novels are in development for movies or TV including *V-Wars, Extinction Machine, Rot & Ruin*, and *Dead of Night*. He's the editor/co-author of *V Wars*, a vampire themed anthology; and is editor for a series of all-original *X-FILES* anthologies, the YA anthology *Scary Out There*, and the dark fantasy anthology *Out of Tune*. His *V-Wars* books have been developed as a board game. He is a popular featured expert on History Channel shows like *Zombies: A Living History* and *Monsters, Myth and Legend*. Since 1978 he's sold more than 1200 magazine feature articles, 3000 columns, two plays, greeting cards, song lyrics, and poetry. His comics include *V-Wars, Rot & Ruin, Captain America: Hail Hydra, Bad Blood, Marvel Zombies Return* and *Marvel Universe VS The Avenger*. He lives in Del Mar, California with his wife, Sara Jo and their dog, Rosie. *www.jonathan-maberry.com*.

Robert E Waters has been writing science fiction and fantasy professionally since 2003 with his first publication in Weird Tales, "The Assassin's Retirement Party." Robert has also published 30 additional stories in various on-line and print magazines and anthologies, including Eric Flint's on-line *Grantville Gazette*, the magazine dedicated to publishing stories set in Baen Book's 1632/Ring of Fire alternate history series. In 2014, Robert published his first novel, *The Wayward Eight: A Contract to Die For*, set in the Wild West Exodus gaming universe. Robert lives in Baltimore, Maryland with his wife Beth, their son Jason, and their cat Buzz. Visit his website as *www.roberternestwaters.com*.

Tonia Brown is a Southern author with a penchant for Victorian dead things. Her work ranges from steampunk to romance to humor to horror, and a healthy mix of these genres. She is the author of *Badass Zombie Roadtrip* and *Lucky Stiff* from Books of the Dead Press, *Sundowners* and *Skin Trade* from Permuted Press, *Hauling Ash* from Post Hill Press, and the *Clockworks and Corsets* series from Kinsington Press, as well as the weird western web serial, *Railroad!* She lives in the backwoods of North Carolina with her genius husband and an ever fluctuating number of cats.

James R. Tuck is the author of the *Deacon Chalk* series and numerous short stories.
He writes the things that keep you up at night.
Find out more at: *www.jamesrtuck.com*.

Liz Colter lives in a rural area of Colorado and spends her free time with her husband, dogs, horses and writing. Over the years she has worked as a paramedic, an Outward Bound instructor, an athletic trainer, a draft-horse farmer and a dispatcher for concrete trucks, but her true passion is her writing. She has been reading speculative fiction for a lifetime and creating her own speculative worlds for more than a decade. Her short stories have appeared in a variety of magazines and anthologies, including *Galaxy's Edge Magazine* and *Urban Fantasy Magazine*, as well as an international contest-winning story in the *Writers of the Future* anthology. In longer works, she has two completed fantasy novels and is working on a third. News of her writing can be found at her website: *www.lizcolter.com*.

As a professional game designer, **Scott Hungerford** has designed great games and told great stories for millions of players world-wide over the last twenty years. But when the job is over for the day, his true passion lies with writing novels mixing the mythic and the mundane.

John G. Hartness is a teller of tales, a righter of wrongs, defender of ladies' virtues, and some people call him Maurice, for he speaks of the pompatus of love. He is the author of *The Black Knight Chronicles* (Bell Bridge), and creator of the comic horror *Bubba the Monster Hunter* series and the *Big Bad* anthology series (Dark Oak Press).

John enjoys long walks on the beach, rescuing kittens from trees and recording episodes of his podcast *Literate Liquors*, where he pairs book reviews and alcoholic drinks in new and ludicrous ways. An avid *Magic: the Gathering* player, John is strong in his nerd-fu.

Diana Pharaoh Francis writes books of a fantastical, adventurous, and often romantic nature. Her award-nominated books include *The Path* series, the *Horngate Witches* series, the *Crosspointe Chronicles*, and *Diamond City Magic* books, and the Mission:Magic series. She's owned by two corgis, spends much of her time herding children, and likes rocks, geocaching, knotting up yarn, and has a thing for 1800s England, especially the Victorians.

For more about her writing, visit www.dianapfrancis.com. She can also be found on twitter as @dianapfrancis.

Ken Schrader is a science fiction and fantasy writer. He spends a great deal of his spare time listening to the characters running around in his head. When he's not doing that, or playing with his dogs, he's been known to take in the occasional super-hero movie.

NYT Bestselling author **Faith Hunter** writes: the multi-book, dark urban fantasy *Skinwalker* series, featuring Jane Yellowrock; the *Rogue Mage* novels, a dark, urban fantasy / post-apocalyptic series and role playing game featuring Thorn St. Croix; and the *Soulwood Trilogy* featuring Nell Nicholson Ingram, a spin-off character of the Jane Yellowrock / Skinwalker series.

About the Editors

Misty Massey is the author of Mad Kestrel (Tor), a rollicking fantasy adventure of magic on the high seas, and *Kestrel's Voyages* (Kindle DP), a set of stories following Captain Kestrel and her daring crew. Her short fiction has appeared in *Rum and Runestones, Dragon's Lure*, and *The Big Bad II*. Misty is one of the featured writers on Magical Words (*magicalwords.net*). When she's not writing, she studies and performs Middle Eastern dance. You can see more of what Misty's up to at her website, *mistymassey.com*, or find her on Facebook and Twitter.

Emily Lavin Leverett is a fantasy, sci-fi, and (occasional) horror writer from North Carolina. Her works have appeared in *Flash Fiction Online, Drafthorse: A Journal of Work and No Work*, and *Athena's Daughters II* from Silence in the Library. She also edits short story collections including *The Big Bad: an Anthology of Evil* and *Big Bad II* with John Hartness, from Dark Oak Press. She freelance edits as well. When not writing or editing, she is a Professor of Medieval English Literature at a small college in Fayetteville. She teaches English literature including Chaucer and Shakespeare, as well as teaching composition and grammar. Medieval studies, especially medieval romance, heavily influence her work. When neither writing nor teaching, she's reading novels, short stories, and comic books or watching television and movies with her spouse and their cats.

Margaret S. McGraw writes fantasy and science fiction; blogs about prompt-writing, con reviews, and book reviews at ; and edits fiction, academic and technical writing. Her imagination draws on her lifelong love of science fiction, fantasy, and anthropology. Her education and experience range from anthropology and communication through web design and IT management. Margaret lives in North Carolina with her daughter and an array of dogs, cats, Macs and PCs, and too many unfinished craft projects. For more details on her writing, friend Margaret on Facebook "Margaret S. McGraw" and Goodreads "Margaret S. McGraw", follow her on Twitter @MargaretSMcGraw, or visit her blog at WritersSpark.com.

THE WEIRD WILD WEST
STAKEHOLDERS

Robby Thrasher, Jay Zastrow, Bonnie Warford, John Idlor, D-Rock, Sheryl R. Hayes, Anonymous, Karen H, Andrew and Kate Barton, Edward Greaves, Keith Hall, Anonymous, Arne Radtke, Leshia-Aimee Doucet, Evaristo Ramos, Jr., Roy Romasanta, Andrew J Clark IV, Gavran, Christian Steudtner, Doug Wardell, Laura Sheana Taylor, John Green, Gail Z. Martin, Amy Bauer, Katy Holder, Pat Hayes, Adriane Ruzak, Amelia, Margaret St. John, CJ Gray, Pam Blome, Melanie C. Duncan, Joy Pinchback, Karen Dubois, Kim R., Cheryl Preyer, Ed Ellis, Jerel Heritage, Brett Hargis, James H. Murphy Jr., Svend Andersen, Axisor, Jim Naeger (c/o Aussie Adventurer Pty Ltd, (www.aussieadventurer.net), Joshua Palmatier, Kit Power, Sasquatch, A Jacob Cord, Missy Katano, Mike Spring, Sheelagh Semper, Chris Imershein, J.R. Murdock, Jennifer Brozek, sure, Travis I. Sivart, Lynn Kramer, Silence in the Library Publishing, Elizabeth Lee, Candace R. Benefiel, Keith Bissett, Wendy Fairfull, Ann Stolinsky, Gontza Games and Gemini Wordsmiths, Christopher S. Sanders, Kelli Neier, Jaime C., Erin Penn, Janito Vaqueiro Ferreira Filho, KDRW, Tina M Good, Tera Fulbright, Paul Bulmer, John MacLeod, Allison M Ketchell, Maggie Allen, Michael Spence, Jeff, Mike Smith, David McCready, Andy Hsu, Simo Muinonen, David Perlmutter, Steven Saus, Sally Novak Janin, Cathy Franchett, Floyd Brigdon, Lennhoff Family, Antha Ann Adkins, Target, Tor Andre Wigmostad, Paul Minturn, Christine Bell, Ib Rasmussen, Jean Marie Ward, David Zurek, Robert Early, Trip Space-Parasite, Steve Jasper, Cynthia Ward, Chan Ka Chun Patrick, Jim Ryan, Elizabeth Inglee-Richards, Wayne L. McCalla, Jr., Anthony R. Cardno, Heather Parra, Sara-Jane Raines, Richard Sargent, V. Hartman DiSanto, Mark Cole, JW, James Elwood, Joshua Megerman, Ken 'Merlyn' Mencher, Vicki Hsu, Andrew Hatchell, Peter Young, Gunnar Hogberg, Brendan Lonehawk, Daniel Frederick Crisman, Ivan Begley, Faye Newsham, Jenn Whitworth, Erica Stevenson, Jan Schumann, Tim Marquitz, Ryan Lawler, Barbara Hasebe, Susan Simko, Ian Harvey, Butch Howard, Wes Rist, JoanneBB, Elaine Tindill-Rohr, JBW, Keith West, Steven Thesken, Darrell Grizzle, James Stubbs, Susan C., V Pallo, Nicholas Ahlhelm, Beth Cato, Paul "Sharps" Ellis, Arnonym, Cindy Gropp Curry, Judith Tarr, Nicholas Diak, Judy Bienvenu, Donald J. Bingle, Komic Brew, Eviltwin, Patrick Dugan, Frances Rowat, Samuel Montgomery-

Blinn, T.Rob, Josette Steele, Duncan Dog, Justin Tappan, Gary Vandegrift, Kristin Evenson Hirst, Stephen Kotowych, Cliff Winnig, Kelly Farmer, Michael Bentley, Peter Darbyshire, Patrick Thomas, KT Wagner, Carissa Little, Stefanie Lazer, Melanie Knight, Rich Bowers, Mary Avinger, Megan E, Jeremy Brett, Rachel M. Thompson, Morgan S. Brilliant, Greg Schauer, Elizabeth, Jon Del Arroz, Robert Greenberger, Little Shop of Horror Durham NC, R.T. Bryson, Mary Spila, Robert E Waters, Charlotte Henley Babb, Paul van Oven, M. Menzies, JD Fitch, Kerry aka Trouble, Jay Wolf, David Boop, Stormsister, Steven Pots, Thomas A. Mays, Rowie McDonald-Moss and Michael Timmers, Chokolatte Jedi, Rebecca D. Flowers, Lara Beneshan, Laura Wilce, Ruth-Hanna Strong, Garrett Calcaterra, Lisa Kruse, Jason and Melissa Gilbert, Inge Formenti, Deidre Dykes, Michael D. Woods, Brian Holder, Trent Walters, Aaron Max Berkowitz, Madison Metricula, Valentine Wolfe, Toby Hansen, David McDermott, Gerty McHenry, Merry Alicia Barton, Patricia deVarennes, Lura Wilcox, Connie Wilkins, Dave McNally, Kala Goriup, Andy Bartalone, Michelle Murrain, Bryan C.P. Steele, Jen M, Wendy Lea WaltzingDog Feldmann, Patti & Joan Holland, Carol Mammano, Ada Milenkovic Brown, James Nettles, Grace Lo, Pepita Hogg-Sonnenberg, Annie Standish, Chad Bowden, Deanna Stanley, Tory Shade, Captain Zorikh, Melinda, Pam Smith, Rie Sheridan Rose, Barb Moermond, Kelly Aguirre, Lang Thompson, Kevin "Wolf" Patti, James M-S Keirstead, Misha Dainiak, William Freedman, T.B. Stahl, Brenda Cooper, Hisham El-Far, Andrew and Monica Marlowe, Amazing Blair Peery, C. Markell Lynch, Becca S, Audrey Hartness Reese, Ashli Tingle, Nellie B, D. C. Wilson, Linda C. Trickey, J.P. Alkema, Marc Rokoff, Larry "Lordlnyc" Nelson, Mike Rhodes, Linda Pierce, Theresa Nitz, Penny McClain, Jeff Young, Kaitlin Thorsen, David Stokes, Eric Avedissian, Nathan Turner, Elisabeth L., Elizabeth Bridges, Paul Cardullo, John G. Hartness, Corrine Vitek, Candice N. Carpenter, Jeanne Wilkins, Max Kaehn, Kenneth Gentile, Janice Hofer, Ragnarok Publications, Tracy Syrstad, Jacalyn Boggs, H Lynnea Johnson, Stephanie Franklin, Jeff Narucki, Rachel S. Vance, Melanie Otto, Eliza Wilcox, Tanya Hamilton, Laura A Burns, Rebecca Miller, Dennis Ti, Meta, Anthony Lowe, Melissa Hicks, Hollybelle Daugherty, Melissa Truhn, Brenda Carre, Bart H. Welch, Master Ogre, Anne Rindfliesch, Kerry Ebanks, Michielle, drey, Karey Greenup Trevizo, Nick Lapeyrouse, Sondra, Melissa Hayden, Danielle Schulman, Ralf "Sandfox" Sandfuchs, Renee McPhail, Sheepy!, Kimberlee A. Hughes, Rebecca McFarland Kyle, Denise Murray, Megan E. Daggett, Denise

(Ducky) Matthews, Mark Knapp Jr, Trevor Curtis, Georgie Coghlan, Alien Zookeeper, Roxanne Bland, Ann Bilbrey, Samantha Corfield, Joel from BourbonPens.com, sure, Adam T Alexander, Tomas Burgos-Caez, Barbara Silcox, Carla "Tigerlibrarian" Hollar, Lisa Barry, Sarah Eyermann, SwordFire

CPSIA information can be obtained
at www.ICGtesting.com
Printed in the USA
LVOW11s0122291116

514863LV00001B/77/P

9 781942 990017